OFF THE GRID

THE LOST PLATOON

Monica McCarty

JOVE
New York

A JOVE BOOK
Published by Berkley
An imprint of Penguin Random House LLC
375 Hudson Street, New York, New York 10014

Copyright © 2018 by Monica McCarty

ISBN: 9780399587726

First Printing: July 2018

Printed in the United States of America
1 3 5 7 9 10 8 6 4 2

Cover art: man © Claudio Marinesco; power plant with
smoke © Nikkytok/Shutterstock Images
Cover design by Rita Frangie
Book design by Laura K. Corless

To Laura, my law school classmate,
Disney half-marathon companion,
and travel buddy extraordinaire,
whom I apparently spend so much time with
that iPhone photos thinks she is in my immediate family ☺*.*
I look forward to many more adventures!

Acknowledgments

A huge thanks to my editor, Cindy Hwang, and my agent, Annelise Robey, for believing in this series and seeing it from my computer screen to bookstores everywhere. Your support, knowledge, and expertise are both valued and appreciated.

The entire team at Berkley Publishing Group has been phenomenal to work with, but I want to give a special and very big shout-out to my incredible publicist, Jessica Brock (you are the bomb); to the art department for the yummy covers (to keep my hot-cover streak alive); and to the production team, including Kristine Swartz and my very hardworking copy editor.

Thanks also to Jami Alden, who is my much-trusted and depended-upon first reader. I have no idea what I would do without you. Please never make me find out.

Prologue

MAY 26, 0130 HOURS

"Travel the world," they'd said. "Have an exciting career while doing what you love."

The navy recruiters who'd come knocking on John Donovan's frat house door eight years ago, when he was an all-American water polo player at University of Southern California, had promised both. John had been thinking more along the lines of Bora Bora or Tahiti—not Siberia—but they'd sure as hell undersold the excitement part of the job.

It was hard to get more exciting than a no-footprint, fail-and-you-die recon mission to a supposedly abandoned gulag in Russia, looking for proof of a doomsday weapon, with not only their lives but war at stake if they were discovered.

Yeah, definitely undersold. But that was why he was here. Retiarius Platoon, one of the two platoons that made up the top secret SEAL Team Nine, didn't do vanilla.

They did exciting and impossible, and this op sure as shit qualified.

But so far they'd been giving Murphy's Law a workout in the "if it can go wrong, it will go wrong" category. They'd lost their unblinking eye in the sky—nicknamed Sauron from *The Lord of the Rings*—lost all comms— aka gone blind—and now that they were finally at the camp and ready to start looking around, something else was going down.

They should be inside the gulag's command building by now, but they'd stopped in the yard for some reason. From his position at point, John took in the other six members of the squad through the green filter of his NVGs: Miggy, Jim Bob, the senior chief, Dolph, the new kid, and the LC.

Whatever it was, it wasn't good. Dean Baylor, the senior chief, had broken the go-dark-on-comms order and was arguing with the officer in charge, Lieutenant Commander Scott Taylor.

Shit, he didn't like this. John shifted back and forth, scanning the ghostly Soviet-era labor camp through the scope of his AR-15. Stalin sure as heck knew how to do grim. This place was bleak with a big-assed "B." But that wasn't what was making him twitchy. It was being out here in the open like this, exposed for so long.

John getting twitchy didn't happen often. It was one of the reasons he usually ended up on point. It was the most dangerous position, and it took a lot to rattle him. Unflappable, cool, laid-back, pick your California-surfer-boy adjective—he didn't let shit get to him.

Usually.

He shot a glance across the camp to the second building—the wooden barracks where the other half of the platoon was reconnoitering. He didn't expect to see anything—those guys were too good and knew how to be invisible—but they were like brothers to him, and if there was something wrong . . .

Fuck. Something was *definitely* wrong. The senior chief ran past him, heading not to the command building, but toward the barracks. The kid—Brian Murphy—followed. The senior chief broke off to the left toward the front of the building, and the kid broke right toward the rear. But the LC was shouting at them—and John—to fall back and get the hell out of there. In other words, it was a Dodge City.

John understood why a moment later.

He heard the whiz an instant before seeing the blinding flash of white light as the night detonated in front of him. The hot pressure of the shock wave made him rear back, his ears thundering with the powerful boom. The first time John had gone surfing, he'd been struck unexpectedly by a large wave and dragged under—the blast felt like that but with fire.

The debris that pummeled his body like bullets and the rock that struck him in the forehead and took him to the ground were secondary. All he could think about was the heat, and feeling as if his lungs had been filled with fuel-fired air.

When the blast of overwhelming heat finally receded, he choked in a few acrid breaths and looked around him in a daze. He couldn't see. A stab of panic penetrated the haze. Only when he tried to wipe his eyes did he remember the NVGs, which were now shattered.

Jerking the goggles off and tossing them to the ground, he blinked as the world came into view. Dust, ash, and smoke were everywhere. It was like every doomsday movie he'd ever seen.

Suddenly he was aware of men around him, pulling at him and mouthing words to him. The world seemed to be moving in slow motion, and it took his brain a moment to catch up. The two men were Miggy and Jim Bob—aka Michael Ruiz and Travis Hart.

"Are you all right?" he thought Ruiz was saying, but John's ears were ringing too loudly to hear anything.

He nodded, remembering that Miggy, Jim Bob, and Dolph—Steve Spivak—had been well behind him when the missile hit the barracks in front of them. John had been a couple hundred feet away. Had he been any closer . . .

He swore, remembering the kid and senior chief running past him. They'd been closer. And the LC?

A moment later his silent question was answered as the LC appeared out of the smoke with Dolph, both dragging the unconscious senior chief. It was hard to see what state Baylor was in in the dark, but if he was half as bad as John felt, it couldn't be good.

Miggy dropped down to look the senior chief over and administer first aid as necessary. Jim Bob was doing the same to John. Their corpsman had been with the other squad, but they all had medical training. SEALs might have specialties, but what made them distinct was that they were trained to do any job. If someone went down, any one of them could step up and fill his shoes.

John finally found his voice. "The kid?"

The LC met his gaze and shook his head. "Murphy was too close to the rear of the building where the first missile hit."

There'd been more than one?

Suddenly, the full importance and ramifications of what the LC said struck. If Murphy had been too close . . .

The other squad, the other seven men of Retiarius, including his best friend and BUD/S brother, Brandon Blake, had been *inside* the barracks building.

The senior chief and Murphy must have been trying to warn them.

John had to do something. He pushed Jim Bob away,

told him he was fine, and struggled to his feet, swaying as he tried to find his equilibrium. Christ, his head hurt. The ground was spinning. He started to run—stumble—toward the orange inferno.

But the LC had guessed his intent and grabbed his arm to hold him back. "It's too late," he yelled, his voice sounding like it was coming from the far end of a tunnel. "They're gone."

Gone. The finality of that one word penetrated his shell-shocked brain.

John wanted to argue. With every bone in his body he wanted to deny the LC's words. But the truth was right in front of his face. The gulag was gone. Both the command and barracks buildings had been flattened. What was left was being incinerated before his eyes.

He'd never been so close to one before, but he suspected what he was seeing: a thermobaric explosion. It was also known as a vacuum bomb, although this one had been attached to missiles. They were nasty shit, frowned upon by the international community for humanitarian reasons. Russia had been accused of using them in Syria, and the US had used them to target the caves in Afghanistan, including one nicknamed the "Mother of all Bombs." They used more fuel than conventional weapons, producing a much hotter, more sustained, and pressurized blast that was far more destructive—and deadly—when used in buildings, bunkers, and caves.

He knew what it meant. Just like that, his best friend, half the platoon, and half the family he had in the world were gone.

It was too horrible. Too hideous to think about.

He couldn't think about it. John had been here once before, and it wasn't a place he ever wanted to go to again. Utter devastation. Feeling as if the entire world had just gone black and he was lost.

He forced himself to look away. To move on and shift

gears. Putting the bad stuff behind him was what made him so good at his job.

But his eyes glanced back to the fire, the instinct to run toward it still strong. SEALs didn't leave their brothers behind. Ever.

"Donovan . . . Dynomite," the LC said, shaking him as if it weren't the first time he'd said his name. Kid Dyn-o-mite from the old 70s show *Good Times*. That was him. "I need you to focus. We don't have much time. They'll be here soon, looking for survivors. They can't find us."

John's head cleared. The heavy weight in his chest was still there, but he was back. The op . . . he had to focus on the op. "What do you need me to do?"

The LC looked relieved. "Get rid of anything electronic. Anything that might let them detect that we weren't in one of those buildings like we were supposed to be." Taylor looked at the other three men around him. "That goes for all of us—and the senior chief as well."

Baylor was still unconscious. He didn't rouse until they went into the river. That was after they'd thrown their electronics into the fire. But fearing that the Russian soldiers—probably their special forces, Spetsnaz—might also be using thermal imaging, they needed to mask their body heat as well.

So, into the icy river they went, taking turns keeping the senior chief afloat. Baylor had come around, but he was still out of it, and every time they had to go under and hold their breath as the Russian soldiers drew near, they feared he might not surface.

But he made it. They all did. Although those hours in the cold river weren't anything John ever wanted to go through again. He'd thought BUD/S had prepared him for cold and uncomfortable. But the Pacific Ocean in San Diego didn't have anything on a river in Arctic Russia.

It seemed as if the bastards would never leave. They

were having too much fun. John didn't need to understand Russian like Spivak did to know they were gloating.

Spivak could only catch a word or two of what they were saying in between breaths, but other than making some kind of joke that John took to be the Russian equivalent of shooting fish in a barrel and having what they needed to make the American "cowboys" pay, they weren't thoughtful enough to mention how they knew the SEALs were coming. If it hadn't been for the LC receiving a last-minute warning—that was what he and the senior chief had been arguing about—they would all be dead.

By the time the Russians left, John wasn't the only one battling hypothermia. But he pushed it aside just like everything else.

He never looked back, only forward.

And forward in this case meant getting the hell out of Dodge—or, in SEAL terminology, exfil.

SEALs had contingencies for contingencies, and this op was no exception. They'd all been well briefed and knew the mission plan backward and forward, but they didn't use their original exfil plan or the backup one. They were going to hump a good seventy miles through the Ural forests and tundra to the nearest city—or what passed for a city in the polar circle—to the old coal-mining town of Vorkuta.

The LC suspected that someone in their own government had set them up, and until he found out who it was, they were going to stay dead. That meant going dark, staying off the grid, and scattering in different directions as soon as they could.

It also meant getting rid of anything that could identify them as American or military. Due to the nature of their mission, most of their gear was unattributable, but even having it could be suspicious, so into the fires it went. They'd even have to ditch their weapons once they got closer to Vorkuta. Fortunately, they'd been trained in how to blend in—low-vis, as they called it. No buzz cuts or clean-shaven jaws for them. Relaxed grooming standards where common in the Teams. Once they had street clothes they would be good to go.

The only thing they saved was food—they would need what little they had—DEET for the bugs that would otherwise eat them alive, and medical supplies.

No one argued with the LC. Not even the senior chief, who had a few burns and was cut up pretty bad but was managing to stand up by himself. Of course, the senior chief could have two broken legs and would likely find a way to stand up by himself. He was one of the toughest sons of bitches John knew, and given that John hung out with Navy SEALs all day, that was saying something.

Senior Chief Baylor was the link—and sometimes shield—between the men and command. If there were problems, the men went to the senior chief. He was their leader, their teacher, their advocate, their confessor, and their punisher all rolled into one. To a man, they would follow him into hell and not look back. There was no one in this world John admired more.

Officers like the LC were part of the team, but their rank kept them apart.

John had mixed feelings about officers. Some were good. Some were bad. But as long as they didn't get in the way or do something to fuck up one of their missions when it needed to be run up the flagpole for approval, he didn't give them too much thought.

He'd known the LC for years and respected the man as much as he did the rank, which wasn't always the case, but he couldn't say he really *knew* him. Officers had to keep themselves apart. They couldn't let personal relationships interfere with or influence their decisions. Taylor could BS along with them, but he always kept himself slightly aloof.

But it wasn't until that moment that John truly understood the weight of the duty and responsibility that fell on an officer's shoulders. There was no head shed—aka command center—to issue orders. Here they were all half-frozen, in shock, mourning the loss of their brothers, six thousand miles away from their base in Honolulu, in a hostile country, where if they were discovered they would hope to be killed quickly, with no one they could trust to help them, and it was on the LC to get them out of it.

John had no idea whether the LC's plan would work, but he had to give Taylor credit—he didn't miss a beat. He didn't show any hesitation or uncertainty in issuing his orders. They might have been on a training exercise in Alaska rather than on the other side of the world in one of the most inhospitable countrysides he'd ever experienced.

The LC knew his role, and he was doing it.

John knew his, too.

As just six of the fourteen men who'd entered the prison camp four short hours before walked out, John took one last look back and forced the heaviness that rose in his chest down. *Good-bye, brothers*, he said to himself, and then aloud, "Hey, LC, I hear they have Starbucks all over Moscow now. Think there's one in Vorkuta? I'd fucking kill for a latte."

There was a long pause before the LC picked up the ball and ran with it. "I thought your discerning palate was too refined for chains?"

John grinned. "You know about the choices of beggars, LC."

"You and your girlie drinks," Baylor grumbled. "If you try to order it with nonfat milk, I may have to shoot you myself."

"Good thing for me the LC is making you toss your gun." John patted his rock-hard abs. "You don't get this incredible body without a little sacrifice, Senior. I have a certain standard to uphold. Just because you don't care what the ladies at Hulas—"

"Dynomite," the senior chief cut him off. "Shut the fuck up. My head hurts enough as it is. I don't need to hear about your Barbie Brigade right now."

But that is exactly what he did need to hear about— what they all needed to hear about. And they did. For two of the most miserable days he'd ever spent, John drew upon every story he could think of to keep their minds off the brothers they'd left behind.

Good thing he had plenty to draw on. But even he was tired of hearing his own voice by the time they reached Vorkuta. He wasn't sure what he expected of a coal-mining town on the doorstep of Siberia, but it looked pretty much like any medium-sized former industrial American city that had reached its height of modernity in the seventies.

They let Spivak, who with his Slavic languages and looks would be the most low-vis, go in first and do a little recon.

When he came back, he turned to John. "Didn't find a Starbucks, Dynomite, but I did see sushi."

"You gotta be shitting me?" It was his second favorite behind Mexican. "Think it would blow cover if I asked for a California roll? Although they probably use that fake crab crap, and avocado in Arctic Russia this time of year might be a little suspect. I know those brown spots are supposed to be safe to eat, but . . ."

This time the senior chief wasn't the only one who was telling him to shut the fuck up. And that was as much normal as John could hope for for a while.

One

Brittany Blake tapped the steering wheel with her thumbs and glanced down at the clock in the dashboard. The bright green LED was just about the only light around on this deserted stretch of road.

Zero dark thirty. That was what they said for twelve thirty a.m. in the military, right? It sounded much more ominous in the movies, which was probably why she'd thought about it. This felt like a movie. A really scary movie where the heroine was doing something supremely stupid and the entire audience was yelling at the screen for her not to do it.

In other words, every horror movie ever.

Why, yes, waiting for a "drop" all alone in a not-so-great part of town after midnight on a moonless night under a highway overpass in an old warehouse area in a spot much loved by drug dealers and other not-so-law-abiding folks sounded like a fabulous idea. Nothing could go wrong there.

Jeez, she'd be yelling at the screen herself.

On cue, a loud crashing sound made her—just like a horror movie audience would—jump. Heart now pounding in her throat, she peered into the darkness but didn't see anything. It had sounded like breaking glass. A bottle dropped by a wino nearby maybe?

She hoped that's what it was, and not some serial killer roaming the streets and breaking the windows of stupid reporters sitting in their cars, asking for trouble.

Slowly Brittany relaxed back into the cloth bucket seat, but her grip on the wheel didn't lighten any.

Sigh. So this definitely wasn't her most brilliant moment, but neither was it the first time she'd been in a sketchy situation. It went along with the job. It was the "investigative" part of the reporting bit.

But if this new source delivered on what they promised, the danger would be worth it—and then some. She had to find out the truth of what had happened to her brother, Brandon.

Tap, tap, tap. The sound of her thumbs hitting the plastic steering wheel mixed with the gentle whir of the AC, which was gradually becoming less and less effective in combating the horrible humidity of the warm summer night the longer she sat here. She was starting to sweat, literally and figuratively.

Her source was—she glanced down at the clock again—thirty-*two* minutes late.

It can't be a hoax. Please, don't let it be a hoax.

The caller had sounded so insistent, so knowledgeable, so official. She'd give them another ten minutes, and then—

Who was she kidding? She'd wait all night if she had to. She needed this. She hated to use the word "desperate," but if the proverbial shoe fit . . .

She *was* desperate. She needed something concrete to prove that her suspicions were correct: that her brother, Brandon, was part of a top secret Navy SEAL team (along the lines of the now not-so-secret-anymore SEAL Team Six) who had gone on a mission and not come back.

"The Lost Platoon," she dubbed them in her articles, after the famous Lost Legion of Rome. Coincidentally—and eerily—they'd both been numbered nine.

She'd thought the title was catchy, and it had certainly captured the public's attention. The three articles she'd written so far—the most recent out this morning—had proved wildly popular, being picked up by the AP, Reuters, and other news organizations worldwide.

Which had turned out to be a double-edged sword. It was great in that it got her the attention she wanted and put pressure on the government and military to explain what had happened, but it also increased the pressure on her to come up with something more than a solid hunch from witness interviews. Preferably a few facts that could be substantiated. Editors liked those. Go figure.

Using the picture in the latest article had been a desperate move, a last-ditch effort to turn up something.

The fact that her brother hadn't called two months ago, on the twelfth anniversary of their parents' deaths, when he'd done so every year previously might have convinced her that something had happened to him, but her boss wanted more.

That she and Brandon hadn't been close didn't matter. Her brother wouldn't have let that day go unacknowledged. No matter what clandestine operation he'd been deployed on that the government didn't want anyone to know about, he would have called or contacted her in some way.

She was so certain of it that she'd flown to Hawaii, where she knew he was stationed, to demand answers.

Of course, at first the navy had refused to talk to her.

When it had become obvious she wasn't going to give up, they'd taken the ignorance route. "You must be mistaken. Your brother is not stationed here." And her personal favorite: "SEAL Team Nine? We don't have a team with that number."

Right. And yet they had every other number between one and ten?

She had found some people who were willing to talk to her. Most were off-the-record, which only made her more certain she was onto something.

But when she'd presented proof of her brother's being stationed there in the form of a handful of very attractive blondes she found at a dive bar called Hulas, who recognized Brandon and the three other men with him in the single recentish photo she had of him—she hadn't seen her brother in five years, but some things apparently never changed—the stony-looking officers who'd been denying they'd ever seen him before suddenly made an abrupt about-face and claimed the information was "classified."

Which was pretty much like holding up a bright red cape in front of an angry bull—her being the angry bull—making her even more determined to find out the truth.

She'd done enough research into America's Special Mission Units and secret soldiers to know that they could be embedded for months on training ops or deployments.

But that wasn't what was going on here. She *knew* something had happened to Brandon and his team—something bad—and the military was trying to cover it up. And she wasn't the only one at the base who thought that. *Proving* it, however, was something else.

The wall of secrecy had gone up, and she'd returned home to DC to try to topple it from a different direction. But so far the navy and the government had ignored her articles. She had to come up with something they couldn't ignore.

She wanted answers. If her brother had died—and every bone in her body told her he had—she wanted to know why. She wasn't going to let them sweep his sacrifice under the rug and cover up whatever mess they'd made. Not this time. She wanted the truth, and she was going to find it. She owed him that at least.

Even if it meant sitting in her car for half the night in a not-so-wonderful part of town, waiting for information that sounded too good to be true. But the handwritten note that had been dropped in her apartment mail slot had promised "proof of what had happened to your brother's platoon."

She started to glance down at the clock again when the beams of approaching headlights reflected in her rearview mirror sent her pulse shooting through her chest again. Temporarily blinded, she looked over her shoulder, but her entire car was filled with light as the car slowly came right up behind her.

At the last minute, the car pulled alongside her. It was a black town car. The kind favored by government officials and airport transport companies everywhere.

Her heart was thumping hard now. This was it. This had to be it.

When the back passenger door was even with her driver's door, the car came to a stop. Whoever was in there, they were important enough to have a driver. Slowly, just like in the movies, the heavily tinted window started to lower. Fortunately, unlike in the movies, the barrel of a gun aimed in her direction didn't appear.

She lowered her window as well.

It was too dark to see inside the other car, but she could barely contain her excitement when a large manila envelope was passed to her. She caught sight of a medium-sized gloved hand—which, as it was about eight hundred degrees, must have been to hide anything identifying—and a dark-wool-clad arm with the telltale gold stripe of a military uniform around the sleeve edge before the window started back up.

"Wait!" Brittany said.

The window stopped with a few-inch gap at the top.

"How can I contact you?" she asked.

There was a long pause. Brittany thought they weren't going to answer, but just as the window started to climb again, someone said in a low voice, "You can't. I'll contact you."

The car pulled away before the window even had a chance to fully close. Despite the effort her contact had made to conceal their identity, Brittany was fairly certain it had been a woman.

She tried to make out the plates as the car drove off, but it was too dark. She flipped on her headlights just in time to see the government plates with a D followed by a few numbers she couldn't read and either a 25 or 26 at the end. She was pretty sure "D" stood for "Department of Defense."

Jackpot! This had to be legit. She pressed the overhead button for the interior light and practically ripped open the envelope.

It was a thin stack—only about four or five pages—but any initial disappointment in size slipped away as she started to flip through.

Oh my God, oh my God, oh my God kept running through her head as she saw the satellite images, heavily redacted deployment order, and news article about a large explosion in the Northern Urals near the border of Siberia picked up by our satellites last May, which the Russians had claimed was a missile test. She recalled seeing it, but as Russians testing weapons these days was not exactly unusual, she hadn't paid it much mind.

She was looking at the redacted deployment order for

something called "Naval Warfare Special Deployment Group" (which must be the official name for Team Nine), when the sound of a very loud muffler reminded her where she was.

She had that horrible moment when she turned the key and the car didn't start right away. *Oh God, please tell me I didn't kill the battery with the AC!* But fortunately, on the second try, the engine roared to life, and she whipped a U-ey to retrace her steps out of here.

Anxious to study the docs in more detail, she headed downtown to her office rather than the hovel she called an apartment across town. Her office was actually more of a cubicle, and the fact that it was less depressing than her home spoke volumes about their relative importance in her life.

She was so excited and busy trying to order the thoughts racing through her mind that it took her a while to realize someone was following her.

Brittany noticed the car behind her when she exited the interstate onto Massachusetts Ave, heading toward the downtown headquarters of the DC News Organization (DCNO), which included her present employer, the *DC Chronicle*, among other media holdings.

There weren't many cars on the road, which was why she noticed the headlights pulling off behind her. But it wasn't until she squeaked through the yellow light at Seventh by the Carnegie Library and the car sped through behind her that she felt the distinctive prickle at her neck.

Her heart took an extra beat or two as her eyes darted between the road and her rearview mirror. She couldn't tell the make and model of the car, but she'd guess an American sedan similar to those used by the police.

Could it be an undercover cop? But why would they

be following her? *Was* someone following her, or was she just being paranoid?

Telling herself to calm down, she switched lanes and flipped on her signal, indicating that she was going to take a left at the next block.

The car behind her did the same.

A spike of adrenaline shot through her. She waited for a car approaching in the opposite direction to pass and made her turn. She was about to take an immediate left again into the circular driveway of a big hotel, when the car behind her suddenly moved out of the turn lane and continued straight.

She let out a long breath, not realizing she'd been holding it. Good God, the meeting earlier tonight must have gotten to her more than she'd realized. She was now officially imagining things.

The heavy pounding of her heart slowed as she continued down the street a few blocks, turned right, and then took another right into the parking lot underneath the nondescript office building.

In the old days a paper like the *Chronicle* would have had their offices in an important stately building. But with the advent of the Internet and online news, those days were long gone. Similar to many papers in this country, the *Chronicle* was fighting to hang on.

They were alike in that regard.

It might not be the most prestigious paper in DC, or the most widely circulated, but it was respected, and coming from where Brittany had been, that was enough.

She found a space near one of the stairwells on the lower level of the garage and pulled in to park. The elevators in the building took forever, but she liked to take the stairs for the exercise.

She'd been slacking off in the workout arena since she'd moved back to DC and started at the *Chronicle* in January. At five foot threeish and . . . what had her friend called it? "Athletically curvy"? . . . with not a lot of time to cook and taste buds that belonged to a teenage boy, she didn't have a lot of room to mess around and needed all the staircases she could get.

Sliding the manila envelope into the nylon messenger bag that she used as a briefcase and purse—she'd had it since college (thus the Georgetown Tigers black and orange) and it was not only low-profile but basically indestructible— she slung it over her shoulder as she got out of the car. There were only a few cars left in the garage at this time of night, and the door closed with a slam that echoed in the cement cavern.

She fumbled with the key fob to lock the doors and swore. She'd left her phone inside. Opening the door, she reached back inside to grab the phone. Before shutting the door again, she decided to toss the lightweight sweater she wore over her sleeveless top in the backseat.

DCNO was cheap, and it cut any flow of cool air into the building at six p.m. sharp, meaning that even after midnight it would be hot and humid in the office.

That was one of the problems with the South and the East Coast in the summer—although usually it was cold rooms inside and hot and humid outside. It seemed like she was always taking clothes off and putting them back on a few minutes later.

She might make a dirty joke about that statement if her love life weren't so pathetic. Weather was the only reason her clothes came off lately. Few minutes or not.

But maybe that would change tomorrow. She'd bitten the bullet and set up her first date using the app her friends had told her about. The guy was smoking hot in his picture, which made her think he must be too good to be true. Guys who looked like that didn't need apps.

She'd just gotten herself all settled and was about to lock the doors when she saw a shadow move behind her in the reflection of the car window.

Oh God. Her stomach hit the floor—along with her heart. She *had* been followed.

Maybe it was because it was the second time Brittany was experiencing panic that night, but her head was clearer, and she knew immediately what to do.

Thank God she still had her keys in her hand. What was the range? Ten feet? Five? She slid off the safety lock, put her finger on the nozzle, and spun around.

The scream died in her throat. Brittany's hand froze only seconds away from spraying the police-grade pepper oil into her would-be assailant's eyes.

But it wasn't an assailant. At least not one who meant her physical harm.

She lowered her hand, her held breath coming in a hard exhale. "What are you doing, Paulie? You scared me half to death! Why are you following me?"

He'd stepped back when he'd seen the spray and had the gall to be eyeing her angrily—or more angrily than usual. Paul "Paulie" DeCarlo, the investigations editor and senior member of the four-person investigative team at the paper, wasn't her biggest fan. To put it mildly. He'd made no secret that he didn't want her as part of "his" team.

"I wasn't following you," he said. "I was on my way to my car and coming over to help you. I can't believe you almost sprayed me with that stuff."

He stared at the hand that was still holding the pink container attached to her key chain.

"Help me with what?" she asked, sliding it back into her bag and telling herself that she had no reason to feel defensive. He was the one who'd snuck up on her.

"You looked like you were having problems, and it isn't safe down here after hours. Didn't you hear about Doris from advertising? She was mugged a few weeks ago. You shouldn't be hanging out in parking lots alone this late."

Brittany sighed, realizing she'd overreacted. That meeting tonight had made her jumpy. But it was hard to believe Paulie would be concerned about her.

She tilted her head, studying him. His face hadn't lost any of its anger. He looked straight out of some seventies cop show. White button-down shirt rolled up at the sleeves, half-done cheap striped tie, dark brown or black slacks (never khakis), untrimmed fluffy mustache, and a tired, been-around-the-block-too-many-times cynicism that made him appear ten years older than his fifty-three years.

"I did hear about it; that's why I picked up the pepper spray." She was taking precautions, but she couldn't let fear keep her from doing her job. "I appreciate the advice, but I've got it under control."

"You sure about that? From where I sit, you don't look like you have anything under control—unless you count a bunch of conspiracy theories. But those are your specialty, right?"

Brittany ignored the jab, but it wasn't easy when it found such a perpetually painful mark. "I'm working on something right now."

Why was she defending herself to him?

"Is that so? It better be good, with a reliable source this time, or you'll be back at that paper in the middle-of-nowhere, writing obits." Cleveland wasn't exactly nowhere (even if it felt like it at times), and it hadn't been obits. But she didn't correct him. The society pages weren't much better. "And next time you won't find another job so easily, even with a boss who wants to get in your pants."

Brittany flushed beet red with anger at the crude insinuation, suddenly wishing she hadn't put the pepper spray in her bag. But he was already walking away.

Paulie was one of those men who had to have the last word. She let him have it this time, mostly because she knew it was jealousy speaking. Her "tabloid style" articles, as he called them, had been receiving a lot of attention, and the old-school reporter—who hadn't wanted her on his team in the first place—resented it.

But she also feared there might be more truth to his accusation than she wanted to admit.

Brittany had worked hard since she had been publicly discredited and fired for allegedly making up a source five years ago. She'd fought her way back, starting as a fact checker and working for almost nothing at a small paper in Arizona, to gradually bigger and better positions at a handful of papers across the country.

But no one had been willing to hire her as a reporter. No one until Jameson Cooper. She'd thought the divorced, fortyish editor in chief of the *Chronicle* had seen something in her. He'd been impressed by the work she'd done up until her fall from grace, and she thought he'd admired her fortitude and determination in working her way back up.

But in the past few months she'd realized that might not be all that he was admiring. She'd caught him looking at her when he didn't think she was aware of it, and lately he seemed to find any excuse to come by her cubicle and chat.

There was nothing inappropriate or creepy about it—and certainly nothing that would be characterized as sexual harassment—he just seemed to like her. *Really* like her.

The worst part was that she liked him, too. He was a nice guy. Funny and smart, easy to talk to, and nice-looking in that bookish, Tom Hiddleston kind of way.

In other circumstances she might have returned his interest. But he was her boss, and she wouldn't go there. Ever.

Women had it hard enough in this business without doing things that legitimately undermined their position. The newsroom might not be the old boy's frat house it had been once, but there was still enough of that around not to want to feed into it. Being accused of sleeping her way to the top wasn't going to happen.

She'd been ignoring her boss's interest and subtle cues, desperation for this job making her hope it wasn't there. But if Paulie had noticed, she couldn't delude herself anymore that her credentials alone had gotten her this job. She may have been a rising hotshot reporter five years ago, but that was a long time ago.

Whatever Jameson's reasons for hiring her, he had taken a chance on her and she was determined to make it pay off for both of them with top-notch work. It was the best way to shut up Paulie as well.

But that wasn't all or even the most important part of what was driving her this time. It was finding out what happened to her brother, and the information she'd received tonight just might help her do that.

Anxious to delve in deeper to what was in that envelope, she was halfway to the stairwell before she realized someone was standing there.

She looked up to see Nancy, another member of the team, holding the door open. From the younger woman's chagrined expression, Brittany didn't need to ask whether she'd heard.

Nancy waited until Brittany was next to her to speak. "Don't listen to Paulie. He's still angry about his protégé leaving for the online job. He wasn't going to like anyone who replaced him."

Brittany smiled at her for trying, but they both knew there was more to it than that. "No, Paulie is right. I need to do better or I'm going to be out of a job." Jameson had as good as told her as much. "But with my next article, I hope to do that."

Nancy's brows lifted in surprise. "You onto something?"

Brittany smiled at her friend, whose eyes looked bleary and red behind thick glasses. "I hope so."

Nancy was a couple years younger than Brittany's twenty-seven, and although she was technically her senior on the team, Brittany had been helping her out lately. Nancy had yet to make her mark in the investigative reporting world. Despite good stories and solid reporting, her articles hadn't really connected with their audience.

She was a talented writer and probably would have found an appreciative audience twenty years earlier, but she didn't know how to spin her stories so that they appealed to the modern forty-character social media reader. Even readers of traditional newspapers, whether in print or online, still needed to have their attention grabbed and held. It wasn't tabloid reporting, as Paulie accused. It wasn't the quality of the story or work, just the way it was presented.

Suddenly, something occurred to her. "You must be onto something, too. It's late."

Nancy shook her head. "I wish. Paulie asked me to stay and help him with some research. It was nothing, but it took longer than I expected. I was just leaving when I heard what he said about you and Jameson." She blushed, hastily correcting herself. "I didn't mean . . . No one thinks . . ."

Brittany could see the woman's discomfort and tried to put an end to it, even as her words filled her with dismay. God, was that what everyone thought? "I know what you meant. Don't worry about it. Besides, I have a hot date this weekend."

"You do?"

The level of Nancy's incredulity might have been embarrassing if it weren't warranted. Brittany nodded and pulled out her phone to show her the picture on the app. "Cute, huh?"

Nancy let out a low whistle. "I'd say. But hockey? I didn't think you were a sports fan."

Brittany shrugged. "Not usually, but we'll see. I just hope he has all his teeth."

Nancy laughed and said good night.

At last Brittany hurried up the stairs, eager to get a good look at the fruit of a long and difficult night.

Two

Who knew relaxing could be so exhausting?

John kicked back on the brown plaid polyester sofa that would have looked right at home in a frat house from the sixties, popped a beer, and put his feet up on the coffee table. He grabbed the remote to turn on the TV and started to flip through the channels.

No one could ever call him a pessimist. Hope sprang eternal every time he sat down to watch TV. But the only sports he could find were soccer and a replay of an earlier track and field meet, which the Finns called "athletics."

He would fucking kill for an A's game. Hell, at this point he was so desperate, he'd even watch the Giants. He just couldn't get behind soccer. He didn't care how many people in the world loved it; watching grown men roll around on the ground in fake pain to try to get a penalty call was embarrassing. Give him a real sport like baseball, basketball, American football, rugby, or water polo any day of week.

Yep, little-known fact: water polo was considered the toughest sport in the world when taking together speed, endurance, strength, agility, skill level, and physicality, beating out Aussie rules football, boxing, and rugby. And that was after the mandatory deduction of man points for the weenie bikini.

Having played water polo for most of his teens and early twenties, John might be biased, but he could tell you one thing: he would have been laughed out of the pool had he ever started rolling around, holding his knee, and crying.

He'd seen enough soccer in the past two months to last him for a lifetime. Settling on a repeat of *The Simpsons*, he sat back to drink his beer. Chilling. Just like he'd been doing every day for two months.

God, he was tired. Tonight he vowed to go to bed before 0200. No resort bars or late-night sauna parties for him— no matter how tempting.

So much for his plan to take it easy and relax while the LC figured out what the hell had gone down in Russia. Being a ski bum in Levi, Finland, had sounded like the perfect job for a temporarily unemployed Navy SEAL who needed to stay off the grid and disappear for a while. Levi was remote—one hundred miles north of the Arctic Circle certainly qualified—his fellow ski bums were too stoned or laid-back to ask a lot of questions, resorts were a mecca for the international labor force who were happy to fill low-paying jobs, and the Finns, like many in the Nordic countries, tended to speak English.

The latter was a good thing, because after two months, John hadn't moved much beyond "hello," "good-bye," "thank you," a few swear words, and "do you speak English?" Which, if you'd ever seen those words in Finnish, was pretty understandable. A few years of college Spanish didn't help much with "*hyvää päivänjatkoa,*" aka, "have a nice day."

His plan had been to find a job on the slopes while the ski season wound down, rent a room in a house with a bunch of guys, and spend his evenings in the local chalets, drinking whatever the Finnish equivalent of a hot toddy was while enjoying the local scenery of the blond, blue-eyed, and long-legged variety.

He'd say one thing for the Nordic countries. They might not know shit about good sports, but they had some of the best-looking women he'd ever seen in his life.

Everything had worked pretty much as he'd anticipated. He'd even managed to get in on some avalanche control, volunteering with the local ski patrol, to keep his skills with explosives fresh—until he'd nearly buried himself in an avalanche when a hand charge had gone off too quickly. Accidents like that happened even to the most experienced patrolmen. If they didn't usually happen to him, John didn't dwell on it. He never dwelled; it was a waste of time.

After the ski season had wound down, he'd exchanged his skis and boots for paddles and a river raft, making money by taking tourists down some not-very-thrilling rapids.

Not exactly his speed, but he wasn't quite running on all cylinders lately. His sleep since arriving in Finland had been crap—especially since he'd exhausted the Ambien supply his roommate had tracked down. SEALs lived on the sleep aid.

Next time he needed to disappear for a while he'd pick a country that didn't have almost twenty-four hours of sunlight. It made it too easy to stay up until two or three in the morning. Of course, the tall, blond-haired and blue-eyed inducements didn't help with early bedtime. What had the inducement's name been last night? Martha? He couldn't remember. That was bad even for him.

Maybe he was going at this relaxing business a little too hard. Apparently, there *was* too much of a good thing. He wasn't in his early twenties anymore; he was almost thirty and way too old to be going out every night.

If Brand were here, he'd be giving him shit for—

John stopped, remembering. No Brand. No any of those guys. They were gone. He had to stop thinking about it, embrace the suck, and move the fuck on.

He finished his beer in one long drink to cool the burning in his chest and popped another, staring so hard at the TV that he didn't hear one of his roommates come in until he spoke.

"What are you doing here alone?" Sami asked. He was the only Finn in the house of five guys—it was a veritable United Nations around this place with a Russian, a Swede, a German, and a fake Canadian (him). "I thought you'd be at Hullu Poro right now, taking your bows before the concert."

Ah, hell, that was tonight? One of his other housemates—the German—was in a local band, and they were playing at the Crazy Reindeer Arena, aka Hullu Poro Areena.

John ignored the taking-bows comment, hoping it would go away, and lifted his beer with a smile. "Just warming up."

"Good," Sami said, tossing him the paper as he unloaded a bag of groceries—or what a twenty-six-year-old single guy considered groceries. There wasn't a shortage of crap around this place. If it weren't for John, these guys wouldn't have eaten a vegetable or nonprocessed food in weeks. "It wouldn't do for the hero of the hour to miss out on his celebration." The young Finn shook his head. "Man, first Marta and now this. You're on a roll this week, my friend."

Marta! That was her name. John's three other unattached housemates, which included Sami, had all been eyeing the pretty new waitress at their favorite resort bar. John hadn't been the first one to ask her out. Actually, he hadn't asked her out at all. She'd done all the asking.

Which was just the way he liked it. He'd figured out a long time ago that some women didn't like to be pursued, and if you waited long enough, they would usually come to you. He'd made waiting an art form; he couldn't remember the last time he'd had to make the first move.

"You going to see her again?" Sami asked.

John shrugged. "Why not?"

Sami shook his head in disbelief. Despite the popular misconception, not all Finns were blond-haired and blue-eyed, but Sami did fit the Nordic mold and could have walked right off a Viking ship with his long hair and scraggy Vandyke-style beard.

Actually, John could have walked off that ship himself, although his hair was a darker blond, his beard was trimmed better, and he was a good half a head taller and fifty pounds heavier than his young friend.

"You're unbelievable. The hottest woman to walk into Levi in months throws herself at you and you act like it's no big deal."

John wasn't acting; it wasn't a big deal. She was a nice enough girl—from what he remembered. And definitely nice to look at. He remembered that. But he didn't lose his head easily. Actually, he didn't lose his head ever.

Once.

"*Paska,*" Sami muttered. "If you don't appreciate her, I'll take her."

Like most Finns, Sami used curse words as punctuation—in this case, *shit*. Finns were reputed to swear more than Russians and Scots. Which was saying something. John had done his fair share of swearing before moving into this house, but with both a Finn and a Russian in the house, it had increased exponentially.

"I'm planning to ask her out again," John said. He might have actually already done so. For some reason Sunday was ringing a bell. He was more tired than he realized, or he might have had one too many beers last night. "But if you want to take her out, I'm happy to stand aside."

Sami muttered a word that John took to be roughly

equivalent to a harsh "asshole" and added, "If I thought she'd say yes, I would, but after today . . ." He shook his head. "None of us stand a chance. They're saying that kid would have died if you hadn't been there."

John shrugged again. It paid to be a winner, as Team-guys liked to say. "Day at the office, man."

Sami gave him a look that was half-amused and half-incredulous. "I'd tell you to stop being modest, but I don't think you are. How long was he under?"

"A minute." Another shrug. "Maybe two."

"I heard it was more like four and that you were under so long they thought you drowned, too."

The kid had had his foot caught between two rocks, which was why his life vest hadn't brought him back to the surface. It had taken some time for John to free him. Not for the first time he thanked BUD/S, which had trained him not just to hold his breath but not to panic. He and Brand . . .

He swore and took another sip of his beer.

"No brain damage to the kid?" Sami asked.

John shook his head. "Doesn't look like it. They're keeping him overnight, but he was alert and talking normally when he left in the chopper."

"The raft dump-trucked?"

John nodded. The guide had taken a big wave too close to the edge, causing the boat to tilt and lose more than half its passengers. In rafting lingo, "dump-truck."

People fell out of rafts all the time. That hadn't been the problem. The problem had been twofold: the wave had been close to a known keeper hole, which, as its name suggested, was a feature on the river when a hydraulic—or hole—is so strong that it doesn't release what goes in it, and the guide miscounted and thought that everyone had been accounted for.

John hadn't been the guide for that raft, but he'd been helping out in one of the three rafts in the tour. He hadn't noticed the seventeen-year-old kid was missing right away either. He'd been helping retrieve another teenage boy who had become hysterical and was being carried toward rocks.

When John acted as a SEAL squad leader, keeping track of his men was second nature. He didn't even have to think about it. But he'd missed the kid.

John had done everything by the book. No one could have found fault with what happened today. But he held himself to a higher standard.

Just like with the avalanche.

Did it mean something?

He was being too hard on himself. Shit happened.

But not usually to him. Unconsciously his fingers went to his forehead, feeling the nearly healed wound that bisected his brow. His only scar from the missile that should have taken his life. He'd walked away with barely a scratch.

Sami was still watching him. "Alexi"—their Russian housemate who had also been on the trip—"said you were . . . what is that English expression? Cool as an ice cube?"

"Cucumber."

Sami frowned. "That doesn't make any sense." He waved his hand and said another word in Finnish, which John assumed was a curse word he wasn't familiar with. "He said you could have been one of those mountain rescue guys. Maybe you should volunteer with the local group? What is it you said you did before coming here?"

He hadn't. No one had asked—or cared. As he said, this place was perfect. "I was at Whistler for the last five years. I did a little of everything."

John had debated picking a more interesting cover than Joe Phillips from Victoria, Canada, but he wasn't very good at language or accents, and he needed someplace not in Europe—which he would never have been able to fake in a place like this—that could explain his skiing ability. His other option had been New Zealand. Canada was definitely easier.

For a guy who was stoned more than half the time, Sami was proving unusually focused. This was almost a grilling and certainly the most sustained conversation John had ever had with him. John was hoping it would end soon. These questions were making him uncomfortable. If too many people had them, he would need to move on.

Surprisingly, a change of scenery didn't sound like a bad idea. All this relaxing was getting to him. He needed to get back to work. Frogman work. To get his war on, as they liked to say. But who the hell knew how long that would be? He'd talked to the LC only once since he'd been in Levi, and that had only been a quick call to give him his number and fill him in on his cover.

The six survivors had scattered, and the LC was the only one who knew where they all were. If it hadn't been hard enough losing Brand and the others, he'd effectively lost Tex, Miggy, Jim Bob, and Dolph as well.

John would never be characterized as impatient, but he felt a twinge of it now.

Fortunately, Sami left the room to take a shower and John was able to finish his beer and the episode of *The Simpsons* in peace.

Only when he got up to hop in the shower himself did he remember the paper. Avoiding electronic devices meant no tablets, smartphones, or laptops, so he'd had to go old-school for his news. He opened it to the international section and swore. The image was grainy, but there was no mistaking the face staring back at him. It looked back at him in the mirror every day.

Damn it, Brit! Can't you just leave it alone? But he knew better than to ask that question. Brittany Blake didn't leave anything alone.

Not for the first time, Brand's little sister was making things difficult for him.

———————

John had been on edge all night, but he apparently didn't have anything to worry about. Either most of the people he hung out with in Levi didn't pay attention to the news—which was a distinct possibility—or he'd changed so much in five years as to become unrecognizable.

The latter seemed to be the case later that night when he brought Marta back to the house for a little late-night sauna action. One of his favorite things about Finland so far definitely had to be the saunas. They were ubiquitous, seemingly more common than dishwashers. Even apartments had them.

He'd left Marta in the living room while he went to get them something to drink, and when he came back she was watching the news. Unfortunately, it was just as they were running a story—with the damned photo—about the "Lost Platoon."

Great, it was on the news now. He cursed Brand's sister again.

Marta's gaze shifted from the grainy image on the screen to his face.

He held his breath for a good long second before he let it go. Not a flicker. Not even one tiny glimmer of recognition.

With the way she'd been staring at him the past couple days, if she didn't make the connection, he doubted any of the others would either.

"What do you think happened to them?" she asked in her heavily accented English.

He feigned ignorance. "Who?"

"The Lost Platoon of American soldiers."

Now, that grated. SEALs were sailors. He shrugged indifferently. "I have no idea. Sounds like a bunch of speculation to me."

He sat down beside her and handed her the glass of

schnapps. He'd stick to beer. He wasn't big on the popular liquor, which tasted like and had the consistency of cough syrup.

"The reporter seems pretty convinced. Her brother is one of the men missing."

John felt the hot pressure building behind his ribs. He didn't want to talk about this, and he knew just how to end the conversation.

He slid his arm around her shoulders and leaned in close. Her dark eyes widened a little. They were a really pretty golden brown framed with long, thick lashes. She wasn't his usual type, but he was up for a change. And it was her mouth he was thinking about now. Red and sweet and gently parted—not with another question but with anticipation.

Perfect.

He waited, and she came to him, leaning in ever so slightly until their lips met.

The kiss was long and slow at first, and just getting mildly interesting when he felt a buzzing vibration in his pocket.

John knew exactly who it had to be because no one else had the number. That was some kind of timing. John had just been thinking it was time to move on, and now the LC—Scott Taylor—was calling. Had he figured out who had set them up? Was it time to get back to work?

The relief caused any blood that had been flowing to instantly stop. He pulled away, and Marta made a sound of protest. "Sorry," he lied. "I gotta take this."

He stood and dug the phone out of his pants. Flipping it open, he pushed the button to answer it but didn't say anything until he was in his room with the door closed behind him. "Johnson's Plumbing."

The code had been his idea. Yes, he was a child. But with what they did, they needed every little bit of amusement—even the cheap dick-humor kind.

"Next time I'm picking the damned code," Taylor said. "I'm so tired of hearing that. It wasn't funny the first time."

John grinned. It was good to hear the LC's voice. That he was clearly irritated and short-tempered didn't bother him—he was usually that way where John was concerned. The LC was always serious. John wasn't. "Did you figure out the source of the leak? Are we all clear to get back?"

There was a long pause. "Not yet. I'm still working on it."

John tried not to be disappointed; it wasn't easy. "What's up, then?"

"I take it you've seen the paper by now?"

The subject caused John's jaw to clamp down. "And the news." Suspecting what this was about, he started to refuse even before the LC asked. "Don't look at me—"

"I need you to shut her up."

John's reaction was visceral. Every bone in his body rejected the idea. He didn't want to have anything to do with Brand's sexy, made-his-blood-run-hot, and definitely off-limits sister. That was a no go. *She* was a no go.

With unusual vehemence for someone who was normally easygoing and agreeable, John said, "No, sir. Not me. Find someone else to take care of it. Sir."

If he thought adding the extra "sir" in there would help, it didn't. "I wasn't asking, Donovan, and the 'sir' crap isn't going to help. Everyone else is busy. Besides, you are the logical choice. Baylor told me you know her."

That was the problem.

"Not well," he lied. Well enough. "What about Miggy? He knows her, too."

The four of them had been hanging out at her brother's rented beach house in San Diego—John, Brand, Miggy, and Tex—when Brittany had shown up for an unexpected visit five years ago. It had been during the time he and Brand were being recruited for Team Nine.

There was a pause. "What's this about, Dynomite? I thought you'd want to help—this is Blake's sister we're talking about, and she could be in danger. She has no idea of the kind of shit storm she's stirring up with these articles. We aren't the only ones who might want her quiet. Did you think of that?"

John's jaw was clenching so hard that his teeth were gritting together. He didn't want to think about that. If he thought about that, he wouldn't be able to refuse. He'd also have to remember his promise.

"You think she's in danger from whoever set us up and told the Russians we were coming?"

"She could be. She's shining a light on something a lot of people want to keep dark. And she's not letting it go."

That was her. If there was anything he remembered about Brand's sister—and unfortunately he remembered a lot, especially those big blue eyes staring up at him as if he'd just stomped all over her heart, which still made him a little sick just thinking about—she didn't back off easily. Once Brit got her teeth into something, she didn't let go. She was the pin-down, box-in type. Which was part of the problem. He didn't do either.

John wanted to refuse, but he knew he was beaten. He might not want to have anything to do with her, but she was his best friend's sister. He couldn't stand by if she was in danger. Besides, it wasn't as if he had to physically come into contact with her. He shivered with something that might actually be characterized as fear.

At least he didn't think he would have to. "I thought you didn't want anyone to know we are alive."

"I don't." The LC stopped to correct himself. "Didn't. Something came up with the senior chief, and I had to bring Kate into it, but no one else can know."

John didn't say anything. He didn't know what to think. Kate was Katherine Wesson. The ex-wife of Team Nine's former chief, Colt Wesson. LC Taylor was supposedly one of the reasons the Wesson marriage had broken up. John hadn't wanted to believe the LC could have done something so effed up as to screw around with another man's wife, let alone a close friend and team member's wife—it didn't fit with Taylor's always by-the-book, run-a-tight-ship persona. But now the one person he'd confided in about this was Kate? John didn't know what to make of that, but he was glad they had someone they could trust helping them—especially since Kate was CIA.

"Then how am I supposed to get her to back off?" John said. "I can't exactly call her and tell her what's up." Nor was he going to threaten or scare her. Not only did the idea make him cringe, but he didn't think it would stop her. Rather, it would probably have the opposite effect.

"You'll think of something," the LC said, apparently unconcerned. "Just do it fast. For her sake as well as ours, this story needs to go away."

John hung up the phone and leaned back against the door, feeling as if he'd just been told to run a marathon in an hour—uphill. Hell, that would be easier. And preferable.

He closed his eyes and thought for a minute, letting the memories come back to him. Memories that he normally kept shut away in a very dark corner, behind a very thick wall. *Not for you.*

His eyes popped open. He had an idea. There was one way he could think of to be sure she heeded the warning. But he was going to hate himself for doing it. And she would hate him more than she already did if she ever found out what he'd done.

Which was definitely saying something.

Three

The hockey player had all his teeth.

Brittany's hot date—Mick—was even hotter than his picture, which meant he was pretty damned hot. Way too hot for her. She was fine-looking—maybe even pretty when she put some effort into it (which she had tonight)—but she was nowhere near this guy's level. A supermodel wouldn't be near this guy's level.

He was gorgeous. Dark, wavy hair, heavily lashed green eyes, chiseled, masculine features, and built. Seriously built, like . . . a hockey player. Tall, broad-shouldered, and stacked with enough hard muscle to make any sane person turn and run in the opposite direction and give proof to his role as the team's enforcer—she didn't need to be a hockey fan to get the gist of that. He bore a distinct resemblance to the actor who played Superman in the new movies and always made her heart beat a little faster.

She didn't know what was more surprising: the fact that her heart was beating at a nice, steady pace (and had been all night) or that Superman—Mick—seemed to be interested in her. Really interested in her. Which might be flattering if she weren't sitting there wondering why.

Good-looking, easy to talk to, a former professional hockey player who'd spent most of his eight years in the minor leagues but had made a few appearances with the Boston Bruins and had gone back to finish school afterward—Harvard, no less—and who was now working as a lobbyist with a big firm in town . . . What was her problem?

She should have been on her knees, thanking God for this gift—for this miracle—rather than wondering whether he had some kind of weird fetishes or some other reason to explain why he wasn't sitting at the bar with a gorgeous woman on each arm.

God, she was cynical. Why did she find it so hard to believe that an exceptionally good-looking guy could be interested in her? Why couldn't she just enjoy herself? And why, for God's sake, was she bored? This was interesting! He was telling her about going back to school as a twenty-six-year-old and . . .

She glanced down at her phone, sitting there temptingly on the chair beside her. She nodded and gave him an encouraging laugh, while surreptitiously touching the screen so that her messages would pop up.

What was she, seventeen? Only teenagers and rude adults checked their phones while at the table.

Suddenly, her eyes widened and her hand went to her mouth to muffle the strangled gasp that snuck out from between her lips.

"What's wrong?" Mick asked, stopping his story to lean across and put a hand on hers. "You look like you've seen a ghost."

She had. Brittany was reeling from shock, trying to control the sudden flood of converging emotions. She looked over at him, trying to think of what to say. "I'm sorry. Would you excuse me for a moment? I . . . I'm not feeling very well."

"Of course," he said. "Is there anything I can do? Something I can get you?"

He was so concerned and sweet, it made her feel even worse. But she shook her head and got up. "I'll be back in a minute. If the food comes, please don't wait for me."

"Of course I'm going to wait for you. Are you sure there isn't anything I can—"

"I'm sure," she cut him off, and then hastily added, "I'm sorry. I'll be right back."

She followed the signs to the restroom, surprised that her liquefactioned legs were keeping her upright and that she wasn't swaying side to side, using the tables to steady her as she made her way across the candlelit restaurant.

Her heart was pounding like a jackhammer.

Her phone felt like a brick in her hand. Maybe she'd been wrong. Maybe she'd read it too quickly. Maybe it was a joke. A horrible, cruel joke.

But not trusting her emotions to stay contained, she waited until she was in the bathroom before checking her phone again. Her hand shook as she touched the screen.

The blood drained from her face all over again. *It can't be. . . .*

But the message clearly said *Brandon Blake* and seemed to be from his personal e-mail account: snowman123. Was it possible he was still alive? She'd been so certain that something horrible had happened to him.

She hit the message and read the words on the small screen. She really needed to get a better cell phone. But it wasn't in her starving-reporter fund. The money her parents had left her had run out a long time ago.

> Brit, I can't take the time to explain now, but you have to stop what you are doing. Your articles are causing me a lot of problems and putting both of us in danger. If you don't stop writing them, I'm going to end up dead.

I'm sorry for not writing you sooner. I know you've been worried. I'll explain everything when I can, but please don't try to contact me. It's too dangerous right now, and both our lives may depend on it. Stay frosty, Brand.

Brittany read the note over at least a half-dozen times. She didn't know what to think. The "Brit" bothered her. He hadn't called her by her childhood nickname in five years. As did the "Brand." That was what his SEAL friends called him, but she'd always called him by his full name. And the note didn't sound like him. It was— she didn't know how to put it—too considerate? Too nice? Their exchanges since their big fallout had been much more stilted and formal.

But the "stay frosty" gave her pause. That did sound like him. The warning to stay cool and not let down her guard was what he was known for and had given him the nickname of "Snowman" in the SEALs. But similar to addressing her as "Brit," he hadn't signed off on messages to her like that in a long time.

She didn't know what to think. She wanted to hope, but . . .

Someone jiggled the handle of the single bathroom, reminding her of where she was. She couldn't do this here. She needed to think, but not in a restaurant bathroom. Dropping her phone in her bag, she unlocked the door, gave an apologetic smile to the older woman whose expression suggested that Brittany had been in there longer than she realized, and returned to her date.

"Is everything all right?" Mick asked, standing as she reached the table.

Brittany didn't sit down. She shook her head. "I'm afraid it's not. I think it's best if I go home." He looked so crestfallen, she added hastily, "I'm really sorry about this."

"Don't apologize," he said. "Just let me take care of the bill, and I'll walk you to your car."

She tried to protest—both on his paying and on him missing his meal—but he insisted. He really was a nice guy, she realized, which made her feel even worse for her attitude earlier.

"Thanks again," she said, getting into her car. She didn't bother saying "see you next time." She knew there wasn't going to be a next time. She'd blown this date big-time. It was too late to regret it. Story. Love life.

"Are you sure you are all right to drive? Do you want me to follow you?"

She shook her head. As great as he was being, she didn't want some guy she'd just met from an app following her home. "I'm sure I'll be fine." He was standing there, holding the door, looking down at her intently. She felt her cheeks grow warm, not knowing what else to say. "I'm really sorry."

"Make it up to me," he said. "Go out with me again."

Surprised, she hesitated. But only for an instant. How could she refuse? More important, why would she want to refuse? She nodded and gave him her number. He promised to call and shut the door.

She left wondering if she would ever hear from him again, and despite the initial lack of spark, she kind of hoped she would. It wasn't as if she had guys like Mick knocking her door down. She hadn't been with someone who was that much of a total package since—

She stopped the thought before it could form. Her lips pressed together in a hard line. If only she'd kept her mouth closed like that back then. She hadn't really been with *him* at all. And John Donovan certainly hadn't been interested in her—the interest had been painfully one-sided. But her brother's friend had been every bit as good-looking as Mick. Maybe that was what explained her less-than-enthusiastic response to her date tonight. Once burned, twice shy.

Putting aside thoughts of John Donovan, she focused

on the mysterious e-mail. As much as she wanted it to be from her brother, something about it didn't feel right. But she couldn't put her finger on what.

It wasn't until she was back at the tiny hovel she called home and read through it again that she figured it out. Brandon hadn't mentioned the missed anniversary of their parents' death in the e-mail. It was the one connection they still had and the only thing that bound them together. It didn't seem likely that he would forget to say something about it.

And what about the satellite pictures she'd received from her new source, showing the explosion in Russia and the deployment orders of a team that she assumed was the didn't-exist Team Nine to Norway, which was a perfect launching place for a mission? Why would this person come forward with information to substantiate her claims if it wasn't true?

The timing of Brandon's e-mail was too convenient. It smelled like a cover-up. Brittany had been in the middle of government cover-ups more than once and knew the lengths they could go to shut someone up. Hacking into an e-mail account would be child's play.

Which gave her an idea. She picked up her phone and dialed.

Mac—as in MacKenzie, her go-to person for anything technology related—picked up on the second ring. "What do you want this time? Spy cameras in your bedroom?"

Brittany wrinkled her nose. "Very funny. You act as if no one has ever asked you to tap their own phone line."

"As a matter of fact"—*snap, crackle, pop*—"no one ever has."

Mac was the best, but a bad smoking habit in high school had turned into a bad chewing gum habit in college. She had been single-handedly keeping Wrigley's Big Red gum in business ever since. Brittany supposed there were worse things than smelling like cinnamon. Smelling like smoke, for example. But Brittany put up with the constant gum smacking not just because Mac was a whiz with computers, but because they'd been friends since high school, when they'd both gone to the same all-girls Catholic school in Baltimore. Rebels needed to stick together.

Brittany had spoken to Mac earlier and asked her to tap her home and office phone lines on the off chance her source decided to contact her by phone. "I need you to try to trace an e-mail for me."

"Who from?"

"Brandon." Brittany heard the stunned silence on the other end. Mac had never met her brother, but she was the one person who knew their history and everything that had gone down between them. "Or someone purporting to be Brandon."

"You don't think it's him?"

"I . . ." Brittany paused. "I'm not sure. Can you take a look at it?"

"Forward it, and I'll see what I can do. If it's not official, it should be easy enough. But if it was him, and he was using official channels, it might take a few days. The military has some decent encryption."

Brittany smiled for the first time since that e-mail had come through. "Only decent? Maybe the military should hire you to design their systems for them."

"They couldn't afford me," Mac said bluntly. Which pretty much summed her up. Mac said what she thought. Not a lot of editing going on there. She didn't have Asperger's, but she touched the spectrum in a few places.

Brittany laughed, although it was undoubtedly true. Mac made millions as a freelancer, hired by corporations to hack into their systems. Not that you would ever know it. She still lived in a shoe box apartment like Brittany— although Mac's was in a nicer area—and also like Brittany, she dressed for comfort not fashion. The only thing she seemed to spend money on was computer equipment.

Brittany had seen the computer room in her apartment once and had felt like she'd walked into a high-tech war room or a teenage boy gamer's wet dream—she couldn't decide which.

Mac had said it might take her a few days, so Brittany was surprised when she heard from her the following afternoon. "That was quick," she said, answering the phone.

"Whoever did this was being careful. It isn't going to be as easy as I thought." Mac sounded a little annoyed—and maybe a little impressed as well, which was unusual.

"Is it military?"

"I'm not sure. It doesn't have the typical military fingerprint—it feels more sophisticated than that. Something more like the CIA would use."

Brittany let that sink in, but she didn't know what to think. "How much longer do you need?"

"I'm not sure, but I have another idea. Something that may get you an answer much quicker."

Quicker was good, especially with her boss breathing down her neck.

Brittany was listening.

Impersonating his dead best friend in an e-mail to his sister was pretty low. And John was feeling guilty, even if it was for Brittany's own good. But what else could he have done? He had to stop her, and God knew—he sure as hell did—the girl didn't take no for an answer.

Case in point, the e-mail that had just come through on the account that he should have deleted on the phone that he should have tossed. But he'd known she would respond, and Kate had routed the account through a special IP address and network. It looked like a popular e-mail account, but that was just a mask for whatever Kate had cooked up to make it impossible—or as close to impossible as possible—to trace.

He'd told Brittany in the note not to contact him, but what had she done? Contacted him, of course. He wasn't surprised she'd ignored him. He was more surprised that it had taken her more than a day to do so.

He stared at the envelope button for a moment. He should probably just delete it. God knew he felt guilty enough already for what he'd done, and she had a talent for making him feel like an asshole, but like some kind of masochist, he hit the button.

The message took a second to load. There was an attachment. A few moments later he was staring at the picture of him, Brand, Miggy, and Tex that had been plastered all over the news. There was a note that went along with it: *If this is Brandon, tell me when and where this picture was taken.*

She was like a damned pit bull. Couldn't she let something go just once? He was trying to help her, for shit's sake.

John didn't hesitate. Jaw clamped, he furiously banged out a response on the keypad.

Only then did he delete the account and toss the phone.

Brittany paled as she read the response: *Fourth of July five years ago at Imperial Beach in San Diego, a few blocks from the beach house.*

Oh my God.

She would have sunk to the couch if she hadn't already been sitting on it. She stared at the laptop screen in disbelief. She'd sent the e-mail while watching a hockey movie on TV—trying to get in the spirit of the second date that she'd agreed to go on next week (Mick had called to check on her that morning)—and hadn't even had a chance to set it aside before the message came through. Could it really be Brandon? Was her brother alive?

She felt tears push up her throat to sting behind her

eyes. One of the hardest things about losing her brother had been knowing that he'd died when they'd barely been on speaking terms and that she would never have a chance to repair their relationship. But if he was alive . . .

There were only a handful of people who could have answered that question—especially so quickly—and most of them were in that picture. She looked at the four faces in the image. Something she rarely did for two reasons. First because the photo reminded her of the big blowup fight she'd had with Brandon. And second because, even after five years, the sight of John Donovan's grinning, I'm-so-gorgeous face looking back at her could still make her chest—and cheeks—burn.

Five years ago had been the second-worst time of her then twenty-two-year-old life. The worst had been when her parents were killed, but she'd had Brandon then. Maybe that was why her first instinct had been to seek him out when life had handed her another big shit sandwich.

She and Brandon had been so close before the car "accident" that took their parents' lives. Their entire family had been unusually close, perhaps because their father's job in sales caused them to move around so much.

They'd all been in the car together when another driver slammed into them, sending their car head-on into an enormous concrete pillar of a highway overpass.

Their parents had died on impact. She and Brandon had been injured as well, but both had been able to tell the police exactly what had happened: the other driver had run the red light and barreled right into them at an extremely high speed.

When they learned from the police that the driver had been drunk and high on cocaine, it had seemed a slam-dunk case of vehicular homicide. Until they found out whom the driver was—or rather who his father was.

It was Brittany's introduction to the horrible abuses of

diplomatic immunity and government cover-ups. The driver was the twenty-two-year-old son of a Saudi "diplomat." She never did find out exactly what the father did. The son had been pulled over multiple times for speeding, reckless driving, and drunk driving. Later she'd heard that he'd been accused of raping a girl he'd picked up at a bar. But the police had to let him go each time with—unbelievably—an apology.

But apparently being given a hall pass for killing her parents wasn't enough. The public pressure to have his son sent back home or for Saudi Arabia to waive immunity angered the father. And he was important enough for the government—her government—to want to appease. Photos from the intersection suddenly materialized showing her father supposedly running the red light.

But far worse was what had come next. Brandon had reversed his statement and agreed with the government's lies and doctored "evidence."

With that she'd lost not just her parents, but her brother as well. At fifteen, she'd gone to live with her aunt and uncle in Baltimore, while the eighteen-year-old Brandon had joined the navy.

She hadn't seen him in years when she'd shown up out of the blue five years ago in San Diego.

Despite all the horrible words exchanged between them after their parents' death, when she'd lost her job, her first instinct had been to reach out to him.

But "lost her job" made it sound nice, when it was anything but. She'd been fired, discredited, and publicly humiliated after being accused of manufacturing "proof" for an article she'd written on backroom deals and corruption on Capitol Hill. Her "deep throat" had disappeared, and the documents were found to have originated on her computer. The circumstances surrounding her parents' death were resurrected, and Brittany was made to seem like a wacko spouting conspiracy theories or as someone with an ax to grind.

Maybe she did have a bit of an ax. But for the second time, she'd come up against the wrong people and paid the price.

She'd reached out to Brandon, but ironically, it had been his drop-dead-sexy friend who'd been her lifeline this time.

She'd never forget the first time she'd seen John Donovan. Not long after she'd arrived, he'd walked into the beach house he rented with her brother, dripping wet, half-covered in sand, carrying a surfboard under his arm and wearing nothing but a killer smile and faded low-slung board shorts, which perfectly accentuated the tanned, muscular torso above them.

Big, bad-assed, and gorgeous. That pretty much summed him up. And even in her depressed state she hadn't failed to notice.

Brittany hadn't been happy to learn that her brother had decided to become a SEAL—the secrecy of the Teams was everything she was fighting against—but she couldn't deny that his friends were built and nice to look at. They seemed to live by the mantra "work hard and play harder."

What she hadn't expected was that the golden-boy player with a capital "P" who'd walked into the house that day would be just as nice on the inside as he was outside.

Or so she'd thought.

She'd been sitting on the beach, wondering if it had been a mistake for her to come, when he'd sat down beside her and started talking. If nothing else, John Donovan was easy to talk to. He was so easygoing, so happy and laid-back, it made her problems seem a little less dire. A little less impossible to overcome. He helped her break things down. Focus on the things she could control and not the things she couldn't. But most of all he made her laugh.

Insta-crush was probably an understatement. Puppy

love? Worship? Maybe a little of all three. He was like catnip—utterly irresistible even when you knew he might not be good for you. He was so far out of her league, but she convinced herself that he'd seen something in her.

When he wasn't at the base, he was with her. For three incredible weeks.

Her brother tried to warn her, but she was twenty-two and thought she knew everything. She really believed that she and John had a special connection.

She was so certain of their connection right up to the point that she saw him on the beach—at that same BBQ where the picture had been taken—with not one but two women.

As she'd said, player with a capital "P."

Hurt, humiliated, and knowing she couldn't stay there any longer, Brittany had gone to her brother's room to write him a good-bye note. She hadn't meant to spy, but the paper was right there on his desk. It had "confidential" stamped all over it, which basically made it like catnip, too. Brandon was being transferred to Hawaii and recruited for some kind of secret SEAL team.

Her brother had come in before she could finish reading it and accused her of spying on him to get her job back. Furious that he would think that of her, she'd lashed out at him, telling him that at least she hadn't lied and betrayed her entire family, including their dead parents. He started to say something. Thought better of it. And then told her maybe it was better if she left.

They hadn't seen each other or done more than exchange a yearly phone call since that day. She should have done something. Shouldn't have let it go on that long. But she was stubborn, and now . . . was it possible that it wasn't too late?

Thanks to the picture, she had a way to find out.

Four

John resisted the urge to fish his phone out of the trash bin he'd tossed it in for a good three hours. Now, twenty-four hours later, with the account restored and still with no response, he could finally throw it back in again and congratulate himself on a job well done. His answers to her photo question must have convinced her of his—Brand's—identity, and she'd taken his warning to heart.

He would be celebrating more if he didn't feel so bad about lying to her about Brand being alive. He was only trying to protect her, but he doubted Brittany would see it that way when she learned the truth. He hoped to be a long way away when that happened. Preferably on an op on the other side of the world.

Who was he fooling? Antarctica wouldn't be far enough. She'd track him down and kill him—which he probably deserved.

Well, he might have to pay the piper one day, but fortunately, that day would not be today. Today he'd gotten rid of her, which was plenty of reason to celebrate. John was doing his best to do exactly that while sitting at the bar of his favorite hangout with a few of his housemates, waiting for Marta. He'd promised her a makeup date after having to cut their sauna party short the other night.

But he might have been going at the celebrating a little hard and had a few too many of Alexi's vodka shots. Most of the bar had had too many of Alexi's vodka shots. Their group had grown with every chorus of cheers. But the next time his housemate yelled out a toast in Russian (they never seemed to be the same—they could be toasting goats for all he knew), John lifted a pint glass of beer instead.

He was pretty buzzed, but not too buzzed to notice that itchy feeling at the back of his neck.

Someone was watching him.

He did a quick scan of the bar, his eyes snagging on that someone immediately. A woman was standing by the door staring at him in wonder and disbelief. He was used to expressions like that on women, but this wasn't that kind of wonder.

He blinked, trying to clear his vodka-hazed vision. He must be more drunk than he realized, because she sure as hell looked like . . .

Their eyes met, and shock punched him in the gut. He caught the flash of emotion behind the trying-to-be-unflattering-but-doing-a-piss-poor-job glasses and knew he wasn't imagining anything. Thick, wavy chestnut-brown hair, big baby-blue eyes, skin like fucking powder sprinkled with a few freckles across her nose, pretty, girl-next-door features, tight, curvy little body . . .

His spine went rigid. No mistake.

He cursed again with disbelief, trying to think of a way to ward off what he knew was an impending disaster. But there wasn't time. The impending disaster was heading his way with a very determined, don't-even-think-about-trying-to-put-me-off expression on her face.

Brittany had changed. It wasn't just the five years

that had taken her from twenty-two and still part girl to twenty-seven and definitely all woman; it was also the hardness of her expression. She'd always been determined, but the last time he'd seen her there had been some vulnerability and lingering innocence—even with everything that had happened to her. That wasn't there anymore. The same thing happened to guys on the Teams. It was part life, part experience, and part disappointment that came with a little too much reality.

He missed that softness. But maybe it was a good thing it was gone. He figured that was what had attracted him so intensely to her. It wasn't that she wasn't pretty—she was—but she wasn't his usual type. The Barbie Brigade had been aptly named. Brittany had stunning blue eyes and plenty of curves, but she had chestnut-colored hair—not blond—and stood about a foot shorter than him. She was also too girl-next-door wholesome. Messing around with someone like that . . . it wasn't right.

Unfortunately, one big mind-of-its-own part of him hadn't agreed.

The bar was small, so it didn't take her long to cross the distance to his stool. He could see the questions and anger in her eyes.

She opened her mouth.

God only knew what kind of insults and accusations she was about to hurl at him, but he couldn't let anyone hear them. He had to shut her up before she blew his cover.

He did the only thing he could think of to do. Leaning forward, he caught her around the waist and pulled her in tight against him. He was mostly leaning on the stool, and she slid right between his legs.

"What are you—" was as far as she got before his mouth closed over hers. He kissed her hard. He knew how good she was at talking—and giving him hell—and he wasn't going to give any of those words a chance to escape.

He filled her mouth with his tongue just to make sure. *Oh, shit.* Not good. *Too* good. He remembered this. He remembered the flood of heat. The tight feeling that came over his entire body. The drowning buzz in his ears that made everything else around him disappear. The way she tasted. Warm and sweet with the faint tinge of the butterscotch Life Savers that he used to tease her about chewing. They were supposed to be sucked.

Damn it, not a great word to think about right now. It made him think of sucking her tongue deeper into his mouth and swirling it around slowly with his own. Tasting every corner and every sweet crevice. God, he really loved butterscotch.

It made him think of another kind of sucking, too.

Really wrong. But too right to stop.

He groaned as his hand slid through her hair to cup the back of her head. It was clipped up in some kind of knot, but enough strands had slipped out to tell him that it was every bit as silky as he remembered. He'd thought he'd been exaggerating it in his mind, but no—he groaned again as he dug a little deeper to pull her head in closer—it was feathery soft and flowed between his fingers like a satin waterfall.

She'd frozen in shock initially, but it didn't take long for that first crack in the ice to appear. Her response was tentative at first. A tiny moan. The softening of her mouth and opening of her lips a little wider. The melting of her body into his as the stiffness left her shoulders, spine, and limbs. The slight movement of her tongue against his.

Oh fuck, yes! You'd think she'd jumped on top of him with the roar of satisfaction that surged through him. He'd never been so happy to have a woman kiss him back. Which maybe wasn't that surprising, since this was the first time he could remember that it had even been a question.

The crack in the ice turned into a chasm as her response grew bolder and more passionate. She was full-on kissing him back now, circling her tongue against his with every bit of the frenzy and hunger that he was experiencing.

It was a heady combination. One that was quickly making him lose all sense of reality. Just like last time. He hadn't wanted to stop then either. All he could think about was sinking in deeper, tasting her deeper, making every second last.

She'd wrapped her hands around his neck, and her soft breasts were pressing into his chest. He slid a hand down to her waist, needing to feel her against him. He was hard and throbbing, and the subtle friction wasn't enough.

He wanted to pull her onto his lap, wrap her legs around his waist, and sink in deep, right here in the middle of the . . .

Bar.

Fuck. When he pulled back suddenly—maybe a little harshly—he wasn't the only one reeling.

She blinked up at him with a hazy look in her eyes that sent the surge of need racing harder through his body. He had to grit his teeth against the urge to pull her back into his arms and keep that haze in her eyes.

The glance that passed between them was of shared shock. A consensus of *What the hell just happened?*

It wasn't a question he wanted to answer. Not here. Not now. Not ever.

Before she could say anything, he stood, threw a few bills down on the bar, told the bartender to call them a ride, grabbed her by the hand, and led her out of there. He could feel the stares of his friends and housemates, but he would answer the questions later.

They stood outside in silence, not even looking at each other as they waited for the cab. It didn't take long, but it was long enough for the shock to wear off and be replaced by something easier to think about: anger.

By the time he was opening the door to his house, John was furious. What was she doing here? How had she found him? And what part of "danger" hadn't been clear?

It took a lot to rile him up, but she'd done it without a fucking word.

He'd been trying to shut her up. That was why John had kissed her. For a moment she'd thought . . .

Idiot.

Brittany didn't trust herself to look at him, fearing that he might catch a glimpse of her stupidity. That he might somehow read her mind and guess exactly what she'd thought. That for one deluded moment, when he'd pulled her into his arms and kissed her, she'd thought she'd walked into her own Hallmark movie. The kind where everything is a misunderstanding and at the very end they realize they were made for each other. The kind where for five years he'd been thinking about her and regretted pushing her away, and now that she'd found him again, they were going to live happily ever after. *That* kind of movie.

You know, fiction.

She didn't understand it. Brittany had never been a fairy-tale kind of girl. She didn't like chick flicks, didn't read romances, and thought words like "destiny," "fate," and "soul mate" set women (and maybe a few unusually sensitive men) up for a lot of disappointment. It wasn't a feminist statement as much as learned cynicism.

But for that one fraction of a heartbeat, when he'd looked into her eyes and pulled her into his arms, she'd been Cinderella, Snow White, and every naive princess in between who believed in "one true love" carrying them away to happiness.

It was disconcerting how an independent woman who'd been on her own for a long time, who *liked* being on her own, could turn into a starry-eyed romantic in the blink of an eye.

The blink of a very sexy blue eye attached to a man who'd gotten even better looking—as if he needed to—in the five years since she'd seen him last.

Yep, Mr. Good Times, aka "Dynomite" as her brother called him, was still in prime form. The center of the party, surrounded by women, and jaw-droppingly gorgeous even with the lumberjack scruff and long hair. The Viking look wasn't easy to pull off—even in Finland—but he somehow managed to make it sexy as hell. *Hello, Thor.*

He'd beefed up in the handful of years since she'd seen him, but from the feel of that rock-hard chest against hers, it was 100 percent grade A muscle.

Of course it was. His body had always been a temple—with plenty of worshipping going on.

It had been a long day, and Brittany wasn't in the mood for John Donovan and his masculine perfection. Everything was always so easy for him. Even in Finland everyone liked him, apparently. Let him dazzle one of the women who'd been hanging on him in the bar when she'd arrived with his good-time-surfer-boy—or, in his case, water-polo-player—charm.

She didn't have the patience for it. Not only was she exhausted from hours of travel—could he have picked a more hard-to-get-to, out-of-the-way place?—but she'd better hope there weren't a lot of storms in her future, as she'd had to use up most of her "rainy day" savings for the last-minute ticket after her boss had refused to pay for it. She was on her own here, with everything—literally—on the line. Job. Reputation. Ability to pay bills.

Was it any surprise that he'd caught her off guard with that kiss?

If only she could convince herself that travel weariness and fears of looming poverty were to blame. But John Donovan had an uncanny ability to make her feel vulnerable in a way she didn't like.

She'd marched across the bar, intending to get answers, and he'd pulled the rug out from under her with that kiss. A kiss that wasn't some kind of romantic moment at the end of a movie, but a kiss to shut her up.

That it had worked so thoroughly—so easily—only made her angrier. She stewed in that anger as the car took them wherever he was taking her—she assumed his apartment. Which was ironic, given the last time they were alone together he couldn't wait to get her *out* of his room . . .

Brittany paced back and forth across the attic-turned-bedroom, pausing every now and then to peer out one of the windows to see if the sound of a car was the one she was waiting for.

But maybe John wouldn't be driving? He'd been drinking heavily before she left. Too heavily. More heavily than she'd ever seen him drink before. Tequila—not beer.

Did that mean something? Was that why he'd done— her heart caught—that?

Tears clogged her throat and raw eyes, threatening to spill again.

She wasn't mistaken in what she'd seen, but maybe there was an explanation. Such as whether the brother she hardly knew anymore had interfered.

Earlier tonight, she had gone down to the beach. It had been a little later than she'd planned, and the bonfire was already jam-packed with people. The guys had a Saturday night off from training, and they were taking full advantage.

She had to admit seeing a dozen good-looking, built guys in one place took some getting used to. She wasn't used to so much testosterone flowing around and didn't think she would ever get over the little primitive flutter of awareness that went through her.

But there was only one guy she wanted to see. She couldn't wait to find John and tell him her news. She'd followed his suggestion and gone downtown to speak with one of the free local papers—one with a liberal bent that didn't dismiss her claim of a cover-up out of hand—and they were willing to give her a shot. It wouldn't be much at first, but it was a start.

She was back in the game. Not even four weeks after, she'd been fired and it had seemed as if her career was over. And she had John to thank for it.

She rose onto her tiptoes, trying to look over the crowd—there must have been forty people here tonight—but didn't see him right away. She saw her brother standing in a circle with a few of his other SEAL friends off to the side near the barbecue, but no John.

She frowned, thinking it strange. John usually took control of the barbecue. He hailed from one of the "culinary meccas" (his words) of the world, the San Francisco Bay Area, and took his food preparation and selection seriously.

Only Brittany knew the reason why. Before she'd died from breast cancer, John's mom had been a sous chef for one of the most important chefs in modern culinary history—Alice Waters of Chez Panisse and "California cuisine" fame.

Brittany tucked that little nugget of knowledge back in her heart, where it had taken up residence when he'd shared it with her. That and the knowledge of how horrible his mom's death had been. John had told her how he'd spent his senior year of high school in a vigil by her hospital bedside. Brittany would bet what money she *had that she was the only person he'd ever confided in about that—including her brother.*

Brandon was wrong.

Her mind turned to the conversation she'd had with her brother the day before. John did care about her. What they had was different. They'd connected right from the start.

She grinned. No one was more surprised than her. The gorgeous golden boy Navy SEAL with "Hermione," as Brandon liked to call her for her supposed resemblance to the actress in the Harry Potter movies, didn't exactly fit.

Brittany wrinkled her nose. She supposed she could see it, but she wasn't sure it was flattering for someone who wanted to be thought of as sexy.

She headed down to the beach, thinking that maybe John was watching the waves as he liked to do—as they both liked to do—when she stopped in her tracks.

He wasn't down by the beach. He was sitting in a low beach chair in front of the fire. The shirt was unmistakable. No one else would wear a Hawaiian shirt that loud and ugly—especially with plaid board shorts.

She just hadn't seen him right away because someone was sitting on his lap. Not just someone—it was Candice O'Reilly. Her twin sister, Barbara, who was never far behind, was sitting on the arm of the chair. Candy and Barbie were just as sweet, beautiful, and vacuous as their nicknames suggested. They had a thing for SEALs and hung out at Danny's Palm Bar in Coronado—a favorite SEAL hangout—but this was the first time Brittany had seen them at one of the beach parties. They'd made no secret that they thought John was "hot," but John had never taken them up on their subtle—or not-so-subtle—invitation(s). He usually stayed away from "frog hogs," as the women who targeted SEALs to sleep with them were known.

Until now.

Brittany froze, watching in stunned horror as Barbie—or was it Candy?—leaned forward and kissed him. John's hand spread over her back, pressed her more firmly against him. Until her sister playfully pushed her out of the way and said something along the lines of "my turn" before exchanging places, his hand still plastered on her sister.

Brittany could live to be a hundred and never forget that hand. The fingers spread wide. Pressing. Marking. Branding.

How desperately she'd longed to feel that hand on her. To have him kiss her like that.

The blood rushed out of her body in one draining wave. Her stomach rose to take its place. She was going to be sick.

She must have gasped, because her hand was already covering her mouth as bile rose in the back of her throat.

Had he heard her? She didn't know, but at that moment he looked over and saw her. Their eyes met and held.

She knew her heart—her breaking heart—was in her gaze, but his was blank. Stark. Maybe a little too stark. It seemed wrong.

Just like the bottle of tequila in his hand, which he lifted to his mouth and took a long drink from. John drank beer. Coors Light, just like the rest of them.

But then he lifted his hand—his other hand—gave her a small wave, and smiled before turning back to the woman—women—on his lap.

That careless wave and smile shattered her heart completely. Brittany turned and ran, making it back to the house before the worst of the tears started.

She'd lain in misery for a few hours, asking herself what had happened and how she could have been wrong, when the answer came to her: Brandon.

That's why she was here in John's room, waiting for him. She had to know. Had her brother put him up to this, or had she been completely wrong about him?

Maybe the right word was "deluded." She knew John had a reputation for having a good time with women—lots of women—but that was before he'd met her. Since almost the day she showed up at her brother's beach house three weeks ago, he'd hung out with her. Only her.

But he'd never tried to kiss her.

Suddenly all the things her brother had said to her yesterday—had warned her about—came rushing back. "He's a great guy—the best—but he never sticks with one woman for long. I don't want to see you get your heart broken."

Too late. Her broken heart started to pound as she heard the back door open and close downstairs.

She thought it might be Brandon, who had one of the rooms downstairs, until she heard the tread of footsteps coming up the stairs.

It was John, and he'd obviously walked back.

She glanced at the clock. Midnight. Early for him. Did that mean something?

He opened the door, stopping in his tracks when he saw her. For one fraction of an instant, she thought she saw sadness in his expression before it hardened to anger.

"You shouldn't be here."

She took a step toward him, but seeing the way he stiffened, she stopped. "I thought I'd give you a chance to explain."

"Explain what?"

"What you were doing tonight with the O'Reilly twins."

His eyes met hers without a flicker. He smiled again, that lazy, cocky smile that seemed to slice her confidence to shreds. "I would think that was obvious. Having a good time."

Dynomite.

Her chest squeezed. If she was wrong about this, she was really *wrong. Cringe-worthy wrong. She took another step toward him, and his gaze darkened with just a hint of wariness.*

It gave her the hope she needed to continue. Maybe he wasn't as indifferent as he appeared.

"I thought . . ." *Her voice fell off as she lost her nerve. She had to force herself to take a big, deep breath and continue.* "I thought you cared about me."

There was a long harsh pause before he suddenly smiled. "I do. You're a great kid. A great friend."

Hammer. Nail. Heart. Straight through. She was twenty-two years old. He was twenty-four. Never had she felt those two years so painfully. She felt like a child—a little girl—in the face of someone much more experienced. Someone who knew what he was doing. Someone who had broken hearts before.

But she wouldn't back down that easily. They weren't just friends. It had been more than that. She knew it in her heart.

To hell with pride. She had to know. "Bullshit." *He flinched, her cursing obviously surprising him.* "That's BS and you know it. We aren't just friends. What has been happening between us is more than that. My brother put you up to this, didn't he? He told you to stay away from me."

John's mouth was clenched so tight his lips had turned white. "It's late. You need to leave. I've had too many shots to deal with this right now. We'll talk in the morning."

This couldn't wait until morning. She took another step toward him, and she swore he would have moved back if he hadn't been against the door. "It's true, isn't it? That's why you were with those women tonight on the *beach. My brother is trying to protect me, so you decided to get rid of me by breaking my heart."*

He looked a little pained at that. But whether it was good pain (as in "you are right" pain) or bad pain (as in "I feel sorry for you" pain), she couldn't tell.

"I'm sorry if you misunderstood—"

"I didn't misunderstand anything."

She knew she was right. So right that she threw caution to the wind—and herself against him.

Instinctively, his arms went around her waist, and just as instinctively, hers looped around his neck. Did she pull him toward her? She didn't know, but the next minute his mouth was on hers, and he was kissing her.

Really kissing her. With lots of groans, lots of tongue, and lots of passion.

Just like she'd imagined it. Better than she'd imagined it.

It was as if the dam had broken, and everything he'd been holding back came pouring out all at once.

It was incredible. A rush of sensation. Heat. God, the heat. It was drenching. And his mouth was . . . intoxicating.

And not just from the faint taste of lime, salt, and tequila. It was everything. The way he tasted, the way he smelled, the way he felt against her. All those hard muscles that she'd admired too many times finally wrapped around and pressing against her.

She moaned as pleasure seemed to infuse every nerve ending. She wanted more. She wanted to feel his hands all over her body, his mouth on her neck, her breast, between her legs.

She wanted to take the hard column wedged between her legs in her hand, wrap her fingers tight around him, and see if he was as big and hard as he felt.

And then maybe she'd take him in her mouth.

She'd never done that before, but she had a feeling

*he'd be happy to show her what to do. It wasn't like there
was a ton to it.*

*But kissing was good for now. Really good. His tongue
was circling deeper and deeper into her mouth, as if he
wanted to devour—*

*She was pushed away so suddenly that it felt as if
she'd been slapped by a snap of cold air.*

*She stumbled back. Wobbled, trying to find the bones
in her legs. And looked up at him in shock.*

"What the hell did you do that for?" he shouted.

*She'd never heard him yell before. She hadn't thought
Mr. Laid-back, "No Worries" capable. But he was drawn
up tight and seething.*

*It was disconcerting. How well did she really know him?
This was the deadly Navy SEAL, not the endless-summer
surfer boy.*

*"I'm sorry. I . . ." She forced her spine to straighten,
but her knees were still wobbly. "I thought you wanted
me."*

*"I'm a man, Brittany. A man who's had way too much
to drink. Throw yourself at anyone in my condition and
you'll likely find a taker. It doesn't mean anything more
than what you saw on the beach tonight." He paused and
added, "Or didn't see."*

*She blinked, unable to believe he'd just said that to
her. Had he really just said that to her?*

*Then the rest of what he'd said hit her with a cold
knife of pain that seemed to go right through her chest.
"Did you have sex with them?"*

*He didn't say anything. He didn't need to. The "What
do you fucking think" expression said it all.*

She felt destroyed. Everything she'd thought . . .

She'd been wrong. Horribly wrong.

*"Look, I don't want to hurt your feelings," he said a
little more gently. "You're a nice girl. But you can't go*

around throwing yourself at men like that. Not everyone will pull away."

Ouch. Direct hit. He didn't need to say it. The "get lost" was clear.

Roger that.

Her confidence was sunk, her heart shattered, leaving only what remained of her pride. "Right," she said flatly. "The next time I decide to do that, I'll make sure it's with someone who has all your experience. It must be tiresome having women always throwing themselves at you."

He gave her an uncertain look, as if he couldn't tell whether she was being sarcastic or not.

She was. "Sorry to bother you, Dynomite." Asshole. "Don't worry. It won't happen again. It was my mistake."

One she wouldn't make again. Ever.

Brittany needed to remember that now. Somehow he'd managed to time-warp her back five years for a few minutes, but she wasn't an impressionable twenty-two-year-old girl anymore. She wouldn't make the same mistake twice—or for the third time, if you counted the temporary lapse of sanity in the bar.

He was gorgeous and a fun guy to be around, but the one guy/one girl thing was totally beyond him. And as she didn't do meaningless sex—or threesomes—she wasn't in danger of falling for his act again.

The fact that she'd very nearly just fallen apart at a kiss didn't mean anything. Of course, he could kiss like a dream. God knew, he'd had enough practice.

By the time he'd pushed her through the door of his house—not an apartment—and plopped her none too gently on a couch that looked as if it had been made out of material from a cheap, rip-off Chanel suit in burnt-orange polyester, she'd recovered *all* of her senses. Even the ones that would normally be a little dazzled by such a gorgeous specimen looming over her and directing all that angry masculine energy at her with eyes narrowed, jaw muscle ticking, and fists clenching.

Did he actually think he could intimidate her?

She would laugh if she weren't so angry. She narrowed her eyes back at him. "I've had a long day, Johnny, and I don't appreciate being manhandled and pushed around. What the hell is going on here, and where is my brother?"

Five

John was so angry, he didn't think. Which seemed to be a frequent occurrence around Brittany. It wasn't just the kiss or that she was here—in Finland, for fuck's sake!—but if anyone found out the truth . . .

"Gone," he snapped.

Dead. Just like they all could be if someone had followed her and learned that not all of them had perished in Russia.

He regretted the harsh response as soon as he said it. Though "gone" could be interpreted a couple ways, she knew instantly what he meant and flinched as if he'd struck her. But her shock seemed to be from the abrupt manner of delivery, not from the content of the message. "He's dead," she said with toneless finality.

John debated lying to her again. He probably shouldn't be confirming or denying anything to her, but he just couldn't do it. She'd somehow known that Brand was dead, and he'd given her false hope. He couldn't prolong it.

He nodded.

But it didn't make the pain in her eyes any easier to

take as she stared at him with that stark, hollow look on her face.

"Damn it," he said, dragging his fingers through his hair. "I'm sor—"

He didn't get the apology out. Suddenly, she jumped up from the couch to face him. It wasn't without effect, but probably not the effect she intended. His nerve endings flared with instant awareness. And all those wrong feelings he'd had from that kiss? They were back. Full force.

This wasn't good. He needed to get rid of her—quick.

"It was you." She jammed her finger into his chest with the accusation. "You sent the e-mail. You pretended to be Brandon." He winced, knowing what was coming next. "How could you be so cruel? How could you let me think he was alive?"

The betrayal in her voice made him want to crawl under the proverbial rock. He felt low enough to do it, too. Clearly he'd killed what little faith she'd had left in him. He was surprised that she'd had any.

He'd known this was coming, but that didn't make it any easier to take. He'd expected to feel like the world's biggest asshole when she found out what he'd done, and that pretty much summed up the gnawing ball of guilt twisting in his chest right now.

It hurt to even look at her, seeing all that "how could you?" betrayal and rage in her eyes. She hated him, all right. And he couldn't blame her. It had been a shit thing to do.

Shit, but necessary.

"You didn't leave me a choice," he said.

He thought she'd been angry before. He was wrong. Her eyes lit with blue fire that went full scorched earth on him—him being the earth.

"Don't you dare turn this on me, John Donovan. I wasn't the one pretending to be my dead best friend. Did they teach you how to do that in your SEAL school?"

They were alone, but he looked around anyway. "Shh," he said. "You can't talk about that here." She knew that. Just as she knew it wasn't a SEAL school but BUD/S. "And my name here is Joe."

She shrugged out of his hold of her arm—he hadn't even realized he'd grabbed her. "More lies and secrets? Is that your cover? Are we being watched?"

Something in her tone pricked through his guilt. Sarcasm maybe? Disregard? He knew the story surrounding her parents' death—the *full* story—and understood the source of her distrust of secrets and government, but it didn't change anything. It only put them at odds. More odds.

"No. We aren't being watched, but it never hurts to be careful. And yes. Joe Phillips from Canada."

She stared at him with those sharp, piercing eyes, which seemed to cut right through him for a long moment, and shook her head. "Still saving the world for Uncle Sam, *Joe*? But that doesn't explain what you are doing here and why you are in hiding—which I assume you are since you are alone, Brandon's dead, and your secret team seems to have vanished off the face of the earth."

He didn't need to ask how she'd learned about Team Nine. Brand had told him she'd seen the paperwork. But John wasn't happy about it. That kind of knowledge made his job harder and put her in danger. Only a handful of people beyond their direct command knew about it.

She also must know he couldn't—wouldn't—answer her. "How did you find me?" he asked.

She crossed her arms, glaring at him. "Your oh-so-thoughtful e-mail."

He ignored the sarcasm. "That's impossible."

She gave him a tight smile tinged with smugness. "Obviously it isn't. I'm here, aren't I? But you can tell whoever did your dirty work for you at the CIA that it wasn't their software."

He didn't show any reaction that she'd guessed his source. But how the hell had she guessed his source?

His eyes narrowed. "Developed a new pastime, Brit? Hacking for fun?"

"Afraid not. But I know people, too. And in this case, it looks like my people are better than yours. That picture I attached? It had a location program built into it."

He swore.

Her smile only got more smug.

He had to force his hands to his sides so he didn't try to wipe it off. What the hell was it about her that made him want to grab her by the shoulders, bring her in nice and tight against his chest, and force her to listen to him? He wasn't ever aggressive with women. They came to him, for fuck's sake.

But she was standing too close already. He took a step back. "You can't stay here."

Her smile fell. "Don't worry. I won't cramp your style for long. I know how you don't like to sleep alone. I'll be on my way just as soon as you tell me what happened to Brandon and why no one has told me that he was killed."

He resisted the urge to reply to the digs. She couldn't be more wrong—on both counts.

He gave her a long look. "You know I can't do that. It was an op gone wrong—that's all I can say. More than I can say. I meant what I wrote in that e-mail, Brit. This is dangerous. Your being here puts both our lives at risk." And other lives as well. "No one can know I'm alive. No one."

"Why? Is someone after you? Is that why you are hiding?"

He'd forgotten how quick she was, and how good she was at pinning someone down. She would have made a killer lawyer. What were those questions when you assumed part of the answer? She was awesome at those.

But he was just as adept at sidestepping and avoiding being cornered—especially by women. "Go home, Brit. Forget you saw me. Put aside your story, and I swear I will tell you everything as soon as I can."

She still had her arms crossed in front of her chest as she stared at him. A body language expert might suggest it was meant to be a barrier, but if that was the intention, she'd neglected to factor in how perfectly they framed in and lifted her breasts, making the already spectacular fucking incredible.

Ah, hell. He shifted his gaze back to her face at the same time as she dropped her arms. The faint pink on her cheeks suggested the timing might not have been a coincidence, that she'd caught the direction of his stare.

She stiffened, straightening her spine and lifting her chin to meet his gaze. It might have been more intimidating if she weren't a good foot shorter than him.

"No. I'm not going to do any of that. You owe me an explanation."

"I don't owe you a damned thing."

There was a sharp silence. John didn't understand it. He was never harsh. Never abrupt. He never said the first thing that popped in his head.

Correction. Never except with Brittany.

She looked at him, and he didn't understand how a look could say so much. How a look could say everything.

He'd known her, what . . . three weeks? Five years ago? And he knew her well enough to read her looks?

Apparently so, because her next words confirmed that they'd both been thinking about what had happened in San Diego. He'd pushed her away without an explanation then, too.

"You're right," she said. "You made that clear the last time I saw you, didn't you? My mistake for thinking that you might feel bad about lying to me. That you might think I deserved an explanation after traveling halfway around the world to see my brother only to find out that he is dead and his former best friend was pretending to be him to stop me from finding out what happened to him. He's gone, John." Her eyes pinned him, pleading for understanding. "My brother is dead. I need to know why."

Those eyes left him nowhere to hide, and maybe for the first time in his life, that was what he felt like doing.

He wasn't going to let her do this to him. He shook off the guilt. He'd done it for her own good. "I was trying to protect you. I lied because I knew you would be like this. I knew you wouldn't be able to listen to reason but would keep digging and digging until you had whatever answer you were looking for no matter who was hurt in the process. If anyone finds out I'm alive, I could be targeted. This is dangerous stuff, Brit. You need to steer clear."

She turned away. "You're just trying to scare me to put me off."

He took her by the arm and hauled her around to look at him. He swore he could feel the flutter of her heart against his. He knew it wasn't fear. Anger maybe? Awareness? Whatever the hell it was, it was magnetic, drawing him in. Taking him somewhere he didn't want to go. He was about ten seconds away from putting his mouth on hers again. Maybe that would make her listen. If he thought he had a chance in hell, he just might try it.

"I'm not," he said tightly. "You don't know what kind of hornet's nest you are stirring up with this 'Lost Platoon' crap, Brit, and I don't want to see you get hurt."

For a moment he wondered if he was getting through

to her. But then she shrugged out of his hold, dismissing him—and the warning. "Thanks for the concern, but it's part of the job. I've been stung before."

"What about me?" Her eyes lifted to his. "If you don't put this aside, I could end up dead."

"You're a big boy, Johnny." She coldly looked him up and down, but somehow it made him hot anyway. "I'm sure you'll manage to land on your feet. You always do. Everything is always so easy for you."

She was right. "It pays to be a winner" had been the story of his life. Things came easy to him. School. Sports. Friends. Girls. Until he'd decided to become a SEAL. For the first time in his life he'd been tested. He'd had to work for something he wanted. Maybe that was why being a SEAL was so important to him. It was the constant challenge.

But he didn't like what she was insinuating. "What's that supposed to mean?"

"You're here, aren't you?"

With that one remark she managed to prick low beneath the surface, beneath layer upon layer of skin, to tap into the one harsh truth that he didn't want to acknowledge. Didn't want to think about. That he'd survived and his friends—and his best friend—had not.

He held her stare, not giving any indication of the raw nerve she'd just struck. "Yeah, you aren't the only one disappointed about that."

Her eyes widened. "I didn't mean it like that. Of course I'm glad that you aren't dead, too."

He'd never seen her twisting her hands before, but she was obviously agitated. He knew the feeling. Everything about her made him agitated.

She uttered a sound of frustration. "I'm not going to let you do this to me. I'm not going to let you confuse me again. You're good at that. But I'm not twenty-two anymore and susceptible to a good-looking face and a killer set of abs. You aren't going to make me feel bad for you and stop me from finding out what happened. If you won't tell me, I'll find out another way."

Good-looking face and killer set of abs? Was that what she'd reduced him to in her mind?

That pissed him off just enough to make him want to return the favor. "Over your little crush, Brit?"

Her cheeks flamed. He thought he heard a "bastard" under her breath before she gave him a tight smile. "Since the moment I left that beach house. But truth be told, it didn't take long. There wasn't much to get over."

She'd gotten even more provoking in her old age.

He took a step toward her. As there wasn't much space between them to start with, that basically brought him right up against her. "You sure?" He reached down lazily to stroke her warm cheek with his thumb, sliding it down over gently parted lips. "You seemed pretty into that kiss."

Her sharp intake of breath only served to stoke that fire a little hotter. But he'd miscalculated. Overestimating his control and underestimating her skill at retaliation.

Hearing her quickening breath and sensing the arousal buzzing through her was playing havoc with his rationality.

She leaned in to him, pressing her body fully against his. Letting him feel the soft crush of her breasts and the gentle friction of her hips against his.

This time it was he who had the sharp intake of breath.

"I wasn't the only one into it. Or is this"—she nudged her hips against the hard column of his erection—"not for me?"

The husky taunt . . . the subtle press . . . John felt a roar rush through his veins. He didn't stand a goddamned chance of letting that go unanswered.

It was for her, all right.

With a groan that was half curse, half relief, he pulled her into his arms and covered her mouth with his.

Brittany didn't tease, she didn't seduce, she was no femme fatale, and she had never pressed herself against a man suggestively like that before in her life.

Had she wanted this reaction? Had she wanted to see whether she had what it took to make a guy like him lose control? Get a taste of the good times he was so famous for?

She didn't know, but the moment his mouth touched hers, it was too late to do anything about it.

She was lost. Consumed. Drowning in the sensations aroused by his lips and tongue. In the heat. In the feel of his arms around her. In the hard body pressed against hers.

God, he could kiss. The long, purposeful strokes seemed to reach deep inside and sent shudders of desire racing through her.

She wasn't usually into facial hair, but the Viking thing was definitely working for her. It made her feel a little naughty. A little ravished and plundered with the gentle scrape against her skin as his mouth moved over hers.

And moving it was. Devouring. Inhaling. As if he couldn't get enough fast enough.

She knew the feeling.

The kiss in the bar had been restrained compared to this one. This one was pure carnal sensuality. Pure eroticism. Pure "I can't wait to get your pants off and fuck you senseless."

Sounded good to her. Sounded *really* good to her.

For someone who was so easygoing and laid-back

all the time, she'd expected him to be more slow and easy. More teasing and relaxed. More detached and controlled.

But the way he was kissing her wasn't any of those things. It was aggressive. Possessive. Determined. And wild. Most of all, wild. It was as if they'd both been caught up in a fierce storm and couldn't break free.

His hands were in her hair, on her breasts, sliding down her back, and lifting her bottom to bring her more firmly against him. Notching them together right in that perfect place.

The perfect fit.

She'd imagined it would be like this. But it was even better. Hotter. Crazier.

He started to move, small, gentle circles of hips to give her a taste of what was to come.

She almost did. The rush of heat between her legs was so intense, she felt her body shudder. It felt like she'd waited forever for this, and now that it was here, she couldn't hold back another second.

Anticipation was overrated.

But from his groans—or was that her moans?—and the frantic beat of his heart against hers, she knew the playacting wasn't going to go on for long.

He wanted one thing. Needed one thing. And truth be told, she did as well. She wanted to feel his naked skin against hers. Feel the hard flex of his muscle moving under her hands as he surged inside her. Gasp at the sensation of that first push. The sweet jolt of shock as his body opened hers. And just for a moment she wanted to feel the connection. She wanted to know what it was like to be close to him, connected if only for a few minutes.

It was going to happen. Not the way she'd wanted five years ago maybe, but she was finally going to have sex with John Donovan.

His mouth slid down her jaw, her neck, her throat. He

didn't stop there, smoothly pushing aside her blouse to reveal the swell of her breasts.

The warmth of his breath on her aroused skin made it prickle. Or maybe that was the anticipation of what she knew was going to come as he worked the buttons down.

When he pushed her blouse back to reveal her bra, he paused just long enough to mutter, "Holy shit," before unhooking the wisp of black lace to show the rest of his admiration with his mouth and tongue.

She guessed he approved of her underwear choice. And maybe the full D cups that were underneath.

She'd caught him checking her out earlier, and it had sent unwelcome flickers of awareness through her body. They weren't unwelcome now.

She arched when he sucked her deep into his mouth. Moaned when his tongue circled and flicked the taut tip. And felt her legs turn to jelly when he slid his hand between her thighs over the denim of her jeans.

She was glad when he leaned her back onto the sofa. It was too much, and she needed to catch her breath—and racing heart. He pulled off his polo shirt before kneeling on the couch over her.

His expression was as intense as she'd ever seen it, his face tight, his gaze fierce with arousal. He'd never looked sexier, which in his case was saying something.

They exchanged a long, heated glance but didn't speak. Speaking would mean acknowledging what was about to happen, and neither of them wanted to do that.

She took a moment—that was all she had—to admire the powerful ridges and planes of his naked torso.

Her stomach dropped. Jesus. If she thought he'd been built five years ago, she had a whole new definition now. In addition to a new tattoo on his upper chest of what appeared to be a trident and net, his shoulders were broader, his arms bigger, his chest harder, and the muscle more defined. Sharply defined. Everywhere. The term washboard stomach? She knew where it came from now.

But she'd have to count the lines in the board later. He was pushing her back on the couch, kissing her again, and the heat and solidness of that chest—the shocking sensation of his skin touching hers—was all she could think about.

That, and what was about to happen next.

She hoped it was worth it, because when this was over—in a few minutes, if she didn't miss her estimate—she was going to hate herself.

Slow down, John kept telling himself. But he couldn't. It was like a freight train of need barreling down on him. He couldn't have stopped if he wanted to.

And part of him wanted to. The responsible, conscientious part that knew this was a mistake. Unfortunately, that part was drowned out by all the other parts that were saying, "Fuck yes," and that were thinking this was incredible. That kissing her, touching her, and feeling her in his arms was about the best thing he'd felt in a long time.

And then there was that lust part. The part that made him feel clumsy and anxious as a teenager who couldn't wait to get inside her.

That part was going freaking nuts. Especially after seeing that bra. Who the hell would have thought that under her modest, businesslike exterior lurked the sexy, slightly trashy underwear taste of a Playboy Bunny— with the chest to match?

Color him shocked. And turned on. Big-time.

Just thinking about those spectacular breasts straining against all that black see-through lace was making his cock hurt.

Or rather, hurt more. He was aching already. Throbbing. Straining against the confines of his jeans.

He didn't have any place left to go. Check that. One place left to go. And he couldn't fucking wait. *Really* couldn't fucking wait. He hadn't had this kind of anticipation, hadn't been this wild for anyone in a long time.

He slid his hand over her stomach and dipped between her legs, nearly growling with satisfaction when she gasped and lifted her hips to meet him.

Her responsiveness was part of the problem. Everything was too seamless. Too perfect. Too right. There was no hesitation, no awkwardness. Nothing to think about and plan. The way they moved together was too natural.

Like the moment he stretched on top of her, propping himself up on an elbow so as not to crush her—and have better access—and she slid right under his arm, tucking in tight against his body as if she'd been locked right into position. Then, when the feel of those incredible tits pressed into his chest proved too much and he reached for the button of her jeans, the feel of her hand on his pants nearly made him burst a blood vessel—the important one.

It was hard to concentrate as he worked her zipper down with her doing the same and her hand so close . . .

Ah, hell. He let out a powerful groan. Her hand was *on* his cock as if it belonged there. She reached down behind the cotton of his boxer briefs and circled that hand around him as if it had done so a hundred times before. As if it had been made to hold him. Stroke him.

He had to grit his teeth against the urge to come as that sweet, oh-so-perfect grip moved from base to tip at just the right beat.

She paused only when his hand pushed aside the black triangle of lace—the thong was every bit as sexy as the bra—and he spread her legs with his hand.

He had the satisfaction of hearing her cry out and arch as his finger slid inside that honeyed warm slit. He slid it in and out, getting her used to the feel of him. Slow and deep, making her wet and ready.

But she was already there.

And so was he. She was stroking him again, keeping the pace he was setting with his hand.

He could feel her straining against him. Lifting. Pushing. Wanting to come. Just as he could feel the building pressure at the base of his spine.

He couldn't take it. He broke away, propping himself up on one knee again over her. Not even bothering to take off his pants, he reached in the pocket of his jeans and pulled out a condom from his wallet. He tossed his wallet on the coffee table and ripped the condom package open.

She shimmied her jeans down her hips, watching him, her eyes on his every move. That was hard enough to take, but when her tongue darted out to run over her bottom lip, he nearly went over the edge right there.

She had no idea how sexy that unconscious gesture was—none. If there were time, he'd let her do what she was thinking. But he knew he had about two minutes. Three if he was lucky.

He rolled the condom down the long length of his erection, trying to get himself under control.

It wasn't working. Especially when he glanced down and saw her waiting for him. Sweater and shirt opened wide, bra unclasped, jeans and thong kicked off on the ground.

She looked like a debauched angel. A sexy-as-hell debauched angel. That couch had never looked so good.

Her body was a fucking wonderland, as the song went. Creamy white skin flushed with arousal, lush, full breasts with pale pink tips turned deeper pink from his sucking,

gently curved hips, taut, athletic limbs, everything com-
pact and neatly proportioned.

He'd seen her in a bathing suit before, but the modest
one-pieces and swim shirts hadn't prepared him.

Or maybe he'd never allowed himself to imagine.
Maybe he knew that no matter how much he liked her,
she wasn't for him.

Their eyes met, and almost as if she could see his
hesitation—see the moment of sanity peeking through
the haze—she reached for him.

Six

If John Donovan thought he was going to leave her hanging like this, he had another think coming. This wasn't the time for second thoughts, and Brittany wasn't going to let him think of any reason why they shouldn't do this.

They were doing this.

So she made sure of it. She took that impressive, suited-up erection in her hand and pulled him toward her.

Of course he had a big dick. What big, bad wolf didn't? *"The better to fuck you with, my dear."* She hoped so. She'd been anticipating this for a long time.

Whatever twinge of conscience he'd had was apparently gone. His face was an intense mask of focus and concentration as he positioned himself between her legs, propping himself over her with his hands on either side of her head.

Okay, that was more like it.

She moved one of her legs around his hips just to make sure he understood, and found a couple of muscles on his upper arms to hold on to as she braced herself for what was to come.

It didn't prepare her for the jolt. For the lightning rod

of awareness that ran up her spine and claimed her whole body as the thick head of his cock nudged between her legs.

He stopped, and her protective instincts deserted her as her eyes found his. Something warm and unwelcome rose in her chest, but she pushed it down. Hard.

It was five years too late for connections. Five years too late for "what does this mean?" That wasn't what she wanted from him anymore.

Still holding his gaze, she smoothed her hands down his rigid arms to his back and then down to his half-clad backside. God, he had an amazing ass. Steel was putting it mildly. How many times had she imagined this?

Too many.

Bracing herself for the shock, she bit her lip and pulled him fully inside her. Gasping, nonetheless, at the sensation. No amount of steeling could have prepared her for the feel of him filling her.

She shouldn't have looked at him then. There was something in his gaze—tenderness? Confusion?—that seemed to penetrate right to the most vulnerable part of her.

But she refused to let those feelings take hold. "Fuck me, John. Please just fuck me."

That did the trick. No more hesitating. He started to move inside her.

Slowly at first, using the long length of his cock to extend every stroke and then adding a small circle of his hips at the end that sent twinges of pleasure radiating through her. Her pulse jumped, her heart pounded, and her breath started to quicken. Those soft little breaths seemed to urge him on.

His skin was hot, and it soon grew slick with perspiration, as the speed of his thrusts intensified.

Oh God. She might have said that aloud. What he was doing to her felt so good, she couldn't hold back. The way he moved . . . the perfect rhythm . . . the thick, solid feeling of him sliding in and out of her . . .

She arched her back. She heard him make a pained sound and managed a glimpse out of her half-lidded eyes of him tensing, holding back, tamping down the pleasure she was bringing him.

She was bringing *him*. She hadn't been all wrong. They were good together. Very good. It might have even meant something once. Something more than that she was about to come.

She felt the hitch in her womb, the slight tensing of muscle, before everything broke apart.

Her cries triggered the same thing inside him. He stiffened, gritted out some kind of muffled curse, and pounded out his orgasm into the shuddering spasms of her own.

It seemed to go on forever. Her body was fighting to hold on to the connection that was every bit as sweet as it was fleeting.

But all good things had to come to an end—isn't that the way the saying went? And this one did. Spectacularly. With a loud banging on the door about ten seconds after he collapsed on top of her.

John was probably crushing her, but he couldn't move. And maybe he kind of liked her under him.

Maybe he liked it a lot. That was . . .

He didn't know how to put it in words. Different? Intense? Fucking incredible?

It was sure as hell quick. That might have been a record for him. Since high school at least. Three minutes had been optimistic. Hell, maybe two had been optimistic. But wow. That had been . . . wow. He'd been seeing stars there for a minute.

Who would have thought that Brittany Blake . . . ?

Shit. His still hammering heart came to a sudden stop. His eyes snapped wide-open as the reality of what he'd done crashed through the lingering euphoria of the one-for-the-books, grade-A-freaking-plus climax.

Blake. As in Brand's little sister. He'd just had sex with his dead best friend's sister—the same sister he'd sworn to stay away from.

No, they hadn't just had sex. That put too nice a spin on it. They'd fucked. Just like she'd asked.

He was about to roll off her and try to think of something to say—though what the hell could he say? He'd screwed up, big-time—when someone started banging on the door.

He cursed, pushing himself off the couch and out of her with a suddenness that he hadn't intended. It felt oddly harsh and final.

Tossing the condom in the trash, he pulled up his briefs and jeans and managed to get them zippered and buttoned before he reached the door.

What had he been thinking? In the living room of the house he rented with four other guys? What was he, eighteen? He should be glad they were knocking.

"Open up, Joe. I know you are in there."

Damn it. Not his housemates. His date—his forgotten-about date, Marta. This wasn't good. This wasn't good at all. And he suspected it was about to get a hell of a lot worse.

"Give me a minute." He thought about grabbing his shirt, but glancing over at Brittany, he knew there was no way it wasn't going to be obvious what had been going on here. She was finishing buttoning her blouse, but even with her clothes back on, she had that just-fucked look written all over her. Her hair was lightly mussed, her cheeks flushed, her lips swollen, and he could see the slight redness on her jaw and neck where his beard had scratched a path.

He'd done that to her. He felt something strange lodge in his chest as he looked at her. Something warm and possessive and unfamiliar. Something a little too primitive.

Something that wasn't him.

He didn't like it. He frowned and turned back to the door, which was being pounded again.

"I know you have someone in there with you," Marta said.

At least that's what he thought she said. Her accent was heavier and harder to understand when she was pissed.

Damn it, nothing to be done. John opened the door wide enough to stick his head out, but hopefully not wide enough for her to see into the living room. "Hey," he said. "I'm sorry about tonight, but I'm afraid this isn't really a good time."

She looked livid and ready to knock down the door, so he made sure it was good and blocked with his foot. The last thing he wanted was a scene.

More of a scene.

"I'm sure it's not." She stood on her toes to try to peer over his shoulder, but he was too tall. "She's in there with you, isn't she? The woman you made out with at the bar? Who is she? Your girlfriend? Wife?"

"No!" Surprise made his response a little harsher than warranted. "Look," he said, starting again in a calmer voice to try to defuse the already tense situation. "It's just an old friend, okay? She arrived, uh, unexpectedly."

Marta held his gaze, and behind the anger he could see the hurt. "And you thought nothing of kissing this 'old friend' and leaving with her when we had a date? How do you think that made me feel to show up tonight and have everyone talking about you and this woman putting on a show in the middle of the bar?"

John swore and dragged his hand through his probably sex-rumpled hair. He hadn't meant this to happen. The thing with Marta wasn't really even a thing, but he hadn't meant to hurt her—or embarrass her. But neither could he explain. He could hardly tell her the truth: "Had to shut her up to prevent her from blowing my cover" wasn't an option.

Nor did it explain this.

"I'm sorry," he said again. He didn't know how to explain. What had happened with Brittany was unexplainable—on so many different levels. Levels he didn't even want to think about.

Marta looked him right in the eye. "Fuck your apologies, Joe, and fuck you, too."

Something inside Brittany made her want to stand and cheer at the woman's parting words. It was no less than he deserved.

Why was Brittany surprised to hear that he'd had a date tonight? She should be more surprised that it wasn't *two*.

Brittany should probably thank the woman for showing up when she did. If she'd been feeling even a twinge of uncertainty about the significance of what had just happened, it was gone.

For the better part of five years, Brittany had wondered what it would be like to have sex with John Donovan. Now she knew. It was every bit as amazing as she'd thought it would be. It was hands down the best sex she'd ever had in her life. No question. He was a master between the sheets—or on a ratty couch, for that matter.

But it wasn't enough. Nor did it change anything. If this had happened in San Diego, she undoubtedly would have been dreaming of wedding gowns and picket fences.

But whatever emotional connection she'd felt for him then was gone. And after the woman had arrived, it was *really* gone.

What they'd had was sex. And meaningless sex—even really hot, explosive, lights-out meaningless sex—was still meaningless.

Part of her had always wondered whether if they'd had sex all those years ago things might have been different. It was a silly question, of course, and impossible to answer. But this had helped her answer a related question. It didn't make a difference *now*. Which put John Donovan firmly in the past where he belonged.

He hadn't changed at all. Five years and he was still a player, still a heartbreaker, and still an asshole.

Same old dog. No new tricks.

Except this time he'd made her feel like an asshole, too. A cheap, meaningless asshole. The "old friend" that he'd screwed, banged, fucked—pick your favorite crude term—when he was supposed to be out with someone else.

If the woman had asked him whether he had the plague rather than a girlfriend or wife, he probably would have sounded less horrified.

Were he and the woman serious? Knowing him, she doubted it, but that didn't make her feel any better right now.

This wasn't her. She didn't fall into bed with men. She could count on one hand the number of men she'd slept with. She wanted intimacy, and that took time she never seemed to have to build. She couldn't spare time for a dog or a cat, let alone a boyfriend. And God knew she'd never find that kind of intimacy with John Donovan, whether it would be in five minutes or five years.

Brittany heard the door close, and he came back in the room. He at least had the decency to look uncomfortable, if not a bit shamefaced.

"I'm sorry about that. I forgot I had, uh, plans to-night."

"Yeah, well, if you want a friendly suggestion, *Joe*, when you find your girlfriend later to explain, you might want to think of another excuse. Most women don't like to be forgotten."

He frowned. "Marta isn't my girlfriend. I barely even know her. This was only our first or second date."

Brittany couldn't hide her outrage. "You don't know how many times you've been out?" She paused. "Or does she have a twin sister, too?"

He gave her a hard look but didn't bite. "It's not like that. Our first date got cut short by something."

Brittany *really* didn't need to hear the details. She just wanted to get out of here. She needed to go back to her hotel room and regroup. Process what had happened. Not just with John, but also with her brother. Brandon was dead. Whatever she'd thought before, there was a finality to it now that she needed to absorb.

She stood to leave, giving him a brief glance. He still didn't have his shirt on, which was a little—a lot—dis-tracting. Especially when she saw what looked like fin-ger marks on his arms. Had she done that when she was . . . ?

Wow. "I should go," she said quickly.

"Wait." He grabbed her arm to stop her, dropping it when she looked at it. "I, uh . . . Don't you think we should talk first?"

She looked up at him, really meeting his gaze for the first time since he'd been on top of her and she'd been about to . . .

Forget it.

"About what? Are you going to tell me what happened to Brandon? Was he killed in the explosion where you got that scar on your brow?"

If he hadn't been holding her, she wouldn't have felt

him stiffen. But if she'd struck close, his expression gave
nothing away. "Stop fishing, Brittany. I didn't say there
was an explosion."

"How did you get it, then? How did my brother die?"

He was clearly frustrated by the questions. "I told
you I can't tell you anything. I've already told you too
much."

She thought so. "Then there isn't anything left to say."

She tried to turn out of his hold, but he wasn't letting
go. "How can you say that? We just . . ." He cursed again
and let her go. "I didn't mean for that to happen."

It took her a moment, but she finally realized what the
real problem was. It was written all over his face. "You
don't need to feel guilty about my brother, John. Brandon
is gone."

"I know he's gone, damn it!"

Right. He would never have done this otherwise. If
she needed any more proof that Brandon was truly dead,
she supposed she had it. "Even if he wasn't, it wasn't his
decision to make. I'm twenty-seven years old. Old enough
to choose who I want to have sex with."

Why she was trying to absolve John of his guilt, she
didn't know. But the mention of sex only seemed to make
him feel worse. He looked mildly ill.

"Just tell me one thing," she said.

"What?"

She looked into his eyes. "Did he ask you to stay away
from me in San Diego?"

Nothing. Not a blink, nothing. Just the steady tic of a
clenched jaw.

She turned away. "Forget it. It doesn't matter anymore."

As she'd said, Brandon was dead. And for all intents
and purposes, so was John to her. John Donovan was bad
news, and she wasn't going to make the same mistake

again—been there, done that—no matter how spectacular he was in bed.

John was at a rare loss. He didn't know what to do—or what to say. He felt as if he were standing in the middle of a minefield and every potential step he took could blow up in his face.

If Marta showing up when she did wasn't bad enough, now Brittany was trying to put him on the spot again, asking him questions he couldn't answer.

She'd guessed right about Brand. Five years ago his friend had given him two options: to state his intentions—and it had better be marriage—or leave her alone. So really, Brand had given him one option.

At twenty-four and a newly minted SEAL tapped for a secret elite team, John sure as hell hadn't been ready for marriage. He didn't know if he even *wanted* to get married. Ever. He didn't like to let things get to the girlfriend stage. He liked to keep things light. The rest of his life was intense enough; he didn't need that in his personal life, too.

Not to mention that a serious girlfriend or wife would mean leaving Nine and going back to one of the conventional teams—or worse, HQ or staff.

No connections. That was the rule for Nine. No one to worry. No one to notice if they were gone for too long. Or gone forever. Brittany was all the proof they needed about why connections were a bad idea, with all the hue and cry she'd raised over an estranged brother.

No, none of that was for him. Things were fine as they were. He *liked* things as they were. He was happy—or he would be soon, when things got back to normal. If that was possible. He needed to get back to frogman work.

He couldn't tell her about his promise to Brand. It might give her the wrong idea.

But what had she meant by it didn't matter? And why was she acting so—he didn't know the right word; blasé maybe?—about the whole thing. Acting like it was no big deal when he was all discombobulated and off-kilter.

They'd had sex, for Christ's sake. Really incredible, mind-blowing sex. They should talk about it for a minute. Make sure there were no, uh, misunderstandings.

"Look, Brit, I know you're upset." She picked up the Georgetown messenger bag that she apparently still used as a purse and turned to look at him. Actually, she didn't look upset at all. She looked perfectly calm and collected. Which couldn't be right. "But we need to talk about this. I don't want there to be any, uh, confusion. This can't happen again."

That last part might have come out a little more vehemently than he intended.

She raised her brows in tandem. "I agree. Once was definitely enough."

He frowned. What was that supposed to mean?

She started walking to the door, and he found himself watching her go. She was just going to leave? Just like that?

What the fuck? "Wait!"

She turned to look at him. He was furious, and he didn't know why. He also didn't know why he'd stopped her.

The story. That was it. He had to stop her from writing any more stories about the "Lost Platoon."

"Remember what I told you. You can't tell anyone about what happened or write about any of this. I mean it, Brit. This is serious."

"Oh, I'm sure you'll forget about this soon enough. But don't worry. I don't write bad porn."

His eyes narrowed. She'd purposely misunderstood him. He hadn't been talking about *that*.

And what the hell did she mean by "bad porn"? It might have been short, but it sure as hell hadn't been bad. It had been bloody, freaking incredible, and she knew it.

Didn't she?

Maybe she hadn't had a lot of experience to compare it to. That must be it.

But he'd had lots, and he was tempted to show her just how wrong she was. Very tempted.

Maybe she realized she was treading on dangerous ground because she dropped the clueless act and sighed. "I heard what you said." She paused and met his gaze. "I won't tell anyone that you are alive."

"And the rest of it?"

"The rest of what? You haven't told me anything. No proof, no story. My publisher has made that very clear."

John nodded. For once it seemed they were on the same page. Well, at least he and her boss were on the same page. But if it kept her from putting out more of those stories, that was fine by him.

She opened the door, and he felt the strangest urge to stop her again. To not let her walk away. But he was in hiding, supposedly dead, and he had to keep it that way.

She turned. He assumed it was to tell him good-bye. But he should have known better. She had to get in one last parting shot.

"Brandon was your best friend. How can you let them do this? How can you let them sweep this under the rug and allow his death—his sacrifice—to go unacknowledged?"

His muscles went rigid, his fists curling into tight balls at his sides. "I don't have a choice. If Brand were here, he would be the first one to agree."

"Yeah, well, I guess I have no way of knowing that, as he's not here to disagree, is he?"

John didn't say anything. What could he say? It was

the goddamned truth—no matter how much he wished it were different.

"I used to wonder if there was anything you really cared about," she said. "I guess I know the answer."

Ironically, Brandon had said something similar to him once. John had thought it might be true. But when the door closed behind her, he wasn't so sure anymore.

Seven

Colt Wesson was drinking whiskey and shooting pool at McNally's Last Chance Saloon. This place had been his favorite hangout between deployments, when he'd been on this coast to see his then wife, who was CIA. At the time he'd been stationed in Honolulu with Team Nine. Ironically, living in different time zones had been the least of their marital problems.

He'd had bars like this in every city when he'd been on the Teams, although this one in DC held some particularly bad memories.

Not much had changed around here. McNally's had the same red vinyl booths, dark "mood" lighting, ancient jukebox playing Patsy Cline's "Crazy" and other depressing country classics, peanut shells on the floor that only seemed to enhance the stale-beer-and-smoke smell—management apparently hadn't gotten the message that you couldn't smoke in bars anymore—and local barflies occupying the stools in front of the wooden bar from midmorning until last call.

The hard-living-looking regulars had given Colt the usual "Who the fuck are you?" stare when he'd walked in, but something about his expression had them turning back to their drinks quick enough.

Either that or they remembered him. He'd occupied one of those stools quite a few times in the dark days around the breakup of his marriage a few years ago. It had been the only place he could escape, though from what he didn't know. Himself maybe? For that "last chance" the name promised?

He supposed he'd gotten both. But not without a lot of whiskey and one-night stands.

McNally's was a good place for the latter as well, as the gritty dive-bar atmosphere attracted a certain kind of female clientele. Tough, no-nonsense women who had been around the block a few times and were happy with exactly what he had to offer: a good, hard fuck. Which is why when he wanted to get drunk and laid—preferably in that order—before shipping out tomorrow, he'd found himself at his old haunt. Screw the memories.

He was already halfway toward his first goal when a decent prospect for the second sauntered her way toward him. Sadie was about thirty, dark-haired, dark-eyed, and had a smoking body that looked good in the skimpy clothes she wore to show it off. She had on a tight and very low-cut shirt that gave him a nice view of a pretty killer rack. Yep, he had to say that so far he liked what he saw.

She clearly did, too, as she'd taken the first opportunity after he'd lost at pool—twenty bucks, but he'd been distracted—to console him by planting herself in his lap.

They would have been off to a very promising start if she hadn't ruined it.

"So, what do you do, Colt?" she asked, taking a swig of her Miller Light.

The questionable taste in beer didn't bother him. It was the conversation. "Government hit man."

She laughed, assuming he was kidding. "What do you *really* do?"

He liked the way she nestled her bottom against his growing erection enough to answer. "Sanitation."

Same difference—getting rid of the trash.

She looked mildly disappointed, which struck him as odd, given their present location. Sanitation was a good, steady union job. There weren't many working-class neighborhoods left in the DC area, but this neighborhood near the old rail yard was one of them. Although if the new housing development he'd noticed going up nearby was an indication, it wasn't going to stay that way for long. Hipsters were the new yuppies of gentrification.

"I thought you might be military," she said.

Off-the-books military, but he was surprised she'd guessed. "What made you think that? My clean-cut, all-American good looks?"

She laughed as he'd intended. He was about as far from that description as you could get. Long-haired, scruffy, and dark—except for the light eyes—with some kind of ethnic mixed in there somewhere. Kate had always thought one of his grandparents or parents must have been Italian, but as Colt didn't have any of them to ask, he could be Mexican or Middle Eastern for all he knew—or cared. His looks had never been a problem. It was everything else. The black cloud, the mean temper, the surly attitude, and the lack of a heart, to name a few, according to his ex.

Why the hell was he thinking about Kate?

He knew why. Because he'd seen her last week for the first time in three years, and he'd been on edge ever since.

Which pissed him off. That ship had sailed—and sunk in spectacular fashion. She'd cheated on him with someone he considered a close friend. As he didn't have many of those, it was a big deal. The fact that Colt had pushed her to it, or that they'd barely been married at the time, didn't matter. Even if he were the forgiving kind—which he wasn't—that kind of betrayal was unforgivable.

Sadie was looking at him thoughtfully. "I don't know. When I saw you, you reminded me of a Ranger I dated once."

Well, nothing killed the mood like being mistaken for an army boy.

She shrugged. "With all the bases around here, we sometimes get military guys in here."

Colt had lost interest and would have eased her off his lap to resume playing pool if he hadn't looked across the room and seen something that made his entire body— and everything inside it—still.

Fuck me.

He must have said it aloud, as the woman on his lap laughed and said something that sounded like "you sure don't waste time," but he wasn't really paying attention. His focus was on the woman who'd just walked into the bar and was standing there staring at him, completely oblivious to the fact that the rest of the bar was doing the same thing to her.

But Kate had always been oblivious to the effect she had on those around her—especially men. It had been part of her charm. And part of what had drawn him to her, since God knew she was pretty much the opposite of the kind of woman he'd ever thought to marry. Not that he'd really ever thought he'd marry.

She couldn't have looked more out of place if she tried. The first time he'd seen her he'd had the same thought as he had right then: *What the hell is she doing here?*

Before he'd moved to the "Special Assignments" department of Task Force Tier One—the secret unit within JSOC that was nicknamed CAD (as in control alt delete)—he'd been chief of SEAL Team Nine. They'd been downrange at a shithole forward operating base in Khost,

Afghanistan. He and the guys were sitting around shooting the shit while waiting for a CIA briefing from some new hotshot analyst, and in walks this icy blonde in a fucking skirt and heels, looking sexy as hell and pretty much like a girlie tropical frozen drink to a bunch of guys who'd been dying of thirst in a desert. He was sure he wasn't the only one fighting off wood just looking at her.

To defuse the tension, he'd made some comment to the guys that she'd overheard. He couldn't remember exactly what he'd said, but it had been along the lines of what the fuck was CIA Barbie doing here? He'd never forget her reply—or the way those icy blue eyes had looked down at him. "Trying to help you do your job, *Chief*, as you sure as heck haven't gotten it done so far."

Heck? With the rest of the team trying not to bust out into laughter, Colt had met that cool gaze with a raised eyebrow and a "Yes, ma'am."

But that was the moment he knew he had to have her. Game fucking on. And it was a game at first. A challenge. An opposite-side-of-the-tracks thing. Bringing the ice bitch down to his level for a while—preferably under him, although if she wanted to be on top, he wouldn't put up much of an argument.

If only it had stayed that way. But the ice bitch hadn't been a bitch at all. She'd been sweet and kind of shy, and had a heart of gold. She'd seen through his shit with alarming speed.

She also hadn't been icy. She'd been hot. Sizzling hot. And he'd been the one to melt.

For a while. She'd almost had him convinced about love and happily ever after. But eventually reality had caught up with them both. He had too many sins to erase, too many demons to tame, and too much baggage to carry.

He'd warned her. But she thought she could change him. Instead, he'd changed her. The woman he married never would have cheated on him. But after four years as

Mrs. Colt Wesson, Kate had found refuge in the bed of their mutual friend Lieutenant Commander Scott Taylor, although he'd been only a lieutenant back then. Colt had trained Taylor since he was a junior officer. He'd been like a younger brother to him.

Ironically, it was Taylor's death that had brought Kate back into his life. Taylor had been the officer in charge of Retiarius Platoon when it had gone missing in Russia. Colt had reached out to Kate to put him in touch with her godfather, General Thomas Murray, Vice Chairman of the Joint Chiefs of Staff, who could get Colt access to the information he needed to find out what had gone wrong and who was responsible. To that end, Colt was going to Russia tomorrow to trace the path of the platoon.

It was just the kind of solo operation he did for Uncle Sam as an operative for CAD, although this was actually unauthorized as opposed to "unauthorized if you get caught." The end result was the same. If he found trouble, he was on his own and no one was going to claim him. But he wouldn't be taken alive.

For a minute he thought Kate might turn around and leave. He didn't need to ask why. Sadie was making herself nice and comfortable, snuggling into his lap and looping her arms around his neck. He wasn't encouraging her, but neither was he discouraging. He let her do what she wanted, which at the moment was kissing his neck, as his ex-wife swallowed her distaste and made her way toward him.

Distaste—not hurt or pain. Those days were long gone. Kate was engaged to someone else now. Someone worthy of her, as her godfather had pointed out.

The dull tap of her heels stopped a few feet away from him. Kate wore her usual uniform of a short suit skirt that looked as if it had been made for her—because undoubtedly it had—silk blouse, and matching suit jacket. This one was in a light khaki, but she probably had one in every color.

Kate was a skirt-and-dress kind of girl. She rarely wore pants. Colt had offered her money to see her in jeans just once, but she'd just laughed and rolled her eyes. With legs like hers, skirts were a good choice, but male admiration wasn't why she wore them. Kate didn't do casual. She hadn't been brought up that way. She was always dressed properly because that was what was expected. She was always on. Always polished to a glossy shine. Dirtying her up a little had been part of the appeal.

Colt was hit by the familiar whiff of perfume. Even the faint floral scent smelled like rich girl. Everything about her screamed privilege, wealth, and genteel refinement. He'd originally thought the scent was roses. But he'd found out later it was peony. A flower he hadn't even known existed before he met Kate.

They were her favorite. Once, after a particularly ugly argument early in their marriage, he'd spent two hundred bucks to have them delivered to her in December. It was probably the only romantic thing he'd ever done in his life. She'd burst into tears with happiness, and he'd never done it again. Making her that happy had scared him; he knew he wouldn't be able to keep it up. He had to keep the bar low.

"I need to talk to you," she said.

Colt guessed why, and it pissed him off. If she had tracked him down, it probably had something to do with Retiarius and, more specifically, Taylor. When she'd agreed to put him in touch with the general, it hadn't been for Colt's sake; it had been for the man who'd ended their marriage and fathered the baby that should have been Colt's.

t was like stepping back in time—and not in a good way.

When Kate walked into the bar and saw her ex-husband sitting on a stool by the pool table with a woman draped all over him, she'd felt a stab of pain so deep it seemed to cut her in half. It might have been three years ago in Hawaii, when she'd flown in to surprise him and tell him the news that she hoped would bring him back to her and resuscitate the last dying breath of their marriage.

Instead it had been like a knife in her heart and the beginning of the end. Or maybe, more accurately, the end of the end. Their marriage had been in trouble for a long time before she'd seen him with the woman draped all over him in the bar.

Three years ago in Honolulu, Kate had turned on her heels and fled the bar in tears. Colt had come after her, but only to accuse her of spying on him. Checking up on him because she didn't trust him. How could he blame her after what she'd seen? He'd claimed it was nothing, but Kate had been crushed. Her last hope destroyed.

She'd told him that she was tired of being the only person fighting for their marriage. If he wanted her, he knew where to find her. She'd flown back to Virginia without telling him about the baby.

She didn't hear from him for two months. By the time she finally did, it hadn't mattered.

But there weren't any tears this time. Kate had loved Colt Wesson with every inch of her heart. But he'd been right when he'd warned her that he wasn't capable of that kind of love—giving or receiving. She'd thought she had enough for them both. But his self-fulfilling prophecy had come true, and eventually the love she'd had for him had turned to hate. When he'd walked away from her that last time, she'd honestly despised him.

Maybe she still did.

She thought Colt was out of her life for good, but Scott needed her to do this, and after all he'd done for her, she couldn't refuse. Even if it meant having to face old demons.

And Colt certainly qualified. But he was still a good-looking devil with that belligerent bad-boy thing he'd perfected. Sexy as sin, drop-dead gorgeous, dark brown, almost black hair that was always too long and scruffy for regulation, with piercing green eyes, he looked like he belonged in an old Western movie. Tough, mean, and a little dangerous. Check that. A *lot* dangerous.

None of it was a facade.

She eyed him coolly and asked her question, not surprised when he refused.

"It's not a good time," he said. "As you can see, I'm busy."

Kate knew he was just being provocative for the sake of being provocative—not because he thought he could get to her. It was just his nature to be a dick.

She smiled tightly. "I'm sure that Miss . . . ?"

She turned to the woman on his lap, who was taking everything in with a wide-eyed look on her face. The woman quickly filled in "Sadie."

Kate gave her a genuine smile of thanks before turning back to Colt. "Miss Sadie wouldn't mind if you step away for a few minutes." She gave the woman another smile. "I promise to send him right back."

As soon as she could, as a matter of fact.

"I don't mind," Sadie said, getting off his lap. "You his wife?"

From the way she asked the question, Kate could tell she thought it unlikely.

Kate gave a small laugh, as if agreeing that the concept was inconceivable. "No."

"Ex-wife," Colt interjected.

His tone gave nothing away, but Kate knew him too well. She could see from the slight tightness around his mouth that her laugh had bothered him.

He'd always assumed that she thought the worst of him; why was he surprised now that she did?

He'd clearly shocked Sadie with his announcement—
and everyone else close enough to hear. She understood
the reaction. They appeared utter opposites. Were this
the '50s, they could have been Sandy and Danny from
Grease. At one time she thought it didn't matter. But four
years of marriage had taught her differently.

"Is there somewhere we can speak privately?" she asked,
aware of the people listening to their conversation.

He unfolded himself from the stool with some effort
and obvious reluctance. Her request appeared to be a
serious hardship. But he led her past the bathrooms to a
back door that led into an alley where the Dumpsters
were located.

The smell hit her immediately. Nothing like rotting
garbage on a warm summer DC night. She didn't react,
but he'd always been good at reading her mind—about
the unimportant things at least.

"Sorry for the smell, but I figured this was better than
the bathroom. There's a private office, but I don't know
the bartender well enough anymore to ask."

But he had at one time. And she could guess why he
would have wanted to use the private office—it wouldn't
have been for talking. She wouldn't give him the satisfaction of wondering whether he'd used that office while they
were married. At this point, what did it matter?

"Careful not to brush up against anything," he said.
"Wouldn't want you to mess up that fancy suit of yours."

"Thanks," she said briskly, pretending she hadn't heard
the sarcasm. She wouldn't be drawn in to this kind of
back-and-forth. She knew better than to try to match him
dig for dig. He would win. His tolerance for cruelty had
always been much higher than hers.

She didn't blame him. It was how he'd been raised and
all he'd known as a child. Lashing out had started as
defense and turned to offense. Her mistake was thinking
that she could atone for that. He was who he was, and she

couldn't change him. It was hard to remember now why she'd ever wanted to try.

But it hadn't always been bad. For a while it had been very, very good. And he wasn't always hard and unapproachable like this. At times he'd let down his guard and let her in a little. But when things got tough those times hadn't been enough to hang on to. Eventually, they'd disappeared completely.

Their differences went from the insignificant—he drank whiskey from a bottle; she liked an occasional glass of chilled white wine—to the fundamental. She'd wanted a family; he didn't. She'd wanted to work; he'd wanted a wife who'd be waiting for him when he got home from his long deployments. She'd wanted him to talk about what was bothering him; he'd wanted to keep it inside and hang out with people who understood—i.e., not his wife.

They'd been doomed from the start. Add the stress of his job as a SEAL . . . He'd pushed her so far away, by the time she'd gone to San Diego to tell him about the baby—the baby he didn't want—she felt like she barely knew him.

"So, what do you want, Kate?"

"I found something," she said, handing him a file she pulled from her oversized purse.

He didn't take it. "What is it?"

"A list of everyone in the chain of command, as well as anyone who might have had access to information about the mission."

He gave her an indifferent "why should I care about this?" look. "So?"

"I think I found something, and I need you to help me check it out."

He shook his head, refusing to take the file. "Can't. Wheels up tomorrow at 0800."

How many times had she heard something similar? It

was the story of their marriage. She needed him and he was gone or shipping out.

But she knew all about this trip to Russia; it was why she was here. She had to stop him.

After Colt had shown up at her house and told her about Scott being killed, Kate had been devastated and had agreed to put Colt in touch with her godfather. But that was before she'd received the phone call from Scott. He wasn't dead. He was in hiding and convinced that Retiarius had been set up. He'd asked for her help to find out by whom.

Aside from the five other survivors, Kate was the only person who knew that not all of the platoon had been killed in Russia. Scott didn't trust anyone. For good reason. The woman who'd warned him and saved the lives of six men had been killed.

Whatever Kate's personal feelings toward Colt, he was an exceptional operator and undoubtedly had connections and resources that could help. Retiarius had been his family—much more so than her. But Scott had been adamant that she not confide in Colt, given his hatred toward Scott for what Colt thought they'd done. Scott also didn't want Colt on their trail, which meant keeping him from going to Russia.

"If I'm right, you won't need to go to Russia." She held the file back out to him. "Come on, it won't hurt to just look at it."

He held her gaze for a moment with a hard intensity that she couldn't decipher. Did he suspect there was more to this than she was letting on?

As she'd said, he was one of the best. She knew she would have to be careful. Despite what he thought of her, she'd never been good at deceiving him. Nor did she like it. But after all Scott had done for her, she owed him this. He'd been her friend and confidant when she'd most needed someone, and he'd sacrificed a lot for it, including his friendship with Colt.

Suspicious or not, Colt took the file.

Kate was following a couple of leads that Scott had given her, including this one. Rear Admiral Ronald Morrison, the head of Naval Special Warfare Command (which had operational command of Team Nine), apparently had a serious gambling problem, which Scott had discovered when the rear admiral's wife had taken to social media to vent. The admiral's dire financial straits—which Kate had set out in the documents she'd just handed Colt—gave him a motive.

She was also following up on the woman who'd died after warning Scott. He wouldn't like it, but she was being careful.

"You think Morrison sold them out?" Colt asked, handing it back to her.

From his tone, she could tell he didn't put much credence in it. "I think it's worth looking into."

He didn't disagree. "Nothing stopping you, but what does this have to do with me?"

"I want you to talk to him."

"Maybe you don't remember too well, but the rear admiral wasn't exactly a fan of mine."

She remembered. Morrison had briefly been the head of Group One when Team Nine was being formed and Colt had been tapped as a founding member—a plankowner.

Most officers felt that way about Colt. His methods had never been conventional even when he was a SEAL. Now that he did whatever it was that he did—she didn't know the details and didn't want to—she was sure their dislike had only grown worse.

"I remember, which is partly why I want you there. You know how to make people angry. If you push his buttons a little, maybe he'll reveal something."

"From what I hear, CIA interrogators are plenty good at making people angry. Read any newspapers lately?"

She refused to bite on his reference to recent scandals within the department of overzealous questioning of prisoners. "You know I'm an analyst. I've never interrogated a suspect."

He held her gaze, again seemingly trying to assess her sincerity. But whether he believed her or not didn't matter. He shook his head. "Sorry. I can't help you out. Everything is already set."

She'd expected this, but it still rankled. How many times had she asked him for anything? It had always been the other way around. *Her* job that had to be sacrificed. *Her* being the one to have understanding. *Her* waiting for him to come back from whatever hellhole he'd been sent to, wondering what kind of horrible things he'd done or seen and what kind of black mood he'd be in this time.

Selfish bastard.

Well, this time he was going to do something for her. "I don't think you are sorry at all. I think you don't want to help because it's me who is asking. I think you still want to punish me and would refuse even if it meant going on a wild-goose chase to Russia and never finding out the truth." His expression gave no hint of his thoughts. It was the same dark look he always gave her. "Your plans can be rearranged. There are other transport flights you can hitch a ride on. I'm asking for a week. That's it. Even if you don't think you owe me anything, don't you owe it to your former teammates—your former men—to follow up on a good lead before getting yourself killed?"

"Is that wishful thinking on your part, your godfather's part, or both?"

Finally he'd managed to prick beneath the shield. How could he think that of her? "I never wanted you dead, Colt." Not even after all the hateful things he'd accused her of—all the words he'd said that could never be taken back: "*Too bad the driver didn't have a few more.*

He could have saved me a lot of lawyer's bills." Even the memory made her ill. "It was the other way around."

Still nothing. It was like looking into a black hole with him. It always had been.

She took a deep breath and tried again. "Can't you put aside your hatred of me for a few days? Or do you hate me so much and the idea of being near me is so horrible that you'd rather go tromping around Arctic Russia?"

Even as she asked the question, Kate wondered if *she* wouldn't rather go tromping around Arctic Russia than spend time with her ex-husband. Being around Colt for five minutes was already stirring up memories that she'd spent three years—and thousands of dollars on therapy—to put behind her. But maybe this was exactly what she needed: closure. Maybe they could find a way to forgive each other.

Right. More likely he would just walk away like he'd done three years ago.

He held her gaze so long she wanted to start squirming, but she forced herself not to reveal any of the turmoil seeing him again had unleashed inside her.

"You have your week. Set up the meeting with the admiral. We'll fly as soon as it can be arranged." He stopped. "Assuming Lord Percy doesn't have an objection to you flying across the country with me? Or maybe you won't tell him."

Percy wasn't a lord, as he well knew. He was a knight. His Excellency Sir Percival Edwards, Her Majesty's Ambassador to the United States.

But Colt was right. Percy wasn't going to like it. He knew what Colt had done to her. He knew what Scott was to her as well, although not that he was alive. She couldn't tell him that. But Percy understood about her job—there were things he couldn't share with her either. Percy trusted her. Which was something Colt had never done.

He'd been jealous from the start. If he only knew how wrong he'd been.

"Why would he have an objection?" she asked innocently. "He knows exactly what you are to me."

Nothing. The slight tightening of his jaw was the only sign that her comment had pricked beneath that impenetrable surface.

Marriage to Colt had taught her something after all. Never show weakness. She needed to remember it.

Eight

John opened his eyes for only a split second, but sunlight found the crack and exploded in his head like a grenade.

God, his head hurt. He felt like crap. What time was it? He blinked again—the pain from the light marginally less excruciating this time—and felt around for his watch on the bedside table.

It could be midnight for all he knew. Finland had taught him that there could be too much of a good thing—who would have ever thought he'd get tired of daylight? But it wasn't conducive to sleeping well. Of course, the nightmares weren't either.

What did help was alcohol, but unfortunately that had a rather unpleasant side effect. Waking up with a head that felt as if it had just gone through a meat grinder, which was pretty much how it felt right now. It was still buzzing with the sound of . . .

Ah, hell, not his head. The phone. That must have been what woke him. Slightly more alert, John sat up and looked around. He saw his watch on the table, but the phone was still in his jeans pocket. He rolled out of bed, fished through the pocket, and pulled it out to answer.

They exchanged the code before the LC laid into him. John was still half-asleep, and it took a moment for his brain to catch up with what Taylor was saying.

"What the hell have you been doing the past few days? I told you to take care of it—of her."

John's mouth flattened. He didn't need to ask whom the LC meant. He'd thought of little else besides *her* since Brittany walked out of here three nights ago.

"I did take care of her," John said, although not in the way he had planned. But he had no intention of sharing that particular detail with the LC. John was doing his best to forget it himself.

A few more nights and he was sure he'd stop thinking about it. Then he'd be out of this weird funk he'd been in. He'd actually lost his temper at work a couple times today with one of the new guys. If he didn't watch it, the senior chief was going to have some competition in the hard-ass category when they all got back to work.

Except they wouldn't *all* be going back to work.

"Then why the hell did I just find out that Lois Lane is in Norway now, asking questions around the base?"

It was John's turn to swear. "At Vaernes?"

"Where else?" the LC said. The air station in Vaernes, Norway, had been their forward operating base for the Russian mission. From Norway they'd hopped on a bird to rendezvous with the ship, which had taken them as close as it could get to Russia before they'd boarded the submersible.

"What did you tell her?" the LC asked.

"Nothing, I swear."

"Then how the hell did she find out about Vaernes?"

"I don't know, but it wasn't from me." John filled the LC in on the e-mail he'd sent and how she'd used the

picture to track him down. He also mentioned her referring to an explosion, although she could have just been
fishing for information.

It took a minute for the LC to stop cursing so John could
explain the rest. John understood Taylor's reaction. The LC
didn't want anyone to know they were alive—and Brittany
being a reporter made her knowledge even more
dangerous.

But his head was killing him, and the LC tearing him
a new one wasn't helping. Taylor only relented a little
when John explained that he had used Kate's tech. Brittany's person had just outsmarted them.

John told the LC that he'd made it clear—very clear—
the danger she would put him in if she continued with
her story. "But other than confirming what she'd already
guessed—that Brand was killed in a mission—I didn't
tell her anything. I thought she understood and was going
home."

He thought back on what she'd said and realized now
that she'd just been putting him off. She hadn't agreed to
anything.

"Well, obviously you didn't make much of an impact
on her."

John's jaw was clenched so tightly his teeth hurt. That
was true in more ways than one. "I guess not."

The LC was silent for a moment on the other line.
"Why do I have a feeling there is something you aren't
telling me? What else happened, Dynomite?"

"Nothing," John said, maybe a little too quickly. "I
told you everything important."

But the LC hadn't been given command of one of the
most elite military units in the US by being an idiot. "Tex
mentioned that he thought she had a crush on you when
she was a kid." Twenty-two was hardly a kid. "You didn't
do anything to piss her off, did you?"

John definitely took offense at that. "Why would you think that?"

"I don't know," the LC said impatiently. "Maybe because I've seen you in action for about five years."

"I don't know what you think you've seen, but I haven't had any complaints."

The LC snorted. "I bet. But maybe I should let Miggy handle this after all."

"No!" Now, that was too quick—and too adamant. If the LC hadn't guessed something was up before, he sure as hell knew it now. "I can handle her, sir."

As a matter of fact, John couldn't wait to get his hands on her.

The LC paused so long that John heard a crack in the plastic of his phone. He released his grip. Cheap, piece-of-crap burner.

"See that you do," Taylor said. "And, Dynomite, I don't think I need to remind you what's at stake."

"Copy that, sir." He knew exactly what was at stake, and Brittany was going to regret not heeding his request the first time.

But this time he wasn't going to be so pleasant. No more Mr. Nice Guy, as the old heavy metal song put it so succinctly.

The young soldier and his friends had been checking Brittany out since she'd walked into the bar and found a seat in a corner booth. She smiled shyly—encouragingly—from behind her menu, and not long after she ordered, he slid into the booth opposite her.

"Hi," he said. "You waiting for someone, or can I buy you a drink?"

His English was very good, but laced with a strong Norwegian accent. She met his ice-blue gaze hesitantly.

"I probably shouldn't answer the first, and I just ordered a beer, so the second isn't necessary."

He grinned as if just having something confirmed. "You are American. I thought you might be."

Brittany wasn't surprised that he'd guessed. The same thing had happened the past two nights. This was her third night mingling with the locals at the favorite hangout of the soldiers who were based at Vaernes Air Station. Either she had some kind of invisible sign above her head blinking "American" or there was something about her clothes and appearance, but the guys who'd talked to her seemed to know before she opened her mouth where she was from. She guessed she could check "spy" off the list of future careers.

"What gave me away?" she asked.

He shrugged and gave her a smile and a conspiratorial wink that if she were a few years younger and not on the job might have made her heart do a little stutter.

He was a nice-looking guy in that blond, blue-eyed, clean-cut Nordic fashion that encompassed about a third of the guys in here. From what she'd seen of Scandinavia so far, they were certainly a good-looking bunch. A little on the homogeneous side, but if big, blond, and Viking were your thing, this was the place to be.

She thought of another big, blond Viking and pursed her mouth. She wasn't going to let *him* run her off. Having Brandon's death confirmed hadn't changed her mind. If anything, it had made her even more determined to find out the truth of what had happened. Her brother's death wasn't going to be swept aside for some governmental expediency. Not like her parents. She wouldn't fail him, too.

And neither was she going to put aside the story of a lifetime without a good reason. And a vague warning that it could be dangerous wasn't enough. She wouldn't say anything about survivors, but if John thought he could use her feelings—her former feelings—for him to get her to bury the story, he was even more full of himself than she thought. He probably assumed she'd been so overwhelmed by having sex with him that she'd fallen in love with him all over again.

Right. No one was that good.

Although admittedly . . .

She had to stop thinking about that. It wasn't helping.

But she'd meant what she told him before she left. There weren't going to be any more Lost Platoon stories without proof—her editor had made that clear. Which was why she was here making friends.

The documents and satellite images from her mysterious source seemed to point to a secret mission in Russia. Given the state of tension between the two countries teetering on war, it made sense that no one would be eager for the information to get out. One of the few helpful clues in the redacted deployment orders had been Vaernes Air Station. If she could prove that Brandon had been here, that would help establish the authenticity of the document, and if he was here right before the purported missile "test" in late May, that might be enough to link SEAL Team Nine to the explosion in Russia. Vaernes was an obvious launch point for an operation in Russia.

Assuming her new source hadn't sent her on a wild-goose chase, as she was beginning to fear. She was still hoping Mac would be able to come back with something more on the license plates, but the car had been a pool car used by any number of people in the Department of Defense. If they kept a list on who took it out, it wasn't electronic.

For now this was her best lead. But so far it wasn't paying off. Hopefully, her luck would change tonight.

"It was your smile," the soldier said. "Americans are

so friendly and confident." He frowned, noticing the change of her expression. "Is something wrong?"

She shook her head, realizing she was still frowning from thinking of John. "No, sorry. I just thought I saw someone I knew."

He didn't hide his disappointment. "Then you are waiting for someone?"

She shook her head. "I'm going to take a chance that you aren't a serial killer scouting bars for victims, but no, I'm not."

He grinned. "Not a serial killer; we don't get a lot of those in Norway. My name is Nils Olsen—Corporal Nils Olsen—I'm stationed at the base." He motioned toward his group of friends, who were watching his progress. "You can ask any of them, and they'll tell you, I'm perfectly safe."

Her mouth quirked in a playful smile. "Brittany Blake. It's nice to meet you, Nils. But maybe I should ask those women over at that table instead? A couple of them keep looking over here."

He blushed. If he was indeed a budding ladies' man, as she suspected, he hadn't perfected the smooth-operator bit. She guessed he was a couple years younger than her—maybe twenty-three or twenty-four. Give him a few years.

Her thoughts slid to another smooth operator before she forced them back to Nils.

Not wanting to scare him away, she changed the subject. "Are you in the air force?"

"I'm with the Home Guard."

From her research on the air station, she knew what the Home Guard was but pretended as if she didn't and gave him a questioning look.

He explained. "It's an *Innsatsstyrke*—what you would call a Rapid Reaction Force. We are trained to respond to all kinds of emergencies, from bomb threats to terrorism. We actually do an exchange with your national guard every year in Minnesota."

"Ah." She nodded. "I think my brother mentioned that." At his questioning look she explained. "He was here briefly with the marines a few months ago."

Brittany didn't think the recent US marine presence at Vaernes was a coincidence. Earlier this year, Vaernes had welcomed three hundred marincs from North Carolina. They were the first US troops to be officially stationed in Norway since World War II. Not surprisingly, Russia wasn't too happy with the arrangement. The marines were on a six-month deployment and the second group had rotated in this summer. The US troop presence at Vaernes would make it easier to hide a team of SEALs moving through.

She let the mention of her brother go and changed the subject when her food and drink arrived. She wasn't hungry, and she was tired of bar food, so she'd ordered a salad and fries. But her attempt at healthy had been foiled by a large glob of creamy dressing.

Oh well.

Brittany was having a surprisingly good time talking to Nils, and it was only after the waitress had cleared the table and brought them each another beer and he'd asked her how she ended up here that she returned to the subject of her brother.

"I was already planning a hiking trip over here with a girlfriend, so when my brother told me about the annual blues festival, I knew I had to check it out. My friend had to go back for work, but I decided to stay on for an extra week to go to the 'Blues in Hell.'"

Hell was the name of a small village near Vaernes, and not surprisingly, the festival took advantage of the catchy name.

Before Nils could ask her any blues-related questions,

she asked him what she'd been wanting to ask since he sat down. "I wonder if you crossed paths with him while he was here?"

It was the same question she'd asked a handful of other soldiers stationed here the past couple nights with no luck. She was trying to be careful, but if this didn't yield something soon, she was going to have to come up with a way to show the picture to more people without drawing attention to it or herself.

She'd always taken the get-more-bees-with-honey approach to her investigating. In her experience, people didn't like reporters—especially aggressive ones—and were naturally defensive around her if they thought she was trying to question them or wanted something. She got a lot more just by talking to people and being friendly.

Flirting wasn't usually part of the repertoire, but with young soldiers it seemed the best way to relate and not seem suspicious. When in Rome . . .

"Maybe," Nils said doubtfully. "What's his name?"

"Brand," she said, and took out her phone. "I have a picture."

It was the same photo from the beach zoomed in on his face. She was going to hold it out to show it to him, but Nils took the opportunity to slide onto the bench seat next to her.

Maybe he was more of an operator than she'd given him credit for. He was sitting close enough for their legs to touch. She could feel the muscle of his thigh pressing against hers. He was tall and lean, but not physically overwhelming like—

Stop.

He took the phone, gave it a brief glance, and then looked back with a small frown. "He looks familiar. When was he here?"

Brittany tried to control her excitement, but her heart

was beating so hard she thought he might hear it. "End of May. He didn't stay very long. But after his description of the area, I knew I had to add it to my itinerary."

He handed the phone back to her, and the way he was looking at her made her realize he was more savvy than his age suggested. "Yeah, I remember him. He and his friends were only here about a week. They kept to themselves and didn't mingle—even with their own guys. I assumed they were some kind of Special Forces."

Brittany acted embarrassed. "I'm not supposed to talk about that." She bit her lip in an effort not to burst out with a bunch of questions. But with her first confirmation, it wasn't easy. "I'm impressed that you remember him. Did you talk to him or any of his friends?"

He shook his head. "Not me. As I said, they weren't interested in meeting the locals, but you do this long enough and you begin to pick out guys like that. Intense, all-business, focused." He shrugged. "My friend Johan drove them to one of our training facilities. He said they barely spoke two words and their uniforms didn't have any kind of military branch or unit on them. Just some kind of patch."

"Johan?" Brittany hoped she didn't sound too eager, but every bone in her body was screaming *"Yes!"* If she could get a description of the patch, it could be proof that Team Nine had been here—especially if it matched the new tattoo she'd noticed on John of the trident and net, which she suspected was some kind of unit or platoon badge. "Is he one of your friends over there?"

She motioned to the group of guys who were still standing by the bar. They'd lost interest in Nils's progress and had concentrated on their own, mingling with some of the women Brittany had noticed earlier.

Nils shook his head. "No. He had a late shift tonight and was just going to hang out at the barrack bar at the garrison tonight." He leaned in a little closer, and his eyes fell to her mouth. Uh-oh, he wasn't going to try to kiss her, was he? He was definitely smoother than she'd thought. "I don't suppose you have any interest in checking it out? It's quieter there."

Definitely smoother than she thought. His hand was stroking the top of her arm and the strands of dark hair that she'd left loose around her shoulders. Her skin was buzzing, but it wasn't with awareness.

It almost felt like someone was watching her. She'd had that feeling a few times since arriving, but every time she looked, it wasn't anything. It was just John making her paranoid. *"You don't know what kind of hornet's nest you are stirring up. . . ."*

Yes, she did. She'd been inside a government cover-up before, but so far the only hornet here was one with eight hands. She'd better watch out or this guy was going to be all over her.

But she couldn't let the chance go to meet someone else who might recognize or have spoken to her brother.

She debated for a minute. "Okay, but just to go to the bar, right?"

"Right."

His brilliant smile made those caution signs go way up. "Did you drive?" she asked. He nodded. "Good. I'll follow you in my rental."

She felt a lot more relaxed and less claustrophobic when he slid out of the seat next to her and stood. She also felt less like she was under a microscope, but she looked around all the same. No one was paying attention to them.

"Where did you park?" he asked.

"In the back." The lot had been packed by the time she arrived. "I'll drive around and meet you by the entrance."

He told her the model of the car, and they walked out the front door. She pretended not to notice the knowing smirks on a few of his friends' faces.

When they got outside, she could see that the skies had darkened with rain. She pulled out her travel umbrella and told him she would see him in a few minutes.

She hurried around the building, trying not to slip in her heeled sandals. Her feet were soaked already. Not the wisest choice of footwear tonight, given the weather, but she'd been going for sexy and had to dress the part. Besides, she was short and needed all the help she could get.

She was about half the distance to her car when the hairs went up on the back of her neck and she got that feeling again. She looked around, thinking it might be Nils, but the parking lot was deserted.

Cursing John Donovan for the umpteenth time, she dug around in her bag for her keys and pepper spray. Ignoring the water sloshing through her toes, she hustled the remaining distance to her car.

Although pepper spray was illegal for private citizens in most of Scandinavia, she'd been able to track some down, thanks to Google after her John-Donovan-inspired paranoia made her think someone was following her the other night. Apparently some sporting goods stores sold it under the table.

Lucky for her, she had it in her hand when someone grabbed her from behind.

Nine

Brittany didn't have time to scream. She felt a hand on her upper arm and raised the pepper spray at the same time as someone—a man—spun her around.

She got off only one short shot before the spray was knocked out of her hand with a muffled word in a language that she didn't need to understand to know it was a curse. Her umbrella was blocking her view of his face, but he was big—about a foot taller than she—and wearing a dark hooded sweatshirt that made him look bulkier than the hardness of the arms grabbing her suggested.

She tried to use the umbrella as a weapon, but it was in her left hand, and her awkward attempt was easily deflected. Like the pepper spray, he knocked it out of her hand with a blow that made her cry out.

She caught a flash of a shadowed profile as he muffled her cry with his hand and drew her in hard against him. He wrapped his arm around her neck so tightly it was cutting off her breath.

Terror was instantaneous and unlike anything she'd ever experienced. It was a primitive reaction that permeated every bone, every fiber, every nerve ending of her being.

She struggled, clawing with her fingertips at the thick, steely arm crushing her throat. But it was immovable. He was strong—terrifyingly strong.

She was so scared it took her a few minutes to realize he was trying to pull the purse that she had instinctively clutched to her side. She released it at the same moment as she stomped down hard on his foot with the point of her heel.

The impractical sandals of a few moments ago were now her salvation. He made a sharp sound of pain and loosened the arm around her neck enough to let in some air. She sucked in a few greedy gasps as she tried to twist away.

But he recovered from the heel stomp too quickly and reached for her—or her purse, which was hanging loose on her arm—again.

Oh God, all she'd succeeded in doing was angering him. She could practically feel the menace wrapping around her and feared that this time the arm around her throat wouldn't stop squeezing.

But instead of tightening around her neck, his arm flexed and she was shoved forward hard against her car. Unable to stop the momentum, she stumbled to her knees and cried out—more from the shock of the force than from pain.

Being on the ground terrified her. Nothing good was going to happen with her like this. The thought of rape permeated the haze, causing her to rally. To fight. She had to get up.

But rape wasn't why he'd pushed her down. She heard the sound of a struggle and realized that someone else was there. She glanced over her left shoulder as she got to her feet, hunched over.

A man in a hooded Gore-Tex jacket appeared to have

just struck the man in the sweatshirt who'd attacked her. Her thought that Nils might have heard and come to her rescue was discarded at the sight of the blue Helly Hansen–style jacket. Nils had been wearing a similar lightweight rain jacket, but his had been a dusky military green.

Her attacker stumbled but shook off the blow and pulled something out of the sweatshirt pocket. She glanced at his face again, trying to make out the features, but the hood of his sweatshirt was pulled down too far. All she could see was a silhouetted profile. Then she was distracted by the glint of metal coming from his pocket.

"Down." She heard the shouted warning and reacted to the voice of her rescuer even as she recognized what the metal was.

She dove forward, hitting the ground flat as a muffled shot was fired. The bullet whizzed right above her head, and she screamed.

She didn't know how long her face was pressed to the wet gravel. She didn't dare move in case he tried to shoot her again. Time seemed to have stopped. She heard scuffling—fighting—the unmistakable crack of a bone, a sharp grunt, and then the clatter of something metal hitting the ground.

A few long heartbeats later someone was at her side and she was being lifted off the ground and turned around into a reclining position.

Fortunately, it was John, whose voice she'd recognized, and not the man who'd attacked her.

He was handling her so gently. Almost tenderly. She might have been a fragile piece of china from the way he was holding her.

"Oh God, are you hit?"

He had her by the shoulders, and she was able to look up at him to shake her head. There was some kind of emotion in his gaze that made her throat squeeze, cutting off her ability to talk.

"Thank God," he said hoarsely, bringing her in tight against his chest.

She felt something pounding against her cheek, and it took her a moment to realize it was his heart.

He'd been scared for her. Scared enough to lose his perpetual cool.

She didn't have time to ponder that as the sound of a motorcycle broke the spell. She looked over John's shoulder long enough to see the man in the hooded sweatshirt speeding away. She also saw the gun on the ground against the wheel of the car, where John must have kicked it after breaking her attacker's arm to release it— that was the crunch she'd heard.

John relaxed his embrace and then held her away from him again to meet her gaze. "You're sure you're okay? He got off that shot before I could reach him." She thought he might have shuddered. "When you cried out, I thought he hit you."

She shook her head again, but this time found her voice. "It just startled me."

He nodded and helped her to her feet. She straightened her clothes and brushed the pebbles off her scraped knees and palms, trying not to wince, suspecting those scrapes were going to hurt later.

She should have guessed from the way he was watching her and the increasing darkness that was coming over his expression that the storm—the real storm—was about to break. Seeing her umbrella and purse on the ground, she put off the inevitable for a moment and bent down to pick them up.

But the rain plastering her clothes and her hair to her body suddenly seemed unimportant. The silence was ominous.

Why was she feeling defensive? She hadn't done anything wrong. "Not that I'm not grateful for your timely arrival, John. But what are you doing here?"

His eyes narrowed. The concern of a few moments ago was evaporating quickly. "I should be asking you the same thing. You were supposed to go home and forget all about this." He took a step toward her, which, if she didn't know him better, she might have considered threatening. "It could be dangerous, remember? Like you could get yourself fucking killed?"

The last two words were practically shouted, and her eyes widened both at his tone and the rage on his face. No, not concerned anymore. That was for sure. Now he was in 100 percent pissed-off-deadly-operator mode.

She had always wondered how someone so laid-back and good-humored could have ended up becoming a SEAL in one of the most elite Special Forces in the world, but suddenly it had become a lot clearer.

She'd never seen him so riled up; it was a little unnerving.

Without her realizing it, he'd pushed her back against the car. "What the fuck were you thinking, Brittany?"

Two fucks in two sentences. Definitely not good.

Her heart was fluttering a little fast, but she forced an even tone to her voice. "I was thinking that since you weren't going to tell me anything, I would have to find out what happened on my own. But that guy who attacked me didn't have anything to do with you or my stories."

Oops. He didn't seem to like that. His face turned really tight and angry. The hang-loose surfer looked like a mean, black-hearted, pillaging Viking.

"Are you out of your sweet, ever-loving mind? I don't know what the hell you've been smoking lately, sweetheart"—*Sweetheart*? She'd never heard an endearment from him before—"but why else do you think he was trying to kill you? This is Norway; they don't do violent crime here."

"He was trying to take my bag."

John was leaning in so close now, she could practically feel the anger reverberating from his tensed muscles. There was rather an impressive lot of them to tense, and her skin prickled in an all-over flush. Unfortunately, it wasn't with fear. It was with something else. Something that was making her blood race, her breath quicken, and really stupid parts of her body tingle.

How could she be turned on at a time like this?

"That guy wasn't a purse snatch. He was a professional. Didn't you see him?"

"Not really." She just had a vague impression. Tall, strong, shadowed features. A smell of . . . aftershave? Soap? She couldn't put her finger on it. But he'd been clean-shaven. Otherwise, with the rain, darkness, and hoods, the two men would have been eerily similar.

She frowned. But that didn't mean he was a professional. John was just trying to scare her. Which he didn't need to do. She was scared enough.

"Well, I did," John said. "And that guy was trained. He sensed my approach and blocked my blow too easily. I was lucky to get the gun away from him." Brittany hadn't seen any of it; she'd had her face pressed against the pavement. "He would have snapped your neck with one twist if I'd been a second later. Do you have any idea how lucky you are that I got here when I did? If the guy you picked up in the bar tonight had taken any longer to persuade you to go home, we wouldn't be having this conversation."

This was a conversation? It seemed rather one-sided to her.

She'd never heard him raise his voice to anyone like this before. And from the way his hands were clenching and reclenching at his sides, she got the definite sense that he was trying to decide whether to shake her or ravish her senseless.

Emphasis on the senseless.

She shuddered, the unwelcome tingling turning to full-fledged clenching. With the length of his powerful body leaning against hers like this, it was too easy to remember how it had felt to have him inside her. Sinking into her with those long, deep thrusts that had possessed her entire body.

She wasn't going to do this. She didn't know whether it was what had just happened, what he was saying, or the desire that was crashing over her, but she suddenly felt overwhelmed, upset, and maybe a little vulnerable.

And she didn't like it. She pushed him back with the flat of her hand on that steely chest. "Stop bullying me, Johnny! I know you are mad that I didn't do your bidding after you went to such great efforts to see that I did, but I'm not twenty-two anymore. I'm not going to put this aside just because we slept together. And you had no right to get rid of Nils whether I picked him up or not!"

She was really stepping in it with him tonight. His eyes turned black. "Don't push me right now, Brittany. You might not like what happens."

She shivered, fearing she'd like it a lot. What kind of warped person was she to get excited by all this raw, masculine anger? She must be going off the deep end.

"You were the one who told me I needed proof," she said. "Well, I'm getting it."

"How? By picking up guys in bars for information and acting like a frog hog?"

If Brittany weren't so furious, she would have laughed. How dared he accuse her of being a slut when he was the one who was indiscriminate in bed partners?

"You have got to be kidding me. This from *you*? One of the biggest players I've ever met? The guy who slept with two women in one night to prove a point? Thanks, Johnny, but I think I'll take my dating advice from someone else."

"That wasn't a date," John said. "That was you pumping some poor kid for information. Just how far were you going to go to get it, Brit?"

John knew he was being an ass, and although he wasn't the player she thought him, he'd had his share of hookups. Okay, maybe a few more than his share, but he couldn't seem to stop himself from lashing out.

He was angry, and worse—scared. He couldn't get that image of her in that guy's hold out of his head.

He'd almost been too late. He'd been so pissed by what he'd witnessed in the bar—and that she was leaving with the young soldier—that he'd finished his beer rather than follow them out right away. And then he'd taken time to get rid of "Nils" first.

Previously-unknown-to-exist jealousy had nearly gotten her killed. It made him sick just thinking about it.

Brittany gasped with outrage at his accusation. She gave him a look that could kill. "It's none of your damned business how far I would go!"

That wasn't exactly what he'd expected her to say. "You aren't going to deny it?"

She lifted her chin—which was too damned cute—and glared at him something fierce. "Why should I bother? Since you have obviously drawn your own conclusions, it would be a waste of time." Those pretty blue eyes pinned him. "But I'm not sure how leaving a bar with a guy equates to sleeping with him."

It didn't. Or it didn't *necessarily*. But it was what had led up to it that had made him crazy. The guy had been touching her. He'd been leaning in tight and had his hands on her. John had wanted to kill something—preferably the other guy.

"So, the flirting and sexy getup is a coincidence—is that it?" His eyes drew down the length of the low-cut blouse, skimpy shorts, and strappy fuck-me sandals, which, given that the rain was making her clothes damp and clingy, wasn't a great idea. She looked hot, and he didn't like it. She needed to go back to businesslike and girl-next-door. "I suppose this doesn't have anything to do with you getting information?"

Her flush deepened just enough to let him know he'd hit a nerve—a guilty one. Or at least a not-so-innocent one.

"You had no right to spy on me. I knew someone was watching me. Where were you?"

He shrugged. He hadn't intended to spy on her. He'd walked into the crowded bar planning to drag her out of there, but when he'd seen her laughing with the guy in the booth, it had stopped him cold in his tracks. He'd felt something hard and tight in this chest. Something that made him feel as if acid were eating away at his lungs. Something he didn't recognize.

He'd taken a seat in the opposite corner of the bar to wait for it to go away, but it had only gotten worse. The burning started to pound through his veins. It felt like anger, but he realized it was a different kind of anger. It was jealousy. And that had taken a couple beers to deal with.

He didn't get jealous. At least he never had before. So why now?

He must be getting old. That was it. Could you have a midlife crisis at twenty-nine?

Maybe when he got home and this mess was all behind him, he'd buy a car. Pathetic old guy in a sport car was better than pathetic old guy getting jealous over some kid.

That wasn't her type, was it? Clean-cut, Boy Scout—
or whatever the Norwegian equivalent—who probably
hadn't done anything more dangerous than lift his gun
in target practice.

She needed someone who knew what to do with all
that intensity and energy she gave off. Someone who was
as strong-willed as she was. Someone with experience.
Someone she could talk to. Someone who could make
her laugh.

John's mouth fell in a hard, grim line, recalling that
she'd been laughing in the booth with Nils.

She seemed impatient and appeared to give up waiting for him to answer. She crossed her arms in front of
her chest, and he had to look down to make sure she
wasn't tapping her foot, which would have really pissed
him off.

"Just tell me what you want, John. I assume you are
here for a reason?"

Looking down again was definitely a mistake. He got
a real good look at those tanned, shapely legs and the
chest that was now straining against the damp linen of her
blouse. Her nipples were hard and pointy, and it didn't
take long to remember how they'd tasted in his mouth.
How he'd sucked, nibbled, swirled, and tongued. How
she'd arched deep into his mouth and moaned.

Yeah, definitely a mistake. He saw a slight tremor rack
her body and suspected she was remembering it, too.

He looked back at her face. Their eyes met. "You
know why I'm here."

She sighed as if she'd had enough of him. *Her* enough
of *him*. WTF?

"Look, it's rainy, I was just mugged, and I'm wet, uncomfortable, and definitely not in the mood for this. If
you came chasing after me to get me to go home, I'm
afraid you've wasted a trip. I'll go home when I'm done
and not before."

He wasn't chasing after her. He didn't chase after anyone.

He frowned. Well, maybe he was *technically* chasing after her, but it wasn't the way she implied.

"I told you that wasn't a mugging," he said. "Now get in the car."

She looked at him as if he'd just told her to jump off a bridge. "What?"

"You said you were wet and uncomfortable. I'm taking you back to your hotel, where you can change"—preferably into something that didn't want to make him rip it off her—"and we can talk about this rationally."

"There's nothing to talk about."

When she didn't pick up the keys, he bent over and did it for her. He also pocketed the gun—a 9mm GSh-18, the sidearm weapon of choice for Eastern operators—hoping to hell he wasn't going to need it. "Fine, I'll drive. Now, get in the car."

She stood there stubbornly, clearly having no intention of doing so.

"I've already taken a big risk being here, Brittany. That picture you published has been all over the news, and your little boyfriend took a long look at me. After what just happened, the least you can do is listen to what I have to say."

The reminder of him saving her ass did the trick. She hesitated, but only for a few seconds before giving an annoyed huff. "Fine. We'll go back to my room and you can say what you have to say, but you aren't staying."

Neither was she, but he kept that to himself.

She got in the car and directed him to her hotel—a large American chain that was right next to the airport and train station.

Her room was on the tenth floor. He was pretty sure they hadn't been followed, but he had her wait in the hall until he cleared the room just to make sure.

She didn't argue, but she gave him a "you are way too paranoid" roll of the eyes when he said it was okay.

But John wasn't going to take any chances, and being paranoid had saved his ass too many times to count. Whether she agreed or not, he knew that the guy who'd attacked her hadn't been an ordinary thief. He'd been trained in hand-to-hand combat. Probably military. Possibly Special Forces.

John had been lucky to get the one solid blow in that he had. If he hadn't landed the perfectly timed kick that broke the other guy's arm while he was focused on shooting, John suspected the other guy would have given him a fight—a *real* fight. And not that he couldn't use that right now, but he'd prefer not to do it when Brittany's life was dependent on the outcome.

He'd have to thank Spivak, who was into MMA fighting—big-time—later. Spivak had competed for a while in the UFC heavyweight class before becoming a SEAL and had taken down the guy who eventually became champ. Water polo players were typical recruiting fodder for SEALs, but Spivak definitely made a case for the UFC ranks.

John hadn't gotten a real good look at the guy, but his first impression had been Eastern European. Which wasn't good for either of them if he was right.

Brittany dropped her bag on the bureau next to the flat-screen and bent over—he turned away from the sight of those shorts creeping higher on those kick-ass legs— to unstrap her sandals, before kicking them into the closet, where the rest of her clothes were half spilling out of her suitcase on the luggage rack.

Good riddance, he thought. Those shoes might have to get lost. From the looks of the mess in that suitcase, she wasn't likely to notice.

She grabbed a few things and told him not to make

himself too comfortable. She'd be right out, and then he could leave.

John ignored the less-than-generous welcome and made himself at home, sprawling out on the small couch that was beside the bed. He noticed the opened bag of potato chips, empty chocolate bar wrapper, and can of Diet Coke on the coffee table and frowned. Some things hadn't changed. He remembered her fondness for junk food. Forget the hit man. She was going to die of heart disease if she kept eating all that chemical crap.

He flipped on the TV and started to scroll through the channels. Even with extended cable, there wasn't much to choose from. At home, he loved the late-night talk shows, but here he had to settle for BBC and the same fifteen minutes of news stories that they seemed to replay over and over.

She came out before the end of the first go-round. Skimpy damp clothes were gone, but bare feet, tight jeans, and a figure-hugging T-shirt hadn't done anything to alleviate the sexy issue. He was way too focused on how good her ass looked in those jeans and how big her tits were in that shirt.

T&A was not what he should be thinking about, damn it. This was Brittany. Off-limits Brittany. The sister of his dead best friend, Brittany.

But the reminders didn't help. Especially when she dragged her fingers through her still-damp hair, tossed it over her shoulders, and came to stand directly in front of him. With him sitting and her standing, it put those spectacular breasts he'd just been trying not to look at directly in front of his eyes.

Was that lace he could see under the shirt? *Damn it, not the Playboy Bunny underwear. Don't think about the Playboy Bunny underwear and the soft, creamy, firm flesh spilling out. . . .*

Fuck.

He looked up. He hoped she hadn't read where his mind had been, but from the way she was glaring at him he figured he'd been caught.

Jesus, he was a *guy*. Put them in front of him and he was going to look. What did she expect?

"All right, John. Say what it is you have to say and get out. I've had a long night, and I want to go to bed."

Her innocent proclamation sent his mind in not-so-innocent directions. He wanted to go to bed, too. But that wasn't going to happen.

Again.

Don't go there. "I'll go just as soon as you promise me that you'll get on a plane tomorrow and go home."

She didn't blink, but just held his stare. "Not going to happen. I'm not done here."

John did exactly what he swore he wasn't going to do. He tossed down the remote and stood, getting way too close to her. He could smell her lotion or shampoo—whatever the light floral scent was that was driving him a little crazy. "Yes, you are. You're going to get on that plane if I have to put you on it myself."

He knew better than to threaten her—it would only make her dig in her heels more—but something about her nonchalant, "you're bothering me" attitude was really getting to him.

He was the one who was supposed to be irritated. He'd had to leave his nice, safe little place in Finland, where everything was going fricking fantastic—wasn't it?—to track her down in Norway and save her sexy ass from some guy who clearly meant to do her harm. And what kind of thanks was he getting? Attitude, and lots of it.

She poked him right in the solar plexus with a hard tap of her finger. It was surprisingly effective at stopping him in his tracks if he'd had any intention of moving toward her—which he might have.

He didn't even recognize himself right now. He was from Berkeley, for shit's sake. He was about as evolved as they came for a Teamguy. His mom had made sure of it. But Brittany had turned him into a caveman.

"I'd like to see you try. You're supposed to be dead, remember?"

Yep, he knew it—digging in her heels even more. He could almost see the dirt flying. He was going to have to change tactics if he wanted to avoid a standoff.

Besides, she had a point. There was only so much he could do without drawing unwanted attention to himself.

But with her so close and every part of his body noticing, he couldn't resist one more volley. "You'd be surprised how inventive I can be."

He hadn't said it with any kind of sexual promise. He didn't need to. Sexual promise was pretty much a given when she was standing this close to him. The air was charged with it.

She got it, and wisely took a step back. He took that different approach. The "let's be reasonable adults" approach. "I know I haven't given you a lot of reason to trust me in the past, but after what just happened, you have to at least *consider* that what I've been telling you is the truth and that if you don't back off this story, people— and not just you and me—could get killed. I know you don't want that."

He was rewarded with the first twinge of uncertainty— or guilt. Whichever one it was didn't really matter if it meant that he was finally getting through to her.

"Of course I don't want that. But neither am I going to back off trying to find out what happened to my brother for no reason—or for vague warnings. Whatever happened on that mission is going to come out at some point, John. Men lost their lives. How long do you think you can keep hiding? *Someone* is going to find out you are alive after this secret mission you went on that went so wrong. Wouldn't you rather it be someone who can be fair?"

She had a point. There were stories of covert operations being kept under wraps for years—in one well-known CIA case, sixteen years—but what had happened in Russia was too big to stay hidden for long. They all knew the clock was ticking. But they needed time to figure out what had happened and who was behind it. He didn't want her anywhere near it when this thing blew.

"*Can* you be fair, Brittany?" he challenged.

She looked taken aback and maybe a little hurt. "What do you mean? I'm a good reporter. I thought you believed me about what happened five years ago. I didn't make up that story."

"I did—I do. But I also think you have an agenda. You have been on a one-woman quest to uncover anything that smacks of a governmental cover-up since the death of your parents. The truth is always good and secrets are always bad—you never stop to consider otherwise. No matter what it costs."

She looked furious. "That isn't true!"

"Isn't it? Why else were you and Brand barely on speaking terms for the past five years?"

"Because he accused me of spying on him!"

"Were you?"

She held his gaze, and despite the anger on her face, he knew he'd hurt her. "Fuck you, John."

That was the second time he'd heard that in three days, and he didn't like it any more this go-round. "Can you blame me for thinking that? You used information you saw in that letter in your 'Lost Platoon of Team Nine' articles."

"Five years *after* the fact. And only *after* I was convinced that my brother was dead and the navy was trying to cover it up, and *after* I heard about Team Nine from a few women at a certain bar in Honolulu." He must have looked surprised. "Your secret team wasn't as secret as you thought it was—or those women weren't as deaf and dumb as you thought they were. But some people had figured it out and heard things. And I'm not the only one stirring things up. There's a woman in Iowa who claims to be pregnant by a SEAL who's suddenly disappeared." John grimaced. He'd heard about Travis's ex from the LC. "To my point: you can't keep things secret forever."

"Maybe not, but I don't want you anywhere near this when the shit hits the fan. God, you were nearly killed less than an hour ago. Someone could be targeting you. I'm not going to stand by and let you get hurt."

She didn't respond right away. She was studying his face in a way that made him uncomfortable. It was as if she was looking for something. "Why?"

"What do you mean, why?"

"Why do you care so much?"

"How can you ask that? You're . . ." What? What was she? "Brand's sister," he finished.

She was a little too quiet, her gaze intense. "I don't need a big brother, John. I haven't had one for a long time." She was wrong about that. "I've been fine on my own for a lot of years."

"Maybe so, but I'm not going to let anything happen to you—not on my watch." Brand had loved her more than anyone in this world—far more than she realized. John owed it to him, and watching out for her was one promise he would keep. "If you won't go home, then I'm afraid there is only one solution."

Her dark eyebrows darted together. "What's that?"

"I'll have to stay with you. Consider me your new bodyguard."

———————

Brittany stared at him, a lump of dread settling slowly to her gut. He had to be kidding. Please tell her he was kidding. "Bodyguard?"

John nodded. "As in never-leave-your-side, up-close-and-personal, twenty-four-seven, stick-to-you-like-glue."

She got it, and that dread started to slide toward panic. John Donovan in her face all day and . . . night? No way. He'd drive her crazy. And not an annoyed "you're bothering me" kind of crazy. A "you are way too good-looking, too overwhelming, and put too much testosterone in the air" kind of crazy. A "you make me think and do stupid things" kind of crazy.

God, she'd actually been wondering if the reason he'd been so upset—the reason he seemed to be so insistent—was because he cared about her. Instead it was some sort of misdirected sense of duty.

For the sake of self-preservation, she needed to get rid of him. She might not be worried about falling in love with him again, but she couldn't say the same thing about falling into bed with him again. The guy was sex on a stick. "Don't you think you are overreacting just a little? That guy could have been anyone. There is no reason—"

She was interrupted by the sound of her phone blasting the theme song from *Hawaii Five-0*. It had seemed like a good idea when she'd done it, but that famous riff had quickly lost its charm. She was too busy—or lazy—to pick a new ringtone. "Sorry. I'd better check this."

Grateful for the reprieve to clear her head (a common issue when John was hogging all the airspace around her), she dug around in her bag until she found her phone. Pulling it out, she frowned, seeing that it was from her coworker Nancy. She'd given her the number for emergencies.

"Hey," she said, answering it. "What's up?"

"I just had a call from the police," Nancy said, clearly upset. "They were trying to find you, and the landlord told them where you worked."

"What's wrong?"

"Your apartment was broken into last night and ransacked."

Brittany forgot how close John must be watching her and paled. "Ransacked?"

"Badly," Nancy said. "Cushions and mattress torn apart with a knife. That kind of thing. And . . ."

Brittany could tell she was trying not to alarm her, but the hesitation wasn't helping. "And?"

"There was a message on your bedroom mirror written in lipstick. It said, 'Stop or die.'"

Ten

Brittany swallowed, but her mouth was dry and the lump wasn't going away easily.

Lipstick on a mirror? Not very original. It was easier to think about that rather than the fact that someone had been in her house, going through her things.

"Is that all?" she asked.

"Isn't that enough?" Nancy said. "You've obviously pushed the wrong buttons with your Lost Platoon articles. It has to be about that, don't you think?"

Brittany was aware of John watching her, and from his ever-darkening expression, it was clear he'd gotten the gist of the conversation. There was going to be no getting rid of him now. After what had just happened, this was too much of a coincidence. Even for her.

When she didn't answer right away, Nancy added, "The police want to talk to you. You need to call them as soon as you can."

"I will. Thanks for the call, Nancy. I really appreciate it, but I'm going to have to call you back."

Brittany hung up without waiting for a response. She

dropped the phone back into her bag before turning to face John.

His expression wasn't as dark as it had been a few moments ago, but the look of icy control was almost worse.

"Someone broke into your apartment," he said flatly.

It wasn't a question, but she nodded anyway.

"What else?" he said with deceptive calmness, although she could tell he was fighting to keep a lid on that temper she'd had no idea he had.

She filled him in on what Nancy had said. He was very still until she got to the part about the message on the mirror, and then the muscle in his jaw jumped.

She was really beginning to dread that little muscle. It seemed to be an indication that something was about to break. Like a levee, but a whole lot worse.

Now was probably not the time to remember how she'd noticed the muscle twitch right before she'd taunted him into having sex with her. That kind of levee break and mad rush she didn't need again.

She bit her lip, giving him a wry smile. "I guess you might have been right about the danger."

Her attempt at placating him didn't work. The "you think?" look he shot her was every bit as foreboding as that muscle tic.

She decided not to voice her question about whether he thought the mugging in the parking lot and the ransacking of her apartment were connected. It was obvious he thought they were. Although she wasn't quite as convinced, it was probably too much of a coincidence not to be.

She could almost see his mind working as he turned over the information in his head. "You said the guy who attacked you tried to grab your bag?"

She nodded.

"They must not have found whatever they were looking for in your apartment. So, what were they looking for? What do they think you have?" He didn't wait for her to answer. "How did you end up in Norway?"

She hesitated. As a reporter, it was almost reflexive to refuse to give information about a source.

He seemed to read her mind, and that muscle jumped again. But all in all, he was doing a remarkable job of holding his temper in check under the circumstances. Somehow she didn't think he would appreciate a gold star at this moment.

"Secrets are bad, remember?" he said. "You can't de-cry cover-ups one minute and then clam up another. If I'm going to keep you safe and try to figure out who wants to shut you up, I need to know what we are up against. You have to tell me what you know and who told you. I'm not going to steal your story. I'm trying to help you."

He was right. The instinct to protect her story and her source was misplaced here. Besides, she didn't even know who her source was to protect.

She went back to her bag and retrieved the envelope. As she handed it to him, she told him how she'd acquired it.

He flipped through the documents quickly, pausing when he reached the deployment orders. His mouth thinned; ob-viously he didn't like what he was seeing.

When he was finished, he handed it back to her and asked her to go back over the drop again, trying to elicit more details. But she'd told him everything she could think of.

"You didn't see the driver?" he asked.

She shook her head.

"But you think it was a woman in a military uniform in the backseat?"

Brittany nodded. "Yes, but other than the fact that there was gold embroidery on the sleeve, I couldn't see anything distinguishing about it. My friend is looking into the car, but she's hit a roadblock."

"The same friend that gave you the e-mail to track me down?"

She nodded.

"I'll put my people on it, too," he said. "But whoever gave you that deployment order was high up. Only a handful of people had access to that kind of information."

She'd figured as much and resisted the opportunity to question him about the op. She didn't think he was in any mood to share more information with her. But she hadn't given up hope on convincing him. Not by a long shot. Especially if he wasn't leaving, which she suspected was off the table for now.

She wasn't sure how she felt about that at the moment. But fear for her life should take precedence over fear of falling into bed again.

Should.

"Do you think that is what they are after?" she asked.

"Maybe." He didn't sound convinced. "It could be that they want to know what you have because they think you are getting too close." He held her gaze. "Or it could be that your stories are drawing too much attention and they just want to shut you up."

From the way she paled, John knew he'd made his point and that she was finally taking this seriously. He didn't like scaring her, but she needed to understand the situation. People who were willing to take out a platoon of Navy SEALs weren't going to balk at getting rid of a reporter. And even if the people trying to kill her weren't the same as those who had tried to kill him, there were plenty who were interested in keeping the story out of the papers. A story that might force the US past the brink of war that it was teetering on with Russia.

In any case, John wasn't going to stick around to find out who was behind the attack on Brittany. If that guy on the motorcycle had friends and they came after them, John was going to be seriously undermanned.

Besides, this place was making him twitchy. There were too many people around Vaernes who might recognize him. The platoon hadn't been at the air station long and they'd kept to themselves, but they weren't invisible, and it wasn't inconceivable that some people around the base might remember him.

He was pretty sure Nils had. But he was also pretty sure Nils understood what he did, which might keep him quiet. He'd definitely bought the jealous-boyfriend-after-an-argument bit—which might not have been as much of a bit as John would have liked.

"Pack your bags," he said. "We need to get out of here."

"Where are we going?"

"I don't know yet, but we can't stay here."

"You think that guy has been following me and knows where I'm staying?"

His nonanswer was answer enough.

She packed in record time, which wasn't surprising as she simply shoved the mess of clothes and shoes flowing out of the suitcase back into it.

After putting on a pair of hiking shoes—the tennis-shoe kind, not the boot kind—she went into the bathroom to retrieve her toiletries. As it was still raining, he was glad to see she had a lightweight raincoat, which was more practical than the umbrella she'd had before.

In an impressive five minutes, they were heading down the fire escape staircase. Exiting into the back parking lot of the hotel, he stopped her from going to her car. "Leave it."

"I have to return it; it's a rental."

"You can call them and tell them where you left it. I don't want to chance it."

"Chance what? Do you think they are out there?" She looked around the empty parking lot as if someone was going to jump out. It wasn't completely dark, but it was about as dark as it would get.

He shook his head. "Not right now, but they could be tracking you."

She obviously didn't like the sound of that and made a face.

"Don't we have to get your things from your hotel?" she asked.

"I don't have a hotel." He hadn't been planning to stick around. "I left a bag at the train station."

Which was where they were headed after he took care of a few things that he hoped would send anyone tracking her in the wrong direction.

It was a quick walk to the airport from the hotel, but her large wheelie suitcase slowed them down a bit. Finally, he grew impatient with her bumping over curbs and picked it up by the carry handle.

"Christ, what do you have in here, rocks?"

She rolled her eyes. "Said every guy everywhere. I wanted to be prepared for all kinds of weather." She looked him up and down in the darkness. "I guess you aren't as strong as you look."

He gave her a wicked grin. "Strong enough for whatever you have in mind, sweetheart."

She laughed, totally impervious to any suggestiveness. He wasn't sure how he felt about that. Five years ago she used to blush when he said things like that to her. She'd grown up. But that wasn't all. He had the distinct feeling she'd outgrown him as well, and that didn't sit well.

"Pack mule is good enough for now," she said.

"I'll remember that," he said dryly.

But this pack mule was about to go on strike.

She wasn't happy when they arrived at the airport and he told her what he wanted to do. "I can't fit what I need in a backpack and a small duffel!"

"It was the biggest bag they had," he said patiently. The

Vaernes airport shop didn't exactly have a broad selection
of travel gear. He'd been lucky to find the packable nylon
duffel. They could be talking plastic shopping bag. "We
need to move around fast, and this"—he indicated the
large suitcase—"isn't going to cut it. Besides, sending
your bag back home will keep them off our tracks."

"But what am I supposed to wear? I don't even know
where we are going."

"Keep it casual and comfortable. You can always layer
things." He grinned and tried not to laugh at her expression. She seemed more upset at the idea of getting rid of
her luggage than she had been at the news of her apartment being ransacked. Maybe she was a little more girlie
than he realized, although he didn't think she'd appreciate him pointing that out right now. "I have a few extra
shirts you can borrow if you need them."

She scoffed sharply. "Not a chance. I've seen your
shirts. I don't do hideous Hawaiian."

He grinned. He missed his shirts. But they did tend to
attract attention. He shrugged. "Not everyone can pull it
off."

"John, not even *you* can pull off garish bright orange
sunsets, turquoise oceans, and lime green palm trees."

He chuckled and was relieved to see her bend down
and open the suitcase to start moving a few things into
the new duffel. He could hear her mumbling under her
breath the whole time and was pretty sure he didn't want
to know what she was saying.

After about five minutes of her putting something in
only to take it out and exchange it for something else a
few minutes later, he said, "How much longer is this going to take?"

And how many pairs of jeans did one person need?
The ones she was wearing were fine.

More than fine.

She gave him a good death glare that didn't quite kill

the surge of lust at thinking about her ass in those jeans again—or out of those jeans, for that matter.

"A few more minutes. It took me more than two hours to pack to come here. You can't expect me to do this in a few minutes. I don't want to forget anything."

"We can always buy something if you need it."

"My credit cards are already maxed out after the last-minute trip to get here."

Which meant he was pretty damned sure she wasn't going to like what he wanted her to do before they went to the freight office to send her bag to her apartment.

"Change my ticket to the next flight?" she repeated, aghast. "Do you have any idea how expensive that is going to be?"

"I'd pay with cash, but I don't want to draw attention to anything." He had a clean credit card in the name of his fake passport, but he avoided using it unless he had to. "We want anyone tracking you to think you and your bag hightailed it home." He paused. "And your phone, too."

If he thought downsizing the luggage or the five hundred dollars to change to the next flight were bad, her reaction at the thought of sending her phone in her luggage was even worse.

Millennials and their attachments to their devices. John didn't get it. He wasn't into smartphones or "i" anything. He probably wouldn't have a cell phone at all if it weren't necessary.

He didn't like being so . . . accessible.

Social media of any type went into the same basket. It wasn't just the job or that he was intensely private— both of which were true—he just didn't think it was a good idea to have even seemingly innocuous information out there for anyone to see. If he wanted someone to know something about him, he'd tell them. Face-to-face. Not over a medium where God only knew who else could see it.

"Do you have a laptop or tablet?"

She shook her head. "No. I didn't bring it with me." She glared at him. "I was traveling light."

He laughed.

She must have recognized that his plan had merit because she only put up a feeble protest before dropping her phone into the inside pocket of her suitcase and zipping it up. From her mournful expression, you would have thought someone had died as she watched the freight agent put the bag on the belt to disappear behind the black rubber curtain.

With her backpack and duffel in tow, they left the airport and followed the sidewalk walkway to the train station. Careful to avoid cameras as much as possible, John retrieved his bag from a storage locker and paid for two tickets on the night train to Stockholm in cash.

Last-minute train fares weren't much cheaper than last-minute air fares, but the agent didn't balk as the wad of Danish kroner passed under the glass.

After a short train ride to Åre in Sweden, they caught the main line to Stockholm. Despite being exhausted, neither of them slept much on the seven-hour journey. Nor did they sleep much more over the next twelve hours as they zigzagged their way across Norway and Sweden before finally arriving in Copenhagen, Denmark, that night.

John had been too amped to sleep. Too watchful. He wouldn't be able to relax until they were safe.

Brittany must have been feeling the same. But once or twice she'd relaxed enough to close her eyes, and somehow her head made its way to his shoulder.

He resisted the urge to put his arm around her and draw her in closer. Mostly because he didn't want to disturb her. But also because he feared how much it would disturb him and his certainty about what this was about.

He caught himself looking down at the dark head and

soft cheek resting on his arm a few times, but the resulting tight squeezing in his chest made him stop.

She just looked so damned peaceful and sweet. And the responsibility of protecting her seemed almost overwhelming. He wasn't intimidated by much, but this . . .

This was different.

He hadn't been able to save his friend, but John swore that he would do whatever it took to keep Brittany safe.

Even from himself.

Eleven

Colt had always known how to keep her guessing. When they'd first met, it had taken Kate months of sporadic dates—and very hot sex sessions—to figure out that he wasn't as indifferent to her as he appeared. In those early days, every time he left, whether it was in the wee hours of the morning after a wild night or on a deployment, she didn't know if she would ever see him again.

Today was no different. She wasn't sure he would show up until she saw him sauntering down the aisle toward her a few minutes before the gate closed.

He was always cutting it close. It had driven her crazy when they were married. She liked to leave plenty of time. Case in point, she'd arrived at six a.m. for their eight a.m. flight this morning.

She'd delayed this trip as long as she could with the excuse that the admiral couldn't see them. But the clock was ticking on the week Colt had given her, and she knew she couldn't put it off anymore.

They planned to fly back on the red-eye to DC later that evening, so he hadn't brought a bag and didn't need to shove anything in the overhead before plopping down in the aisle seat beside her. Just like that the oxygen around her was gone. His size—his sheer physicality—had always overwhelmed her.

The flight attendant immediately came by to ask him what he wanted to drink. Proving his continued appeal to the opposite sex, she gave him a lingering smile and an unabashed look of interest, which he ignored. Kate knew it wasn't for her benefit. It was just the way he was. He didn't flirt. He didn't play games. If he wanted a woman, he would make the first move.

But maybe he had changed a little. The old Colt would have ordered a Bloody Mary after a long night at the bar, but he just asked for water.

He stretched his legs out in front of him. "Nice seats. As I'm sure Uncle Sam didn't spring for this, Lord Percy must be treating you right." He paused to look at her. "I'm just surprised that I'm not sitting in the last row rather than the first."

He knew very well that she didn't need Percy's money, and the jibe about him being a lord wasn't funny the first time. Colt was just trying to make Percy seem stuffy and pompous, which he wasn't. Usually. "If you'd rather, I'm sure someone would be happy to switch. You were doing a favor for me, so I thought I'd try to make it as pleasant for you as possible. But if you want to sit somewhere else, please don't let me stop you."

She turned to look out the small window, studying with fierce intensity the guys loading the luggage into the plane next to theirs. Her heart was pounding hard in her chest. How could he still get her so angry so quickly?

"Hey." He put his hand on her arm. She was so surprised by his touch that she flinched. He removed it immediately. "I shouldn't have said that. Thanks for the seats. It's a hell of a lot more comfortable up here than it is in steerage."

That hurt more than it should. Her heart squeezed. Steerage had been an inside joke between them. It had started on their honeymoon, when her godfather had lent them his private plane. Colt had had only a couple days off, and it had enabled them to eke out as much time as possible in Cabo.

On boarding Colt had taken one look around at the luxurious leather bucket seats and shiny wood and quipped, "I'm going to have a hell of a time going back to steerage after this, Kiki." They'd done one of those "what's your stripper name?" games, and guess what hers came out to be? "The manner I've grown accustomed to has just gotten a little pricier for you in a divorce."

It had been funny then. But maybe joking about divorce on their honeymoon had said a lot more than she realized. He was already setting them up for the fall.

Ironically, as much as he'd given her a hard time about "steerage" and the lifestyle in which she'd been raised, he hadn't wanted a penny of her money in the divorce.

Her godfather had been furious when she'd married Colt without a prenup. But she'd been right: she hadn't needed one.

Of course, she'd been mistaken about the reason. Once she'd finally sold Colt on the idea of marriage and gotten him to the altar, she'd been sure it would be forever.

Forever hadn't even lasted to their fifth anniversary.

He was studying her so intently, she wondered if he was remembering as well. But it wasn't likely. If there was one thing she could say with certainty about her ex-husband: once Colt was done with something, he never looked back. He just cut it off. She was as good as dead to him.

Kate acknowledged the rare apology with a nod. "You're welcome." She paused, hesitating. It probably wasn't worth it, but she would at least try. "Do you think you could put aside how much you hate me until this is over? I don't want to spend the rest of the day fighting with you or exchanging veiled taunts. Can we just try to be . . . ?" She didn't know. What could they be together after all they'd been through? "Professional, maybe? I know you're good at this kind of thing, and we both want the same thing here, don't we?"

He stared at her so long without saying anything after her little speech that her cheeks started to heat.

"What is it you want, Kate? We can't bring them back."

There was more emotion in his voice than she'd heard in a long time. She knew how much the deaths of the men in Retiarius must mean to him, and the fact that she was keeping the knowledge of six survivors from him turned that self-conscious flush to a guilty one. "An answer. Justice."

"There is no justice in this world, Kate. I thought you might have learned that by now. But we'll do it your way. I'll play along. You've got four more days before I leave. Until then, we'll see what we can find out and I'll be on my best behavior." He held up his hand. "Scout's honor."

She shook her head. "You were never a Boy Scout, and it's three fingers, not two. In your line of work, mistakes like that could get you killed."

She was surprised when he smiled and gave a small laugh. It had been so long since she'd seen him do that, it caught in her chest and stuck there, jamming everything.

How could she despise someone so much and still feel regret? When he smiled, she could almost remember the man she'd fallen in love with before everything had turned so dark and ugly.

"You're right. That was sloppy. They threw me out of Cub Scouts after one meeting."

"What did you do? Burn down a forest trying to earn your fire badge?"

"Not exactly."

She waited patiently, as she'd done in the old days. He would tell her if he wanted to or not tell her if he didn't. Nothing she did would make a difference.

He shrugged. "The scoutmaster thought that a nine-year-old foster kid was fair game. The pocketknife I put through his hand told him otherwise."

He said it so matter-of-factly it took her a moment to realize what he meant. Colt had never sat down and told her about his past, but piece by piece over the years, with little tidbits like this, he'd painted a horrible picture.

She knew better than to feel sorry for him. He despised pity. But she couldn't hide her revulsion. "He touched you?"

"Once."

"And you didn't tell anyone what happened?"

He did laugh this time, but it was devoid of humor. "I tried. But this was in the days before stuff like that was acknowledged. I was the one who was punished for making up such 'horrible lies.' But the truth eventually came out. I hear he put a bullet through his head." A cold smile turned his lips. "Maybe there is a little justice in this world after all."

Clearly disappointed to see him talking to Kate, the flight attendant told them to get ready for takeoff, and it wasn't until they were up in the air that Kate spoke again. In truth, she didn't know what to say. When they'd been married, she would have put her head on his shoulder and silently cried for him, wishing she could make it better.

But her heart wasn't his anymore. It was firmly shut no matter how tragic and horrible his childhood. He didn't want or need her comfort or understanding.

So she didn't say anything.

Professional, she reminded herself. With that in mind,

she spent a good part of the flight preparing Colt for the meeting with the rear admiral.

Colt would lead the questioning, taking the role of bad cop—no surprise—and she would intervene if necessary to be the voice of understanding.

The six-hour flight landed early, and they had some time to grab lunch at the airport before hopping in the taxi to meet the rear admiral at his home at the appointed one p.m.

As much as Kate had been dreading spending time with Colt, the morning flew by with remarkable speed. After all they'd been through, she was surprised at how easy it was to be around him again and how well they worked together.

They hadn't exactly gotten off to the best start the first and only time they'd worked together in Afghanistan. She probably would never have gone out with the darkly sexy SEAL chief at all after that CIA Barbie comment if he hadn't saved her life.

Not long after she'd arrived at the "safe" (relatively speaking) base, local insurgents had sent a suicide bomber in a car to ram the gates and detonate as soon as he was inside, hoping to take out the guardhouse. She'd been standing too close and probably would have been killed if Colt hadn't jumped on top of her. He still bore scars from the shrapnel he'd taken for her that day.

Even the "this isn't the way I had planned to get you under me" line that he said when he was still bleeding on top of her hadn't turned her off. The bluntness had actually made her laugh. Her willingness to go out with him might have also had something to do with her not being completely unaffected by having a really good-looking guy with a body as hard as a rock on top of her. The physical appeal had always been there. The saving-her-life part hadn't hurt either.

But once they'd become involved, they'd been careful

to avoid any appearance of conflict or fraternization by making sure their ops didn't overlap. If she worked with Team Nine, it was through Scott. That was how she'd gotten to know him so well.

She'd forgotten how insightful and smart Colt was. Not book smart like Percy but savvy—especially about human nature. Street smart, she supposed they'd call it. But he also had an almost photographic memory and was good with numbers. He went through the spreadsheets she'd put together of the rear admiral's complicated finances and found the discrepancies far quicker than she had—and she had an accounting background. Before she'd been recruited for the CIA she'd thought she wanted to be a CPA.

He could have made a fortune on Wall Street. But he'd put his skills to good use in the military. He was one of the best—and not just because of his mental quickness, his physical strengths, or his skill with weapons. He was also cold, methodical, ruthless, detached, secretive, and at times deceitful. The problem for her was that those qualities might make him a great covert operator, but they made him a horrible husband.

By the time they arrived at the rear admiral's home—she'd stressed that it was better not to meet at the base when she'd called last night to set this up—and were shown into his office by his wife, Kate was wondering if this might be more than a wild-goose chase to stop him from going to Russia as she'd first thought. Could Rear Admiral Morrison be responsible for what had happened to Scott and his men? She had thought it was a long shot, but after going through everything with Colt, she couldn't deny the motive.

She watched as Colt tossed the file on the desk in front of the rear admiral and leaned over with just the right amount of anger and threat to start questioning him. She was about to find out.

Colt had spent enough time in San Diego to be familiar with the ritzy Rancho Santa Fe neighborhood, where the rear admiral lived, so when they were shown out about an hour after they'd been shown in—with a decidedly less friendly slam of the door from the rear admiral's wife that made him wonder whether she'd been listening—he suggested they walk to a coffee shop that was near the golf course on which Morrison lived.

It was a typical San Diego day. In other words, a perfect seventy degrees, slightly breezy, and sunny blue skies. Since they had time before returning to the airport to catch their flight back, Colt needed to burn off some energy.

He wanted to think his agitation was from the meeting that had just taken place, but he knew that wasn't all of it.

Having been pent up with his ex all day was having more of an effect on him than it should. He'd forgotten how much he used to like her. The attraction hadn't been all of it. Not by half.

Despite her heels, Kate didn't object, and they walked along the treelined street of mostly Mediterranean "residences" (apparently calling them homes wasn't distinguished enough) toward the shopping center that was just outside the gates.

Kate was quiet and thoughtful. Probably, like him, processing the meeting that had just taken place. She was playing with the single strand of pearls at her neck, as she tended to do when she was lost in thought.

He'd never seen another woman under seventy or who wasn't named Barbara Bush wear pearls, but on Kate they looked right. "Chic" is what he'd heard someone say about her once—which about covered it.

"What did you think?" he asked.

Despite the sun beating down on her fair head, she

looked as cool and crisp as she had when he'd sat down on the plane seat beside her in one of those linen sheath dresses she wore when she wanted something more casual than a suit.

He had on his typical T-shirt and khaki cargo shorts. That was his dressy.

Even their clothes had never fit right together. What the hell had he been thinking? They'd never been in the same league.

She glanced over at him to answer, a wry smile on her face. "I think that if the goal was to push the rear admiral's buttons, I couldn't have picked anyone better to go with me. You really know how to go for blood, don't you?"

Her tone was lighthearted, and he responded similarly. "Yes, that particular skill has some positive uses at times."

She laughed. "I'll say. I thought he was going to burst a blood vessel when you started digging in about the online poker, his kids' tuition bills, and Mrs. Morrison's 'anonymous' posts on social media. But when you started insinuating a possible connection to Retiarius . . ." She shivered. "I was glad he didn't have a gun."

"I was too. He was pissed off."

"Pissed-off-you-offended-my-honor or pissed-off-guilty?"

Colt shrugged. "I don't know. As much as I'm not a fan of Morrison's, I'm not sure I could see him selling out a platoon of men like that to cover his ass."

"Even if he is being threatened by the people who lent him money?"

"We'll see. He's been poked. Now we have to see how he reacts. I assume you have everything in place?"

She nodded. He suspected Kate hadn't asked permission to hack into the rear admiral's computers and phone lines, but she'd done it anyway. Being CIA had its advantages. Although he suspected she wouldn't be CIA much longer if they found out what she was doing. He was pretty sure she was on her own on this.

If he needed more proof of how much Taylor had meant to her, the fact that she was willing to risk the job that was so important to her—the job that she hadn't been willing to sacrifice for him—was it. Which shouldn't still burn so much.

School must have just gotten out because there were all kinds of kids waiting to cross the main street as they approached. Most of them seemed to have a parent or nanny attached. He was tempted to steer clear of the kid chaos, which definitely wasn't his thing, by crossing at the next block, but Kate had already worked her way into the crowd and was smiling down at a young girl.

He felt something sharp stab him between the ribs and turned away. She used to do the same thing when they were married, and it had always made him uncomfortable. Guilty, maybe because he knew how much she wanted a baby. But he'd told her straight out before they married that he never wanted kids. She'd said it didn't matter.

But it had.

He noticed an older teenage girl talking on her phone with one hand while pushing a stroller with the other. He assumed there was a kid in there, although he couldn't see around the front. A little boy of about five or six—presumably the one she'd just picked up from school—was standing on the curb next to her. He looked like he wanted attention, but she was too busy talking to give it to him.

As this wasn't exactly the neighborhood for teenage mothers, Colt assumed she was the babysitter or nanny.

He didn't know why he noticed the kid, much less why he was still watching him when the light turned. Maybe he knew what it was like to want someone to pay attention to him. Or maybe he sensed the disaster that was about to come.

The light change from "don't walk" to "walk" acted as a trigger. The kid stepped off the curb into the street without a pause, and if Colt's reflexes had been any slower, the little boy would have been run over by the SUV that went blowing through the light.

Colt heard Kate scream as he lurched forward and grabbed the kid to pull him out of the way. But the SUV was so close that one of the side mirrors caught Colt and sent both him and the little boy headfirst into the asphalt.

He felt the pavement connect with the skin of his arm as he tried to turn the kid away from the ground.

They seemed to slide for a while, or at least the burning down his side seemed to last for a while. When they finally came to a stop, he heard more than a few screams as chaos turned to pandemonium.

Kate was already beside him when he looked up. "Oh my God, are you all right?"

She looked so upset—so concerned—it somehow made him angry. It was too late to pretend she cared now.

"I'm fine," he snapped. Then, realizing the kid in his arms was squirming and starting to bawl, he held him out to her. "Here, take him and make sure he's okay."

The babysitter (or nanny) suddenly made her appearance—phone no longer attached to her ear—and was clearly on the verge of hysteria, saying "Oh my God" over and over and "It wasn't my fault" to anyone who would listen.

"Someone call nine-one-one," Colt said, trying to unpeel himself from the pavement.

Apparently, someone already had. He could hear the sirens blaring. In the neighborhoods he'd grown up in, they'd have been waiting hours for an ambulance or for the police to show up for something like this. There were too many shootings and stabbings to take precedence.

Colt temporarily lost sight of Kate after the police arrived. He gave his statement—using his real name, which would show an honorable discharge from the SEALs three years ago—and was letting the paramedics patch him up a little when he looked over and saw Kate standing by the ambulance rocking a baby in her arms.

She was smiling and cooing and looked so fucking happy it made his lungs burn with pain that was infinitely worse than the one that had torn a good portion of the flesh from his arm and lower leg.

Kate was obviously taking care of the baby while the babysitter/nanny was in hysterics and the little boy was being tended to. According to the paramedics, the kid only had a few scrapes. Colt had taken the brunt of it. He was a real hero. Right. It would have made him laugh if he wasn't so pissed off at the sight of Kate and a baby.

It sent him into a cold rage that he didn't understand. It was born of guilt and jealousy and maybe, in a very dark, hidden place that he would never acknowledge, hurt.

The anger got worse when a young couple wearing scrubs came bursting through the temporary barricade that had been erected for the investigation in an obvious panic.

Colt didn't need to ask who they were. The woman doc practically ripped the baby out of Kate's arms before bursting into tears as they ran toward the ambulance that held the little boy.

Colt made the mistake of looking at Kate's face. The look of heartbreak and pure longing drove that knife of rage deeper into his gut.

He knew just how badly she wanted a baby and how much she'd mourned the one she'd lost. The baby that hadn't belonged to him. She'd been hit by a drunk driver when she was a few months pregnant and had been inches away from dying.

The baby hadn't been so lucky. He'd never forget racing

into that hospital thinking that he might lose her—calling himself every kind of fool for trying to push her away—and seeing her and Scott together. He'd wanted to kill them both.

Almost as if she sensed him watching her, she looked over and caught his gaze. She gave him a small bereft smile and came walking toward the back of the fire truck—yes, a fire truck for a small accident—where one of the paramedics was giving him instructions on changing the bandages. Colt didn't bother explaining that he'd had more experience with blood and gore and patching up wounds than the woman would see in a lifetime.

Kate waited patiently until he was done, which gave him a little time to settle down before she spoke. "That nanny owes you big-time. I think she just had the scare of her life."

"She'll forget about it tomorrow."

Kate smiled. "Still a wild-eyed optimist, I see."

"She's a teenager. They are missing the consequences-and-perspective chip."

"I didn't realize you knew so much about child psychology."

He didn't. But he'd been that age once. "We should go if we are going to make our flight."

"The boy's father said he would call a limo. I suspect it's going to be filled with champagne for the hero." She didn't give him a chance to say "hell no." "Don't worry. I knew you wouldn't want a fuss. I told him I'd already called the cab company. But what you did back there, Colt." Her voice got all thick and her eyes teary. "It was amazing."

He didn't like seeing that look on her face, so he brought up the subject that he knew would take it off. "I saw you and the baby over there. You look like a natural. I assume you and Lord Percy won't wait too long to get going on the heir and the spare."

She froze. Any admiration she might have been feeling for him for saving the kid slid from her face.

It took her a moment to respond. She gave a slight shake of her head and said, "No . . . No. I don't think so."

There was something about her response that was off, but he read it wrong. "You aren't that old—or is it the ambassador? He has a couple of kids from his first marriage, right? Two and out, is that it?"

He didn't think she was going to respond. She held his gaze until he felt like squirming. He who had withstood hours of interrogation (i.e., torture) training and never flinched.

"There were complications after the accident. I can no longer have children."

Was there accusation in her tone, or did he just imagine it? He didn't know, but whatever it was, it made him want to strike back.

It was what he did. What he always did. "Karma's a bitch."

She stood there just staring at him. She was so still he didn't think she was breathing.

He used to be so good at reading her, but her expression was so blank, so stark, she might have been dead.

"Thank you for that."

And with that she walked away.

They barely spoke on the return flight to DC. It was what he wanted.

He didn't understand why she'd thanked him at first. But then he realized that if she'd been softening toward him, the remark had reminded her of who he was.

Twelve

Brittany had been so wiped out by the time they'd finally opened the door to the hotel room in Copenhagen that she'd barely registered the king-sized bed. She'd been too tired to care, protest, or act missish about sleeping in the same bed with him. It was big enough to spread out and leave a nice safety-zone buffer in between.

Besides, John had slept even less than she had in the past forty or so hours since she'd gotten out of bed yesterday morning—and he looked even more exhausted than she felt—so sex was probably the last thing on his mind.

He'd been strangely untalkative—almost brooding—since they'd gotten on the train, and she suspected he needed sleep even more than she did.

They both did the bare minimum in terms of preparing for bed—a few minutes in the bathroom to wash and the removal of outer layers of clothes—before collapsing in an exhausted heap on the bed.

But at some point during the night that nice safety-zone buffer disappeared. Brittany must have inched her way across no-man's-land because when she woke, she was practically sprawled on top of John's chest. His *naked* chest.

It was worse than that, she realized, as her mind slowly lost the fuzziness and awareness came barreling in with all the subtlety of a freight train. Their legs were entwined, and his hand was cupping her bottom as if to hold her in place.

Her body temperature seemed to shoot up a good eight hundred degrees—at least. He radiated heat like an inferno, and with her plastered to him like this, it was flowing directly into her.

She knew exactly the moment he woke. She had her cheek pressed to the smooth, bare skin of that incredible chest, and his heart, which had been beating nice and steadily in her ear, started to pound.

She froze, hoping he wouldn't realize she was awake. But her cheeks were burning.

So much for staying away from him. Apparently he was catnip even in her subconscious.

Mortified at finding herself in this position, Brittany was trying to think of ways to extricate herself when things went from bad to worse. If possible, his body heat seemed to go up a couple notches, from scorching to red-hot, and his hand spread across her bottom and began to lightly caress it over the jeans she hadn't bothered to take off.

But that wasn't all. She was suddenly aware of the significant bulge hard against her hip and experienced the overwhelming urge to press herself against it.

He must have been having the same idea because the hand on her bottom suddenly grew a little more insistent. He was lifting her, pressing her . . . or maybe that was her lifting and pressing. She didn't know.

And she didn't really care. Her body was getting that heavy, languid feeling. That insistent pull toward pleasure that made her limbs limp, her pulse quicken, and the place between her legs warm and melty.

One little press wouldn't hurt. But it did. It sent a flood of wanting racing through her.

She was saved from doing something *really* stupid by the bell. Or in this case, the phone.

She thought it was hers, but then realized it wasn't *Hawaii Five-0* and her phone was on the way back to DC.

John swore and gently eased himself out from under her. "I've got to take this."

She pretended to be half-awake, unaware of what was going on, and grumbled sleepily as she rolled onto her side facing away from him.

Freedom!

"Yeah," she heard him say. Someone must have started talking, but John stopped them. "Wait. Give me a minute."

She heard him fumbling with clothes, presumably putting his shirt, socks, and shoes back on, and shortly after that, the door clicked shut.

She wondered who was calling him. Was it another survivor? *Were* there other survivors? Who else knew he was alive? Someone had helped him with that e-mail account.

Whoever it was, John obviously didn't want to talk with her around.

Normally that would make her even more curious, but right now she was just grateful to have escaped major—major—stupidity.

This had been a wake-up call. Big-time. Obviously she needed to be much more careful around him if she didn't want to end up another notch in Mr. Donovan's never-ending bedpost.

One notch was enough.

Although, apparently, given her reaction to being on top of him, not all of her was on board with that plan.

Maybe they could just do the sex thing? He was good at that.

But she didn't think she could handle the meaningless aspect that went along with it, and she quickly discarded the idea. It would only confuse things, and with her luck she'd end up falling for his shenanigans again. Which would put her right back where she was five years ago: all alone with nothing but a broken heart.

No, thanks.

The best thing to do would be to get far away from him, but as they were stuck together until they could find out whether someone really was trying to hurt her—and who—that wasn't an option.

In the clear light of day, after a solid twelve hours of sleep, she had to wonder if she'd let John get to her and overreacted by fleeing Vaernes like that. He'd clearly wanted her away from Nils and the air base.

But even if going on the run to protect her from bad guys fit with his objective, she couldn't completely discount the possibility that the attack in the parking lot and the ransacking of her apartment were related.

She would give it a few days. Maybe she'd try to get in touch with Mac and see what she could find out.

Until then she'd concentrate on her next article. She wished she had been able to meet Nils's friend, but his confirmation of the platoon's presence at Vaernes closely before the "missile test" in Russia was a good start in tying the two together. If her brother was killed on a secret mission to Russia that the government now wanted to cover up, Norway made sense as the place from where they'd launched the op. It might even be enough to satisfy her editor.

She pulled out the small laptop she carried with her everywhere from her messenger bag. She felt bad that she'd lied about it to John, but she knew he would have made her get rid of it, and she wasn't going to be without the means to write her story. But she wasn't stupid. She had it in airplane mode, and she would keep it that way.

She took it, along with her bag, a change of clothes, and her toiletries into the bathroom. She wanted to get started on her next article before jumping in the shower.

She wasn't hiding it from him as much as avoiding an unnecessary confrontation. As much as he might want to think differently, he wasn't her master or her commander, and she didn't have to take orders from him.

Although she didn't relish reminding him of that.

But one thing was for sure: no more sharing beds.

In retrospect, the sharing-the-bed thing had probably been a bad idea. If the LC hadn't called when he did, John was pretty damned sure he would have forgotten his vow for the second time. Wake up with a warm, sexy female in his arms and his body was going to react.

But he knew that was BS. There was react and there was *react*, and with Brittany it had been hard and fast. Really hard and fast. He'd been a few seconds away from rolling her on top of him and going for round two. Which he had hoped would go a little longer than round one, but with the way he'd been feeling a few minutes ago, he wouldn't put money on it.

What the fuck was the matter with him? What happened to his control? He wasn't exactly a teenager anymore. But tell his dick that. It seemed to have forgotten the past fifteen years.

Once he left the room, John hustled down the hall and didn't speak again until he entered the stairwell. As their hotel room was on the fourteenth floor, he figured the chance of someone walking up or down the stairs was pretty unlikely.

"Sorry about that," he said to the LC. "Brittany was

in the room, and I didn't want you to say anything she could overhear through the phone."

There was a long pause. "You sounded like you just woke up."

"I did."

John knew that needed an explanation, so he told Taylor how he'd gone to Vaernes and found Brittany asking questions in a bar. He left out the part about him glowering in a corner while she flirted with a soldier. He also left out the part about finishing his beer before following her out to the parking lot and fighting off the attacker.

The LC cursed under his breath. "I'm guessing the attack wasn't a coincidence."

"I don't think so. She got a call from a coworker not long afterward, telling her that her apartment in DC was ransacked. The guy in the parking lot tried to grab her purse, so I figure they were looking for something."

John repeated everything she'd told him about the drop, including the car, the license plate, and the woman wearing a military jacket. He also told the LC about the documents she had.

"You've got to be fucking kidding me. A redacted deployment order? Only a handful of people would have had access to that."

Pretty much exactly what John had said.

"I'll have Kate look into it and see what she can find out," Taylor said. "Maybe finding Brittany's source will help us find the leak." He didn't sound overly optimistic. "Anything about the guy in the parking lot?"

"It was raining and hard to see. He was wearing a hood, so I didn't get a good look at him. But he was about my size and build and knew how to fight."

All of which were significant. Not a lot of guys had a build like his. He was in top physical condition—or had been two months ago.

"One of ours?"

"I couldn't rule it out, but if I had to guess, I'd say Eastern European." Team Nine had trained with some guys in Crimea once, and Brittany's attacker reminded him of that.

"Russian?" The LC asked grimly, as if he already knew the answer.

"Could be."

Taylor didn't say anything, but John knew what he was thinking. If the Russians were trying to stop her, what did that mean? Were they trying to protect a source—maybe the same source who'd leaked the mission—or did they just want to avoid the public relations disaster of having it be known that they wiped out a platoon of US soldiers?

Retiarius might have been on Russian soil—which made it look bad for the US—but President Ivanov had vowed to go to war under that very scenario. If what had happened became public, he'd lose considerable face or be forced to go to war. Humiliation or a war with the biggest superpower in the world. For Ivanov, that was what you called a no-win situation.

"Did he get a look at you?"

"Not a good one. It happened fast. I was wearing a hood, too. With any luck, he'll just assume I'm one of the locals."

And without luck they were screwed. Like Brittany, they would be targets for anyone who wanted their op to stay a secret, and it would make finding out who had set them up a hell of a lot more difficult.

"Do you think they were tracking her?"

"Probably. I didn't want to take any chances, so I got her out of there fast." John explained about her luggage and phone, as well as the zigzag train rides.

"Where are you now?"

"Denmark."

"Good. Sit tight for a couple days. I'll be in touch once

I've seen what Kate can dig up on Brittany's source. I'll also see if anyone checked into an emergency room with a broken arm. But I'm not holding my breath on that." Neither was John. A professional would have his own resources. "I assume I don't have to worry about any more articles?"

It wasn't really a question. It was more of a "you better have done your fucking job." But the LC didn't know Brittany. She wouldn't give up so easily. Not with something like this. If she thought the government was trying to cover up her brother's death—which admittedly it was—she would be relentless. No quit. As that pretty much summed up every SEAL John knew, he might admire her for it if that same quality in her didn't wind him up so much.

"Brittany kind of has a mind of her own when it comes to things like this."

"What the hell is that supposed to mean?"

He sighed. "It means I don't think she's put aside the idea."

Taylor swore a few times at that. "What more does she need to understand the danger?"

"She understands the danger fine." John paused. "I think she's more like Brand than either of them realized."

In other words, she was like them. They didn't run from danger; they ran toward it. He wasn't one of those guys who thought women couldn't hack it in war. His mom had made damned sure of that. She'd been a strong woman—and a fighter. He'd never seen anyone do battle the way she had in the hospital. But he'd never understood how such a smart woman—and a feminist to her bones—could fall in love with a guy like his father.

It was one reason John had no intention of getting married. He'd never do to a woman what his father had done to his mom.

The LC cursed in frustration before responding. "Well,

do what you can to convince her, but if you can't do that, then at least keep her *occupied* and too busy to think about anything else," the LC said. "Put some of that skill you are supposed to have with women to good use for once."

"How am I supposed to do that?"

"I'll leave the details to you, but I'm sure you can think of something."

The LC wasn't suggesting what John thought he was suggesting . . . was he? "Sleeping with her is off the table, LC. I'm not going to seduce Brand's sister."

He left out "again."

"At ease, Donovan. Don't get your choir boy robes all in a twist. I wasn't suggesting you sleep with her—although good to know you do have a few lines you won't cross when it comes to good-looking women. I was referring more to your tour guide skills." He paused. "Interesting assumption to make though. Have something on your mind, sailor?"

Ah, hell. John decided to cut his losses and change subject. "You and Kate any closer to figuring out who did this?"

"We're still working on a few leads."

In other words, no.

"Weren't you the one complaining about lack of leave the past couple of years?" Taylor asked. "Well, you got it. So I suggest you take advantage of it while you can."

"Let me guess, by sightseeing in Copenhagen?"

"Exactly." The LC sounded like he might be smiling. "Keep me posted."

John hung up and started to head back to the room. But recalling who was waiting for him, he took the elevator downstairs instead to talk to the front desk.

When the maid made up the room later today, that king bed was going to turn into two twins.

Thirteen

Brittany took a sip of her Austrian beer in its Edelweiss logo glass and studied the man across the picnic-style table.

"What?" John said. "Do I have mustard on my face or something?"

She smiled. "No. I'm just surprised, that's all. I wouldn't think that bratwurst was on the John-Donovan-approved menu list. Didn't you give me a long lecture after I ate that hot dog at the Padres game about how unhealthy they were?"

He'd taken her to a baseball game to cheer her up not long after that first time he'd sat down next to her on the beach. She'd made a comment about the only thing they ever had on the TV being baseball, which had to be about the most boring sport known to man and mentioned that she'd never been to a game. He insisted on correcting that "defect" in her Americanness immediately, and they'd spent a Sunday afternoon baking in the warm San Diego sun. She still didn't like baseball, but being at the game with him had been the most fun she'd had in years. They'd argued playfully all day.

Much like today. Which had also been one of the most fun days she'd had in years. He was funny and charming, easy to be around, and so sexy he made her eyes hurt. Too many times today it had felt as if they were a couple. It had been the same way five years ago.

He put down the enormous roll loaded with sauerkraut, mustard, and some kind of weird curry ketchup and gave her a look of acute disappointment that hadn't lessened any in five years. "Anyone who eats a hot dog at a Padres game when there are some of the best fish tacos to be had doesn't deserve an answer."

She made a face. "I told you, I'm not big on fish or on Mexican food—except for nachos."

He gave her a long, hard look. "I'm going to pretend I didn't hear that, but plastic cheese sauce isn't Mexican food. Nor is Taco Bell, which, knowing your teenage-boy eating tendencies, is probably what you are basing your judgment on." She rolled her eyes even though he was pretty much right. She knew better than to get him on a discussion of Mexican food, which he considered God's gift to the planet. "But to answer your question, there is a vast difference between a fresh brat and a hot dog—namely discernible meat. By the time those things are emulsified and processed, God only knows what you are eating."

"Who cares? They taste good." She dipped a fried potato wedge—cooked with bacon—in the weird ketchup and popped it in her mouth to emphasize her point and smiled.

He shook his head, apparently giving up on her lack of a palate. "Finish your fried chicken, Brittany, so we can go on more rides before the park closes."

They'd spent the morning at the Viking Ship Museum in Roskilde, and then they'd visited the National Museum of Denmark in the afternoon before walking to the famous Tivoli Gardens, one of the oldest amusement parks in the world.

It was a magical place, and she hadn't been surprised at all when John had told her Walt Disney had once visited and had used it as inspiration for Disneyland. The better word might be "modeled," as there were so many parts of the park that looked a lot like the Anaheim theme park. They were eating dinner at the Biergarten restaurant that was next to the Bjergbanen Mountain Coaster, which bore a distinct resemblance to the Matterhorn Bobsleds.

"It's not fried chicken," she said. "It's schnitzel." Which was obviously much healthier. "And I'm not leaving without dessert. You can't eat in an Austrian restaurant and not try the strudel."

"Is that a rule?"

"If it's not, it should be."

He smiled. "For once, when it comes to food, we agree on something. Apple strudel is one of my favorites."

She realized just how much of a favorite after he devoured his and then finished off the second half of hers. The chef, a seventy-plus-year-old Austrian woman, overheard him complimenting the waiter and came out to accept the praise in person. This precipitated a good ten-minute conversation about the proper way to make a true Viennese apple strudel.

"How does an American know so much about strudel?" the chef asked, her rosy cheeks dimpling.

He didn't correct her assumption that they were American. "It was one my mother's favorites."

"Did she have family from Austria?"

Brittany suspected that the woman was getting ready to whisk him away if the answer was yes. Alas, Brittany wouldn't be getting rid of him that easily. John shook his head. "No. Her family was Danish. They were from a town not far from here."

Brittany stilled, her heart jamming in her chest. Was that why they were here? She'd thought they'd ended up in Copenhagen by chance, but had he picked it for a reason?

She stared at him. Almost as if he knew what she was thinking, he wouldn't look in her direction.

It wasn't until they were walking out of the restaurant that she asked him about it. "I was wondering how you knew so much about Copenhagen. Were you here before with your mom?"

He shook his head. "No. She never had the chance. But it was her dream to come here one day." He smiled. "She used to read guidebooks cover to cover. We talked about doing a trip together after I graduated from SC."

Brittany knew his mother hadn't lived that long. She'd been diagnosed with a vicious form of breast cancer when John was a senior in high school. He'd missed so much school to stay by her bedside that he probably shouldn't have graduated, but his teachers had taken pity on him. He'd passed, but barely.

His mom had died a few months after she was diagnosed. John had to live with his water polo coach and his coach's wife for the remainder of his senior year, as he didn't have any other immediate family.

Brittany had asked him about his father when he'd told her about his mom. It was the first time she'd ever seen him angry. He'd said his father was a selfish bastard and a walking cliché who'd left them to marry his twenty-two-year-old secretary when John was nine years old. He was on his fourth wife now and had three other kids whom John had never met.

He'd played his father's abandonment and mother's death off as no big deal, but Brittany knew otherwise. She knew what it was like to be orphaned at a young age. It must have been difficult to go off to college alone. What had he done during holidays? She'd at least had her aunt and uncle. And Brandon. Though they hadn't seen much of each other in those days—or the days after—she'd always known he was there.

Brittany had never had the courage to ask John about where he'd gone during the off times during college, as she suspected he would think she felt sorry for him. Maybe he was right. But her heart had gone out to him anyway.

She'd been touched that he'd confided in her about his mom at all. As much as he talked and enjoyed being the center of attention, John actually didn't say much about himself. That he'd shared something so personal with her meant something.

She suspected that despite his matter-of-fact, no-big-deal, everyone-has-shit-to-deal-with attitude, his mother's death was a painful subject for him that he tried to block out or not think about at all. Maybe that was how he was able to move on—by pretending it didn't happen.

In other words, she'd convinced herself that beneath the outwardly "no big deal" exterior, things did matter to him. His mom. Brandon and the other guys on the team. Her.

At least that's what she'd thought until that day on the beach. But what if she'd been right in the beginning and he did care?

"Is this your first time here?" she asked.

He nodded.

She tried to stop her heart from squeezing, but it wasn't easy. She told herself it didn't necessarily mean anything that he'd chosen to visit his mother's special place with her, but she couldn't make herself believe it was a coincidence that they'd just ended up in Copenhagen. They could have stopped anywhere in Scandinavia.

What did it mean?

It meant that if she didn't get a grip, she was going to find herself headed down a dangerous path again.

She had to stop inventing feelings for him and just enjoy the moment because she didn't delude herself: John

Donovan was not long-term material. As soon as it was safe, he would walk out of her life and not look back.

She couldn't forget that, no matter how special he made her feel. That was his superpower. That was why women were drawn to him.

With a broad smile that might have been a little forced, she turned to him. "Which ride next? And if you say the roller coaster, you are riding by yourself. You crushed me every time we went around a curve."

He returned her smile, seemingly glad to be back on playful-not-serious ground again. "You can't fight the laws of physics, Brit."

"He who has more body mass wins?"

He laughed. "Exactly. Want to compare muscles?"

She rolled her eyes. She didn't need any reminders. She had a feeling every one of those muscles was going to be imprinted in her mind for a very long time. "No, thanks, but next time remind me to finish my dessert."

The problem with John doing his best impression of Rick Steves was that not only was he running them ragged by exploring every inch of this pretty damned incredible city, but he was also spending way too much time with her—which wasn't good.

He'd forgotten how easy it was to be around her. How much he liked to be around her. How good she was at giving it back to him.

What he hadn't forgotten was how it felt to have her under him. To be inside her. To have her fingertips digging into the muscles of his shoulders and arms. The soft little cries she'd made in his ear as she came. The taste of butterscotch melting in his mouth.

The first night after they'd closed down Tivoli Gardens, they'd returned to their hotel room and collapsed on the beds. The *twin* beds. She'd looked so relieved by the new sleeping arrangements that he almost regretted talking to the front desk. The rest of the time she seemed so indifferent to him, it was driving him nuts.

Because he sure as hell wasn't indifferent to her.

It had taken everything he had to stay in his own bed that night. He wanted her, and that wanting wasn't going away. It was getting stronger. He'd been awake most of the night reminding himself of why it was a bad idea to screw around with his dead best friend's sister, and that if he were alive, Brand would kill him for even considering it. Although if Brand were alive, John would probably already be dead for having done it the first time.

Day two had been pretty much a rinse and repeat—which only made that wanting worse. They'd been sightseeing all day. Initially she'd balked, claiming she needed to find an Internet café to do some work. But he'd distracted her with mermaids and palaces. Hans Christian Andersen's *Little Mermaid* statue in Langelinie Park and Kronborg Castle, made famous in Hamlet, to be specific. Afterward, they'd walked around the colorful buildings that lined the canal at Nyhavn and had dinner at one of the waterfront restaurants.

He was having so much fun that he forgot it was only a distraction. She, however, hadn't forgotten a damned thing. While he was lingering over his wine, reluctant to end the day by returning to their beds—their *separate* beds—her mind was still on one track.

And that track didn't have anything to do with him or the torture of their sleeping arrangements.

"If you ever get tired of saving the world, you have a brilliant future as a tour guide. I guess you've seen a good part of the Baltic countries now: Denmark, Norway, Finland, and Russia. I hear Sweden is beautiful. Ever been to Stockholm? What about Estonia?"

Maybe it was the wine. Maybe it was the relaxing of his guard after a long, exhausting day. Or maybe it was

just his ease of being around her, but John almost answered before he realized what she'd done.

Russia.

His eyes narrowed ever so slightly as he eyed her over
the candlelit table. Why had he chosen this place anyway? It was too damned romantic! "Well, if things at the
paper don't work out for you, you have a hell of a future
ahead of you as a lawyer."

She blinked innocently, which he didn't buy for a minute. "What do you mean?"

"You are good at asking questions with lots of facts
not in evidence."

"What facts are those?"

"I never said I've been to Russia."

"You didn't need to. Where else would you have gone
from Vaernes? I also don't think it's a coincidence that
you were in Vaernes for a week or two right before those
satellite images of an explosion in Russia were taken."

She'd done it again. More fact assumptions. "What
makes you think I've been to Vaernes before I went there
to save your sweet little ass?"

She put down the wineglass she'd been sipping from
all night. She wasn't much of a drinker. He'd had most of
the rest of the bottle himself.

"Nils recognized my picture of Brandon," she said.
"If my brother was there, I know you were there, too. The
reason that I was leaving the bar with Nils that night was
to talk to a friend of his who'd transported you guys to a
shooting range while you were there. His name was Johan. Do you remember him?"

John was good and pissed off and didn't bother trying
to hide it. "Unlike your young Norwegian friend, it's going to take a hell of a lot more than a low-cut top and
tight jeans to get me to spill my guts, Brit."

She had the nerve to smile at that. She tried to hide it,
but he saw it. Damn her.

There was also something calculating in that smile that scared the crap out of him. He'd thrown down that gauntlet without really thinking about it. There were ways she could try to press him that he wasn't so sure he could fend off.

They sure as hell didn't teach how to resist spilling information under sexual duress by a woman he could barely resist even in the best of circumstances. Great. He had his own personal Mata Hari.

He was relieved that she let it go.

"The way I figure it, Vaernes was where you launched the mission. Probably by helicoptering or flying to the coast to hop on one of our subs in the area. Getting to that part of Russia isn't exactly easy, but my guess is you either parachuted or swam in. Given how good you guys are at swimming, my money is on the latter." She paused, completely unfazed by his expression, which had darkened to good and black by then. "Am I warm?"

He was practically seething. Warm? She was on fire. That was pretty much exactly how it had gone down. She was only missing the submersible launched from the sub. "We aren't going to do this, Brit."

She shrugged. "I don't really need you to corroborate. I've got enough to go on already. I wonder what I'll find when I look into what subs were in the area at that time."

The goddamned Internet! That kind of information was too easily available.

John wanted to shout, but he forced his voice to a low rumble. "Have you forgotten about what happened in Norway? Are you trying to get yourself killed?"

"Of course I haven't forgotten, but I'm not going to put this aside until I find out the truth about what happened. What kind of reporter would I be if I let someone intimidate me so easily?"

"A breathing one," he snapped. "You keep talking about the truth as if it's this great panacea. But this quest you are on isn't going to give you what you are looking for. It isn't going to bring your brother back—or your parents. It's just going to get more people killed."

"You keep saying that, but you won't tell me why."

"You just need to trust me."

"When you won't trust me?"

Their eyes held. He wasn't sure who looked away first.

"I don't expect you to understand," she said dejectedly.

"What do you mean?"

"Look at what you do for a living. Your entire life is cloaked in secrets."

His jaw practically cracked his teeth were clamped so tightly together. "For a reason."

"So you say. I know all about the 'need for secrecy to keep America safe' arguments—I heard them enough times from Brandon. But I'm not as ready to trust the government as you are. Secret government is the antithesis of democratic government. The press is a big part of what keeps our government in check. Free and open, remember? That's the real red, white, and blue. So I'm not going to take anyone's word for anything until I know what happened."

"There's a bigger picture here that you aren't seeing. Sometimes the greater good requires secrecy. It's a balancing act between national security and the free flow of information. You can't have a very effective military or national defense if your enemy knows what you are doing. I wouldn't be able to do my job in the open."

"But that's just it. There isn't a balance. Much of our military action has shifted to secret warfare now—covert ops by special forces rather than traditional ground forces. You may need secrecy to function, but I question whether you should be functioning at all. I bet most of the American public would be surprised to hear the level of military action being undertaken by our Special Forces around the globe right now. We should be given the right to ask questions about whether this is what we want. Congress is supposed to make war, not the president or some general at the Pentagon." She gave him a hard look. "But even if I accepted what you said about needing secrecy to do your job, you aren't operating in a vacuum. You have to be willing to answer for your actions after the fact, and the government has to be held accountable for what it does in our name." She paused. "Such as an illegal covert operation to Russia."

To protect the US from something potentially far worse. But he didn't show any reaction to her statement that was really a question.

John heard what she was saying—and he didn't disagree with all of it—but he knew constitutional principles weren't all that was at work here. She might believe in freedom of the press, but that wasn't what was driving her. It was misplaced guilt and the fear that the same thing that happened to her parents would happen with her brother's death. That justice would be denied.

But John wouldn't let that happen. Someone would pay for what had happened to Brand and their seven other teammates. Justice might be delayed, but it would come.

"That's the problem," he said. "It isn't after the fact." He gave her a solemn look. "This isn't over."

When it was, he would tell her what he could. She deserved to know the truth.

Whatever the hell the truth was.

Brittany didn't expect John to understand. She and Brandon had fought enough about his job as a SEAL for her to know the arguments. But strangely, it seemed as if he understood a little—or at least he wasn't as vocal as her brother had been in disagreeing with her.

"Thoughtful" wasn't a word that she would have attributed to John Donovan, but maybe there was more depth to him than she gave him credit for.

There she went again. Inventing feelings for him and fitting him into that silly, unrealistic, fantasy image she had of looks-like-Mr.-Bad-Boy-on-the-outside-but-is-actually-Mr.-Sensitive-on-the-inside. She had to stop doing that. It was hard enough as it was to keep her head on straight when they were spending all this time together.

Here they were on the run, with someone potentially trying to shut her up permanently, and it felt as if they were a couple on the vacation of a lifetime. He had the uncanny ability to make stressful situations feel not so intense. He defused tension with humor and just by being so utterly relaxed and in control.

She could see why he was a great guy to have on the team—or in the locker room or frat house, for that matter. They all kind of blended together in her opinion as bastions of testosterone, which might have been an instant turnoff if he weren't so otherwise evolved. She suspected it was because of his upbringing in Berkeley with a single mom. He respected women and their opinions in a way that most guys only gave lip service to.

Every hour they spent together, it was getting harder and harder to remind herself why he was no good for her. She'd laughed more in the past two days than she had in the last year. He was outrageous, charmingly arrogant (she never thought those two words would go together), shameless, and utterly incorrigible. Unfortunately for her and her story, he was also sharp. She'd been trying to get something out of him for two days, but he seemed to see her coming a mile away.

She'd forgotten how considerate and gallant he was. Almost old-fashioned. Hold the door open, help her get out of the car—that kind of thing.

No wonder women fell for his shtick. A genuinely nice guy with that big, protective alpha-male thing going on—not to mention serious eye candy? He was pretty much irresistible. Female catnip, as she'd said before.

Especially with that uncanny ability to make you feel as if you were the most important woman in the world.

It was exactly the way he'd made her feel five years ago. Except she was wiser this time.

Wasn't she?

She sighed. She wasn't so sure anymore. The past few days he'd been chipping away at the protective shield she'd wrapped around her heart, and she had to admit there might be a few cracks. If she didn't watch it, she'd start believing that this was about more than some kind of misdirected sense of duty. That John might actually care about her.

She looked at him over her glass of half-filled wine as he handed the bill and a stack of kroner back to the waiter who'd come up just after John made his ominous pronouncement about it not being over.

The scruff and longer hair looked good on him. Really good. He smiled at something he said to the waiter, and it was like a shot straight to the heart.

Oh God, what was she going to do?

Even if she could let herself believe that he did care about her, where did that get her? Did she really want to fall in love with someone like him?

It wasn't just the too many women or the "nothing gets to me—don't look to me for anything but a good time" personality. As they'd just talked about, could she really see herself with someone who couldn't tell her anything about what he was doing (which she probably didn't want to know) or where he was going? She hated secrets. Did she want to be with someone whose job—whose life— was dependent on them?

It would drive her crazy.

And then there was all the danger and stress that came with being a SEAL. Did she want to say good-bye to him every time he left and wonder if he was ever going to come back? Her brother had been gone for months at a time. One year Brandon said he'd spent less than a month at "home." Could she handle someone being away so much?

There was a reason the divorce rate was so high among Special Forces guys. They might look and act like superheroes, but being married to one would take heroism of its own. John might make it seem as if nothing bothered him, but how could he not be affected by the things he did and saw? By the deaths of his friends?

She suspected he was affected—far more than he wanted to let on. She saw how much he drank, and she didn't think he was sleeping much. Last night he'd been restless, and she thought she heard him mumbling something. It had woken her up. She'd tried to ask him about it earlier, but he'd brushed her off, claiming that the room had been too hot.

She didn't know what was worse: if he really didn't feel anything or if he did and just bottled it up or tried to self-medicate with alcohol. He'd obviously been drinking heavily for a while, as he could have five or six drinks and not show any effects. He was a big guy, but that was a lot of drinks for anyone.

No matter how many good reasons she came up with for why this wouldn't work and why she shouldn't fall in love with him, Brittany knew that if this went on much longer, she might not have a choice.

She had to do something. Staying away from him would be a great start. Tomorrow, no matter how much he tried to entice her away with some fantastic thing that "she had to see," Brittany wasn't going to let him. She was going to find an Internet café and get in touch with Mac and do a little more research for her article.

Of course, she had to get through tonight first. And when she returned to her room—their room—and the beds that might have been pulled apart but were still far too close for her peace of mind, the night had never looked so long.

It seemed that she'd just closed her eyes, when they shot open again. Her heart jumped to her throat at the sound of a hoarse cry. "I have to try, damn it! I can't just leave them . . ." He made another sound, this one more of a low moan. "Oh God. Please . . . no."

The raw emotion in his voice broke her heart. She climbed out from under the duvet—apparently they didn't believe in sheets in Scandinavia—and crossed the short distance between the two beds.

She knew he was having a nightmare—or more likely reliving something—and she had heard enough about PTSD to be cautious. He could react violently.

He was on his side with his back to her, squeezing a pillow in his arms as if he were about to tear it apart. She could practically feel the tension of coiled-up muscles. Tentatively, she put her hand on his bare shoulder.

He was burning up as if with fever. Whatever memories he was wrestling with in his nightmare, they were taking a physical toll on him. It was like putting her hand on the lid of a pot of boiling water.

But he didn't flinch or lash out. Instead his body stilled.

Emboldened, she sat down on the bed beside him and moved her hand over his back in gentle little caresses, almost as if she were trying to quiet a baby.

"It's all right," she said soothingly. "You're just having a nightmare." He seemed to relax into her hand. "Go back to sleep."

He turned to look at her. Or maybe he was just responding to the sound of her voice, because the next moment he'd pulled her down onto the bed in front of him and brought her in tight against his chest. His arms went around her and held her there.

She was instantly enveloped in heat and muscle and

the scent of a man who'd just done battle. Of course, just as everything else about him, he even sweated sexily. John Donovan didn't stink; the soapy smell of his skin was just intensified.

Suddenly, he sighed. Deeply. As if utterly contented. He fell into what sounded from his breathing like a deep sleep.

But he held on to her as if he would never let her go. She felt like a beloved teddy bear. Which just might be the most awesome feeling in the world.

Brittany didn't sleep. She just listened to the steady flow of his breathing until dawn, her heart breaking for him the entire time. John might not want to admit it, but whatever had happened out there was hurting him.

He was mourning the death of her brother maybe even more than she was—which wasn't all that surprising. Other than the three weeks that summer, she could count on one hand the number of times she'd seen her brother in the past twelve years since their parents had died. John and Brandon had been best friends since they'd gone to SEAL training together—BUD/S, or whatever they called it—eight years ago.

Brandon had been more John's brother than he'd been hers. She envied him that relationship even as she saw the pain it was causing him now. Brittany mourned Brandon, too, but not in the same way. Not so immediately. More in that she regretted their estrangement and the loss of the brother she'd known and loved as a young girl. But there had been a hole in her life where Brandon was concerned for a long time. Now it was permanent.

About an hour before dawn—such as it was in the land of the midnight sun—Brittany crept back to her bed in the semidarkness. It felt as if everything had changed. The question was what she was going to do about it.

Fourteen

Kate tried to get a little sleep when she returned home to Arlington from the airport after the red-eye. She tossed and turned for an hour before giving up. A shower, an omelet, and a triple-shot latte made her feel almost human again.

She decided to work from home for the day rather than go into the office. Percy, who had been living with her since their engagement, had been tied up with a morning meeting and had sent a driver to the airport to pick her up, but he'd checked in on her later that morning with a phone call.

"You're sure you are okay?" he asked after she filled him in on what had happened in San Diego.

Or, rather, *most* of what had happened. She left out Colt's last cruel dig, which had felt something like a jagged knife opening an old wound. An old wound that for a moment had been very raw and very painful.

How could she have let him get to her like that? She couldn't put her shield down even for a moment when it came to him. But she'd been lulled into a false sense of complacency. They'd been getting along so well, she'd actually thought that maybe she didn't hate him as much as she thought. That maybe they could work together like two rational adults. Which was idiotic, as there had never been anything rational about the two of them.

She'd made a mistake in a moment of weakness, which she attributed to the accident. Seeing that child nearly run over and then holding the baby until her parents arrived had stripped her to her core and left her unusually vulnerable.

"I'm fine," she assured her fiancé. "Just tired. You know how I don't sleep well on planes."

If Percy didn't quite believe her explanation, he was too polite to disagree with her. Sometimes his very proper Englishness could come off as coldness or aloofness, but right now she was grateful for it.

"Don't forget about the party tonight. The car will be there at five to pick you up."

"You aren't coming home to change?"

"I brought my tux with me."

"I'll be ready." She wasn't looking forward to a formal party tonight, but she knew it was part of her duties as the soon-to-be Mrs. Ambassador.

They'd met while she was briefing him on a joint US/UK operation. There had been some pushback from both sides about security issues when they'd started dating, but because she was a counterterrorism analyst and not a field agent (aka a spook), they had only been asked to give an occasional report on their dates.

Marriage was more problematic. A CIA agent marrying a foreign national—even from our closest ally country—was frowned upon, which is why she hadn't formally told her superiors yet. They could try to revoke her security clearances, although she thought it unlikely since she didn't do clandestine work. Percy intended to retire from the diplomatic service when his posting was up. She knew he wanted to return to England, but they hadn't really talked about that. They hadn't talked about a lot of things. She paused. "I was hoping we might have time to talk along the way."

"About what?"

"Have you had a chance to look over the information I gave you?"

He paused for long enough to let her know that he wasn't keen on the conversation. "Not yet. I thought it was agreed that we would discuss a possible adoption after my posting was complete. I'd like you to spend some time with Poppy and George first."

Percy's kids lived with their mother in England. Kate had met them only once.

She knew what he was hoping. That she would fall in love with his children and not feel the need for her own. But she wanted both. She loved that Percy had kids, and she couldn't wait to get to know them better, but they were in their teens already. She wanted a baby or a young child to raise.

"I don't think I want to wait," she said quietly, remembering how it had felt to have the baby pulled out of her arms yesterday. She hadn't wanted to let go.

"What brought this on, Katherine? Does it have something to do with seeing your ex-husband?"

It was not said unkindly. Percy could be abrupt and standoffish at times, but he was a genuinely nice man. And he cared for her. She did not doubt that. He just liked their life, and a child would disrupt that.

"It has nothing to do with Colt. I gave you that material weeks ago." Although Colt and what happened yesterday had brought it to the forefront. "I'm almost thirty-five."

"You have plenty of years left to be a mother. There is no need to rush."

Kate let it go for now. She didn't want to press him. But it had become blatantly clear that she could not wait a few years. She wanted a child now. Today. Yesterday.

Three years ago.

Don't go there. . . .

She said good-bye, telling him she would see him later, and hung up. She spent most of the morning and early afternoon trying to figure out more about Natalie Andersson—the woman Scott had been involved with whom she wasn't supposed to be investigating. Scott would be pissed when he found out.

Natalie had been killed shortly after warning Scott of the danger to the platoon, and he didn't think it was a coincidence.

Neither did Kate, which was why she was pursuing it. If she could find out who killed Natalie, it could presumably lead her to who set up the platoon.

Given what had happened to Natalie, Scott thought it was too dangerous. He was probably right, but it was also their best lead. Kate would be careful not to leave any trace of her snooping.

Scott had left out some rather pertinent information about the woman he wasn't supposed to be seeing (members of Team Nine weren't supposed to have any ties), such as the fact that she worked at the Pentagon as an executive assistant to the Deputy Secretary of Defense. Talk about having a girlfriend in high places. The commanding officers of Team Nine wouldn't have been the only ones objecting to their seeing each other. With her security clearances, fraternization with a SEAL, or anyone in the military, would have been frowned upon.

Jeez, Scott, nothing like making your life even more complicated.

But she knew better than anyone that the heart didn't always follow the path you wanted it to.

Understatement.

Kate had finally accessed Natalie's personnel folder—which had been difficult even for her to get to—when she looked at the clock and realized she'd better get ready. Percy wouldn't be happy if she was late.

She'd just stepped out of the shower when her cell phone rang. Seeing the "unknown" caller, her heart jammed in her chest. Was it Colt? She didn't think she was ready to talk to him.

But what if it was Scott?

Tentatively, she picked it up and answered. She sighed with relief at the sound of the voice on the other end of the line.

"How did it go?"

It was a simple question, but she could hear the concern in Scott's voice. He knew how hard it would be for her to see Colt. She knew he would never have asked her if there had been any other way.

"Fine." She gave a brief overview of their meeting with the rear admiral and the accident that had followed. She didn't mention Colt's cruel dig or the fact that he'd managed to get to her.

"You've got to be kidding me. Wesson always did have a knack for being in the wrong place at the wrong time."

"It was the right place for the little boy," Kate said quietly.

Maybe too quietly. Scott had heard something. He swore. "I never should have asked you to do this. He did something, didn't he? What aren't you telling me?"

"Nothing," she said quickly. "Seriously, I'm fine. I can handle him."

That was a flat-out lie. No one could handle Colt Wesson, least of all her. God knew she'd tried.

But Scott chose not to call her on it—at least right now. "What did you think? Was there anything to Morrison's gambling?"

"I'm not sure. Colt did his job and made the rear

admiral furious, but so far Morrison hasn't made any calls or logged into his computer."

She could practically hear Scott frowning. "That's odd—even for someone who isn't guilty."

Kate agreed. But she'd double-checked her equipment and programs, and everything seemed to be in order.

"Something else came up," Scott said. "I was hoping you could run it down for me and see what you can find out. It's about Blake's sister—the reporter who is causing a lot of problems. She apparently has a source high up in the DoD."

Scott passed on what John Donovan had told him, and Kate agreed to see what she could find out.

"You know how to reach me," he said, and then paused. "Are you sure you are okay?"

"I'm fine," she repeated, this time more forcefully. "Really. You worry too much."

"It comes with the job, Katie. And when it's about Wesson, I worry a lot. I know what he's capable of."

"Well, he's not going to be happy with either of us when he finds out the truth."

"What else is new?"

They both laughed, but it wasn't really funny. It was true.

She hung up and finished getting ready. When the doorbell rang at a quarter to five, she assumed it was her driver—which was why she was totally unprepared to see Colt standing there.

She gasped, and just for a moment she forgot how much she hated him. Her heart lurched the way it had always done when he'd shown up unexpectedly on her doorstep. It was always right about that time that she'd convinced herself she could do fine without him.

He took in her formfitting, slightly sexy gown with a long, cool look. "Sorry to interrupt, but this won't take long. Is there somewhere we can talk?"

"You should have called first."

"I did. You didn't answer. I left a message."

She pulled out her phone from her evening bag and saw the voice-mail indicator. He must have called when she was in the shower or on the phone with Scott.

"You could have waited for me to call you back."

"I wasn't sure you would, and like I said, it's important."

She waved him into the vestibule and closed the door. "Say what you want. There is no one else here."

He didn't hesitate. "Morrison was found at his desk this morning with a bullet through his head. Looks like the rear admiral killed himself."

Fifteen

Brittany's resolve to get some work done lasted through breakfast. She was lured away by a boat ride. An exhilarating, wild, open-it-up-full-throttle RIB boat ride to be specific.

But admittedly, after what had happened last night, it wouldn't have taken much to tempt her. Though John seemed to have no recollection of what had occurred, she remembered every minute. He'd turned to her and revealed a part of himself, even if he didn't realize it.

She was worried about him, but her attempts to broach the subject with him at breakfast had been brushed aside. When she'd mentioned his restlessness, he'd said he'd had a nightmare. Everyone had them. "It's no big deal."

She might have believed him if she hadn't felt the tension in him last night so viscerally. That had been no ordinary nightmare.

Once they boarded the boat, there wasn't much opportunity for talking. She was holding on for her life, trying to not fly out of her seat as they slammed over the waves, laughing until the tears blended into the dampness of the sea spray on her face. She was glad for the dry suits the boat company had given them—she would have been soaked without one. She'd tied her hair back in a ponytail, but it was still flying all over.

But the tangles were worth it. The scenery was take-your-breath-away stunning.

Once the boat had taxied out of the harbor, the group of twelve had passed a couple of tiny islands on the way out to sea. It was a sunny day, and the varying shades of blue were almost unreal. This was where descriptive words like "cerulean" and "sapphire" came from.

John appeared to be enjoying himself, too, but he was watching her more than the scenery. She wished she was a mind reader. His expression—at least when he looked at her—didn't reveal much. Every now and then, when he wasn't watching her, she would catch him glancing at the captain of the boat. It wasn't too difficult to guess what he was thinking then—he wanted to be at the helm. If what she'd read about SEALs was true, she suspected John would be the far more skilled of the two.

She was still smiling as they got rid of the dry suits, which looked more like puffy coveralls, and walked away from the dock. The boats left from the canal area of Ny-havn, where they'd had dinner last night, which was probably how he'd gotten the idea.

"I take it you had fun?" he asked.

If she'd had dimples, they would have been dimpling. "That was a blast. Well, except for the nearly-flying-out-of-the-boat parts." He gave her a sidelong glance with a very skeptical lift of one eyebrow. "Oh, all right, those parts were fun, too. Although I noticed that you didn't seem to have as much problem keeping your seat."

"Age and experience, little one."

She rolled her eyes at his tone. "More like body mass again."

He grinned back at her. "Maybe a little. But you haven't ridden in an RIB with your brother. He can take one of those things sideways and almost flip it. . . ."

His voice fell off, and a shadow crossed his features as he realized what he'd said. Can. Present tense.

She put her hand on his arm, experiencing that same overwhelming desire to comfort him she'd felt last night. Her heart had never felt this big before. "I miss him, too," she said.

He held her gaze for a minute before turning away.

That was the only acknowledgment she got before he started to walk again. He took the narrow set of stairs to the street level and held his hand out to help her up. She took it even though she didn't need it.

But she wasn't ready to let the moment go. "Maybe you could show me how he did it sometime," she said. He glanced in her direction again, his expression neutral. She was feeling a little silly. A little like she'd ventured out too far into the future. "I saw the way you were eyeing the wheel. I was surprised you didn't offer to take it from him."

Apparently relieved that she hadn't been talking about at home—which she had been—he smiled. "I did. I offered to pay him the kroner equivalent of a hundred bucks if he let me take it for a spin, but he said he'd be fired if anyone found out." He shrugged. "It was worth a try."

They'd reached the building where they'd met the group for the RIB tour. It was a restaurant, which hadn't been open earlier. It was now.

She turned on him with an exaggerated groan. "I'm sure this isn't a coincidence?"

A flash of very white teeth appeared in a very wide grin. "You mean lunch? I hope you are hungry."

She had been. "Only you would find Mexican food in Denmark."

"The world's greatest cuisine is everywhere, Brit," he said, putting his arm around her shoulder to lead her inside. "I don't want you to get your hopes up too high though. This place is supposed to be the best in Copenhagen, but Europe and Mexican food don't always mix right."

She groaned again in case he hadn't heard her the first time. "Then why are we going here?"

"One thing you need to learn about me is that I'm an eternal optimist when it comes to Mexican food."

She gave him a sidelong look. "You sure it isn't more like an addict needing a fix no matter how bad the crack?"

He laughed, pulling her in a little closer. "Yeah, well, maybe that, too."

She liked the feeling of his arm around her a little too much. It felt right. It felt strong and protective, as if it could stay there forever.

She heaved a dramatic sigh. It wasn't capitulation, she told herself. "All right. But this time you aren't ordering for me. What was that nasty soup you got me last time?"

"Menudo. And you liked it at first."

She made a face. "Until you told me what it was, and then I nearly threw up. I'm not eating cow stomach again—or whatever nice word you called it by."

"Tripe. Duly noted, but I didn't realize you were so pedestrian."

She knew he was baiting her, and it was kind of working. "Only when it comes to food."

She hadn't meant it provocatively, but when their eyes met she knew that's how he'd taken it.

Normally that would have guaranteed some kind of naughty, suggestive response from him. But surprisingly, he let it go. She wasn't sure whether she should ascribe any meaning to that, but for some reason it felt significant. As if maybe she wasn't the only one feeling that what was between them wasn't normal.

It was different.

———

By the time they finished their late lunch, it was nearly time for an early dinner.

"Admit it," John said as they were walking back toward the hotel along the canal. "You liked it."

Looking down, he saw her nose wrinkle under the faded edge of her Bulldogs baseball cap. He probably should have told her to ditch the hat. It wasn't that it practically shouted American—which it did, even if you didn't know the Georgetown mascot; it was also sexy as hell.

Which he knew was ridiculous. There was nothing that should be sexy about a ponytail, ball cap, T-shirt, and jeans, but all he had to do was look at her and he was thinking about sex.

Fuck.

Exactly.

"I don't know whether I liked it. After three margaritas anything is going to taste pretty good." Her eyes narrowed as she looked up at him. "I'm onto your ploy—or should I say *ply*."

He chuckled. She didn't like to admit defeat. Which was a personality flaw he could get behind, as he was guilty of it himself. "I didn't order you that third one— that's on you. And I saw you chowing down those tacos well before the second foo-foo drink arrived."

She shot him an angry glare. "Strawberry margaritas are not 'foo-foo,' and for someone who is reportedly so good with women, you would think you would know better than to use the term 'chowing down' when it comes to the way we eat. You make me sound like a frat boy at a chili-dog-eating contest."

He shrugged. "If the shoe fits."

She gasped with outrage and slugged him in the arm.

Hard. He was laughing even as he grabbed his arm. "Ouch, that hurt."

She batted her eyes, doing her best Southern belle—which was surprisingly good. "Why, a little ol' girl like me hurt a big, strong man like you? What would all the other guys say?"

"They'd say you throw a mean punch," he said dryly.

She laughed. "Don't be such a baby, Johnny. You're gonna lose your alpha card."

He puffed up at that. "Glad to see you finally recognize your place in the natural order around here."

She groaned, realizing she'd walked right into that one. "You're incorrigible, and I've had too much tequila to match wits with you right now."

"I'll have to remember that the next time you're irritating me."

She looked up at him, her big blue eyes wide and guileless behind the sultry haze. "Do I irritate you?"

He sighed. "All the time."

"Good. You irritate me, too, when I'm not thinking about—"

She stopped suddenly, her cheeks turning bright red.

Now, that wasn't just sexy; it was really damned cute. It made him want to make her blush like that all over. Maybe when he stripped her naked and told her exactly what he thought of her body. Part by part. Starting with the chest he was trying not to look at.

It wasn't his fault. It was the damned V-neck T-shirt, which had an opening that was practically right in his line of sight every time he looked down at her.

They were still walking along the canal, but it wasn't the touristy part. When he took her arm and turned her toward him, he realized no one else was around. "What?" he demanded. "When you aren't thinking about what?"

She tried to pull away with an embarrassed laugh. "Nothing. I'm drunk. I don't know what I'm saying."

Bullshit. She wasn't that drunk. She had been about to say something revealing—that was the problem. And he wanted to hear it. He shouldn't, but damn it, he did.

"Tell me," he said. It came out as more of an order, which she would typically ignore or countermand. But buzzed, she didn't seem as indifferent as she usually did to him. He was beginning to think she might not have outgrown him as much as he thought. That maybe she was just as affected as before but had just grown better at hiding it.

Her blush deepened, but she answered him. "When I'm not thinking about being with you."

"You're with me right now."

She tried to look away, but he wouldn't let her. He held her chin to face him. Those eyes. God, those eyes. He seemed to get lost in them.

"Not like that," she said in a soft, husky voice. "Being with you . . . intimately."

The last word was whispered so softly that he almost didn't hear it. Or maybe that was just the freight train of desire that suddenly came roaring through his ears.

Her mouth was right there. Tilted toward his so temptingly. He couldn't help himself. He had to kiss her again. Just to see if it was as sweet as he remembered.

He lowered his mouth to hers.

She had time to react. Time to part her lips and give a little gasp of anticipation.

A gasp that went straight to his cock. Everything about her went straight to his cock. But that wasn't the only place that blood was rushing. His chest was feeling that tightness, too. It must be his lungs. Yeah, his lungs.

But his lungs weren't what was pounding.

He stilled at the contact. The softness of her lips, the

warmth, the sweet taste of strawberries coupled with the tangy edge of salt stopped him in his tracks. For a moment, he forgot what to do. He was too busy savoring every incredible sensation.

His hand was still on her chin, tilting her mouth to his and holding her at a perfect angle to sink in his tongue deep and take a big sweeping drink of her. But he didn't even want to take a breath, as if he could hold on to the moment forever. As if the connection afforded by a single kiss would be all that he needed.

That was crazy. Wasn't it?

She made a sound. A whimper? A moan? He didn't know, but the effect was the same. The lust that had been pounding in his blood came racing back full force. He knew exactly what to do.

But when his mouth started to move over hers there was something different about it. His movements were slower. Softer. His lips were savoring and lingering with every gentle caress.

It was as if every kiss, every soft circle and stroke of his tongue, were trying to elicit something.

Or trying to say something.

Never had a kiss felt so revealing, so expressive, so . . .

Intimate. Just like she'd said.

He pulled away almost as if he'd been zapped like a finger in a light socket.

What the hell was he doing?

She wobbled a little, which he attributed to the alcohol. Although the soft and hazy look in her eyes as she gazed up at him didn't look anything like tequila. It looked like the wrong impression. It looked like emotions he didn't want to see.

"We should get back to the hotel," he said, his tone abrupt. Or maybe it just seemed abrupt because of what had been happening a few moments before.

She blinked up at him, obviously confused. A state he understood only too well.

"All right," she said, far too huskily for how hot he was right now.

"I'm going to try to get a workout in before dinner," he explained.

Lifting weights and a good five-mile run on the treadmill should help. He was out of sorts because he hadn't worked out in a few days. He needed to burn off some energy. Lots of energy.

Maybe he'd better make that ten miles.

He was so distracted he forgot that he was supposed to be distracting her and keeping her busy. Fortunately, she didn't try to sneak off to the Internet café. She said she was going to lie down for a while and then take a bath.

She was still in the bath when he returned—hot, sweaty, and on edge. He had to wait for his cold shower.

She sure took long baths. When she finally came out, it seemed she'd taken most of her belongings in there with her.

"Sorry," she said, her cheeks still rosy from the steam. She'd put on some makeup and done her hair, but she was still wearing the hotel bathrobe. Which pissed him off. Didn't she know how easy it was for him to take that thing off? "I hope you weren't waiting long."

He grumbled something and barely even looked at her as he took refuge in the icy-cold waters of his shower. After BUD/S, he swore he'd never take a cold shower again. That was before he'd met Brittany.

He was more relaxed by the time he emerged, and he managed to make it through a pretty decent dinner at a local French-style café before some of that earlier tension returned. It wasn't the long night ahead of him that confronted him when he looked at the two beds as they came back into the room—although that sure as hell bothered him; it was the turn their conversation took.

At dinner, she'd been almost cautious in conversation topics. As if she knew something was bothering him. But as soon as they returned to their hotel room, all that restraint fled.

"Are you going to tell me what's wrong?" she asked.

"Nothing's wrong."

"Then why are you acting like this?"

"Like what?"

Brittany had never had a high tolerance for his or any other BS. He shouldn't have been surprised when she cut right to the quick.

"Like you didn't kiss me earlier."

"It was only a kiss, Brittany. Don't make one of your federal cases out of it, like you do everything else."

Five years ago she would have flushed with embarrassment, but not now. Now it was anger. "And what about me sleeping in your arms last night? I guess that didn't mean anything either?"

"What the hell are you talking about?"

"You cried out. You were having a nightmare. I went over to see if you were okay, and you pulled me into bed beside you. You held me cuddled against your chest all night long."

John was the one who was embarrassed now. It was like she'd just thrown a pitch and dropped him into the dunking booth of shame. It washed over him in a hot rush of anger. The nightmares and talking in his sleep were why he'd avoided overnight female companionship since the op in Russia.

What had he said?

He didn't want to know. But most of all, he didn't want *her* to know.

"I was *asleep*, Brittany. I didn't know what I was doing. You could have been anyone."

He'd said something like that to her once before, but this time she called him on it. "That's crap, John, and you know it. You knew it was me. Just like you knew it was me when you kissed me like that." Her gaze held his in an unyielding challenge. "I'd wager you've never kissed anyone like that in your life." She didn't give him an opportunity to play dumb. "Like you cared." And just in case he didn't get the point. "Like you cared about *me*."

"I do care about you."

"You know I don't mean it like that."

"Then why don't you say what you mean, because I feel like you are talking in some kind of language I don't understand? And if you are expecting me to say something, you're going to be waiting a really long time."

Eyes wide with shock, she blinked. But it didn't quite hide the hurt.

He felt like an ass. But this was exactly what had happened before. She was trying to get too close. Trying to pin him down. "Look," he said. "I'm sorry about last night. It won't happen again. And I shouldn't have kissed you earlier. You were drunk and obviously mistook my intentions."

"I didn't mistake anything, and I wasn't drunk. I was a little buzzed, but not drunk."

A drink was exactly what he needed. He started toward the minibar, but she stepped in front of him, cutting him off. "Alcohol isn't going to help, John. It isn't going to make you forget what happened, and it isn't going to bring them back. I'm worried about you. The drinking, the nightmares. You need to talk to someone."

He snapped. This was exactly the kind of crap he didn't need. She wasn't his girlfriend; she needed to stop acting like one.

He took one long look at her, standing there with her eyes too full of concern, as if she fucking understood. She didn't understand anything. "Fine. I won't drink here. I'll be back later."

He'd finally shaken her confidence. Now she looked

worried. As if she'd overplayed her hand and he'd called her on it. "Where are you going?"

He lifted an eyebrow. This time it was his gaze that was challenging. "Does it really matter?"

They'd been here once before. He knew exactly how to make sure she didn't have the wrong idea.

"I don't know what you think you have to prove, but you don't need to do this." She moved away from the bar. "Stay and have your drink. We can talk about it."

That was the last thing he wanted. He'd done all the talking he was going to do.

He grabbed the jacket he'd tossed on the chair when they'd walked in a few minutes ago and headed for the door. "Don't wait up."

The slam of the door behind him sounded final. Even to him.

Sixteen

Brittany forced her eyes closed so she wouldn't stare at the clock as she lay in bed not sleeping in the mostly darkened room. It was after midnight, and John had been gone for hours.

She didn't need to ask where. She knew exactly where he was going and what he planned to do when he said he was leaving. The only question was whether he would find anyone at the bar to pick up.

Which was a stupid question. Of course he would. He could probably draw numbers, there would be so many volunteers. Knowing his luck, he'd find twins again.

She never should have pushed him. She knew how much he didn't like to be cornered about anything personal. As soon as she got too close, his first instinct was to do something to push her away.

Just like last time.

She tugged the duvet over her head and squeezed her eyes in frustration. Why did she care what time it was or what he was doing right now? She should be grateful that he'd reminded her of how much of a dog he was before she got too attached.

Well, he could drink himself into oblivion and never sleep another night for all she cared. The big jerk.

She refused to wait up for him. She had to go to sleep.

But her body wasn't cooperating. Especially her pounding chest, her tight throat, and her burning eyes.

Damn him.

She hated herself right now almost as much as she hated him. How could she let him do this to her?

The red glow of the clock seemed to taunt her with each passing minute: 12:17. How long was she going to do this?

For another minute—that was when the door finally opened.

She held her breath, glad she was facing away from the door at that moment. She wasn't sure what she would do if she had to look at him. She didn't want to see him right now. If there was any sign of what he'd been doing, she might not be able to control herself.

She'd probably do something horrible like burst into tears, and she wouldn't embarrass herself like that. He didn't deserve half the tears she'd already wasted on him. She wasn't even a crier!

She heard him go into the bathroom and pulled the covers over her head again, trying to calm the frantic pace of her heart. The toilet flushed. The sink turned on for him to wash his hands and brush his teeth. When it went off, she braced herself.

She heard footsteps as he crossed the room and the creak of the bed as his weight landed on the mattress.

A moment later she heard a deep sigh. It sounded enough like contentment to make her snap. All her good intentions flew right out the window.

She tore off the covers and jumped out of bed. "Get out of here. Find another place to sleep, because you sure as hell aren't sleeping in the same room as me."

For maybe the first time ever the fact that he wasn't

wearing a shirt didn't matter. He disgusted her right now. She didn't even want to look in case there were marks on him. Had someone else been digging their fingertips into his arms and shoulders when he made them come?

Her stomach turned. God, she hated him right now.

John looked taken aback by the vehemence of her attack. She probably looked like a crazy woman looming over him, but she was beyond caring.

"Hey, take it easy," he said. "There's no reason to over-react."

That sent her flying right over the edge. For someone who was reportedly so good with women, he didn't have a clue with her. You don't tell a nearly hysterical woman to calm down and not to overreact!

He'd climbed out of bed to face her, and when he tried to move toward her, she pushed him away. "Don't you dare tell me how to feel or how to react. Just because *you* don't feel anything or act as if nothing bothers you doesn't mean that's normal. News flash, John. It's actually *normal* to have feelings. And it's even normal to show them sometimes. Like when your mom dies, when you lose your best friend, or when you care about someone."

He went utterly stone-faced—full icy Viking. "I don't know what you are talking about. I have feelings."

"Do you? You could have fooled me. How could you leave like that and do what you did? God, I . . ." Her eyes were burning too hard to fight it anymore. The blasted tears started to fall. "I am not going to let you do this to me again. You need to get out of here." And just in case he hadn't understood, she put both her hands on his ridiculously perfect chest and gave him a push. "Now."

"I'm not going anywhere," he said, circling her wrists with his hands. Her push hadn't budged him an inch. Stupid muscles! "We're going to talk about why you are so upset."

The fact that he sounded so calm only served to light

another fuse to a fire that didn't need stoking. "Why I'm so upset? Jeez, I don't know, John. Do you think it might have something to do with the fact that we've been spending time together like two people who care about each other, but as soon as I start to get too close, you run out of here like a scared rabbit and find someone else to have sex with so you can prove to me how much you don't care about me? Well, you know what? I got the message last time." She might have shoved him in the chest again. She was crying too hard to know. "You don't care about me. Got it."

She was clearly past the "nearly" and on her way to full-fledged hysterical. And what was his response?

"Ah, hell."

He tried to pull her into his arms, but she fought against it. "Don't touch me. God, just leave me alone!"

She was seriously losing it now.

Despite her best efforts, his arms were around her and her damp cheek was pressed against his bare and very warm and cozy chest as he stroked her hair. "I didn't sleep with anyone tonight."

It took a few moments for his words to penetrate her emotions. When they finally did, she seemed to freeze mid-choking sob. She looked up at him, trying to read his expression in the semidarkness of the room. "You didn't?"

He shook his head. "I wanted to, but . . ."

Her heart, which had lifted for a second, sank. For a minute she'd thought . . . Her gaze dropped. "No suitable victims, huh?"

"No. It wasn't that."

Of course it wasn't that. She looked back up again. "Then why?"

He shrugged. "I don't know. I just couldn't. I didn't want to."

"Why not?"

"God, I don't know," he said, using his thumb to sweep tears from her cheeks. "It just didn't feel right. Can we leave it at that for now?"

He sounded so uncomfortable she took momentary pity on him. "But you wanted me to think that you had."

It wasn't a question, but his shrug seemed to be an affirmation.

"Why?" she asked.

"I guess I didn't like what you were saying."

"About the drinking and nightmares?"

He paused and then nodded. He took what seemed a very long and deep breath. "Maybe everything isn't as great as it seems."

Knowing what those words must have cost him, Brittany felt something inside her chest break. But it was a different kind of heart breaking—more an opening. It was a feeling that might make her terrified if her concern weren't directed on him. "Why would it be great? You just lost your best friend, and I'm assuming other men you were close to as well."

"It's part of the job. Shit happens. Lots of shit. You have to be able to move on."

"Of course you do, and I get that. But moving on doesn't mean you aren't allowed to mourn a little or be sad. You can't bury your feelings and pretend they aren't there."

One corner of his mouth lifted. "Who says?"

She smiled back at him. "Me." She paused, sobering. "Do you want to talk about it?"

He looked like he wanted to run for the door, but instead he shuffled his feet. "There isn't much to talk about. Men died. *Good* men died by the luck of the draw. I didn't." He forced a laugh. "It pays to be a winner."

She'd heard the saying a few times when they were together in San Diego. It was usually meant motivationally in a competitive situation—work hard to be a winner—but he was using it more ironically.

Brittany suspected there was a lot more in what he'd said than he realized. She wasn't a psychiatrist or a therapist, but it sounded as if he was experiencing not just the loss but also a good old-fashioned case of survivor's guilt.

"Could you have done anything to change what happened?"

He shook his head. "Not unless I figured out how to see the future."

"Did you do everything you could to help them?"

He seemed taken aback even by the question. "There was nothing anyone could have done."

She feigned shock. "Not even you? You mean you aren't Superman?"

He realized what she was doing and got the point. "I hate to disappoint you—I know how superhero big I loom in your mind—but unfortunately, no leotards and phone booths for me."

She wrinkled her nose. Even John Donovan might have a hard time pulling off a leotard. But a leather Thor suit? She may have shuddered a little. He could definitely pull that off. Big-time. Move over, Chris Hemsworth. And for her that was saying a lot.

"You aren't to blame for not dying, John."

"I know that."

"What if the draw had come out another way? Would you want Brandon to be feeling guilty because you were the one to die?"

He looked at her as if she were crazy. "Of course not. That's not how it works."

She gave a sharp nod. "Good. Then remember that."

Somehow her head was back on his chest and his hand was caressing her back. She could feel him chuckle when he responded, "Aye-aye, Captain."

She looked at him sideways. "I like the sound of that."

"Well, don't get used to it. We've already established

the command structure around here, and I'm not always so accommodating."

She snorted at the command-structure comment. Right. "You are never accommodating. You pretty much do what you want."

"Not always."

It took her a moment to figure out what he meant. But when she felt something hard jutting against her stomach just as he let her go, she understood. He wanted her, but he still wasn't going to act on it.

And she'd be willing to wager everything she had in the bank—which admittedly was about a hundred dollars—that it was more than wanting. Which brought her back to their earlier subject.

He'd taken a step away from her, but she closed the distance quickly. The bed was behind him, so there was no place for him to move. He might not like to be cornered, but too bad. She wasn't going to let this go. "Why didn't it feel right at the bar tonight?"

He had that pained look on his face again. "I thought we weren't going to talk about that."

"I never said that." She leaned into him a little so their bodies were barely touching. "Does it feel wrong with me?"

He definitely wasn't liking the turn the conversation was taking because he bit back a curse before he responded. "It should."

"But it doesn't because you care about me, don't you?"

"You already know that."

"And you know that's not the kind of caring I meant." She slid her hand between them until her palm was lying flat on his chest. Pretty much right over his heart, where she could feel the heavy beating. "You feel something for me."

He shot her an angry glare. "I think that's obvious. I

feel like I'm going to explode, I want to fuck you so badly."

She might have been annoyed by the bluntness if she weren't feeling the same thing herself. It was more than that, but how much more she didn't know herself.

But tonight had proved that she wasn't quite as over him as she wanted to think, and maybe he wasn't as incapable of feelings as he appeared. But could she let herself care about him again?

Did she have a choice?

She didn't know. But something told her she couldn't let this moment go. She had to hold on to the closeness.

He'd turned to her last night in his sleep and kissed her today as if she were the most important thing in the world to him. He couldn't make himself go through with what he had planned tonight, and then he'd confided in her about something she was sure he didn't even want to acknowledge to himself. That had to mean something.

It meant she was going to do something potentially really stupid or really wonderful again.

Or maybe both.

She stood on her tiptoes to whisper softly in his ear, "Then why don't you?"

The hand resting on her hip and back gripped a little harder. She could feel the restraint in each press of his fingers, and when he spoke, his voice came out just as hard and tense as his body. "I'm not going to do this, Brit."

She let her mouth roam near his ear and down his neck, pressing soft little kisses everywhere she went. God, he smelled good. She could still catch the hint of the soap he'd used earlier. He didn't smell like smoke or alcohol, which made her wonder where he'd been for so many hours. But that was a question for another time.

Now all she wanted to ask was, "Why not?"

———

Good question. One John didn't have the answer for right now. Not when those soft, warm lips were pressing against his skin and sure as hell not when the tight little body that seemed to meld right into him started to press provocatively against an erection that was definitely all in.

It just felt too damned good. Too damned right.

But he wasn't going to think about that either.

How could he when he was suddenly kissing her and she was curling in his arms with little sounds of delight as his tongue delved and circled deeper and deeper into her mouth?

He was consumed by kissing. Savoring every stroke, every taste, every response. He loved how her body slid into his. How her breasts crushed against his chest, how her arms wrapped around his neck, how her soft body stretched out against his.

How they felt together.

He loved it even better when she pushed him back on the bed and she was on top of him. Their mouths never separated. They didn't stop kissing even as their limited clothes started to land in a heap on the floor.

He didn't want to let her go. Even to lift off her T-shirt. He might have torn it off her if she hadn't pushed herself away with a laugh.

She was sitting upright, straddled over him. "You aren't going to ruin my favorite T-shirt."

Once she lifted the seen-better-days Georgetown ringer over her head, any response he might have had fell aside. He was too busy trying to contain himself at the feast before his eyes. To hell with the *Playboy* underwear; the bare breasts in front of him were infinitely more enticing.

He couldn't hold back a second longer. He slid his hands up the smooth skin of her stomach to cup the heavy mounds of sweet flesh in his hands.

He gave a low groan of pleasure. He'd died and entered man heaven. "I hope you don't take this the wrong way, sweetheart, but if *Playboy* ever does an annoying-reporter issue, you could have the centerfold."

Just to make sure the annoying-reporter remark didn't get his hands removed, he started to squeeze and rub his thumbs over the perfect pink tips.

She must have liked it because she arched a little deeper into his hands before she replied. "How could I possibly take being objectified to serve as men's spank material wrong? But I will accept the sexist remark in the complimentary way that it was intended."

He feigned offense. "Hey, I read it for the articles. And the pictures are art."

She made a sound that showed how much she believed that. "And I'm not annoying, *sweetheart*. I'm persistent. They aren't the same thing."

He grinned, deciding not to press his luck by arguing, and went back to admiring her flawless creamy skin, which was getting a nice rosy flush from his efforts, the hard pink tips, and the incredible feel of all that very feminine weight in his hands.

She arched and stretched with his ministrations, but as soon as her hips started to lift, he knew playtime was over. He had to be inside her.

He reached for his wallet on the bedside table, found the condom inside, and started to take it out of the package.

She stopped him. "Let me. I want to do it."

He wasn't sure that was a good idea, but he handed it to her anyway.

She took her own sweet time. Kneeling over him.

Playing with him. Stroking him in her hand until he was just the way she wanted him. And then slowly rolling the prophylactic down the turgid beast that she'd just created.

He was ready to jump out of his skin. When she traced the long, bulging muscle along his cock with her finger, he was straining so hard not to come that he started to sweat.

He was in trouble. Real trouble. As in might-not-make-it-past-the-start-line trouble.

"Jesus, Brit, you done yet? You're killing me."

Their eyes met. She looked so damned sexy. Her mouth was still swollen from their kisses, her sparkling blue eyes slitted with arousal, her silky, dark hair hanging around her face as she bent over his prone body. Naked. Yeah, especially the naked part.

He was utterly helpless and at her mercy. And they both knew it.

She gave him a feline smile that definitely boded trouble. "Had enough already? I was looking forward to a little lesson."

From the way she licked her lower lip, he told himself not to ask. But he couldn't help it. "In what?"

"Fellatio."

He made a sound that wasn't half as tortured as he felt. Just the thought of her mouth on him made him pulse a little. Okay, a lot.

But as good as that sounded, he wouldn't last a minute. And he was determined to make it last longer than that this time. "Rain check?"

She arched a brow. "You so sure there will be a round three?"

He didn't like that. And he was done with messing around. Before she knew what was happening, he flipped her around under him.

She let out a startled gasp as he pinned her. The tables had been turned. She was at his mercy now. But if the grin on her face was any indication, she didn't seem to mind the change in leadership positions.

SEAL training came in handy in more ways than one.

"You saying there won't be?" he asked.

"I'm not the one with all the qualms."

"Yeah, well, I'm not feeling those so much anymore." He should be, but he wasn't. He was all in—all of him.

"Good. Then I'm looking forward to my lesson."

"So am I," he said before his mouth closed over hers again.

No more talking. Although he had to admit he kind of liked it. He'd never talked so freely—so effortlessly—with someone in the middle of sex before.

Hell, the extent of his sex talk had been, "How does that feel? Do you like that?" That kind of thing. He didn't do conversations when he was turned on—especially when he was Brittany-level turned on.

Except that apparently he did. It made it more . . . He didn't know. Fun maybe?

That was part of it, but not all of it. He didn't quite know how to explain it, but it was different. It was a level of closeness he'd never experienced before.

It was easy, comfortable, and natural, yet at the same time, whenever he touched her—or she touched him—the intensity of sensation was both fierce and powerful.

It didn't make a lot of sense. But he wasn't going to give it much thought right now—not when he had more important things on his mind.

He slid his hand down to find the slick opening between her legs. She gave a sexy little moan as his finger—and then fingers—slipped inside of her, stroking . . . probing . . . gently stretching.

He raised his chest enough to watch her face as he pleasured her. But too soon her gasps and fluttered eyelids became more than he could take. He had to be inside her.

He fisted his cock to position himself at her entry. He teased them both for a moment with the tip. Circling, caressing, sliding in the plump head just a little.

The sensations were incredible. Body-shuddering incredible.

He didn't know who he was torturing more. He was so turned on that the urge to thrust was almost overwhelming.

But even more overwhelming was the urge to draw it out. He wanted to see each euphoric expression on her face. Each gasp of surprise. Each groan of pleasure as their bodies came together.

He pushed inside slowly. Inch by inch. Holding her gaze the entire time, while biting back his own pleasure of her body gripping him tightly. Oh, so fucking tightly.

He was really sweating now. His body was a furnace of need. The pressure and pounding at the base of his spine intense.

Only when he was fully seated inside her, when he'd pushed as deep as he could go with that final nudge of possession, did he start to move. Sliding in and out with long, slow strokes. Watching as her eyes fluttered, her head fell back, and each sensation played out on her face.

He didn't know how he did it. Usually when he was this turned on—although it had been a long time since he'd been this turned on—he wanted to close his eyes and pound hard and fast.

He did want to do that. But he wanted to see her reactions and building pleasure even more.

And she was digging it. Really digging it. Her hips were lifting to meet his every stroke, her fingertips were pressing into his arms, and her back was arching as if begging him to give her what she wanted. The way she moved with him was so smooth and silky, so sexy, it was almost like a dance. The hottest, most sensual dance he'd ever experienced.

But it was her eyes that drew him in and wouldn't let go. Holding him captive with the proof of just how much she liked what he was doing to her. The long, slow strokes. The circling thrusts. The deep hitch of possession.

She really liked that. He held still, just letting himself fill and beat inside her, as her body found its peak. As she grinded herself against him to a powerful climax.

He kissed her as she came, telling her how sexy she was—how hot she made him—letting the cries and moans of her release flow inside him, as his tongue circled to match the rhythm of her spasms.

He didn't let her come back down. He took her over the peak again, but this time he let himself go along for the ride.

Slowly and purposefully, he increased the pace. He wanted to feel every touch, every caress, every stroke. It built so powerfully and to such heights that when he finally came, it came over him like a freight train. It was as if his whole body had come apart.

He'd never felt anything like it. He was completely shattered. Drained of every last ounce of strength. His bones seemed to have dissolved from his body.

But he'd never felt such a sense of satisfaction. Not even when he'd finished the infamous Hell Week of BUD/S training. He might as well have climbed Mount Everest.

Make that Mount Olympus. Because he'd just seen a god—lots of them.

Somehow he managed not to collapse completely on top of her, but rolled to the side a little so she was only half under him.

Her eyes fluttered open to meet his. They stared at each other for a long moment without saying anything. He wasn't sure what to say. *Wow? Shit?* Both somehow seemed appropriate.

Because even as he was aware that he'd just had the most incredible sexual experience of his life, he was also aware that it was different. And he wasn't sure what that meant. If it meant anything.

But there was something in his chest. A wave of tenderness that almost humbled him.

He reached out, ostensibly to sweep a lock of hair from her forehead, but he really just needed to touch her. To let his thumb caress the soft skin of her brow. And look into her eyes to make sure she was okay. She'd been more upset than he'd expected earlier. Her feelings for him weren't as over as she'd made him believe. He was happier about that than he should be, knowing that it would definitely complicate things. This.

"Hey," he finally said, his voice oddly thick.

His blood had stopped pounding every place but in his chest. That was still beating hard and heavy.

"Hey," she repeated with a tentative smile. She searched his face for something. "Second thoughts?"

He shook his head. "No."

He wished he could say he regretted it, but he didn't. He hadn't intended to end up in bed with her again, any more than he'd intended to spill his guts earlier—they both just sort of happened.

No, regret wasn't quite what came to mind. Hot, insane, blow his fucking mind? That was closer. But it still wasn't all of it. There was something more that he was feeling. Something strong and possessive. Something that made him want to tell her things that he'd never told anyone else in his life. Something he wasn't sure he liked. He liked to keep things light and fun. Brittany was fun, but nothing about how he was feeling right now was light.

Maybe she understood more than he wanted and took pity on him. When he followed his no with a "You?" she shook her head.

"No," she said. "But I think you might be able to wear that red cape after all. That was real superhero stuff right there, John."

He laughed, grateful for the turn back to light. "Keep talking like that and I'll be strutting around here with my chest thrust out."

She rolled her eyes. "Like you don't already?" She pushed him off her. "I knew I shouldn't have said anything. Now you'll be impossible—more impossible," she corrected herself.

There wasn't much room in the twin bed, so he got out to push the two beds together and tossed the condom in the wastebasket while he was at it. She didn't object when he slid down beside her and tucked her in against his chest.

Might as well save time. He was pretty sure she'd end up wrapped in his arms anyway.

Seventeen

Kate missed Percy's big party.

After Colt's proclamation about Rear Admiral Morrison's suicide, she'd been too upset. Had their meeting with the rear admiral sent him over the edge? Was his suicide an admission of guilt? Who else knew? Did this mean Scott and the others were in the clear and could come out of hiding?

She voiced all but the last question to Colt. He didn't know, but they spent the next few hours trying to find out, using both her connections and his.

They hadn't come up with much more than they'd already had. Colt learned that the investigation was being kept quiet so far—the circumstances seemed cut-and-dried. She found out that the rear admiral had cleared out the last of his bank accounts a few days earlier, but she still hadn't been able to locate any accounts that were in the green. By her calculations he was more than two hundred grand in the hole. That gorgeous home they'd visited on the golf course? Mortgaged to the hilt and purchased at the height of the market about five years ago. If he'd tried to sell the property, they'd have been underwater.

Colt left before Percy got home from the party, which was a good thing, as Percy was furious enough. Seeing Colt would have made that stiff-upper-lip facade crack even more.

She'd embarrassed Percy by not showing up and more so by not calling with an explanation. Did she realize how that looked?

Kate could explain the first but not the latter. She could have called; she just hadn't thought of it.

Which in a way was worse.

He'd been worried. Although not worried enough, she realized, to call her.

They'd argued. Did she understand his position and the duties that she was agreeing to as his wife?

Of course she did. But that didn't mean those duties would take precedence over her own work.

When Percy hadn't agreed, she'd been floored. Apparently, he thought they did take precedence.

When he decided to sleep on the couch downstairs, Kate didn't object.

Things had been better in the morning—he'd apologized for losing his temper—but when he left for work, he told her that if she was having second thoughts about their marriage she needed to be honest with him—and herself.

She knew he was right. She'd fought long and hard to get over her heartbreak with Colt, and she desperately wanted to make her relationship with Percy work. Maybe a little too desperately. Had she worked *too* hard? Percy was a good man. In so many ways he was everything Colt wasn't—kind, loving, respectful of her job and life. She cared about him deeply, but . . .

There shouldn't be a "but."

Kate pushed the errant thought away. She couldn't think about it right now—not with Hurricane Colt confusing her. She was meeting him first thing the next morning to plan out their course of action. If Mrs. Morrison alerted the police to their visit, it wouldn't be long before the investigators came knocking and wanted to know why they'd met with the rear admiral hours before he'd killed himself. They needed to come up with a plausible explanation and get their story straight.

Fortunately, he'd agreed to put off his trip to Russia until everything was sorted out.

But today she had to clear her tracks. She'd gotten rid of all the surveillance programs she'd had on the rear admiral's electronics last night, but she wanted to make sure she got rid of any trail at work, too. She was well aware of the fact that what she was doing might be construed as illegal—destroying evidence—but as her surveillance had been unsanctioned, that ship had probably already sailed. Besides, protecting Scott came first.

To that end, she spent most of the afternoon and into the night looking into the reporter and her source at the DoD. Kate needed only half that time, and a glance at the pool car logbook, to connect the dots.

She saw the name of the woman who'd requested the car and driver on the date in question and couldn't believe her eyes. Nor did she believe in coincidences.

When she walked into the coffee shop the next morning after only a few hours of sleep, Colt must have realized she was upset. He stood and reached for her as if he still had a right to touch her without realizing what he was doing. As soon as he did, he dropped his hand.

The tightening in her chest wasn't as easily disposed of. That protective look, the concern, the I'll-make-all-your-troubles-go-away certainty had always taken the edge off what was bothering her. It had made her feel as if they were a team. She'd counted on him in a way she'd never allowed herself to count on anyone before.

She'd forgotten how much she missed that. But she couldn't let herself get confused. He'd shown her who he was; she had to believe him.

"What's wrong?" he asked. "What did you find out?"

"I'm not sure," she said. "But we need to go see my godfather."

The last place Colt wanted to go was Castle Murray—or whatever the hell the general's "estate" was called. But he understood Kate's insistence when she explained what she'd found: the general's longtime assistant had requested a car on the same night Brittany Blake had met with her "source."

What he hadn't understood was Kate's reaction to his question about how she'd learned of the reporter's source at all. It had clearly jellied her. She'd claimed that she and Brittany had crossed paths when she and Colt were married and become friends. But to Colt's knowledge, Blake and his sister had been estranged for a long time.

He was almost certain Kate was lying to him.

But the question of why would have to wait. Jeeves, or whatever the hell the butler's name was, welcomed Kate at the door with a smile and a fond kiss on the cheek. He acknowledged Colt with a pursed mouth and a slight inhaling of his nostrils, as if something unpleasant had just been stuck under his oversized nose. Unlike the last time Colt was here, they were admitted to the inner sanctum of the general's private office immediately.

"My dear!" Murray said, rising from his seat behind the desk. He came around to give Kate a big hug. "What a pleasant surprise."

The last was said with a sharp glance toward Colt. Clearly it was a surprise to see him as well, but not a pleasant one. Colt was supposed to be in Russia. And the general probably wasn't happy to see him with Kate, either.

But the old guy needn't have any worries on that account. Colt and Kate were working together because they had to. Nothing more. If Colt had any regrets about his "karma" dig from the other day, he wasn't going to admit it—even to himself. All he'd done was establish the lines of the playing field.

Whatever unwanted feelings and attraction had been resurrected by being around his ex didn't matter. That grave was buried under six feet of ice. It would take a hell of a lot more than a raging hard-on to chip through it.

Although it was an impressive hard-on.

It was that damned dress. His eyes had nearly popped out of his head when she'd answered the door the night of Percy's party. Kate had never dressed sexy when they'd been married. He probably wouldn't have let her walk out of the house in a dress like that—it would have been ripped off her well before she left the bedroom. The slinky red silk had clung to every slender curve. Her hips. Her ass. Her tits. She might as well have been poured into it. He'd had to move to the opposite side of the room after he'd caught a few too many glimpses of creamy skin in the low-cut gown when she'd leaned forward at the computer.

She wasn't wearing a bra.

He'd always loved her breasts. They weren't big, but they were big enough and perfectly round and firm. Way too firm for a woman of almost thirty-five. But it was the delicate softness of the skin that had always gotten him. It had been fucking unreal. Flawless. Still was from what he could tell.

"Wesson," the general said with a rotting-fish curl of his mouth.

"Sorry for barging in on you like this," Kate said after the general released her. "But it's important."

The general indicated the two chairs opposite his desk for them to sit.

When he'd settled back in the chair behind his desk, Murray said, "What's this about?"

Kate got right to it. "Janet."

He seemed taken aback. "My secretary?" The twenty-first-century term was "executive assistant," but Janet O'Brien had been with the general for so long, she probably had been hired as a secretary. "Did she do something wrong?"

Kate gave him a hard look. "You tell me. Did she pass confidential information to Brittany Blake on her own accord or because you asked her to?"

If the general was surprised by the allegation, he didn't show it. He barely blinked. "On my request," he said. "How did you find out?" He shot an accusing glance to Colt, obviously assuming he was to blame for Kate's involvement.

Maybe he was, although not about this. Colt intended to find out how she'd learned about the reporter's source himself.

"It doesn't matter," Kate said. "What does matter is why you would do such a thing. I thought the government and military wanted to keep Team Nine's mission secret."

"They do," the general admitted.

"But you don't," Colt finished for him. "You want the truth to come out."

Kate had obviously suspected why as well. "This is about TJ, isn't it?" TJ, or Thomas Junior, was the general's son, who'd been shot down by the Russians a few months ago when his plane had "accidentally" veered into Russian airspace. "You couldn't convince President Cartwright to retaliate against Russia for shooting down his plane, so you used the press to do your work for you and try to sway public opinion."

Having clearly spent too much time in the political arena, the general decided to split a few hairs. "The reporter was already on the right track—I just helped her along a little."

"By leaking classified information?" Kate challenged. "If anyone finds out, it could put an end to your career and any hopes you have for the vice presidency."

The general shrugged. "Maybe, maybe not. With all the mudslinging that goes along with political campaigns these days, it's hard to find the line between truth and fiction. And most of my supporters would be in favor of military action against Russia." His expression darkened. "They shouldn't be allowed to get away with what they've done—to my son or Retiarius Platoon. Those boys deserved better. They deserve justice." On that point, Colt actually agreed with him. "Ivanov is probably laughing his ass off. He got away with killing fourteen SEALs and no one is going to say a damned thing—not the Russians or the Americans."

Kate frowned. "Russians?"

Colt knew what he meant. "After the plane was shot down, Ivanov vowed to declare war on the US if there were any more 'incursions.'"

Kate nodded. "I remember. So, it's in Ivanov's interest, too, that the truth not come out. Pride might force him into a war he doesn't want." She gave her godfather a sharp glance. "This is your way of tweaking his nose as well."

The general didn't deny it. "You shouldn't have involved her in this," he said to Colt.

"I wouldn't have needed to if I'd thought you'd agree to see me without her help."

Kate obviously didn't appreciate being talked over. "*She* is sitting right here and didn't need permission from either of you. I want to find out what happened to Scott and the rest of Retiarius, too."

The general frowned and looked between the two of them, obviously taking note of Colt's reaction at the mention of the other man.

"Scott?" the general asked. "You mean Lieutenant Commander Taylor? I didn't realize you knew him."

"Oh, she knew him really well." Colt couldn't resist adding with more than a snide undertone, "She and Taylor were *very* close—wouldn't you say, Kate?"

Kate didn't flinch. There wasn't a tinge of a guilty flush on any part of her cheeks. She turned to look at Colt, her expression perfectly composed. "Yes, we were. He was there for me when my husband wasn't."

Turned out, Colt was the one who flinched. He didn't flush with guilt, but he might have felt a prick of it along with the knife that slid right between his ribs.

Guess she wasn't denying it anymore. Why did he suddenly feel sick? That shit was dead and buried. But she was twisting him up in all kinds of angry knots again, and he didn't like it. For three years he hadn't felt anything. He liked being impenetrable. It was the way he'd been before he met her.

Turning back to her godfather, Kate added, "We found out we had a lot in common. My father and his mother used to summer near each other on the Cape."

Colt hadn't known that. But he wasn't surprised. Taylor's blood was as blue as Kate's. In other words, the type "to summer." He didn't know much about Taylor's family history other than that they'd been loaded.

"I'm sorry," the general said to Kate, sounding as if he meant it. "I didn't realize that. But I would rather you weren't involved. It could be dangerous. There are a lot of people who might not want the truth to come out."

"If you knew that, then why did you involve Brittany Blake? You could have made her a target."

"She made herself a target. She wasn't going away—with or without my help."

"Not like the woman in Iowa," Colt said, watching the general's reaction.

But it was Kate who looked at him sharply. "The woman who claimed one of the missing SEALs got her pregnant?"

Clearly she thought he'd been holding out on her.

Maybe he had, but he'd only just seen the bank statement, and it hadn't been foremost on his mind after the rear admiral's suicide. Colt nodded. "I assumed the government paid her off to keep her quiet."

If the general knew about it, he wasn't giving anything away. "It wouldn't surprise me. She was creating a ruckus like the reporter, but why do you think she was paid off?"

"Five thousand dollars landed in her bank account a few days ago, and she's taken down her social media posts."

"That's not much of a payoff," Kate said.

"Maybe not for you," Colt said. "But it was for her."

Colt hadn't meant it as a dig, but he could see she'd taken it that way. But when he'd been growing up, five thousand would have seemed like a fortune.

"Any idea where the money came from?" the general asked.

"Not yet," Colt said.

Seeing Kate's increasingly annoyed expression, he was glad when the general asked, "Have you found out anything else about what happened to Retiarius? Any proof that the missile the Russians claimed was a test was actually directed at them?"

Colt exchanged a glance with Kate. Apparently the silent communication thing was still intact, as she understood that he would leave what they shared up to her.

"Not directly," Kate said. "But we thought we might have a lead in how the mission was compromised."

"You mean how the platoon was detected by the Russians?" the general asked.

Kate shook her head. "I don't think they were detected."

Murray understood what she meant right away. "You think they were betrayed?"

"You don't sound surprised," Colt said.

The general gave him a hard, don't-piss-me-off glare. "I've been in this business too long to not have considered every angle, including espionage or an inside job from one of our own." He turned back to Kate. "What did you find?"

"I assume you've heard about Rear Admiral Morrison's death?" Kate said gently, aware that the two men were friends.

He nodded somberly. "I was informed yesterday." Realizing where she was going, he said adamantly, "His suicide had nothing to do with this."

"He was in debt," Colt said. "Lots of debt."

Murray's glare in his direction grew darker. "I know."

"You did?" Kate asked, clearly surprised.

"A few people in command have been aware of his gambling problem for some time. Measures were taken."

Colt knew what that meant. Morrison would have been watched and probably compartmentalized. Meaning he wouldn't have been given sensitive information until it was need-to-know. Probably at the last minute for this op.

Kate must have realized what it meant as well and couldn't hide her relief. Colt knew the timing of their visit to Morrison had been weighing on her. They hadn't put a gun to his head; he'd done that on his own. But she clearly hadn't seen it that way.

It was a good thing she didn't do fieldwork. Guilt didn't fit into the job description.

"If you were thinking that he sold the platoon out for money, you are way off base," the general said. "Ron killed himself because he was more than two hundred grand in the hole and just lost the only money he had left in the bank on a 'can't miss' bet that—no surprise—missed."

"We went to see him that afternoon," Kate said. "To question him about Retiarius."

The general swore. "You should have told me." He gave Colt a look that told him whom he blamed. "The police will want to talk to you, but I'll see what I can do to put them off for a while."

Something is going on here, Colt thought. The wily bastard knew more than he was saying. Not that Colt blamed him. He wouldn't share more than he had to with the general—or anyone, for that matter.

"If Morrison didn't do it, then who did?" Colt asked him.

"I don't know."

Colt kept him pinned with his gaze. "But you suspect someone."

The general shrugged. "It's nothing I can prove."

He had their attention.

"But . . . ?" Kate prompted.

"But when I was going through the list of people who might have had access to the classified information, one name stuck out."

"Why?" Colt asked.

"Because she was killed in a car crash right after the platoon went missing." Colt didn't want to turn his eyes from the general, but Kate seemed to have gone rigid beside him. "I knew her and liked her. She worked for the Deputy Secretary of Defense, but he relied on her as if it were the other way around. I wondered whether they were having an affair. She was an extremely beautiful woman."

Colt looked at Kate, who'd gone strangely mute. He frowned. She also looked a little pale.

"You are talking about Natalie Andersson," he said to the general. Colt had met her a few times. Murray was

right. She'd been a stunning woman. He'd heard about
her death.

"Yes, but that wasn't the name she was born with." The
general paused. "Her real name was Natalya Petrova."

Kate felt ill. What her godfather was insinuating couldn't
be right.

Was it possible that the woman Scott had secretly been
dating, who'd warned the platoon of the danger, was a
Russian spy? Why would she have warned Scott if she'd
been spying on him?

According to her godfather, Natalie had been adopted
from Russia when she was a child. Her adoptive parents—
from Minnesota—had given her their last name and
changed her name to the more American-friendly Natalie. But other than the accident and her Russian birth, the
general hadn't been able to find anything incriminating.
Nothing to support that she was some kind of a twenty-
plus-year Russian sleeper agent.

It was ludicrous. That kind of stuff only happened in
movies and novels. Russian birth didn't make someone a
spy. There were presumably thousands of kids adopted
from Russia—were they all suspect? Of course not. But
Kate had been CIA too long. Coincidences were never
good. And there was no question that Natalie had had
access to sensitive information about the mission. She'd
warned the platoon, after all.

Kate couldn't wait to get home to see what she could
find out. But first she needed to talk to Scott. As much as
she would prefer to tell him after she'd cleared Natalie of
any wrongdoing, Kate needed to know everything she
could about the woman he'd been seeing in secret.

But she already knew that he wasn't going to like what
she had to say.

Kate didn't realize how much her thoughts were showing on her face—or how closely Colt was watching her.

The moment they got into the car, he turned to her.
"What's wrong?"

"Nothing."

"Bullshit."

She looked at him. "Can you just take me home?"

"I would, but I don't have the keys. You drove."

Her face heated as she realized she'd sat in the passenger seat. He'd always driven when they were married,
and she'd unconsciously slipped into their old roles. But
as they'd met close to his hotel, they'd taken her car from
the coffee shop.

"It's keyless," she said. "The engine will start as long
as the keys are in my purse."

Of course, she knew he wouldn't make it that easy. He
didn't make any move to start the car. "Tell me why the
mention of Natalie made you so upset." He paused. "Did
you know her, too?"

She heard the note of sarcasm and understood the reference. Clearly he hadn't bought her explanation for how
she'd come upon the information for Brittany Blake's
source. She should have known better than to try to lie
to him, but he'd caught her off guard. She should have
just told him what she told him now. "It's none of your
business."

"If you want me to help you figure this out, you need
to tell me everything."

"Just like you tell me everything? What about the
woman in Iowa? Seems as if you forgot to mention her."

"I just found out about that, and I didn't think it was
important."

"Right," she said. Did he think she would believe
that? "You've never trusted me, Colt. Why would you
start now?"

"Did I have reason to?"

It was hard to believe anyone's eyes could get that hard and glittery. But she met the icy accusation unblinkingly. She knew it wasn't really a question, but she answered anyway. "Yes, you actually did."

Colt had always hidden his emotions well, but she could detect the signs of his anger in the tightening of his mouth and the flare of his eyes. His hands were gripping the steering wheel so hard she thought he might pull it off. "You would say that even now? After what you fucking did?"

She didn't say anything. She just stared at him. Stared at the darkly handsome features of the man she'd thought she would love forever. And just for an instant, all the feelings, all the longing, came rushing back in a hot tidal wave of emotion.

Why? She wanted to scream at him. Why had he done this to them? Why had he pushed her away? Why had he been so ready to believe the worst?

She would never have been with another man. Colt had laid claim to her body as thoroughly as he had her heart. She'd never been so fiercely attracted to anyone. Just looking at him or standing close to him used to turn her into a syrupy mess.

Even now the effects of being so close to him in the car were making themselves felt. The unwelcome prickle of awareness that sent a buzz of warmth along her skin and a pulse quickening through her heart. One gasp of air and she could breathe him in. The spicy masculine scent that had been as familiar to her as her own perfume. She could almost taste the mint of his toothpaste. Feel the grit of his stubble on her skin as he kissed her. *Ravished* her like some marauding medieval knight.

That was him: medieval. Dangerous, merciless, and utterly unforgiving. Maybe a little primitive in his emotions, but also sexy as hell in a fiercely masculine way.

Humiliated, she wanted to turn away. But she couldn't.

Because in that moment of awareness, she could see that he felt it, too. That the draw was just as powerful and overwhelming for him. It had always been like that between them—passion that was every bit as fierce, explosive, and dangerous as he was, coming out of nowhere to hit her with the force of a . . . hurricane.

She could also see that he didn't like it any better than she did.

But he was going to act on it.

His hand slipped around to grip the back of her neck and pull her toward him. Every hair prickled, and she shuddered at the rough but achingly familiar feel of his workingman hand on her skin. How could she remember after so long? How could her body flood and pulse with yearning with one touch?

Three years of hatred—of telling herself she was over him—dissolved in an instant.

But only for an instant. When his mouth dipped to hers, when he was only seconds away from touching his lips to hers, the memories returned. The pain of heartbreak. The feeling that she would never know another moment of happiness. The deep depression of losing a child, nearly dying, and having the man she'd given her heart to turn to her not with compassion and love but with cruelty and abandonment.

She couldn't do this. She couldn't let Hurricane Colt back into her life.

"No!" She put her hand on his chest and pushed him— or herself—away. "I'm engaged to someone else, for God's sake!"

She didn't know whether she was reminding him or herself. She hadn't thought of Percy until that moment. It was self-preservation and not her fiancé that had kept her from falling into her ex-husband's arms again.

What that said, she didn't want to think about right now.

He smirked as if the rejection didn't mean anything to him—which it probably didn't. She wasn't fool enough to think this was about anything other than physical attraction for him. He saw opportunity and homed in for the kill. Just like any predator.

But he wouldn't just let it go. "Still like slumming it, eh, Kiki?"

The nickname was like a jolt of pain applied directly under her skin. She hated that he would use it now—like this. When he was being cruel, not holding her in his arms as if he would love her forever.

"Not anymore," she said softly. "I outgrew mean and ugly." She looked back up into those razor-sharp eyes that could be so blind. "Right after you left me in the hospital to mourn the death of our daughter alone."

He barely flinched. But she could see the tiny lines of witness around his mouth as his jaw tensed. "How do you know it was a girl? You were only a few months pregnant."

She hadn't meant to say "daughter." She didn't owe him the explanation that he'd never asked for. He'd just assumed the worst and reacted in his scorched-earth way, which left no room for mistakes or regrets.

She looked away, staring out the car window at the circular flagstone driveway of Blairhaven. She wanted to lie, knowing it would be easier. But maybe her ex-husband deserved to suffer a few pangs of regret. "I was almost five months pregnant."

When his eyes flickered, she knew he'd done the math. Scott had been in Hawaii during that time, and Colt had been with her in DC.

He might have paled a little. It was hard to tell in the car. "The nurse said you were only a few months along."

"I have no idea what the nurse said, but if you had asked me or the doctor rather than storming in there, threatening to kill Scott, you would have seen that I was in my nineteenth week." She already regretted saying anything. She didn't want to talk about this now. Ever. "Can we go now?"

"God, Kate . . . I . . ."

The buzz of her cellphone cut off whatever he was going to say. She reached down to pull it out of her bag. Seeing the "unknown caller" on the screen, she felt a wave of relief.

Not only did she want to talk to him, but Scott's was exactly the calming voice she needed to hear right now. She opened the car door and got out as she answered, closing it behind her to prevent Colt from overhearing anything.

But she wasn't outside for long. The call was short and sweet.

"I'm here," Scott said. "How soon can I see you?"

He was here? Kate's excitement to see him in person was only tempered by the information she would have to impart. "Give me an hour. Tell me where you are."

Thankfully, Colt didn't argue when she got back in the car and told him that something had come up at work and she needed to get to Langley. He tried to bring up her pregnancy again, but she cut him off. "What does it matter, Colt? It's dead and buried."

Just like the child he'd never wanted.

Eighteen

Brittany was still half-asleep when the door closed. The click, and the resounding jolt of her heart with it, brought her to full awareness. John had left her alone in bed, and it was too reminiscent of a bad one-night stand where the guy can't wait to slink away for her not to feel a pang of uncertainty.

She sat up and looked around. Her heart fell again when she didn't see any kind of note.

She told herself not to be ridiculous. He wasn't running away.

At least she didn't think he was. But had last night freaked him out even more than she thought?

God, she wasn't going to do this. She wasn't going to overreact or make too much out of everything he did, including what had happened last night. It was just sex.

The most incredible, tender, passionate, sweet, romantic sex she'd ever had in her life, but still just sex.

Except that it wasn't. She knew that, and if the concerned look on John's face afterward was any indication, he knew it, too. Last night had meant something.

What, she didn't know. She wasn't sure of her own

feelings, let alone his. But this time she wasn't going to make the mistake of trying to pin him down and force something from him that he wasn't ready to admit—to her or to himself.

She could do "take it as it goes." She would hone her inner dude and not make too much out of the fact that he was opening up to her in a way that she was pretty damned sure he'd never opened up to anyone before, that he'd wanted to hook up with someone else but couldn't, and that when she'd had her little freak-out—okay, major freak-out—he'd handled her so sweetly and gently before and after making love to her.

Yes, making love. It wasn't just sex or the fucking he'd declared he'd wanted. You didn't stare into someone's eyes with that kind of intensity—with that kind of emotion—while slowly bringing them to the height of passion (twice!), conveying importance and significance with every stroke . . . did you?

Oh my God, Brittany, put up the mental stop sign already! Clearly, she was going way overboard on the analysis. With the vow she'd made only seconds ago to take it as it goes already in jeopardy, Brittany forced herself to get up—ignoring the soreness in places she shouldn't be thinking about—and gathered all her stuff before slipping into the bathroom.

She'd take advantage of John's morning-after abandonment—*absence*—and try to get a little work done before taking a shower. She wanted a bath but knew that soaking in the warm water would be too relaxing and her mind would likely wander back to last night, where she didn't want it to go.

No, better to focus on work and the job she needed to keep. Aside from finding out what happened to her brother—which was a big aside—she didn't want to blow the opportunity she wasn't sure she'd ever get again to be an investigative journalist. She was desperate and not too proud to admit it.

She tried working on her article but didn't get very far—she didn't have much to add. She was tempted to turn on the Wi-Fi on her computer for a minute to send an e-mail to Mac, letting her know what was going on and asking if she'd found out anything, but John's paranoia had spread to her.

She'd go the Internet café route just to be safe. After quickly showering, Brittany put on her clothes and makeup and was sitting on the bed tying her shoes when the door opened and John walked back into the room, sucking all the air right out of her lungs along with the room.

He took in her clothes, shoes, and messenger bag, which was beside her on the bed, with a glance and frowned. "Going somewhere?"

With her own quick glance at him, she took in the coffee carrier with two drinks in his left hand and the bag of food tucked under the same arm. She felt an unmistakable surge in her chest. He hadn't run away; he'd left to get breakfast. A heap of Danish pastries if the size and heavenly smell emanating from the bag was any indication.

"I have a few things I need to get done for work," she said, trying not to feel as if *she* had been the one running away.

His frown deepened as he set down the food on the hotel room bureau. Pulling one of the drinks from the holder and handing it to her, he said, "Work can wait. You need to eat."

Feeling guilty for thinking he was trying to get away from her when all he'd done was go get them breakfast, which was actually really sweet, Brittany took the latte and the pastry that followed.

She took one bite of the tender cinnamon-flavored concoction with sugary icing and tried not to groan. "God, these are delicious. I guess the Danes are famous for their pastry for a reason. I'd be eight hundred pounds if I lived here."

He grinned. "I doubt it. With the amount of crap you and your teenage-boy metabolism demolish, I think you'd be just fine." He gave her one of those long, hot looks that made her insides quiver. "Very fine."

She tried not to blush at the reminder of how much he liked her body. She shrugged. "I don't like to cook, and not all of us need to be a finely honed weapon of war."

"Finely honed, huh?" He popped the last of the second pastry into his mouth. "Guess you'll have to finish the last one. I wouldn't want to disappoint you."

He said it jokingly, but there was something in his eye that made her wonder if he might be thinking about last night. But how could he need any reassurance about that?

Right. As if John Donovan needed reassurance about anything.

Still, their eyes met, and she found herself saying, "'Disappointment' is the last word I would use."

The slow, broad smile that spread across his obscenely good-looking face made her wonder if she'd been right. He looked happy. Really happy.

"Finish your breakfast," he said. "I have a surprise for you."

She almost said "What?" before remembering her plans. "It will have to hold until I get back. There are some things I need to take care of first."

"I'm sure they can wait a day or two."

She didn't like his dismissiveness; but telling herself not to be oversensitive, she smiled. "Not if I want to have a job when I get back. I need to get in touch with my editor and tell him what's been going on."

And what progress she'd made on her article, as well

as get in touch with Mac. But she wasn't going to tell John about either of those, so he couldn't object.

He did anyway. "I don't think that's a good idea—not without knowing how sophisticated these guys are and how they were tracking you. Let's wait a few days, and—"

"No," she said, mentally putting her foot down for the first time since they'd arrived. "I'm not going to let you distract me. Whatever risk there is to someone tracking all the e-mails at work has to be small and . . ."

Her voice fell off. *Distract me.* Suspicion flooded through her in a horrifying deluge.

No. That wasn't what he'd been doing.

Was it?

Her eyes shot to his, catching them just as his gaze shifted. But not before she saw the flicker of guilt that popped the bubble of hope in her chest like a pin on an overstretched balloon.

"Oh my God, that's it, isn't it? That's what all this is about. You've been giving me the full-court John Donovan press to keep me from writing any articles."

And she'd fallen for it hook, line, and sinker.

God, did she have idiot written on her forehead? It sure as hell felt like it.

John took one look at her expression and knew he'd better explain or this conversation was going to go downhill fast. Very fast.

It wasn't like that.

He winced. Or not exactly like that.

"What happened between us has nothing to do with that."

So maybe that wasn't the best thinking on his feet that he'd ever done because she took his words as an admission.

She stood up to face him, her expression incredulous. "So, you admit it? You were trying to distract me?"

He held her by the shoulders, trying to get her to calm down and listen before she started drawing all sorts of wrong conclusions. "I don't want you to write any articles about this—you know that. And I may have been trying to keep you busy, but with sightseeing, Brit. Not with anything else."

She drew back, stunned—or maybe the better word was "struck." Obviously, she wasn't seeing the distinction. Or if she was, she wasn't buying it.

"So, the traipsing around town together was all an act, but not the seduction part—is that it?" She put her hands on his chest and pushed out of his hold. "God, you are such an asshole! This is a new low—even for you, John."

Christ, wasn't she listening to what he was saying? He gritted his teeth, trying to stay calm. It wasn't easy. She made him so damned . . . irritated. "I didn't seduce you, Brit."

She sneered with disgust, but he wasn't sure whether it was at him or herself. "No, of course you didn't. You didn't have to, did you? I came to your bed willingly enough. But it was all a seduction, wasn't it? You pretended to want to be with me and made me care about you again."

Given how angry she was with him, he shouldn't be so happy to hear it aloud. "I care about you, too. You know that. And just because I may have had more than one reason doesn't mean I didn't want to spend time with you or that I wasn't having fun. I did and was."

His words—which were as much of an admission as he'd ever made—seemed not to have had any impact. She had that look of impatience. The kind where she was probably mentally crossing her arms and tapping her toes.

"I'm supposed to believe that?"

Her sarcasm brought out a flare of his own temper.

"Yes, you are. And if you had been reasonable about this in the first place, none of it would have been necessary."

The incredulous look was back. "What is that supposed to mean?"

"It means that *reasonable* people might stop doing something when it is putting them in danger."

She arched a delicate eyebrow. "Is that what you do?"

He clenched his jaw with frustration. He should have seen that one coming; he'd pretty much said the same thing to the LC. But it was one thing to be pro-feminism with other women and another when it was his woman, damn it.

When he didn't respond right away, she added, "And how do I know you weren't exaggerating the danger just to get me out of Vaernes and keep me from following up with Nils's friend? Is that for my own good, too?"

"That guy in the parking lot wasn't an exaggeration. If I hadn't shown up when I did, we wouldn't be having this conversation."

"Maybe, maybe not. But unlike you, I'm not going to live in hiding forever. I'm going home."

"What do you mean, you are going home?" Actually, it was pretty obvious what she meant. And the finality of her tone sent alarm, if not something distinctly resembling panic, flickering through him. "You can't go home yet."

"Why not?"

"It might not be safe."

"I'll take precautions."

There weren't any precautions she could take that would make him okay with her leaving. "No, you won't. You aren't going anywhere."

Yep, definitely not thinking well on his feet today. He knew it was the wrong thing to say even before she gave him a long, hard look.

"Are you giving me an *order*?"

"Yes!" he shouted angrily.

"Nice try, John. But you don't have any authority over me."

He took a step toward her, tempted to prove just what kind of authority he did have. But as he was pretty sure that would only make him the subject of more ridiculous accusations afterward, he restrained himself—barely. But he might have to remind himself a few times why he couldn't just tie her up. Like to the bed.

He forced his rising blood pressure back down and clenched his fists at his sides instead of touching her.

He could be rational even if she couldn't. "I'm asking you to trust me. Give me a few more days. If we don't find something out by then, you can go."

She shook her head. "You had your few days. And asking me to trust you when you don't trust me about anything isn't exactly fair."

"What do you want from me?"

"A little honesty to start."

"I'm being honest with you. You're dead wrong if you think anything about last night had to do with distracting you."

She held his gaze for long enough to believe him. "Fine. I believe you. But it doesn't change anything. It's been a nice few days, but I need to get back to the real world—and my job."

He heard the determination in her voice and knew she wasn't going to be easily dissuaded. Whatever trust she'd had in him had obviously reached its limit with the sight-seeing/distraction revelation.

How could he make her understand that he wasn't ex-aggerating the potential danger?

She turned, grabbed her duffel bag, and started throwing things into it. "Wait," he said. "Hear me out first. If you still want to go after hearing what I have to say, I'll take you to the airport myself."

She paused long enough to turn to look at him. He

waved to the recently vacated edge of the bed where she'd been sitting previously.

She must have heard something in his voice because she actually did as he requested and sat.

This went against every bone in his body—not to mention direct orders. The LC was going to be pissed when he found out. But John had his back up against the wall. He had to make her see the danger and restore some of her eroded trust in him. "You want me to trust you? Well, I'm about to do that. But you have to promise me that you won't repeat or print one word of what I'm about to tell you."

Her eyes widened a little, obviously guessing where this was going. She nodded. "I promise."

He gave her a sharp nod back. "Good. I'm going to hold you to that."

Nineteen

Brittany sat on the bed waiting while John paced back and forth a few times, obviously struggling with what to say.

This better be good and not another one of his distracting tactics.

Though her pride wasn't stinging quite as hard as it had been a few minutes ago—she was inclined to believe him about last night (she didn't think he was *that* good of an actor)—she still couldn't believe that she hadn't guessed what he was up to. She'd been having too much fun and assumed he was as well. He'd certainly seemed to be.

Had it all been an act?

She didn't know, but it didn't matter anymore. Now that she knew what this little seemingly romantic getaway to Copenhagen was all about, she wasn't going to let him put her off any longer.

Not without a good reason.

She was just glad she hadn't let herself get carried away after last night with all kinds of silly ideas. It was her pride that had been hurt, that was all. The swift kick in the gut, the hot tightness in her chest, and the crashing feeling of disappointment hadn't lasted longer than a few moments.

A couple minutes at most.

Damn it, she had to get out of there and away from him or she was going to be in real trouble.

John finally stopped pacing and took a position opposite her, leaning back on the bureau to look at her. "Other than the men who made it out of there like me, there is only one other person who knows about this. One, Brittany, so I hope you realize the level of trust I'm putting in you."

She nodded, her pulse quickening a little. She was excited, anxious, and nervous all at the same time. She desperately wanted to know what had happened to her brother, but at the same time feared what she might hear.

"You were right. We were on a mission to Russia, searching for proof of a doomsday device." A doomsday device? Was he kidding? He must have read her skepticism. "I know, I know. Iraq WMDs all over again. But we had actionable intelligence this time—good intel. Given the recent hostilities with Russia, including our plane being 'accidentally' shot down, I don't have to tell you that this was a highly classified operation. Literally a handful of people beyond the platoon knew about it and one of those was the president."

Though she'd suspected as much, confirmation was still a shock—and the implications. An illegal covert mission to—and invasion of—a country we were already teetering on the precipice of war with? Brittany's mind was reeling with dozens of questions, but she put a mental zipper on her lips, not wanting to interrupt him.

"The satellite pictures you saw with the explosion were taken in the area of an old gulag we had been reconnoitering. We'd split off into two teams not long after arriving to check out two buildings in the camp. My team was delayed in the yard. We'd lost communications, but one of our officers was able to retrieve a message—a warning that the Russians knew we were there. I was on point, so I didn't know what was going on at the time. A couple of our guys tried to let the other team know, but it was too late. The camp was destroyed by two thermobaric missiles."

She gasped, feeling tears spring to her eyes. "Oh my God!"

She knew the destructive power of those kinds of missiles. No one in those buildings would have had a chance.

Poor Brandon.

John gave her a long look, as if he knew exactly what she was thinking. "Eight men were killed. The entire team that was already in the building and one member of our team, who died trying to warn them. But without that message, there would have been no survivors."

"Who sent the message?"

"I'm not sure." The LC hadn't confided the person's name when he'd told John what had happened. "But they won't be of any help."

"Why not?"

"They're dead."

Brittany gasped again, her eyes widening as she grasped the implications.

He held her gaze with a fierce intensity. "You can see why I said it was dangerous. Whoever it was that leaked the information about our mission is obviously taking care of loose ends. Right now no one except you and the person who is helping us knows there were any survivors. It's safer for us that way, and until we figure out who was responsible for the Russians knowing we were coming, we have to stay dead."

Even though he hadn't said it, Brittany immediately grasped the implications. "You think the information could have come from the inside?"

John's mouth fell in a grim line. "It's one possibility. Not the only one."

Brittany finished for him. "But it's the one you think is most likely."

He didn't say anything, which she took as agreement. She was glad she was sitting down because her mind was reeling.

This was far bigger than anything she'd imagined.

The Russians taking out half a platoon of Navy SEALs on a covert op that probably violated scores of treaties and international laws was huge enough, but if the information that had led to their deaths had been leaked from the inside? That was Watergate, Iran Contragate, name-your-favorite-gate huge. She'd probably be nominated for a Pulitzer if she broke this story.

And now that she knew the truth—or some of it—she was even more convinced it was a story that needed to be told. If the government was running illegal operations in America's name, they needed to be held accountable for those actions. No wonder they didn't want anyone to know what had happened.

And once again someone she loved had been caught up in the cross fire of the government trying to protect its interests at the expense of law and justice.

But even as she wrestled with all the implications, she understood why John had been so furious when she'd tracked him down. She believed him about the danger and certainly didn't want to do anything to see him or anyone else killed.

"Who would have done such a thing?" she finally asked.

"I have no idea, but people are looking into it."

"Who?"

"I can't tell you that. I shouldn't have even told you what I did, and I'm not going to say anything that could get someone else killed."

She guessed she could understand that. For now. "Do these people have any leads?"

"They are looking in a few directions."

"In other words, no."

He didn't say anything.

"You can't stay in hiding forever, John. The ski-bum life is going to get old after a while."

She suspected it was already. He was a Navy SEAL, and as much as he projected the hang-loose, beach-boy vibe, that wasn't him. She knew that about him now. He thrived on challenge.

"I won't have to. We have someone helping us now. It won't be much longer."

Was he trying to convince her or himself? He was living on borrowed time. Whoever was responsible for setting them up obviously had resources if they'd killed the person who'd warned them and now were going after her. "And what if the wrong people find out first that you survived?"

He shrugged again. "It wouldn't be the first time I had a target on my head."

How he could so coolly and calmly talk about someone trying to kill him, she didn't know. She was scared for him, even if he wasn't for himself.

Really scared.

Aside from whoever had set them up, there was a host of other players who might not be happy to hear that there were survivors of the doomed mission. Both the US and Russian governments were probably only too happy to sweep it under the rug and pretend it never happened.

Well, she wasn't. And she had an idea. One he most certainly wasn't going to like. "You do have one lead," she said.

He frowned. "What's that?"

"Not what, who. You have me."

John stared at her as the realization of what she meant sank in. Was she out of her sweet, loving mind?

"No. Fucking. Way." He said each word with a hard finality that told her exactly what he thought of that idea. "Get it out of your head. You are not going anywhere near this. If I have to tie you to that damned bed, I will."

She rolled her eyes as if his anger—and attitude—were to be expected and were nothing to worry about. She was dead wrong about that. He meant every word.

"Don't be overdramatic, John."

He gave her a long look and then shifted his eyes to the headboard behind her. "I assure you I'd like nothing more—for more reasons than one."

If he'd hoped to make her blush, it had worked. She got an adorably embarrassed look on her face for a moment before giving him a Sunday-school-teacher glare. "It makes perfect sense. And I'm already involved. *If* the person who attacked me in the parking lot and went through my apartment does have something to do with this, they aren't going to just go away." He could hardly argue otherwise when he'd been telling her how much danger she was in and why she couldn't go home for the past few days. But that was why he wanted her to stay here—with him. "What if they are the same people who set you guys up? You can't let this opportunity go by. You might be content to live in hiding forever, but I'm not."

"I told you it wouldn't be forever," he snapped. "All I'm asking for is a few more days."

"We could lose the advantage we have if we wait. Right now no one knows you are alive. Who's to say that will be the case in a few days? We can set a trap and take them by surprise."

"With you as bait? It's not going to happen."

He was practically shaking with fury, but she just sat there on the bed with her head tilted to the side ever so slightly, staring at him. Those big blue eyes penetrating and seeing far more than he wanted her to.

"Why not?"

"That should be obvious. It's too goddamned danger-ous. If these are the same people, they aren't going to be fucking around. They will shoot to kill, and I can guar-antee they won't miss like they do in the movies."

Just the thought made him almost physically ill. If anything happened to her . . .

He'd lose his freaking mind. Hell, just thinking about it was testing his sanity.

She continued to stare at him with a knowing look in her eyes that he didn't like. "I'm sure we could come up with some kind of plan to minimize that risk. What is this really about, John? Is it because I'm a woman?"

"No." But it didn't hurt. Jesus Christ, look at her! She was tiny—or tiny compared to him. And unless Her-mione had a magic wand tucked in the back pocket of her jeans, she didn't have any superpowers.

Clearly she didn't believe him. "If I were one of your guys we wouldn't be having this conversation."

"You're right, but that's because my guys are trained. They are some of the most elite operatives in the world. You are a reporter!"

"I trust you and whoever you are talking to on the phone to protect me."

He didn't deserve or want that kind of trust. "It's not going to happen, Brit."

"If I were anyone else, you wouldn't be acting like this. You are letting your personal feelings blind you to what needs to be done. This isn't just about you; it's about the other survivors as well."

She was right about his personal feelings. She was

Brand's sister; he'd promised to look out for her, and using her as bait sure as hell didn't qualify.

But he knew that wasn't all of it.

"I want to do this, John. Not just for me or you or your teammates, but for Brandon. If there is a way I can find out who is responsible for his death, I have to do it. You can see that, can't you?"

No. He wasn't seeing anything right now except her lying in a pool of blood, and that sure as hell wasn't going to happen. He was breaking into a cold sweat just thinking about it.

But he wasn't as deaf or blind to her argument as he wanted to be. She was right. If it were anyone else, he might consider it. But it wasn't anyone else. It was her, and she was . . .

Fuck.

She must have seen the slight opening and gone in for the kill. "Call the guy you are always talking to on the phone. See what he says. If he thinks it's a good idea, we go forward."

"No."

"John, you are being—"

He cut her off. "If he thinks it's a good idea, I'll consider it. But only if I can be sure that nothing can go wrong."

But he knew that was impossible. Something always went wrong.

Twenty

John stared down at the clouds from the airplane's small window and wondered what the hell he was doing. How had he let them talk him into this?

He hadn't slept the entire eight-hour flight from Copenhagen into Toronto. He was too on edge, and his head was spinning.

He wasn't thinking about his travel documents (they should hold up) or about sneaking across the porous Canadian border into the US (which was almost child's play with his training), or even about returning to Washington, DC, where he'd spent enough time to know exactly how dangerous it would be for him to be there.

He was thinking about the promise he'd made to Brand if anything were to happen to him. Somehow John didn't think using his sister as bait qualified as watching out for her. He didn't want to think about the earlier "stay away from her" promise he'd already broken.

Twice. Pretty spectacularly.

He looked down at the head resting against his shoulder and felt something inside his chest hitch right up to his throat. He'd probably break that promise a third time, as it seemed he had no control when it came to the woman sleeping like a baby without a care in the world next to him.

Brittany was putting way too much trust in him, and it was making him uneasy. Despite his joking to the contrary, he wasn't Superman. He didn't have any special powers. If something went wrong, there was no guarantee he'd be able to keep her safe.

The now-familiar knot of fear twisted in his gut again. He'd be lucky if he came out of this little op with just an ulcer.

Him. The guy with no cares in the world and who never let anything get to him. An ulcer. The world had turned upside down. Or rather, his world had turned upside down since Brittany had walked into that bar.

She made a small sound of contentment in her sleep and shifted against him. He felt a wave of something powerful crash over him, dragging him down a black hole he wasn't sure he could pull out of—even if he wanted to.

He was in trouble. He'd let himself get too close. He cared too much.

Which made him something he'd never been in his life: unsure of himself. In other words, exactly the opposite of how he usually was when heading into an op.

This wasn't good; it wasn't good at all.

Brittany shifted again, waking up this time when the flight attendant call buttons chimed and the pilot came on to announce their initial descent.

The instant smile on her face when she looked at him only increased the unease gnawing in his gut. He should have ended it when he'd had the chance, letting her think he'd slept with someone at the bar. But he hadn't been able to make himself do it. Not this time.

"Did you sleep at all?" she asked.

"A little."

She gave him a frown that told him she knew he was

lying. "I thought you said it was going to be a long day when we got there and we needed sleep." It was true; his mind just hadn't cooperated. "Are you still mad at me?"

"I'm not mad at you." He wasn't. He was mad at himself for agreeing to this.

Brittany smiled. "Not even for ganging up on you?"

John should have known better than to run it by the LC. Taylor thought using Brittany to trap the people who were after her—and possibly therefore connected to what happened to them—was a great idea. In fact, he'd been pissed that he hadn't thought of it himself.

"I'm worried, Brit. Not angry."

"I didn't think you got worried."

He didn't. Except apparently when it came to her. "Yeah, well, I guess there's a first time for everything."

They didn't even have a fully formed plan. The LC said he was still getting everything in place. John's job was to get them both to Washington, DC. Taylor would see them there and fill John in on the rest then.

He wasn't all that surprised to learn that the LC would be meeting them in DC. John didn't know where the other survivors had scattered for operational security reasons. But he'd suspected Taylor was in the US. Maybe even in DC, tracking down leads.

When the wheels hit the ground in Canada, John's twitchiness only got worse. He was back on the grid and the clock was ticking. He just hoped to hell time didn't run out.

For both of them.

Brittany was glad for every hour of sleep she'd gotten on that plane. By the time she opened the door to the big conference hotel John had picked near Dulles Airport, she felt as if she'd been on every mode of transportation between DC and Toronto for the past fifteen hours, including a boat, a train, a bus, a couple of taxis, and a pair of very tired feet that had walked more miles than she wanted to count.

It had been an adventure, all right, and she was exhausted. She wished she could have gone back to her apartment, but that was out of the question until John and whoever he was working with made sure it was safe.

She took a nice long bath—for real this time, as she was too tired to work—while John made a call. He was still on the phone, talking in muffled monosyllables, when she came back into the room, dragging a comb through her still damp hair. He glanced over, taking in her borrowed terry robe and slippers with an amused grin. Hey, that was what they were there for. And they were comfy.

She sat on the edge of the bed while he finished, only half-listening. She knew he wasn't going to say anything that he didn't want her to hear. He would have left the room to make the call otherwise. He'd fill her in later on what he thought she needed to know, which probably wasn't anything close to what she wanted to know.

She'd finished combing her hair and started to put lotion on her legs when he ended the call. He was staring at her legs with an unmistakable gleam in his eye, which sent a tickle of warmth running up her thighs.

"You're distracting," he said accusingly.

"Is that good or bad?"

"Depends on how tired you are."

"I'm pretty tired."

"Then bad."

She smiled. "You gonna fill me in on what's happening?"

"In a minute. I need a shower."

He didn't take much longer than that. She was still rubbing in lotion when he came back out, a towel slung around his waist.

Low around his waist.

She took a long, slow eyeful, letting her gaze trail over the broad shoulders, muscular arms, and tanned washboard stomach, searching for a flaw. There wasn't one. He was, as the phrase went, seriously put together. What was that men's fitness magazine? He could be on the cover.

And from the grin on his face, he knew exactly what his incredible body was doing to her.

She shot him a glare, knowing why that towel was slung so low. It was sexy as hell and gave her a glimpse of his low ab muscles, which led right to . . .

He gave her a suggestive lift of an eyebrow. "Still tired?"

She tore her eyes away from that happy trail. She couldn't let him win that easily; he would be unbearable. Or, as he was already unbearable, more unbearable.

She yawned, taking in those killer abs as if they were the most boring thing in the world when all she wanted to do was slide her fingertips up and down and count every tight rope of muscle. "Yep. I can barely keep my eyes open."

"Is that so?" he drawled, with a smile that reminded her of a gunslinger daring his opponent to go ahead and make his day. "Anything I can do to wake you up a little?"

His gaze lowered to the opening of her robe, landing in a place between her legs that turned her insides to quicksand. Just the thought of what he was suggesting was enough to make her hot. She had to squeeze her thighs together a little not to quiver with anticipation. The thought of his mouth and tongue on her the way she might have imagined more than once . . .

Oh God, she couldn't help it. Her body quivered.

He saw the movement and gave her one of those "I have you right in the palm of my hand" smiles.

Not so fast. She wasn't going to fall to pieces just because he said he would go down on her. She had her pride, didn't she?

At least a few minutes' worth. She forced her thoughts away from slow nuzzles and long slides of tongue.

And gunslingers with big guns.

"How about you tell me the plan?" she said with an impressive matter-of-factness.

He lifted an eyebrow and closed the distance between them. "I didn't take you for a play-by-play dirty talker, but if that's what you want. First I'm going to put my mouth—"

She pushed him away with an embarrassed laugh. "Not *that* plan. What's happening tomorrow? Is everything ready for us? Did we get the green light?"

His eyes narrowed dramatically, and the arms she'd been doing her best not to admire too openly might have flexed a little. She must have sounded too excited.

"This isn't fun, it isn't exciting, and it sure as hell isn't a damned TV show. It's dangerous. Got that? *Dangerous.*"

Okay, maybe the green-light business was a little Hollywood, but she was just getting into the spirit. She resisted the urge to say "Copy that." She didn't think he'd appreciate the attempt at humor. Which was odd, as he was exactly the guy who should. Keeping things light when things were dangerous was his job. His pranks were legendary. But he was pretty much Mr. Stone Face humorless right now. And wound up way too tight. He needed to relax. But she was smart enough not to tell him that.

"Dangerous," she repeated. "Got it. I promise to be suitably terrified the whole time. Now will you tell me?"

He gave her a look that told her he knew she was humoring him. Sitting on the bureau opposite where she sat on the bed, he crossed his arms and stared at her intimidatingly for a few moments.

She forced herself to keep a suitably contrite and serious look on her face. It wasn't easy. Something about this angry, overbearing, way-too-serious John Donovan made her want to push and see what it revealed. Although she'd vowed not to try to pin him down on his feelings for her this time, they were becoming more obvious each day they spent together.

But as heady as it was realizing that he cared for her, Brittany knew it was far more than John admitting his feelings working against them. There were also their respective jobs. She couldn't imagine a life of secrets, his history with women (lots of them), his hang-up about her being Brandon's sister, and the fact that he was in hiding because someone had tried to kill him—and was now maybe targeting her. Yeah, there was *that*.

Which brought her back to the plan. Her restraint paid off when he spoke. "The guys who will be watching your apartment will be in place tomorrow. We'll head over in the morning to retrieve your phone and computer. You will call, text, and e-mail everyone at work, letting them know that you are meeting your source tomorrow, who has promised to give you something 'explosive.' That should pique the interest of anyone listening. We'll set up a drop with our guys covering and hopefully whoever has been following you will show up to spring the trap."

"Who are these guys? Can you trust them?"

"I trust hardly anyone right now. But I've been assured by someone I do trust that they are the best. But if you want to back out, just say the word."

Clearly that was exactly what he was hoping she would do.

"I don't want to back out," she said.

"If you change your mind at any time, all you have to do is say the word. But you'll be well covered. Your job is just to go about your day and try to act as natural as possible."

"And what will you be doing?"

"Not letting you out of my sight."

That was what she'd figured. "And don't you think

anyone is going to wonder why I have a six-foot-four bodyguard following me?"

"No one will notice I'm there."

She gave a sharp laugh. "Um, you kind of stick out, Johnny."

He frowned. "You can tell people I'm your boyfriend."

"Right." She rolled her eyes at the obvious. "Like anyone will believe that."

He looked indignant. "Why wouldn't they?"

Was he serious? Oddly enough, he seemed to be. "You're kind of hot."

Actually, there was no "kind of" about it.

"So are you."

She smiled. "Thanks, but it's a level-of-hotness thing. Me, I'm about here." She leveled her hand at waist level. "You are here," she said, lifting it above her head.

"That's superficial bullshit." He honestly looked pissed off. "Are you with me because of how I look?"

"It sure doesn't hurt."

He didn't seem to appreciate her flip response, and she wondered when he stood up to reach for his clothes if maybe she'd hurt him unintentionally. He had to know how incredible he was. Didn't he?

She grabbed his arm to stop him. "Of course I'm not. I like being with you because of how you make me feel, not how you look. From the first time you sat down on the beach next to me five years ago, you made me laugh. You make me . . . I don't know, better somehow. Calmer. More relaxed? You slow me down and make me want to smell the roses—or get a cat."

He didn't get that one. "A cat?"

She flushed. "I've always wanted a cat or a dog"—or a boyfriend—"but I've never had the time." Fearing she'd revealed too much, she turned the conversation back. "But other people won't see any of that."

Her words seem to mollify him. "Good," he said gruffly. "And you don't need to worry about convincing anyone. It will be obvious to anyone who sees how I look at you."

He pulled her up against him, and from the heated intensity in his eyes she guessed he was giving her a demonstration.

"And how's that?" she said, her voice suddenly husky.

"Like you are mine and I can't wait to get inside your pants."

"I hate to state the obvious, but I'm not wearing any pants."

"Hmm . . ." Which in her imagination actually kind of sounded like "yum." "Is that so?"

It didn't take much for him to slide his hand under her robe and continue the hands-on demonstration.

Very effectively. It nearly convinced her.

She groaned when he cupped her possessively, his finger dipping between her legs with the confidence of a man who already knew her body and was staking a claim. A very deep, penetrating, and thorough claim.

Her robe slid off her shoulders as he gave her a few more thrusts of his finger before laying her back on the bed and replacing it with his tongue.

He took her apart bit by bit. Nuzzling, delving, and flicking until she had nowhere to go. Until her heels dug into his back and her thighs clenched around his face as he finally gave her the pressure and friction that sent her soaring over the edge. He devoured her ecstasy with his mouth, making sounds as if he couldn't get enough.

Turned out, he couldn't. He took her over the edge again before he let her take a breath.

But she had her revenge. Deciding he looked a little bit too much like the proverbial cat who ate the canary, she sat up on the edge of the bed, lifted him to his feet, and pulled off his towel.

What she was interested in was right at mouth level and looking like it might need a little lightening of the pressure. It was thick and hard and very, very red.

"Poor baby," she said, making commiserating sounds over his obvious discomfort. She looked up at him coyly. Their eyes met, and for maybe the first time in her life she felt as sexy as any femme fatale. "I think you mentioned a rain check on that lesson?"

His expression was so fierce and his jaw clenched so tightly he couldn't even get out the words. Instead, he groaned as her mouth covered him.

It turned out she didn't need much of a lesson after all. All she had to do was follow the sounds, clenches, and pulsing throbs of a very long and bulging vein.

The latter she did with her tongue. A slow, delicious pull from root to tip that ended with her taking that big blunt plum in her mouth and milking him until he came with a fierceness that undid them both.

Afterward, sated and weak from pleasure, they lay naked and entwined on the bed in a weird kind of post-euphoric silence. It wasn't awkward or uncomfortable; it was more a sense of awe and humbleness. As if maybe something bigger than either of them realized was taking hold.

What's happening?

She didn't realize she'd spoken aloud until he answered. "I don't know."

But it was clear to both of them that something was. And as she fell asleep with her cheek pressed to the steady beat of his heart—a heart that wasn't running for the hills—she suspected the answer.

She was falling for him all over again. He'd better not disappoint her. The landing would be much harder this time.

Twenty-one

Kate burst into tears the moment he opened the door. It was as if all the emotion of the past couple of weeks—ever since she'd received that horrible phone call from Colt telling her Scott was dead—which she'd been carefully keeping at bay, burst through the dam. All it took was one look into the navy blue eyes of the man whose face was nearly as familiar to her as her own—no matter how he attempted to disguise it.

She threw herself into his arms and didn't let go until the heavy, choking sobs slowed to a few sputtering sniffles.

He'd closed the door behind her, but otherwise he hadn't moved, content, it seemed, to just hold her until she got it all out.

When she finally pulled back to look up at him through blurry, swollen eyes, he was grinning down at her. "I take it you're glad to see me?"

She swatted at him playfully and wiped her eyes. "Don't joke about this. I was so scared that I'd lost you. When I heard . . ." She let her voice fall off. "It doesn't matter. You're safe, and that's all that matters."

Scott pulled out a chair from the desk, indicating for her to sit.

After dropping Colt off at his hotel, she'd driven straight to the address Scott had given her. It hadn't taken long, as the hotel was also near Capitol Hill and only a few blocks away. Both men had picked large chain hotels favored by businessmen—she suspected it wasn't a coincidence and was only glad they hadn't picked the same one.

She gave an involuntary shudder at the thought of them accidentally crossing paths. Scott's subtle change in appearance wouldn't fool Colt any more than it had her.

Scott went into the bathroom and came out with a few tissues, which she made good use of.

He sat on the desk and looked down at her. "Why do I think this isn't just about me? Wesson's been giving you a hard time, hasn't he?"

She looked away, avoiding his gaze. "He gives everyone a hard time. I'm nothing special."

"Kate . . ." He had that impatient-father tone in his voice.

"I don't want to talk about Colt. I want to talk about you." She reached up and tugged on his short beard. "I've never seen you with a beard before. You look different."

It roughened the edges of his patrician features, making him look a little more rugged and not so clean-cut Nantucket.

A wry smile turned his mouth. "That's the point."

"And your hair is darker."

"A little help from Just For Men."

She took in the blue button-down shirt and gray slacks—neither of which were tailored and hid his well-honed SEAL physique behind bad pleats and extra fabric. She knew from her marriage to Colt that muscular, broad-shouldered guys needed to have their shirts tailored or they would blouse when they were tucked in, making them look a little Stay Puft Marshmallow Man.

The pleated dad-pants didn't help, although she suspected that was the intention. Scott looked like all the other slightly paunchy, out-of-state businessmen in this hotel.

Okay, well, maybe not quite like them. Even with the ill-fitting clothes, he was strikingly good-looking. Ken to her Barbie, Colt had once accused. *"You look like fucking Ken and Barbie Country Club edition."*

It hadn't been a compliment—especially with the nasty way in which he'd said it. But Colt had been half-right. They did look alike, but there never had been anything romantic between them. Only love and friendship forged from a deep, unexpected connection.

Scott grinned, obviously taking in her scrutiny. "You like the outfit? It's not Savile Row."

She snorted. Like her, Scott was always impeccably dressed. She knew he had more than one bespoke suit from England. His wealth made hers look like pocket change. But most of the time he ignored it. It had brought him comfort, but not happiness. Only guilt. "Definitely not, but it does the job." She paused. "Now, tell me what's going on. Why are you here?"

"We have a lead. I told you about the reporter being attacked in Norway. Well, it doesn't look like a coincidence. Her place in DC was ransacked. We're setting up a sting to see if we can lure whoever is responsible out."

Kate muttered a curse under her breath. "Brittany? I found out who was feeding her information."

"You did?"

She nodded and filled him in. He swore a few times, but she wasn't sure whether he was angry or pleased. She suspected a little of both. Her godfather's interference had definitely made things harder on him, but he'd also been the only one willing to stick up for them and not let their sacrifice be swept under the rug.

She also filled him in on the rear admiral's suicide and what they'd learned from her godfather that made his involvement seem unlikely.

When she mentioned the woman in Iowa, he looked 100 percent angry again. "That was Jim Bob's high school girlfriend." At her look of confusion, he said, "Travis Hart. One of the young guys who made it out with us. Apparently it wasn't as over as he led everyone to believe. You think someone in the government paid her off to keep her quiet?"

"Sounds that way, but I'll look into it when I get a chance." She suspected Colt was ahead of her on that.

Then she got to the difficult part. The part she wasn't looking forward to. "My godfather said something else."

Scott gave her a sharp look, something in her voice obviously alerting him. "Yeah? What's that?"

She took a deep breath. "It was about Natalie."

A look of acute pain crossed his grim-set features. But suddenly his expression filled with alarm, and he swore. "Does he know about the text? Does he know she warned us?" His voice lowered. "Not that it really makes a difference now."

"No. At least I don't think he knows about that. But with my godfather you never know. He worked in intelligence a long time before joining the Chiefs of Staff." She paused, the biting of her lip betraying her anxiousness. "He said she was adopted when she was a child and that her real name was Natalya Petrova."

It didn't take him long to process the significance, and when he did his face darkened with rage. "No fucking way. Whatever it is you are thinking, it's way off base. Nat didn't have anything to do with this. She warned me, for fuck's sake. She saved my life and five other men's lives. I don't care what her name was. She was born somewhere else. So what? A lot of people were. It doesn't mean anything. It's a coincidence."

"All right," Kate said quietly, knowing he was too angry and too shocked to think rationally right now. He was right, but this was too big a coincidence to discount.

"I mean it, Katie. Leave her out of this."

"All right," she repeated, but they both knew she would follow up on it. She had to. He would understand that . . . eventually.

"What do you need me to do?" she asked.

"What you are doing. Keep Wesson out of our way and off our tracks."

As if getting Colt to do anything was that easy. "I'll do my best. But with the rear admiral not a suspect anymore, I don't know how long I can keep him from getting on a plane to Russia."

"Well, then, let's hope this fishing expedition Donovan is on catches something big."

Kate stayed for a little while longer, but eventually she had to say good-bye. Scott was getting things lined up for tomorrow, and Percy was waiting. They had some talking to do. Some talking that she might have put off for too long but that she couldn't put off anymore.

The shock was like a punch to the gut. A sucker punch, hitting Colt when he wasn't expecting it.

Though why the hell he hadn't expected it, he didn't know. She'd done it to him, hadn't she? Lord Percy wasn't even married to her yet and she was already cheating on him.

Called back into work, my ass. Colt had seen her face after that phone call. He'd seen the elation. The eagerness. He'd known she was lying.

She was meeting someone.

So he'd followed her. She'd dropped him off, and he'd

hopped in a cab and followed her. Even when she'd handed her keys to the valet and practically ran into the lobby to the elevator, he hadn't wanted to believe it.

He'd nearly missed the little lovers' reunion. He'd had to wait to see what floor she stopped on, and then, at the last second, some asshole jumped in the elevator he was holding open, causing the closing doors to reopen. Colt had stopped him before he pushed a button on four—two floors lower than the sixth, where she'd gotten off.

Colt walked out of the elevator just in time to look down the hall and see her launch herself into the arms of a man who'd obviously been waiting for her. Colt didn't get a good look at him; he'd closed the door behind them too quickly, as if he couldn't wait to . . .

Anger seethed through Colt's veins. Why the hell was he so upset? This had nothing to do with him. He knew she was a liar. Nothing new there.

Almost five months old.

She'd probably been lying about that, too. Hadn't she?

But what if she hadn't? What if the baby she'd lost had been his, just as he'd thought that entire, hideous plane ride across the country after he'd learned that she'd been in a car accident. When he'd stupidly vowed to do anything to repair the wreck that their marriage had become. When he'd told himself he would give her the benefit of the doubt and ignore what every sign—the secret e-mails and meetings, the whispered calls, the unexplained absences, the flushed cheeks and heartfelt stares she thought he didn't see, and then the final blow, discovering they'd both been in DC together—pointed to: that she was having an affair with Taylor.

But all those signs were corroborated when he'd arrived at the hospital and was told that her husband, the father of her child, was already with her and talking to the doctor. Colt still wouldn't have believed it if he hadn't seen with his own two eyes the way Taylor was holding her in his arms. Lying next to her in that hospital bed as if he belonged there.

Comforting her.

Loving her.

Would it make a difference if the baby had been Colt's? Would it change anything?

When she'd told him earlier, it had felt as if the rug had been pulled out from under his feet and he was looking around for something to stand on.

He'd found it when the door opened to the hotel room.

Whether the baby was his didn't change the fact that she'd cheated on him. And now, apparently, on the ambassador.

Colt shouldn't have stayed. He should have gone back to his own hotel and drunk himself into oblivion there. Not sat there hunched over on a barstool in the lobby bar, drinking whiskey and waiting for the elevator door to open two hours later. Even then he could have let her go. Let her walk away oblivious to what he'd learned.

But he'd never been very good at doing what he should where Kate was concerned.

She'd taken only a few steps out of the elevator before he was in front of her.

She gasped. "Colt!"

Taking advantage of her surprise—and the fact that she was trying to back away from him—he maneuvered her back into the elevator.

Blocking her exit with his body, he pushed a button as the doors closed.

"Wait. What are you doing?"

He waited for the elevator to climb a few floors before stopping it and disabling the alarm so that it couldn't sound. His job had its benefits.

"Stop!" She realized what he was doing, but it was too late. Not that she could have stopped him. "What is this about? Why are you keeping me here like this?"

"I wanted a little privacy, but if you'd rather, we can talk about this in your room—unless you rented it by the hour. What was it, 6307?"

He remembered too well she liked to meet in hotel rooms. They'd done it themselves when they'd first started dating. He'd teased her that she liked the illicitness of it. The tawdriness. She'd said it was to protect their privacy—a believable explanation with their respective jobs—but the blush on her cheeks had made him wonder.

She blanched at the recitation of the room number but recovered quickly. "I don't know what you thought you saw, but this has nothing to do with you."

"You're right. Does the ambassador know you're screwing around on him?"

He'd closed the distance between them without realizing it, until her chest started to heave against his and he realized everything in a hot pull of lust fueled by anger. Anger that felt as fresh as it had three years ago.

"I'm not screwing around on him," she said through gritted teeth.

She was angry. Maybe just as angry as he was.

But Colt wasn't listening. "I almost feel sorry for him," he said, backing her up against the handrail. "Although I'm not surprised he couldn't satisfy you. Does he know what a naughty girl you are yet, or does he still think you are as prim and proper as you look?"

She tried to push him back, but his arms were pinning her on either side of the brass handrail that circled the elevator. If looks could kill, he'd be lying in a pool of blood. "You're a bastard, Colt. You've always been a bastard. A vile, crude, cruel-hearted bastard."

"And you've always been hot for it. Even now I can see it on your face. You're turned on. You like it a little rough. A little dirty. That's why you wanted me."

Years ago she would have denied it. She would have said she wanted him because she loved him. She didn't say

that now. She stood there, eyes blazing, cheeks hot, heartbeat pounding, not saying a damned thing. Angry, turned
on, but yet oddly detached in all the ways that mattered.

He didn't like that at all. He wanted to get to her. To
prick beneath that haughty facade the way he'd always
done.

He bent his mouth closer, grazing the soft strands of
her hair as his lips swept over the even softer velvet of
her flushed skin. "Does he know how you like to be
sucked?" he whispered, his lips hovering close to her ear.
The shiver that racked her body only egged him on.
"Does he know how to make you cry out with the flick
of a tongue between your legs?"

She sucked in her breath in a gasp that was more of pleasure than of shock, and Colt found his body responding.

Fuck that. His body had been responding since that
elevator door had closed behind them and he'd caught the
scent of that damned perfume.

He hated peonies.

But they fucking smelled like heaven. They smelled
like sex. With her.

He wasn't supposed to be getting turned on. He was
supposed to be pissing her off. Outraging her. Angering
her the way she'd done him.

But he'd miscalculated. His lips made full contact
with the silky skin of her neck as her hands circled his
head and brought their bodies together in a sizzle of raw
heat. Like water hitting a pan of oil with a hard snap and
a burning splatter. It almost hurt.

His hand skimmed down over the familiar slender hip
and the firm, tight ass. "Does he know how much you
like it from behind? How you like to be on your hands
and knees when I ram into you?"

He could almost feel her opening for him. Feel her
dampness as his rigid cock rubbed against her. It felt so
fucking good. He wanted to groan at the contact.

Maybe he did. He didn't know because his mouth was on hers and he was kissing her. Devouring her like a man who'd been starving for three years.

Longer than that. It had been a long time since they'd kissed with this kind of intensity.

His tongue was in her mouth, fighting with hers for dominance. For depth. For how much they could take of each other.

He was on fire. The elevator was on fire. It had become a sauna. A sensual den of erotic pleasure.

He was out of control, and she was meeting him stroke for stroke, thrust for thrust. But it wouldn't be enough until he was inside her. Until he was pounding and she was grabbing and lifting and demanding more.

Demanding everything.

But as quickly as the spark had ignited, it was snuffed out. "Stop!" she said, pushing him away. "Damn you, stop! I can't do this."

He might have protested otherwise if he hadn't seen the glint in her eye. The glint of tears.

He stepped back. Where his body had been hot only seconds earlier, it was now ice.

What was he doing?

She wasn't the only one who couldn't do this. But she'd gotten to him. She'd gotten to him after everything she'd done.

He was every bit as disgusted with himself as she was. Except she didn't look disgusted; she looked shaken. Fragile. As if the kiss had destroyed something inside her.

He knew the feeling.

He didn't want to look at her, but he forced himself to meet her gaze. The tightening in his chest was even worse than he had braced himself for. "I'm sorry."

She held his stare until he thought he would die from lack of oxygen in his frozen lungs. "I—I . . ." She stumbled. "I just want to go home."

The desperation in her voice sent a knife through his ribs. Home wasn't him anymore. Home was to someone else.

Colt didn't say anything. He just nodded and returned to the elevator panel. In a few seconds it was going again.

He hit the button for the lobby, and a few moments later he was watching her walk away from him. After what had just happened, it probably should be for the last time. But somehow he knew it wasn't. There was unfinished business between them, whether either of them wanted to admit it or not. That kiss had just ripped open a scar that wasn't fully closed.

Twenty-two

Brittany heard the mutter of curses and a few angry huffs behind her as she clambered up the fire escape stairwell to her fifth-floor apartment the next morning. She waited at the top, holding the door open as John rounded the last turn below her with the bulky suitcase they'd retrieved from her building manager.

She smiled. "Everything okay?"

"Peachy," he said with a grunt, dropping the wheeled duffel to the floor. It landed with a heavy *thud*, which wasn't surprising, as it must have weighed about seventy-five pounds, thanks to the stack of yellow pages that had been sitting in the mailroom. She'd jammed in as many as she could when he wasn't looking. "How long did you say that elevator has been on the blitz?"

She shrugged. "A couple weeks. I told you I didn't mind carrying it. I hope it wasn't too heavy for you." She smiled sweetly as he shot her a disgusted glare. "I thought you guys carried big packs when you go . . ." Seeing his warning glare, she modified her comment to, "To work."

"Sometimes, but on our backs. But this thing is a pain in the—"

The sound of the elevator chime stopped him. The door opened, and her manager walked out. "I forgot to give you the new key I had made after the break-in," he said, frowning at the suitcase at the top of the stairs. "Why didn't you take the elevator?"

"It's broken," John replied, although his gaze had slid to hers.

Busted.

"Broken?" the manager repeated with a frown. "I had it replaced last year. It's practically brand-new."

Brittany fought a smile—pretty unsuccessfully. "Is that right? I would have sworn it was down last week. But Joe doesn't mind a little exercise. Do you, Joe?"

Brittany might have had her fun—she hadn't forgotten his comments about the rocks in her bag—but from the look on John's face, he was already planning his payback. Wait until he saw the phone books.

Bring it on, Johnny. She could take whatever he dished out. And when his gaze slid hotly and possessively down her body as her manager unlocked the door, she was looking forward to it. A lot.

She'd taken him in her mouth again this morning, waking him slowly and gently with the sensual kiss until he was as big and hard as a spike and straining against the urge to push deeper into her mouth. She'd tortured him with the long, slow sucks and pulls until his body was shaking with need and he started to beg with small pumps of his hips. Only then did she suck him hard and deep, pumping him as fast as he wanted.

Nope, no lessons needed.

But he gave her one anyway in the shower. A lesson in how not to slip when a man had his tongue buried between your legs and you were coming until your legs gave out. Or when he bent you over to brace against the wall while he took you from behind.

But all thoughts of their morning sex-fest fell by the

wayside when her manager opened the door and she walked into her apartment.

Or what had been her apartment. There wasn't much left of the place she remembered. The few pieces of furniture she'd had—mostly IKEA remainders—had been torn apart, with the stuffing pulled out and strewn across the floor or, in the case of the wood, broken into pieces. It was as if a cyclone had hit it.

But from the level of destruction, it was more than that. It felt almost malevolent. As if someone hadn't been just looking for something but had wanted to destroy.

John swore.

Brittany felt oddly numb. It hadn't been much of a home, but it had been the only one she had.

The manager, an older man who'd lost his wife a few years ago and seemed pretty checked out most of the time, seemed to suddenly see it as well. He turned a chair upright. "I didn't want to disturb anything," he apologized defensively.

"I understand completely, Mr. Polonsky. I'm sure the police had their investigation and you didn't want to throw out anything that might be important."

The old man was obviously relieved at the out she'd given him. "That's right."

"We can take it from here," she said. "Joe is going to help me clean up."

The manager took in the big, strong-looking SEAL, obviously concluded that she was in capable hands, and gave her a nod. "Good. Let me know if you need anything."

He shut the door behind him, and Brittany looked around. "Lots of trash bags," she said to herself.

Glancing up, she saw John watching her. "You okay?" he asked.

"I'm fine. Or I will be as soon as I get some new furniture."

He must have picked up on the malevolent aspect of

the destruction as well. "You're safe, Brit. I won't let any-thing happen to you. And there are a half-dozen guys watching this building right now. No one is getting in or out of here without us knowing it."

She nodded, the reminder definitely making her feel better. But it wasn't the half-dozen guys posted around the building that steadied her; it was John's presence.

He swore again. "I never should have agreed to this. I'm going to call my guy and tell him it's all off."

"You'll do no such thing," she said, putting her hand on his chest. She wasn't the only one who needed steady-ing. "It was just a little bit of a shock. I'm fine—or will be when we get some of this cleaned up. Okay?"

She didn't give him a chance to answer and went to work. They spent the next hour clearing the worst of it, filling a few trash bags and salvaging what they could. A couch with one cushion, a couple wooden chairs, and her breakfast table. Fortunately, her dishes were mostly melamine and she only had a few broken coffee mugs that she had to toss, including a SAVE A REPORTER: BUY A NEWSPAPER gag gift that Mac had given her for her birthday last year.

There was only one time the tears that she'd kept tight in her throat threatened to spill, and that was when she saw her clothes all over the floor of her bedroom and realized someone had gone through her underwear, socks, pajamas, and everything else in her drawers. That made it personal. Violating.

Fortunately, John was still in the living room and didn't witness the moment of weakness or he might have called it off for good this time.

She threw all the clothes in a laundry bag to be washed, but she wondered if she'd wear any of them again.

Once the worst of it was straightened, John asked her to see if she could find anything missing. What limited jewelry she had—a few necklaces and earrings that had belonged to her mother—had been tossed on the floor, but thankfully appeared undamaged. This hadn't been a robbery; it had been a hunt.

She didn't have much by way of electronics, but the TV and the alarm clock that served triple purpose by functioning as a phone dock and stereo speaker had been knocked over but seemed okay.

Her desk mostly served as a place to rest her laptop. She didn't store files at home, so nothing important would have been taken. Her personal papers consisted of bank and credit card statements and tax documents. Nothing worthwhile there. The would-be thief must have agreed because those appeared to be opened and strewn across her desk—the only pieces of upright furniture in her apartment aside from the bed—but intact.

She panicked for a minute when she couldn't find the silver frame with the photo of her parents that she kept on the desk, but it was on the floor by her bed. The glass was broken, but she cleared it away and placed the frame back on her desk.

She didn't realize John was watching her. "You look like your mom."

She nodded, smiling wistfully at the woman who looked so young and happy in the picture. "Who do you look like?"

He didn't answer right away. "My dad."

Clearly, he wasn't happy about that. "Well, I looked like my mom, but I was more like my dad. I'm sure you're nothing like your father in the ways that matter, John."

He didn't look so sure, but he let the subject drop. "Anything missing? Laptop? Anything else like that?"

She shook her head. She had that on her—although he didn't know about that. Before he could follow up, she remembered. "My phone! I can't believe I didn't check it yet."

She wasn't as tied to her phone as some millennials, but after a few days she should be jonesing big-time. After rescuing it from the suitcase John had dragged up the stairs, she had to plug it in for a few minutes to start it. There were three progressively angrier messages from her boss, one from Nancy making sure she was okay, and two from Mac wondering where the hell she was. There was also a message from Mick the hockey player, checking in to make sure they were still on for their rescheduled date tomorrow. She'd called before she'd left for Finland to push their makeup date back a week. Not surprisingly, she'd forgotten all about it.

She didn't realize John was listening so closely until he said, "Who the hell was that?"

She turned to look at him, hearing the angry edge to his voice. No, "angry" wasn't quite the right word. "Ice-cold" was a little better. His eyes were positively glacial.

She arched an eyebrow, taking in his reaction. Interesting. *Very* interesting. Mr. Casual wasn't acting so casual. He was acting jealous.

Deciding to test her theory, she said, "Just a guy I've been dating."

Half a date, but who was counting?

"You've been dating someone?" he shouted, looking as if his head were about to explode. "Why didn't you say anything?"

Okay, maybe it was juvenile to be happy when a guy was jealous, but that didn't stop her. She wanted to grin like a thirteen-year-old.

Instead, she shrugged. "I didn't think it mattered. It's not as if you and I are exclusive or anything."

"Who the fuck said that!"

His shouting was getting louder and angrier. "I just assumed. You aren't exactly a one-girl type of guy, John."

His eyes narrowed to slits. "You aren't dating him."

"I assume the same goes for you?"

"I won't date him either."

She'd walked right into that one. "You know what I mean."

He finally seemed to realize that she was teasing him, but surprisingly, rather than accuse her of trying to trick him or pin him down, he pulled her into his arms. "Consider this exclusive."

Brittany tried not to get carried away, but it happened anyway. She knew what a big step it was for him to make that kind of commitment to her, and her heart swelled.

Not even his hastily added "as long as we're together" could put a rein on her soaring hopes. Especially when he sealed that promise by covering his mouth with hers in a fierce kiss that left no room for argument.

Not that she intended to make one. Exclusive was fine by her. It was more than fine. It was what she'd wanted but hadn't let herself think about.

Just like she wouldn't let herself wonder how long "as long as we're together" would be.

"I won't be too late," John said. "There are guys posted at every exit, on the roof, and one in that car over there." He pointed to the midsized American-made sedan parked across the street with a perfect view to her living room window.

The LC had essentially given them their own private army. The guys—all former operatives—had been sent from the biggest defense contractor in the country. Apparently, the senior chief, Dean Baylor, had hooked up with Steve Marino's stepdaughter—more than hooked up, according to the LC—and they essentially had carte blanche/no questions asked with his hired men.

John would have to thank Tex later for the fortunate

taste in girlfriends. *After* he gave him shit for hooking up with a "do-gooder." The senior chief with an environmental activist? John couldn't believe it. After all the pinko Berkeley crap John had taken over the years from him, he was looking forward to some payback.

Brittany practically pushed him out the door. "Get out of here. I'll be fine. It's like Fort Knox at this place. Besides, your hovering is driving me nuts."

He frowned. What was she talking about? "I'm not hovering."

She stared at him, challenging that assessment with crossed arms and a sharply arched eyebrow.

One corner of his mouth lifted, which was about as close to a smile as he'd had since this damned plot had been hatched. "All right, maybe I've been hovering a little."

"You taste-tested my peanut butter and jelly sandwich!"

He made a face. "You mean the ninety-nine percent grape jelly and one percent thin layer of overly processed brown crap that belongs in a candy bar on the pieces of white Styrofoam? You know, it's just as easy to make your own peanut butter in a food processor, and it tastes like actual nuts."

"Food processor? You're kidding, right? Did you look at my kitchen? There's barely room for a microwave. And before you tell me that I don't need a microwave"—he slammed his mouth shut, having been about to say exactly that—"I happen to like my microwave. It's perfect for reheating TV dinners."

His eyes narrowed. She was messing with him, wasn't she? But with her fast-food eating habits, he couldn't be completely sure. Making a note to check the freezer for any form of Salisbury when he got back, he let her push him out the door with only a few more warnings before the door closed behind him.

He hated the idea of leaving her alone even for a few hours, but he had to scout the drop area and go through the mission plan before game time tonight.

For most ops SEALs spent weeks, sometimes months, practicing and going through every permutation, often using actual ships, helicopters, and buildings. Before Operation Neptune Spear—the bin Laden raid—Team Six had spent weeks training in North Carolina, in a building constructed to replicate the compound in Abbottabad, and in Nevada to replicate the high altitude for the new stealth Black Hawks.

A couple of hours wasn't anywhere near enough.

But it was all he had; the op was set for 2200 hours.

Brittany had sent her e-mails and texts and made her phone calls earlier to her boss and coworkers, informing them that she was meeting her source tonight and had "explosive proof" of what had happened to the platoon of SEALs.

If he'd thought she'd been exaggerating her job status, after he heard some of her boss's response while she was talking to him, John realized she hadn't been exaggerating at all.

Apparently, her boss, Jameson Cooper, was being pressured by the head of the investigative reporting team to get rid of her, and if she didn't come up with something soon, he was going to have to move her to the metro news desk.

There was something in "Jameson's" voice that John didn't like—he sounded a little too familiar—but John put it aside for now. Brittany had hidden her worry from him, but he knew it was there.

It made him momentarily uneasy, given all that he'd confided in her about what had happened in Russia, but she'd promised him, and he knew he could trust her.

It was strange how he didn't question it. But he trusted her in the same way he had her brother—with his life.

And as she was trusting hers with him, he intended to do everything he could to ensure that nothing went wrong.

The LC was standing by if he needed him, but this was John's op.

He met his contact at the highway underpass where Brittany had met her source the first time. Had he been more familiar with DC at the time, he would have had a hell of a lot more to say about her business practices. Did she have a fucking death wish? This place was crime central, and hanging around here was asking for trouble. Thinking of her sitting here alone in her car at night made him furious.

He'd been forced to leave the gun he'd taken from Brittany's attacker in Norway behind, and even he breathed a little easier once Buddha—they were all using code names—handed him the bag with the weapons, body armor, and gear he'd asked for. For the first time since the explosion in Russia, John felt like himself again.

The biggest danger with the hired army was that one of the former operators would recognize him. Over the years he'd crossed paths with a number of SEALs who'd gone into the private sector when they'd decided not to re-up or retired from the Teams after getting their twenty years. But among the sixteen men Buddha had gathered in the abandoned warehouse to sketch out the details of what was going on tonight, John didn't see any familiar faces.

Buddha—it seemed as if every team had a guy named after the ancient sage—reminded him of a stockier, thicker-necked version of the senior chief. They had the same take-charge, no-nonsense, hard-ass, Spartan-throwback personality that immediately put John at ease. This guy knew what he was doing, and he was good at his job.

For the next few hours they scouted the terrain, made note of entry and exit points, and tried to cover as many potential scenarios as possible to mitigate the risk of something going wrong.

Basically running it like any other op. Except that John was keenly aware that it wasn't any other op. With Brittany at the center of it, this private army—who were damned good even if they weren't his Team Nine brethren—weren't going to be enough to make him relax.

Nothing was going to make him relax until this was over, the bastards who were after her were caught, and she was out of danger. If anything happened to her . . .

He couldn't even think about it without breaking out in a cold sweat. John had never been in this position before, and he didn't like it. He didn't like feeling vulnerable. It reminded him of the months he'd spent in the hospital sitting by his mother's bedside. He'd never felt so damned helpless in his life. He never wanted to feel like that again.

But he was coming close now. He wanted to tell himself it was because of the promise he'd made to Brand to keep Brittany safe, but he knew it was a hell of a lot more than that. How much more he didn't know. This was *Star Trek* territory for him, as in "never gone before."

He almost didn't recognize himself. Brittany had turned him into some kind of less evolved, possessive, jealous version of John Donovan. Just hearing the other guy's voice in the message and thinking of her dating someone else made him feel like smashing something— preferably the other guy's face. He'd had to do something. So he'd found himself setting down a line he'd never set down before. The one guy/one girl kind of line. As in boyfriend/girlfriend. As in exclusive.

As in something he'd always avoided.

It scared the hell out of him. But for the first time in his life, John realized that he wanted to share more than a bed and a few laughs with someone. He wasn't sure what it meant—or whether it would be enough to keep from hurting her. And maybe that bothered him most of all. Not only had he broken his promise to Brand by messing around with his sister, but he could end up doing the very thing his friend had feared he would do by breaking her heart. For real this time.

At the very least, he owed it to Brand not to do that. But despite John's attempt to qualify "exclusive" with an "as long as we're together," he suspected it might already be too late. He'd seen her face. She thought he was making promises.

But he wasn't ready for promises. He wasn't sure he'd ever be ready. He didn't know whether he had what it took for that kind of relationship—the permanent type.

He hadn't exactly had a good role model in that arena. His dad had broken every promise that mattered to his mother. John had seen how it destroyed her and vowed to never let himself do that to anyone. He didn't want to be anything like his father, so he'd never put himself in the position to be like him.

Until now.

Just how much of the old man did he have in him? He looked just like the bastard, and what bothered him most was that he might be like him in other ways too. *Blood will tell*. Isn't that how the saying went?

To hell with that. He was nothing like his dad. And he'd prove it by being the best damned boyfriend—no matter how temporary—and doing everything in his power not to hurt her.

But first he had to get her through this op safely and catch the guys that were trying to hurt her.

John spent the rest of the afternoon assuring himself that no one would be able to slip through their net. By the time he left to return to Brittany's apartment, he was satisfied—or as satisfied as he could be in an afternoon—that she would be covered. But he still couldn't relax. He wouldn't be able to relax until this was all over.

The trap was set. Now they just needed someone to spring it.

B rittany took advantage of John's absence to put the finishing touches on her next "Lost Platoon" article. Even without using anything that John had told her, the documents, photos, and identification by Nils of her brother at the base in Norway painted a pretty compelling case of a secret SEAL team sent on a covert mission to Russia and targeted by a missile strike.

It should be enough to satisfy Jameson.

Should.

Of course, the second version of the article with the section about the six survivors who were in hiding because they weren't sure whether someone on their own side had set them up to die was even better. If only she could publish it.

But she wouldn't do that until she had John's permission. Which she was hoping to get tonight if all went as planned.

She read through the articles one last time and then backed them up with a trick she'd learned from terrorists: saving it as a draft in a private e-mail account—i.e., a dead-drop e-mail. It was a little paranoid, perhaps, but she had learned to be cautious with her work after what had happened five years ago, when her files had been sabotaged. She also didn't want anyone—including her boss and her coworkers—reading her articles before they were ready to be published.

She'd just finished shutting down her laptop and putting it back in her messenger bag when she heard a commotion outside her door. Two voices—a man's and a woman's—were arguing.

"What do you mean I can't go in there? Who the hell are you, and what the heck is going on around here?"

Brittany grinned, and despite her assurances to John that she wouldn't open the door even if it were the Pope dropping by for tea, she undid the dead bolt and threw it open.

Mac was a hell of a lot more tenacious than the Pope—and much less understanding. She was also a lot louder, and Brittany knew that she'd have every neighbor in the place wondering what was going on if she didn't let her in.

The sight that met her eyes was almost comical. Her tiny friend, who was all of about a hundred pounds soaking wet and not much taller than five feet, was standing toe-to-toe with a guy a good foot and half taller than her who looked like he belonged in the WWE. He was huge. He was also clearly packing—the casual clothing didn't quite hide the bulge of the sidearm under his jacket. She could also see the wire of his earpiece under his Yankees baseball cap.

None of that seemed to bother Mac, who had her finger jabbed against his impressive chest. She turned as soon as the door opened, and the relief in her eyes filled Brittany with guilt.

"Thank God."

Mac had clearly been worried about her; Brittany should have tried harder to get her a message. But if she'd asked to use John's phone he would have had questions, and Brittany knew Mac didn't like people knowing about her. She was almost a mythic figure in the dark web, and she liked to keep it that way. Very few people knew what she did for a living.

"It's okay," Brittany said to the burly giant, who, with his handlebar mustache and neck tattoos, looked like he could have doubled for a guy in a motorcycle gang. "She's a friend."

Mac crossed her arms and scowled at the man who was still blocking her path. "Just like I said: Move aside, tough guy."

The tough guy didn't look convinced. "I need to pat her down first." His voice was deep and held just a hint of Jersey.

"The hell you do! Put one hand on me and I'll rip it off."

Mac's threat elicited no more than a raised eyebrow and maybe a glint of amusement in his dark eyes. With his accent and coloring, Brittany was going to go out on a limb and say Italian. Brittany also suspected he'd been messing with her friend just to get a reaction.

"Feisty little thing, aren't you?" He didn't wait for a response—Mac was too busy sputtering obscenities— and looked back at Brittany. "Call out if she gives you any trouble." He looked Mac up and down calculatingly. "I wouldn't mind taking Tinker Bell here down."

Brittany dragged her friend inside before she could retaliate.

"Pig!" Mac said as the door closed behind her. "God, I hate guys who think a couple inches and a few muscles give them a right to push people around." Brittany decided not to point out that it was way more than a couple or a few. "And Tinker Bell? How demeaning is that? I don't look anything like a fairy." Brittany didn't comment. With her tinted violet hair—which actually looked cute—and her pixie features . . . "Why do you have a guy like that watching your door? He was on me out of nowhere as soon as I got out of the elevator." She didn't give Brittany a chance to answer. "God, I was so worried about you. I thought you'd been killed. What is going on around here?"

She gazed around at the cleaned up but still obviously destroyed apartment.

"Sit down," Brittany said. "I'll tell you what I can."

Leaving out John's role and what he'd told her about Team Nine, she filled Mac in on the attack in Norway and the not-so-coincidentally timed break-in at her apartment. She said that they had a plan to try to catch who was responsible and that the man guarding her door was one of the good guys.

Mac snorted at that.

"What about the e-mail?" Mac asked. "Did you find your brother?"

Brittany was surprised by the sudden well of emotion and tears that filled her eyes. She shook her head.

"Then who sent it?"

"I can't say. I'm sorry, but when this is all over, I promise I'll explain everything."

Mac must have heard the pleading in her voice and didn't press.

Brittany apologized for not getting in touch before, explaining that she feared her phone and e-mail were compromised.

"Do you have your phone?"

Brittany nodded and retrieved it from the kitchen counter.

Mac pulled out a laptop, hooked it up to the phone, and a few minutes later, after a flurry of keystrokes, shook her head. "It doesn't look as if it's been cloned and I don't see any spyware."

"Other than yours, you mean?"

Mac smiled. "Hey, it was your idea."

"I assume that's how you knew I was back?" Brittany asked.

Her friend nodded. "But that doesn't mean someone hasn't been monitoring your calls—all they need is your phone number and some good software. And hacking someone's e-mail takes about fifteen minutes of watching a video. There are tutorials on this stuff all over the Internet."

"How reassuring," Brittany said dryly.

Mac grinned.

"Did you find out anything more about the driver of that car?" she asked.

Mac's expression changed quickly to one of frustration and annoyance. "Not yet. But I'm still working on it. I can't believe in this day and age that our government is still using a logbook." She paused. "Wait. Maybe I can."

They both laughed.

Mac didn't stay around for long. After exacting a promise that Brittany would do a better job at staying in touch, she pulled a flip phone from her bag and handed it to her.

"What's this?"

"A burner."

"You keep them in your purse?"

"All the time. I have boatloads of them. Let me know if you need anything. If that cretin out there is any indication, you seem to have plenty of muscle. But you might want to rely on more than the CIA for brains."

Brittany didn't have much more faith in their government than Mac did, but she had faith in John, and that was all that mattered.

Twenty-three

Brittany's heart was pounding as she approached the overpass. She didn't know whether it was nervousness or excitement. Maybe it was a little of both. It was hard to believe that it had been almost two weeks since she'd driven her car to this exact spot to meet her unknown source.

It seemed like a lifetime ago. So much had changed. She wasn't scared like last time. Of course, last time she hadn't had a small army watching over her and a one-man army lying low in the backseat.

John had insisted on accompanying her in the car. She hadn't argued; she felt safer with him there. She'd forgotten how scary this place was—not that she was going to bring that up to John. She'd gotten enough of an earful from him about it earlier.

"What the hell, Brittany? You shouldn't be driving through a place like that by yourself at night, let alone sitting in your damned car for God knows how long!"

She'd tried to explain to him that it went with the job, but he hadn't been in the mood to hear it. As they didn't see eye to eye on many of the finer points of her being a journalist—or the bigger points, for that matter—she'd let it go. But she knew she couldn't do that forever, and at some point they were going to have to talk about it. Being a reporter was important to her. As important as being a SEAL was to him. If they were going to have any chance, they needed to figure out a way to deal with that. She didn't have to like what he did any more than he had to like what she did, but they needed to respect each other's jobs.

She'd also had an earful about her visit from Mac, which he'd apparently been briefed on by the guy in the stairwell before he entered the apartment. She'd let him bellow, knowing it would make him feel better. He'd needed to let off some steam. He was too wound up. Which was still almost surreal to think about. John Donovan. Wound up. Because of her. Who would have thought?

John waited for the car to stop before he asked, "See anything?"

She bent down and pretended to fiddle with the radio before responding, "Not yet."

"Okay, but stay—" He stopped all of a sudden.

She didn't need to ask why. "Frosty," she finished for him, her voice soft and gentle.

John didn't say anything. He didn't need to. She knew what he was thinking. The familiar saying had resurrected her brother between them. No doubt John was feeling guilty again, blaming himself for getting her into this mess. But it had been her decision.

"I'm sure," she said, anticipating his next question. It was the same thing he'd asked half a dozen times since they'd gotten in the car: *"Are you sure you want to go through with this? It's not too late to back out."*

John made a not-so-happy grunt. "If you see anything that doesn't look right, let me know right away."

She listened as he made radio contact with the men surrounding them. It had been a shock to see him all geared up. Though he wasn't in a uniform, the dark ball cap and clothing, earpiece, armored vest stuffed with gear, and gun had given her a good idea of what he must look like when he went on an op.

When he'd walked out of her bathroom, it had taken her aback. The grim-faced mercenary didn't look anything like the laid-back surfer. She knew how big and strong he was physically, but kitted out G.I. Joe John was a very different kind of big and strong.

It was a little intimidating.

And a lot sexy. A *whole* lot sexy. Which, given her feelings about his being a SEAL, was unexpected. But primitive instincts were primitive instincts, and hers had gone a little hog wild. She'd wanted to drag him right back in that bedroom and strip him down piece by piece. Or maybe she'd just let him take her while he was all kitted out.

Was she messed up or what?

She adjusted the vest he'd made her put on, which was bulky, heavy, and uncomfortable. "I can't imagine running or walking long distances in one of these things."

"Try dropping out of an airplane, fast-roping down from a hovering helicopter, or swimming a few miles in one. But those plates have saved my life more than once."

She didn't like to think about him being shot at. Nor did she really want to think about herself being shot at. It was just a precaution, he'd told her when he handed it to her. It was better to be safe than sorry.

Of course, it would be useless against a shot to the head, which was probably not something she should be thinking about right now.

Knowing they shouldn't talk too much in case someone was watching them from afar, Brittany sat quietly watching the clock creep forward minute by minute. It was 10:17. Seventeen minutes after the appointed time and nearly a half hour since she'd parked. The wait was agonizing and interminable.

What if they didn't show up? What if this was all for nothing? What if . . . ?

She jumped when her phone rang. She didn't recognize the number, but it was local. "What should I do?"

"Answer it," John said.

"Hello?"

"Finally! I was beginning to think you disappeared on me."

She recognized the voice and cursed silently. "Hey, Mick. I'm sorry I didn't get back to you, but it's not a good time right now."

John said something she was sure she didn't want to hear, and she was glad he wasn't sitting next to her.

"Sorry to call so late, but I'm just checking to make sure we are still on for tomorrow night?" Mick said. "I thought we could go to that new Italian restaurant in Georgetown."

Brittany didn't get a chance to respond. At that moment all hell broke loose in front of her. She could hear the quick exchange of voices through John's earpiece. The men who'd been watching from the shadows poured out into the street and dragged someone from what looked like an abandoned car parked next to the building opposite her.

John was already out of the car. Brittany paused long enough to tell Mick she would have to call him back, but then she was right behind him.

She let out a sharp gasp when confronted with the hired soldiers who'd been protecting her. If she thought John was intimidating, a dozen G.I. Joe Johns were even more so. John was only minimally geared up compared to these guys. They were dressed in black from head to toe and armed to the gills with all sorts of weapons. Each guy looked bigger and stronger than the last.

Brittany had read a lot of stories in her research about black ops and secret warriors, but seeing these guys put it all in perspective.

Without realizing it, she took a step toward John.

Mistaking the source of her fear, he said, "Get back in the car. You shouldn't be out here."

She didn't bother to respond, but she wasn't going anywhere. She needed to be here. She needed to see who was trying to kill her.

The guy they'd pulled from the car was dragged forward. She could see John and one of the black-clad soldiers exchanging glances. But she didn't need to ask what the problem was. She could see it for herself.

The guy they were holding didn't look anything like the guy who'd attacked her in Norway. He was about half a foot shorter and fifty pounds thinner for one. "Scrawny" came to mind. He was also in his midforties and wearing thick glasses that looked completely wrong with the black stocking cap and black leather jacket.

What was going on here? This guy was clearly not a professional hit man—or any kind of hit man.

"What the fuck?" John said to the soldier he'd exchanged a glance with.

Brittany assumed he was the head honcho. He looked at one of his guys, who said, "I thought he had a gun."

Someone else came forward, holding something up. "It was a camera. It fell to the ground when we pulled him from the car."

"If that lens is damaged, you're paying for it," the man they'd pulled from the car said.

"What were you doing out here?" John demanded. "Why were you in that car with a camera?"

"It's none of your business."

John took a step toward him. "Try again."

The guy looked at the men circling in around him, and his pale face lost some of its defiance. "I'm meeting someone, and I saw the car pull up. I thought it looked suspicious—"

John didn't let him finish. He reached down, grabbed

him by the collar of his jacket, and lifted him a few inches off the ground as if he weighed no more than a wet cat. "Maybe you don't understand the seriousness of your situation right now. But if I were you, I'd think about the next words out of my mouth."

Brittany shivered at the cold menace in his voice. The guy's eyes bulged, and whatever bravery he'd shown dissolved comically fast. "I'm a PI. I was hired to follow her."

"Hired by who?"

"I don't know."

John tightened his grip and lifted him higher so they were almost eye to eye and the private eye was hanging a good foot off the ground.

"One of her coworkers," the PI couldn't say fast enough. "She gave me a fake name, but it was Nancy something."

Brittany was completely floored. Paulie she might have believed, but Nancy? "Why?"

The PI looked at her. "She wanted to know where you were getting your information."

"So you broke into her apartment?" John growled.

The guy nodded nervously. "Looking for her laptop or documents. But I didn't find anything. The woman told me to make it look bad."

Nancy had gotten what she paid for. Brittany was still too stunned to process it all. Her friend—the woman she'd tried to help—had hired someone to spy on her? Terrorize her with scary messages in lipstick?

"And you followed her to Europe?" John said.

The guy shook his head, obviously confused. "No. The woman didn't pay me enough for that. She didn't pay me enough for any of this."

John questioned him a little longer, but it was obvious the guy was telling the truth. It was also obvious that they'd made a mistake. What had happened to Brittany wasn't connected to John's platoon and what went wrong in Russia at all. This was about a jealous coworker trying to discredit her or get the jump on her story. The attack in Norway was what Brittany initially thought it had been: an attempted mugging.

She didn't know whether to be disappointed or happy. No one was trying to kill her, but neither were she and John any closer to finding out who was responsible for setting up Team Nine and killing her brother.

She had one more idea, but she knew John wasn't going to like it.

Twenty-four

"No." John was furious even at the suggestion. Brittany had waited until after they'd gotten back to her apartment and he'd called the LC to fill him in on what had happened to spring her "idea" on him. "What I told you was in confidence. You swore that you wouldn't print anything."

"I said I wouldn't print anything that you told me," she said. "And I won't, but I think you should listen and think about it before you say no. It could be a way to shake things up and see what comes loose."

John couldn't believe it. He'd thought she understood. He'd told her the information in confidence. He didn't want to hear her rationale, even if it made some sense.

Although the LC had Kate helping them, a full-scale investigation from a "leak" could lead to an answer much faster. And even though the LC didn't think they could trust anyone, John could think of plenty he would trust with his life—including Colt Wesson, Kate's ex-husband and John's ex-chief.

But it wasn't just his life; it was the lives of the five other men who'd survived with him. And it wasn't his call to make.

"It could also put a target on my head." Not to mention the other survivors.

"I don't have to say there were survivors. But I could say that it looked like a setup. That the Russians knew you were coming. It might start an investigation."

"No, damn it! You aren't going to say anything!"

John didn't realize he was shouting until she took a step back and looked up at him with a wounded expression on her face that made him want to crawl out of his own skin. "It was only an idea. I was trying to help. But if you don't want me to say anything about what you told me, I won't."

"I don't want you to say anything at all."

She didn't respond. But he knew. He fucking *knew.* "You're still planning to write another story, aren't you? I can't believe it. After everything that just happened?"

"But that's just it. Nothing just happened. I'm not in any danger. What happened at my apartment and in Norway had nothing to do with you. I can't put this aside."

"Yes, you can. Very easily. You just don't write the damn story. Simple."

"This is my job, John, and I owe it to my brother to uncover the truth and see that who is responsible is punished."

"So this is all about lofty ideals? It doesn't have anything to do with you making a name for yourself? Or maybe I should say remaking a name for yourself. This is a great story. It would do a lot to get back some of your lost credibility. You've already used intel you saw on that doc in Brand's room."

She flushed with anger. And maybe a little guilt. "I explained about that. It was already a not-very-well-kept secret."

"But you made it *not* a secret. How do I know you won't rationalize the same thing with what I told you?"

She looked struck—and hurt. As if the accusation had

wounded her. "I would never betray your trust. You should know that."

"What I know is that you have a one-track mind when it comes to uncovering 'the truth' and that nothing else matters when you think you are onto something. But you've let your search for justice for the people who are dead interfere with the living. First with your parents and Brand and now with me. You are so busy looking behind you that you don't think about what you are doing. Not all cover-ups are bad cover-ups. Sometimes there are things more important than the truth."

She was clearly furious. "You have no idea what you are talking about."

"I know a hell of a lot more than you do. You were wrong to turn your back on Brand. You should have trusted him."

"What are you talking about?"

He shouldn't have said anything. "Nothing." But he couldn't leave it there. "Sometimes justice isn't meted out right away. Sometimes it takes longer."

"Like the justice for my parents? I'm still waiting for that, John, and it's been twelve years. And while you're lecturing me about living in the past, what about you? At least I care about something and don't mind showing it. Your mom died and you acted as if it were no big deal. Just like you did with Brandon and the others you lost in Russia. Just another day at the office, right, Johnny?"

A flash of white heat shot through him as fierce and riveting as a lightning bolt. He stiffened. "Don't try to psychoanalyze me, Brittany. You aren't my—" He stopped.

But she guessed what he'd been about to say. Girlfriend. Wife. Someone who had a right to intrude.

He hadn't said it, but that didn't seem to matter. She looked just as crushed as if he had.

"Me, try to get inside the great John Donovan's head? I wouldn't dream of it."

He didn't like her sarcasm, but he also knew he'd better put a stop to this before they both said something they would regret.

He sat on the couch, trying to calm down. It had been a shit night. He'd been so certain the apartment and attack in Norway were related. But now they were back to square one, and he was still . . . lost.

But he might not be for much longer if he didn't convince her to put her story aside.

"Look, Brit. I know you think you have a duty, but what about your duty not to inflame an already precarious situation? The US and Russia are teetering on the edge of war. Do you really want to be the one to push us into it? I've been there once. I don't have any interest in going back anytime soon." He looked over to where she stood by the kitchen table and met her gaze squarely. "I'm not asking you to put it aside forever. I'm just asking you to be patient for a little longer." He paused. "For me."

Brittany couldn't believe he was doing this. He was trying to manipulate her. If not with guilt for inciting a war, then with her feelings for him.

"You don't have any idea what you are asking."

"I know exactly what I'm asking."

"You want me to bury another government cover-up and let my brother's death be swept aside just as my parents' were." *Because you know how much I care about you.* "You want me to ignore my job and the story of a lifetime. Yes, a story that could give me my career back. I'm a journalist, John—as much as you are a SEAL. Searching for the truth, uncovering secrets, holding the government accountable . . . this is exactly the kind of story that I went into this business to write. It's what I've devoted my life to."

"Too much of your life, from what I can see."

"What is that supposed to mean?"

"Look at this place. There's hardly anything personal around. And didn't you say something about a pet?"

She flushed. Even if that were true, he had no right to comment. "You are one to talk. You've devoted your life to being a SEAL just as much as I've devoted my life to my job. What if I asked you to put it all aside for me?"

"This is different. My job isn't going to get you killed."

"But your job could get *you* killed." He didn't bite, but she could tell he didn't appreciate her flip response. "No one is looking for you right now, John. No one knows you are alive. My articles haven't changed that. You are asking me to put aside everything I've believed in and forgo justice for yet another family member's death." She paused. "What you are asking isn't fair. If you cared about me, if you loved me as I love you, you would understand that and would never ask this."

I love you. She hadn't meant to say it; it just sort of slipped out. So much for not rushing things. But for her it wasn't rushed at all. It was the realization of what had been growing between them five years ago and had reached full maturation over the past ten days that they'd been together.

But it didn't take her long to regret the words. His reaction was every bit as horrible as she might have imagined. Instant discomfort. Avoiding her gaze. Something like panic in his. And mentally racing for the door. All that was missing was a cold sweat.

It was just like last time. She might have been standing in that second-floor bedroom of the beach house he shared with her brother, having her heart ripped to shreds all over again. But this time was worse. This time she'd thought . . .

No. She stopped herself. She hadn't been all wrong. He did care about her.

Just not enough.

But it turned out that being partially right didn't stop her chest from feeling as if an elephant had just stomped on it.

She couldn't stand the silence, so she rushed to cover it. "But I guess that's hypothetical, right?" She tried to smile, but it came out wobbly. "That was rhetorical. I don't expect you to say anything. You didn't do anything wrong. You never made me any promises. I get it. You don't need to go find a set of twins again to prove it to me."

The joke fell flat. But he finally seemed to come out of his daze. He stood and reached for her, snagging her arm before she could spin away. "Look. I care about you. I don't want to hurt you."

Then don't.

But if he heard her silent plea, he didn't answer it.

To hell with playing it safe. She couldn't take the words back. She might as well deal with them. "What are we doing here, John?"

"I'm trying to keep you safe."

She'd always thought the dagger-through-the-heart thing was just a romantic metaphor. Too flowery. Way too silly for a serious writer like herself. But she felt it now. Digging sharp and deep. Words could cut.

That was what this was about to him. Keeping her safe. And, apparently, keeping her quiet. She'd been building a relationship, while he'd been fulfilling some kind of duty.

She sucked in her breath sharply. The answer obvious. She should have known. "Let me guess. Brandon made you promise to watch over me if anything ever happened to him."

John had finally recovered enough from the shock of the "L" word to realize that this conversation was in a nosedive, and if he didn't do something to pull himself out of it soon, it was heading for a death spiral.

"No . . . well . . . yes. But that isn't why—"

She stopped him. "Forget it. You don't need to explain. I get it."

Clearly she didn't. But how could he explain? He was here for Brand, but he was also here for himself. He reached for her, cupping the side of her face with his hand and forcing her to look at him. The pad of his thumb slid over her bottom lip in a tender caress. "I care about you, Brit. And I don't want to hurt you, but I can't make any more promises than that."

She pulled away. "Then don't."

"What do you mean?"

"Don't hurt me any more. I'm not in any danger. You kept your promise to my brother. You don't need to stay here anymore. Leave before it gets worse."

Wait. That wasn't what he wanted.

She read his hesitation but misinterpreted it. "If you are worried about keeping me quiet, don't be. You win. Consider the article buried."

Now, that *really* jellied him. "What?"

"I won't publish another Lost Platoon article. Isn't that what you wanted?"

That was exactly what he wanted. So why did he feel like shit? Why did he feel as if he'd just asked her to cut out her heart and hand it to him on a plate? Why did he feel as if he should never have asked it of her?

If you loved me . . .

He felt the walls closing in on him again. As if he were being backed into a corner. But for the first time, he didn't feel like running.

He knew that if he ran now, there would be no coming back.

But Brittany had other ideas. She wasn't trying to hold on to him; she was trying to force him out the door. Literally. She crossed the room and opened the door. "Go now, John. While your conscience is clear. You've kept your promise. But if you stick around, you might not be able to say the same."

But maybe he would. Maybe he wouldn't end up hurting her at all. Maybe he would make her promises and keep them.

Was maybe enough?

"Leave before it gets worse."

He was hurting her. And without the justification of protecting her, he didn't really have an excuse to stick around any longer.

Had it all been an excuse? Had he overreacted to what he'd seen in Norway? Seen danger that wasn't there because of who she was?

He didn't know anymore. And after the war party they'd mobilized tonight, and the risk of discovery that he'd taken, it felt as if his senses had let him down. Not getting emotionally invested was the only way he could do his job.

He needed to do what he always did: put it aside—put *her* aside—and move on.

Except he didn't want to.

"Johnny, you're going to break some poor girl's heart one day." He could still hear the sadness in his mom's voice when some girl in high school was calling him all the time. He knew what she was thinking. That he was like his old man. Even his mom who'd loved him more than anything had seen it.

Without more to offer, was that fair to Brittany?

He knew the answer. With one last look, he walked out of the apartment. "I'm sorry."

"I know."

And then the door closed, and it was too late to wonder if he'd made a mistake.

Twenty-five

It wasn't supposed to happen that way. He wasn't supposed to leave.

But you asked him to. You practically pushed him out the door. You played the noble card and he took it. Why are you surprised?

For all his ladies' man reputation, Brittany knew John Donovan was an inherently decent guy. When faced with a choice between hurting her more or hurting her less, he was going to take the less.

She'd asked him to give her a guarantee when there weren't any. Love didn't come with guarantees. It came with hard work and commitment. It came with understanding and patience.

It came with trust.

None of which she'd showed him. Instead, she'd given him an ultimatum: tell me you love me and will never hurt me or go. So he'd gone. What had she expected?

She'd wanted everything wrapped up. But life didn't come with pretty bows. It came with snags and tears and knots. Sometimes lots of knots that needed to be untangled.

Still, in those first horrible minutes after the door closed she'd tried to convince herself it was for the best. He didn't *really* love her. He couldn't. Not if he could use her feelings for him to manipulate her into putting aside her story when he knew how important it was to her.

"I'm not asking you to put it aside forever."

But he shouldn't have asked her at all . . . right?

Understanding and patience—wasn't that what she'd said?

Brittany sat down on the couch, suddenly feeling a little queasy.

She had to stop this. She'd done the right thing. Saved herself a lot of future pain. There were too many uncertainties, too many ways it could go wrong. Their respective jobs for one. His difficulty in dealing with his feelings for another. The fact that he was at the center of one of the biggest military disasters in US history, which could potentially turn into one of its biggest scandals—or a third world war.

What chance did they have? Was she really going to be okay being with someone who lived a life of secrets? Who couldn't tell her anything? Who might be involved in the kind of secret operations that she was trying to shine lights on?

But maybe she wasn't asking the right questions. Maybe she should ask herself whether she would be okay with a guy who went to work every day willing to put his life on the line for others, who served his country with distinction, and who was willing to make the ultimate sacrifice for his country, his friends, and the people he loved.

Would she be okay with a guy who wanted to protect her, who would do anything to keep her safe, who didn't want to hurt her? Who could make her laugh even in the darkest of times? Who listened and understood? Who was as strong and sexy as he was gentle and considerate?

Who both respected her and disrespected her at exactly the right times—the latter when they were naked?

Yeah, she'd be okay with that guy. She'd be more than okay. She'd be lucky and proud.

Now it was too late to tell him that.

It's for the best. But no matter how many times she said that, it didn't feel like the best. It felt miserable. It felt lonely. It felt as if she'd just lost the only man she'd ever love.

And if a broken heart wasn't enough, when Brittany's life went to hell, it *really* went to hell. In the space of one wretched evening she had no John, no story, two coworkers who wanted to be rid of her—one so badly she'd hired a PI to investigate her—and probably no job.

Saving her job. *That* was what she had to think about. Brittany wiped the tears away. Not whether she'd done the right thing. Not whether she should have given him a chance.

Not whether she'd made a mistake.

It was too late for second thoughts. John was long gone, and she knew she would never find him again. Not unless he wanted to be found.

But it wasn't too late to save the only thing she had left.

Five years ago, when she'd thought her career was over, John had shown her how to open her eyes a little wider. Reminded her not to give up too easily. He'd made her see that what felt like rock bottom might actually have a few feet of water above it.

Brittany walked into the paper the next morning prepared to do battle with a new story idea.

But that few feet of water evaporated quickly.

"So, let me get this straight?" Brittany looked directly at Nancy. "One of my coworkers hires a PI to break into my apartment and spy on me, and I'm the one defending myself?"

When Brittany had walked into Jameson's office, both Paulie and Nancy were sitting there, waiting for her. They'd taken the two seats on the other side of the desk, leaving her to stand and feel as if she were on trial.

Apparently she was.

Realizing that the jig was up, Nancy had gone on the offensive, joining forces with Paulie to discredit Brittany before Jameson. Nancy had admitted to hiring the PI because she was worried that Brittany was manufacturing evidence . . . again.

Nancy turned to Jameson. "I admit it was extreme—"

"Extreme?" Brittany was outraged at the understatement. "He destroyed my apartment and threatened me!"

Nancy looked at her as if she were being dramatic. "He looked through a few drawers, which I believe the situation warranted—especially with her history of conspiracy theories. I was worried about the integrity of the team—about the integrity of the entire paper. I don't need to explain what it would do if it became known that one of the paper's investigative team reporters was manufacturing 'proof'—it would destroy our credibility."

"That's a serious claim to make," Jameson said calmly. "What proof do you have?"

"She doesn't have any proof," Brittany interrupted. "Because there isn't any. I am not making this up."

"Then where are your sources?" Nancy said smugly. "Weren't you telling us all yesterday about a big meeting last night and some 'explosive proof.' Where is it? According to the guy I hired, no one showed up last night."

Brittany opened her mouth, but quickly realized the problem. If she admitted it was a sting and that she'd lied about the meeting, she would have to explain why or she would sound like . . . a liar.

She would also have to explain the men who were with her. Nancy had obviously talked to her PI and realized that no one had called the police. By not doing so,

Nancy realized that Brittany didn't want the police involved. She must have guessed that Brittany wouldn't be able to reveal who they were.

She was right.

"They must have been scared off by your PI," Brittany said.

"Or there wasn't any meeting," Nancy replied. "And you were lying about it to support your next article."

There was no next article. Not a Lost Platoon one anyway. But she couldn't let that go.

"I'm not lying," Brittany said to Jameson. She pulled out the file of documents she'd received from her mysterious source and handed them to him. "You'll see the deployment order. Naval Warfare Special Deployment Group has to be Team Nine. In Norway, I found a man who was able to place my brother there at about the same time."

Jameson flipped through the documents quickly and handed them back to her. "I guess you haven't read the morning paper yet?"

Brittany shook her head. She'd skipped coffee at home and come straight to the office. "No. Why?"

He handed it to her. She looked at the headline: FOURTEEN SEALs LOSE THEIR LIVES IN A TRAINING EXERCISE.

Her stomach dropped. "What is this?"

"The navy has acknowledged your brother's death," Jameson said. She gazed down at the list of names, seeing Brandon's staring back at her—and John's—among a couple others she recognized from her time in San Diego. "They don't say it," he continued. "But it's clearly a response to the public interest spawned by your articles and the ruckus in Iowa by the woman who claimed to be pregnant by one of the missing SEALs."

Brittany was reading it for herself. There was no mention of secret teams or clandestine missions, only "the tragic loss of life" of "fourteen SEALs" in "one of the worst training disasters ever to befall the US military" off the coast of Alaska when a storm caused their helicopter to go down. There were no further details, only that the incident was under investigation.

"This is ridiculous," Brittany said, handing the paper back to him. "It's obviously CYA. They don't even say when it happened."

"Maybe so," Jameson said. "But it's the official statement, and you need something more than a redacted order that mentions Norway—not Russia—to disprove it. I went out on a limb for you, Brittany, but you are leaving me hanging out to dry here. If we don't publish something more—something with proof—to refute this, we are going to look like idiots."

It was clear he wanted to believe her, but she also needed to give him something concrete. Something she didn't have.

"Why don't you give it to him?" Nancy said.

"Give him what?"

"Your next article," she said. "The one about the six survivors who were warned by an inside source of the trap waiting for them in Russia."

It was hard to tell who was more shocked by Nancy's bombshell: Jameson or Brittany. Even Paulie looked surprised. Obviously, Brittany's e-mail drop trick wasn't as fail-safe as she'd thought—or Nancy's PI wasn't as inept as he looked.

"You hacked my e-mail?"

Nancy shrugged. "I didn't need to. I saw you type in your password once. Your name with one-two-three after it isn't very original."

"Nancy, that is out of line—way out of line," Jameson said. "We will discuss what happens to you later." He turned to Brittany. "Is she right? Did you write an article about survivors?"

"It was a draft article," Brittany said. "It wasn't meant for publication."

"Not until you can make up some sources?" Paulie said snidely. "Or do you have more 'proof' that we don't know about?"

"My PI said you were with a man. Was he one of them?" Nancy asked.

Brittany didn't know whether Nancy's comment was a shot in the dark or just an effort to make Brittany look silly, but it didn't matter. The thought of John being unmasked or someone learning that he was alive made her blood run cold. If he was hurt or killed because of her . . . because of something she did . . .

She couldn't even think about it.

Which made what would seem like a horrible choice of defending her work and breaking her promise to John or letting her boss believe what her coworkers were accusing her of easy.

There wasn't a choice at all. John was right. In her quest for the truth, she sometimes lost sight of the human costs. The truth did have limits, and she'd just come up against hers. She wouldn't do anything that would put him in more danger. Even if it meant lying. Even if it meant covering up a story. Even if it meant the job she loved.

He'd asked her to give him the trust she hadn't given her brother. *"You should have trusted him."* John was right. She should have. It was too late for Brandon—and she would regret that every day of her life—but it wasn't too late for John.

She responded to Nancy first. "He wasn't one of them because there were no survivors. He was that hockey player I told you I was dating who came to help me out." *Thank you, Mick.* She took a deep breath and turned to Jameson. "There isn't any proof."

Brittany thought that would be it. But apparently

Jameson had more faith in her than she realized. He seemed to suspect she was hiding something. "Let me read it. Maybe there is something we can use."

Brittany shook her head numbly. She knew what she had to do. But it wasn't easy to get the words out, knowing what they would cost her. "I'm sorry. I can't do that."

"Why?" he asked.

She wanted to cry. Her last chance to restore her reputation and have the career she loved was about to go up in smoke. "Paulie and Nancy were right. I made it up. I made it all up."

The silence in the room was deafening. She'd surprised even Nancy.

Of course Jameson fired her. She'd left him with no other choice. Brittany was so ashamed, she couldn't even look at him.

She returned to her cubicle—escorted—to pack up her things, realizing that no one would ever take a chance on her again.

She'd hit rock bottom enough times in the past to know what it felt like. But then she'd had her brother—and John. Her three feet of water.

Now she was touching rock and had no one to blame but herself.

Twenty-six

John woke feeling even shittier than he had the night before. And for once it wasn't from drinking himself into oblivion. It was from *not* drinking himself into oblivion and having some of the worst dreams he'd had since fleeing Russia. Instead of seeing his SEAL brothers' faces in his nightmares, he'd seen Brittany's.

She was running in the darkness and smoke was everywhere. She was yelling for him to help her, and he couldn't find her. Every time he closed his eyes he'd see her crying, telling him she loved him, and himself standing there paralyzed with fear. Wanting to do something but too damned scared to move. He'd been scared in his life before, but he'd never been a coward.

"What the hell is wrong with you, Dynomite? Are you listening to anything I'm saying?"

The LC's voice penetrated the haze of his sleep-deprived brain. John hadn't been listening. He needed to snap out of it.

When Scott Taylor had shown up at his hotel room this morning, John had been stunned. And so damned happy to see him, he could have cried.

For more than two months he'd been telling himself it
didn't matter. It didn't matter that he'd lost his best friend
and half the family he had left. It didn't matter that the
survivors had been forced to scatter to different corners
of the globe. It didn't matter that he was sitting on his ass
alone—in fucking Finland—doing none of the things
he'd been trained to do.

It didn't matter that he was alive when his best friend
wasn't.

But that was bullshit. Brittany had known that and
had called him on it, but it wasn't until he'd seen his commanding officer standing in front of him that he knew
how much he'd been fooling himself.

You couldn't just move on from something like that.
Any more than you could just move on and forget losing
a parent to cancer.

Those feelings were still there. Buried but ready to
surface at any time. Like the overwhelming punch of
emotion that had hit him on seeing the LC.

But if Taylor had been surprised by the exuberance
of the bro-hug John had subjected him to, he didn't
show it. Actually, John suspected the always-serious,
do-it-by-the-book officer was just as happy to see him.
SEALs were pack animals—the lone-survivor stuff
sucked.

John wasn't sure why the LC had decided to risk
meeting in person, but he wasn't going to question it.

"Sorry," John said. "I didn't sleep much last night." As
in at all.

"Is this about Blake's sister? I thought you said she'd
agreed to keep quiet."

John nodded. "She said she would bury the article."

He'd won. He'd gotten what he wanted. But he didn't
feel as if he'd won at all. He felt as if he'd used the love
of the only woman he'd ever cared about against her.

"If you loved me as I love you . . ."

He could still see her face when she'd told him that she loved him—and the hurt and disappointment when he hadn't replied. He felt that gnawing in his gut again. That swell of unease that he just couldn't shake.

Coward.

"I can keep a few guys on her if you are still worried about her being a target."

He was still worried, but he didn't have any reason to be. Of course, when it came to Brittany, he and reason seemed to part ways more often than not.

"Yeah, I'd appreciate it." The break-in and attack in Norway might not be related, but he still couldn't forget that guy. He'd been a professional—of that he was certain. But it seemed as if it was a coincidence.

Or maybe he was just inventing more excuses to go back to her.

"So, what's this about, LC? Does Kate have something for us? Are we any closer to finding out what the hell happened out there?"

Taylor shook his head and filled John in on everything that had happened the past few days with the rear admiral and discovering that General Murray, Vice Chairman of the Joint Chiefs of Staff, was Brittany's source.

"You're fucking kidding me."

The LC shook his head. "Nope. He wants the Russians to pay for what happened to us and for his son's death."

"Even if it means war?"

The LC nodded.

"So, Kate and Colt are working together?" John asked, watching the LC's expression.

He didn't give away anything. "She's keeping him from getting on a plane to Russia."

"And you're sure that's a bad idea? Maybe he can find something."

"That's what I'm worried about. He could blow this thing wide open."

John hesitated. "Maybe shaking it up to see whether something comes loose is what we need."

John was aware that he was repeating Brittany's argument, but he didn't care. She hadn't been all wrong.

The LC shook his head. "Forget it. I'm not risking any of your lives. We just need to be a little more patient. Kate will find something." As if on cue, his phone buzzed. "That's her now."

John could only hear half the conversation, but from the "no" and occasional curse, he knew it wasn't good.

As soon as the LC disconnected, John asked, "What happened?"

"The military has declared us dead. Apparently, it was on the news and in the papers this morning."

They turned on CNN. It didn't take long for the "training accident" story to appear. It was surreal to see his name and face on the screen.

"Guess we're officially dead now," John said. "What do you think it means?"

"That they are nervous. That your reporter was making it too hard for them to keep this under wraps." He paused. "And that we probably both should get out of DC before someone recognizes us."

John shook his head. "I can't do that, sir. Not yet." Not while he couldn't shake this unease with Brittany.

The LC eyed him, clearly suspecting the reason. "Yeah, that makes two of us. So, what do you say we put our heads together and see what we can come up with?"

For the rest of the day they did just that. Going over every angle of the operation at least a half-dozen times. It was damned good to be back in the saddle again, but John was still distracted.

He went into the bathroom to take a shower to clear his head while the LC ordered more room service, but he came out a few minutes later when the LC called to him.

"You gotta see this," Taylor said. "She *really* buried the story."

"What are you talking about?"

"Blake's sister." The LC nodded toward the screen, where the reporter was talking.

John listened, stunned. "In light of the navy's statement this morning about the training accident, investigative reporter Brittany Blake, who published a series of articles for the *DC Chronicle* about the so-called Lost Platoon of a secret SEAL team, has been dismissed for fabricating the stories. The *Chronicle* has posted a retraction. This is the second time Ms. Blake has been let go under the cloud of suspicion and wrongdoing."

John was glad the bed was behind him. "Ah, hell," he said, sitting down.

The LC was looking at him. "Man, you must have really persuaded her for her to fall on her sword for you like that."

John was too numb to say anything other than, "Yeah."

He'd done a number on her, all right. She'd sacrificed everything she'd been fighting for to protect him.

And what had he done? He'd accused her of betraying him and then stood there, paralyzed, like a fucking coward when she told him she loved him, too scared to admit what he was feeling.

John wasn't his father. His first impulse when she'd gotten too close in Denmark was to go to pick someone up, but he hadn't done it. He couldn't do it. He hadn't wanted to, and he'd known that if he did, she would never forgive him—and he would never forgive himself.

He hadn't been able to do it five years ago either.

Because he'd been falling in love with her then, too.

"I gotta go talk to her," John said to the LC.

He just hoped to hell that she would want to see him. That she would give him long enough to explain before slamming the door in his face.

He couldn't blame her.

"Go," the LC said. "Do what you need to do, but be careful."

Brittany couldn't stand the thought of going back to an empty apartment, so she'd gone to the National Portrait Gallery and sat in one of the rooms staring at the paintings. Her mother had always loved museums and galleries, and sometimes Brittany came here to think. It made her mom feel not so gone.

But George wasn't helping much today. She looked up at the famous *Lansdowne Portrait* of the first president, by Gilbert Stuart. Her mother had always preferred the English and Continental artists—Gainsborough, Reynolds, Renoir, Monet. But there was something about the wise and serious countenances of the founding fathers that had always appealed to Brittany. Their strength, commitment, and certainty in the country they'd set up were somehow reassuring.

A psychiatrist would probably have a field day with that, given her personal crusade with the First Amendment.

But Brittany wasn't finding much solace in anything today. Eventually, she gathered up her belongings, including the personal items she'd removed from her cubicle—all of which fit in her bag—and returned to her apartment.

She parked her car on the street. Her building didn't have a garage, but there was plenty of resident-permit parking around. She was almost to the door of the building when she looked up and saw a man standing there.

For one incredible heartbeat she thought it was John. She saw the tall, broad-shouldered form in the dark clothes and ball cap and thought he'd changed his mind.

But then the man looked over. The dark hair and slight crook in his nose made her realize that it wasn't John; it was her Internet date, the hockey player Mick.

Brittany swore under her breath and walked toward him. She'd forgotten to call him back and cancel their makeup date tonight.

He grinned, seeing her. "Hey, there you are. I've been buzzing a while and was starting to think that you'd forgotten about tonight."

"I'm sorry to say that I did," Brittany admitted. "I've had a lot going on this week, and I should have called to cancel."

His expression changed, the easygoing, lady-killer smile replaced by a tinge of annoyance. "But I came all this way—and I made reservations—and you already canceled on me once."

He looked around—which she thought was odd—and took a step toward her. She caught the hint of his aftershave. It smelled familiar, although she couldn't place the scent.

"Here," he said. He started to reach for her bag with his right hand, but then switched to his left. "Let me help you with that."

Brittany looked down at his right hand and saw the cast on his arm. "What happened?"

"Pickup hockey game," he said with a crooked smile.

He was standing a little too close, and it was beginning to make her uncomfortable. She looked around instinctively. There was a man walking on the opposite side of the street, but he wasn't looking in their direction.

Should she call out?

Almost as if Mick could read her mind, he moved to block her view of the guy.

Had it been intentional?

Her heartbeat made a sudden lurch and started to race. Her instincts that something wasn't right flared even before she realized what it was. "That's okay." She pulled her bag in closer to her body. "I really have to go up now. Call, and we can reschedule."

Not.

She started to move away, but he grabbed her arm. "Sorry. Rescheduling isn't going to work for me."

That was when it clicked. The profile, the scent of aftershave, the broken arm. Mick was the guy who'd attacked her in Norway.

It happened so fast that she didn't have time to react. He tucked her against his body and dragged her into the alley at the side of her building. She saw the car waiting and tried to yell. Tried to kick. Tried to do anything to get away.

But her second of hesitation had cost her. The guy across the street was gone.

She felt the sharp pinch of a needle in her neck and tried to break away, but she could feel the rush of fluid pouring into her body. Too late. "What are you doing? Mick! Stop!"

"Not Mick," he said softly, his face swimming above hers. "Mikhail."

Oh God . . . he's Russian.

It was the last thought Brittany had before she catapulted into unconsciousness.

Twenty-seven

Percy had known there was something wrong as soon as Kate walked in the door.

It was no wonder. She must look like a wreck. Hurricane Colt had struck again. She'd been completely destroyed by that kiss.

How could she still respond to someone she hated?

She couldn't. That was the problem. She didn't hate Colt. She hated what he'd done, but not the man. She didn't need to. He hated himself enough for both of them. He'd never believed he deserved to be happy, so he'd seen that he wasn't.

And heaven help her, she still felt drawn to him. Still felt that maybe she was the one who could get through to him. Was it arrogance or idiocy? Maybe a little of both.

But what about her? Didn't she deserve to be happy, too?

She knew the answer, and she also knew that she wasn't going to find it with Percy. Not if he didn't want a child with her.

And not if he couldn't do that to her with a kiss.

The conversation was painful but over quickly. For the first time, Kate told him how she felt. She wanted to adopt a child. Not in the future but now. As soon as they were married. If that wasn't something he wanted, he needed to tell her.

He did. He didn't want to be a father again. He loved George and Poppy, but he was ready for a new stage in his life. One that didn't involve diapers and parent-teacher meetings. He wanted to enjoy all the benefits of his being in the diplomatic service. The travel. The parties. All the opportunities that wouldn't be as easy with small children.

When it was over, Kate couldn't help but think how civilized it all had been. There hadn't been tears or accusations or anger. There hadn't been slammed doors or yelling or any signs of emotion. It hadn't felt as if her limbs were being torn from her body and her heart had been burned to an ashy crisp.

It hadn't felt anything like before.

But in one way it had been brutally the same. Neither man she thought she loved had been willing to fight for her—or for them. They'd both walked away and not looked back.

In the aftermath of Percy's departure, Kate took up residence in her home office. For the next few days, when she wasn't working, she pored over everything she could find about Natalie Andersson, aka Natalya Petrova.

There wasn't much.

She fell asleep on the sofa bed, and when she woke up, she made a pot of coffee and went at it again.

Calling in favors, she scoured every kind of record she could find. Credit card statements, utility bills, phone bills, employment records, medical records, social media accounts—especially social media accounts, which were usually a hotbed of information.

But there was nothing. Either Natalie was good or Scott was right—it was a coincidence.

But Kate didn't believe in coincidences and something about it didn't feel right.

It was only after Scott called her to tell her about the bungled sting and the PI who'd walked into it that Kate shifted her attention back to Brittany. She'd pulled Brittany's cell phone records a couple days ago and decided to look at them again.

There was something niggling, but she couldn't put her finger on it.

Kate scanned the numbers of the recent calls and stopped, the niggle turning to a fully formed buzz. 0125. The last four numbers of one of the calls. January 25th. Her father's birthday. To remember important numbers—such as phone numbers—she'd used memory tricks like birthdays, anniversaries, or other important dates.

She'd seen that number before.

She pulled out Natalie's phone records again, and halfway down the page of the last bill before she died, there it was again a few times in the weeks leading up to the Russia mission. The number matched. A few more hours of digging and Kate had the missing link that connected Brittany and Natalie.

She called the number Scott had left for her. He answered on the second ring.

"What's up?" he asked.

"I found something." She paused. "You aren't going to like it."

"If this is about Natalie, I told you—"

"I know what you told me and I know she tried to help you, but she was involved, Scott." She quickly brought him up to speed. "Natalie and Brittany had texts and calls from the same number."

She could hear the dead pause on the other side of the

call. "I assume you were able to trace the number and have more than a common phone number?" he asked, his voice flat.

"Yes. It belongs to a hockey player named Mick Evans. Brittany met him on a dating app. I haven't been able to find out how Natalie knew him, but his number shows up a few times in the weeks before she was killed. I did some digging into his background. He was adopted as a child, too."

Scott didn't say anything for a moment, but then he filled it in. "From Russia?"

"It looks that way—I'm tracking down the records now."

"So, what, you think there's some baby-spy network with Russian orphans? That's ridiculous."

"I don't think anything. I'm just putting together the information."

"You didn't know her, Kate. Nat wasn't a spy. I was going to fucking ask her to marry me, for Christ's sake."

He was fighting, but she could tell his certainty was wavering. One coincidence could maybe be explained, but not two.

Kate's heart went out to him. She knew better than anyone what it was like to have the person you thought you loved betray you. "I'm sorry, Scott. But you need to warn John. Brittany might not be out of danger if this guy is who we think he is."

Scott swore. "He left a while ago to find her. Hold on a sec. I'll try to call him from another phone." He was back on a few moments later. "He's not answering. I left a text as well, but I'm going after him."

She knew better than to try to talk him out of it, but John was going to need some help.

Twenty-eight

John was in a cab when the call came through. Recognizing the number, he heaved a sigh of relief. He should have gotten rid of his phone after he left Brittany's apartment, but he was damned glad he'd followed his gut and not protocol.

"Brit," he said, answering. "Thank God. Where are you? I need to talk to you."

"Sorry to disappoint you. I knew you wouldn't get rid of the phone. Good thing for her I was right. Sloppy, Donovan. But I guess even SEALs have weak spots. Good thing I found yours."

John went cold at the man's words. He processed instantly what had happened. Brittany had been taken, and whoever had done so knew who he was. "If you hurt her, I'll kill you," John said.

It wasn't a threat; it was a promise.

"You aren't exactly in a position to be bargaining right now. I hold all the cards—or the only card that matters." He laughed. "And I owe you for my broken wrist. Maybe I'll fuck her when you get here so you can watch. Again."

Oh God. John's chest twisted. Every bone in his body ached at the thought of her being hurt like that.

She was alive; he had to focus on that.

John didn't know whether the guy was telling the truth or trying to get to him, but he wasn't going to show how much he had. "That was you in Norway," he said. "I should have killed you."

"You should have," the guy agreed. "But you didn't finish the job. You were more concerned with making sure she was okay. You can be assured that's not a mistake I will make."

"What do you want?"

"Simple. An exchange. Your life for hers."

The irony wasn't lost on him. Brittany was bait again, but this time he was the fish. "Where?" John asked.

The guy gave him an address of a warehouse near the docks. "I don't have to tell you to come alone. I won't be—I'll be well covered—but I bet you figured that out. Be here in thirty minutes."

The call disconnected.

John had figured it out, all right. Whoever was holding her didn't have any intention of letting either of them walk away. And thirty minutes wasn't enough time to get anything in place. Not that he was going to take the chance.

But then his phone buzzed again. He didn't recognize the number but took a chance and answered.

Brittany woke to the sound of distant voices. Her head felt as if it were stuffed with cotton and her mouth was dry. She blinked, but it took her eyes a while to focus. She was lying on the ground in a damp, dank-smelling room. It was dark—lit only by what remained of the daylight streaming through a small oval window on the wall opposite her. The walls and floors appeared to be made of steel.

There was a banging sound above her that echoed strangely, and she knew at once where she was. They weren't moving, but she was sure she was on a ship.

All of a sudden it came back to her. Mick—Mikhail—had stuck her with something and taken her. His was one of the voices she was hearing. Her back was to the men speaking on the other side of the room behind her, and she dared not turn and alert them to her consciousness. But it took everything she had not to cry out when she realized whom Mick was calling—and what he intended to do.

He must have taken her phone from her bag. She looked around on the ground before her and saw the contents of the messenger bag spread out on the floor in front of her. Her computer and the files she had in her bag were gone as well.

Panic raced through her, but she knew she had to do something. Mick knew who John was. He must have recognized him from the picture she'd posted in the paper when he'd seen him with her in Norway. She wished she'd never published it, but she couldn't have imagined something like this.

She also knew that she couldn't let John walk in here and sacrifice himself for her.

The fact that Mick had been using her phone made her think her guess was right that they probably weren't out to sea. If he had cell service, they must still be docked somewhere.

If only she had a way of warning . . .

Oh my God. She did. She just prayed Mick hadn't found it.

She felt around the front pocket of her shorts, and it was there. The burner phone Mac had given her. It had been sitting on her counter when she went to leave for work this morning. She'd stuck it in her pocket almost as an afterthought.

Thank you, Mac! Brittany owed her big-time. Although a few moments later, as she was painstakingly
texting out a message using the number keys, she was
wishing Mac's supply of burners was smartphones.

But she managed a short message: *Kidnapped. Being
held on a ship. Tell John not to come.* She sent the message and then thought again. She knew better. *Tell him
not to come alone.*

She knew him well enough to have no doubt that he
would come for her—no matter what she said. But she
would do everything in her power to help him.

After pressing a couple keys, she slipped the phone
back in her pocket and turned around, pretending to
wake up.

She had to try to find out what Mick intended. Even if
it meant drawing attention to herself.

She shivered as she saw him walking toward her, the
look of cold purpose on his face almost making her
reconsider.

She just prayed someone was listening.

Twenty-nine

Brittany had done everything she could. She just had to hope that it was enough.

On seeing that she was awake, Mick had her hauled up and tossed in a metal chair. Her hands had been tied behind her back and her feet were bound.

He'd then proceeded to question her about what she knew about John and his mission. When she didn't give him an answer he liked—which was most of the time— he struck her across the face.

"Wrong answer."

"I can't tell you something I don't know. John didn't tell me anything."

One of the four other men she'd seen going in and out of the room—the guy who was looking at her computer—came over and whispered something in Mick's ear that caused him to hit her again. This time with his fist on her cheek with enough force to draw blood.

She'd been trying not to make a sound, conscious of people listening, but she couldn't stop herself from crying out this time. She saw stars—or more accurately, black spots and flashes of light.

"You're lying," he said. "We just found the unpublished article on your computer. You know the one to which I'm referring—the one where you mention survivors. Who are they?"

Obviously, her rudimentary attempt to hide her articles hadn't been much of a deterrent, but her paranoia hadn't extended to this type of situation. God, what had she done?

"If you were spying on me you should know that I made that up. I lost my job because of it. Didn't you read the paper?"

"Your boyfriend's alive. Were you lying about that, too? Why shouldn't I believe there were others?"

"Even if there were, do you honestly think he would have divulged information like that to me?"

"Then what reason do I have to keep you alive?"

"None."

He laughed at her bravado. "No. There you are wrong. I suspect your boyfriend will be much more forthcoming with information when you are the one suffering for his answers."

"He isn't my boyfriend. If you were watching me as you say, you would know that."

He shrugged indifferently. "Maybe not. But for your sake, I hope you are wrong or you are going to have a very long and unpleasant death."

Brittany was doing her best to be brave, but there was nothing she could do to stave off the chill of terror at the thought of being tortured to death. But he'd just given her the opening she needed to convey to anyone who was listening the number of men she'd seen. "Are you sure it won't be your death?" She looked around. "I hope you have an army hiding on this ship. Five men versus one SEAL aren't very good odds."

Mick just laughed. "I think I like my odds—even with

a broken wrist." He held up an impressive-looking gun, which he'd pulled from his waist, and pressed it to her temple.

But her terror turned outward when she heard a voice on a radio. "He's here."

Mick radioed back. "Is he alone?"

A pause. "Looks that way."

"Make sure. Then bring him over. Search him first. Search him well."

Mick's men were watching the warehouse from the ship, ready to unload if John attempted a rescue. But he'd come alone. Exactly as she'd warned him not to.

She prayed Mac had gotten her message and was listening. But she dared not check the phone in her pocket.

God, what if she'd accidentally turned it off with the moving around?

As much as she didn't want to see him, Brittany couldn't prevent her heart from leaping to her throat when John was led into the room. He still managed to look intimidating, even with his hands zip-tied behind his back and being led in at gunpoint by one of the men who'd been in the room earlier.

None of the other men had spoken to her directly, but from what she'd heard, they spoke English as well as Russian. With the tattoos and leather, they looked more like Russian Mafia than soldiers, but from what she knew of the Russian Mafia, that might not be a good thing.

John didn't even glance in her direction. He kept his eyes fixed on Mick.

He must be furious with her for getting him into this. She wanted to apologize. Wanted to tell him she was sorry for not listening to him. Sorry for writing that stupid article in the first place. She'd never meant for anything like this to happen.

"I'm here," John said calmly. "Now let her go."

Mick laughed. "Right. You didn't really think that was going to happen?"

John held his stare. "No."

"And still you came alone?"

"What choice did I have?"

"You could have left her to her fate. It's what you should have done."

There was a soft *thud* outside the door. Mick's head turned at the same time as the door opened.

"And you should have brought more men," John said as the room exploded in gunfire. Brittany was pushed from the chair to the ground as John launched himself between her and Mick.

Two SEALs—one with his hands tied and no weapons— against five armed guys wasn't exactly best-case-scenario territory, but it was a damned lot better than the worst-case scenario John had been facing before he'd received the call from Brittany's mysterious friend, who'd only identified herself as Mac.

Mac had been the one to give Brittany that tracking program attached to the photo.

She'd also—thank God—given Brittany a burner phone that Brittany had managed to access. It not only pinpointed where she was being held, but it had also given Mac an inside voice into what was happening on the ship. Brittany's voice.

Mac had been feeding him information, but John realized that she'd been keeping information from him. Like Brittany getting the crap beaten out of her.

John hadn't trusted himself to look at her, but even out of the corner of his eye he'd seen her bloodied cheek and bruised face.

He was relieved when he heard the body drop outside

and knew that the LC had successfully snuck onboard—for a SEAL there wasn't a better place to rescue a hostage than a ship—as he was having a hard time not launching himself at the bastard who'd hurt her.

He hoped Buddha and his crew weren't far behind, but for now it was just John and the LC.

They had the advantage of surprise. Mick and his crew had anticipated a rescue attempt at the warehouse, not on board the ship, as they didn't realize John knew where Brittany was actually being held.

With his hands tied behind his back, John used his body like a battering ram, knocking the bastard off his feet and into the wall. He followed with a kick to the head that landed with a satisfying crunch.

John heard the sound of two shots behind him and knew that the LC had taken care of the two other guys. "The big one," John said, turning over his shoulder. "He has a knife."

The LC fumbled around while John kept his foot on Mick's neck. He was unconscious, but the LC wanted him alive. A few seconds later, the LC had the knife and John's hands were free.

"He's mine after you are done with him," John said to the LC. He was already heading toward Brittany when the LC nodded.

The next few moments were a blur. John cut the zip ties that had been used to bind her feet and arms, and then she was in his arms. He didn't know what he was saying; all he knew was that she was safe.

"God, I'm so sorry," he said. "I love you so much. I never should have left."

The bruised and bloody face that looked up at him was filled not with wonder and happiness at his words but with outrage. "You have got to be kidding me. I've been waiting for five years to hear those words out of Mr.

Good Times' mouth and *now* you say them? In a room full of dead guys and me looking like *this*?"

John tried not to smile, but it was damned hard. "I think you look beautiful." He stroked her bruised face gently with the pad of his thumb. "These will heal, but you are alive."

She was trying not to smile, too, but her eyes were glistening with tears. "If you think you are getting away with telling me you love me like that, you are more crazy than he is." She waved at Mick, who was being interrogated by the LC.

From the look of anger on the LC's face, he didn't seem to like what the bastard was saying.

"Should I hire a marching band?"

"That would be a good start." Her expression softened, the teasing slipping away. "I was thinking more along the lines of you cooking dinner, a glass or two of wine, and . . ." She leaned up to whisper something in his ear that sounded really good.

He couldn't wait to get her in bed again and show her how good.

"You're on." But he wasn't going to let himself off the hook as quickly as she had. When he thought . . . He shuddered. "God, when I think of what you've gone through. I'm so damned sorry."

"I heard what he said to you," Brittany said. "He didn't rape me."

John was relieved she'd escaped that. But her poor face. His chest squeezed as he wiped some of the blood from her cheek. "He's still going to pay for this." He gave her a long look. "I really do love you, Brit."

"I know." She gave him a wistful smile. "I just wasn't sure you ever would." Suddenly her expression changed. "Oh no!"

"What?" he asked.

But she was already pulling her phone out of her

pocket as she said, "Mac, are you still there?" Pause. "Oh my God, I don't know how I'm ever going to thank you." She listened for a while before turning back to him. "She thinks I let you off too easily."

He lifted a brow.

Brittany grinned. "She said you should be crawling naked with the marching band and twirling a baton."

He was about to reply with a joke that any guy would make when hearing the word "baton" in the same sentence as "naked," but that's when the room exploded for the second time.

They'd made a mistake. There were six guys, not five. The LC had cleared the ship, but there must have been another guy keeping watch from the warehouse. Maybe one of the guys had warned him on the radio before being killed. John didn't know. All he heard was the shot from the door, and the LC's grunt of surprise as he went full plank to the floor.

Before John could grab the LC's gun and take down the shooter, there was another shot from outside. The shooter fell.

John had the gun in his hand and aimed at the door when a woman ran through it. Fortunately, he recognized Kate and the man who came in after her—his former chief, Colt Wesson—before he pulled the trigger.

She screamed when she saw Taylor lying on the ground and ran toward him. "Oh God, Scott, no!"

Colt came to a sudden stop as if he'd just run full speed into the proverbial brick wall.

Which was why it was John who reacted when Mick raised a gun and pointed it toward Kate.

John fired. He heard Brittany cry out as the bullet hit Mick right between the eyes, taking a good portion of the top of his head along with it.

She buried her head against him and sobbed. John comforted her even as his gaze met the LC's.

"I'm okay," Taylor said.

"No, you aren't," Kate said. "You're bleeding."

"It's a flesh wound. I'll be fine."

Kate turned to Colt, tears streaming down her cheeks. "You were a corpsman. Do something to help him."

Colt looked as if he'd just seen a ghost. Two ghosts actually. "You let me think they were dead. All this time. How could you fucking do that?"

"Because I asked her to," the LC said. His face was getting paler, and despite his protestations, John suspected it wasn't just a flesh wound.

Kate was getting more and more upset. "Are you just going to stand there and watch him die? Do something. For God's sake, Colt, do something. *Please.*"

John wasn't a corpsman, but they all had some medical training. He started to look around for supplies.

Colt stopped him. "There should be a medical bay somewhere. See what you can find." He rattled off a list of items to look for as he knelt down and started to help Kate pull off Taylor's shirt.

John started to tell Brittany he'd be right back, but she shook her head. "I'm coming with you. I want to help."

The commercial fishing vessel didn't have a medical bay, but in one of the storerooms they found most of what they needed. By the time John and Brittany returned with the supplies, Colt had already stopped the bleeding and the LC looked much better.

John helped him as Colt used what they'd found to clean out the wound—the bullet had gone straight through his shoulder—and bind it.

"Good to have you back, Dynomite," Colt said as they finished up.

"Good to be back, Chief," John said. Colt might not be on the Team anymore, but he was still a SEAL.

They helped Taylor get to his feet. "Thanks," Scott said to Colt.

There was an awkward pause as the two men who had once been as close as brothers exchanged a long look. John didn't know exactly what had happened, but what he suspected didn't reflect well on the LC.

Colt shrugged in explanation. "She loves you."

His words seemed to make Taylor angry. He turned to Kate. "This has gone on long enough. He still loves you. Tell him. There isn't a reason to keep it a secret anymore. If you don't, I will."

Kate's mouth thinned with defiance. John thought she might argue. But after exchanging a glance with Taylor, she must have seen that he meant what he said. "Of course I love him," she said to Colt. "Scott is my brother."

Well, motherfucker. John let out a low whistle of surprise. That was the last thing he would have expected to hear. Who would have thought?

Apparently not Colt. He looked as if he'd just been the one to get shot.

Brittany nudged John and gave him a "what's going on?" look. He shook his head, signaling that he'd fill her in later.

It was at that point that the cavalry arrived. Buddha and the other hired operators would see to the cleanup. "Go," Colt said to them. "I'll take it from here. The fewer people that see you, the better until we figure out what the hell is going on."

"I'll take them to my place," Kate said.

"What about the ambassador?" Colt asked.

"He's gone," Kate said.

Colt nodded with an even more grim set to his mouth, and John suspected his former chief was having a hard time assimilating the information coming at him. John didn't blame him. John wouldn't want to be him right now. Colt had fucked up—fucked up big-time, from what John could tell—and now he'd have to pay for it.

John had been in the same position an hour ago, and it wasn't fun. But even if it took the rest of his life, he would make it up to Brittany.

"Is it over?" Brittany asked. She'd washed most of the blood off her face, and Colt had fixed her up with a few butterfly bandages. John was relieved to see the cut wasn't too bad. The bruises would fade. But he knew the memories were going to be harder to erase.

He took her into his arms and kissed her. He knew what she meant: was it safe for him to come out of hiding? He wasn't sure yet. But Mick's involvement pointed to Russia being behind the leak. "I sure as hell hope so."

"Can we go home?"

Home. He knew exactly where that was going to be. "Soon, sweetheart," he said with a kiss. "Very soon."

Thirty

I could definitely get used to working like this.

Brittany set her computer down for a moment, not only to take a sip of wine but also to enjoy the view. It didn't get much better than the ocean at sunset from a rooftop deck with a gentle breeze sifting through the warm California air.

Since she'd arrived, her story seemed to be writing itself. She just may get that Pulitzer yet. Although that had never been what it was about. It had been about finding the truth, and she'd done that. Since she no longer had a job, she decided to tackle her next story freelance. Although, thanks to Kate, the door was open if she wanted to go back to the *Chronicle*. Kate had spoken to Jameson and explained that for national security reasons Brittany had had to bury the story, but as soon as they had the okay, she would have the exclusive.

But Brittany wasn't sure she wanted to go back. The freelance idea had merit—especially if that meant she could stay in California. For almost a week Brittany had been in San Diego at Brandon's old beach house, which unbeknownst to her, he'd bought a few years ago. There were so many things she didn't know about her brother, but she hoped John would help fill in the blanks for her when he arrived later tonight.

Brandon had rented the beach house out to some of the local SEALs while he was stationed in Hawaii, but he'd planned to come back to it someday. Now, with his death, it belonged to her. As the SEALs who were renting it out were currently deployed overseas, John thought it was the perfect place for her to recuperate while he and the other survivors decided how to handle the discovery that Russian agents were apparently behind the failed mission.

No one knew she was here. Although Mick was dead and appeared to have been acting alone, she still had a couple teams of SEALs looking out for her. John hadn't been able to call in favors, as he was still supposed to be dead, but his former chief, Colt Wesson, had done so on his behalf. The guys stationed at the base in Coronado were only too happy to keep any eye on a former Team-guy's sister.

Brittany thought it was one of them "stopping by to check in on her" when the doorbell rang.

It was UPS, and whatever it was required a signature. She signed illegibly, and the delivery guy came back with two big boxes. One was addressed to the family of Brandon Blake and the other to the family of John Donovan. They'd been sent from the base in Hawaii.

Brittany reeled back as if she'd just slammed her recently healed face into the door, realizing it was their personal effects.

She opened John's first—he could accuse her of being nosy later. There was a letter addressed to her brother, which she didn't touch, but her heart squeezed, realizing that her brother had been his only family, too—that's why he'd had his stuff sent here. Now they would have each other.

The rest of the items were mostly clothes, including a stack of very ugly Hawaiian shirts that she was tempted to toss in the garbage. She wasn't surprised that there wasn't much that was personal except for a framed picture of him and his mom taken at one of his water polo games. He had a gold medal around his neck and his mom was beaming.

The lack of the personal didn't surprise her, but she vowed that would change. For both of them. She reached down to pet what she hoped would be the beginning of that: their new kitten, which John didn't know about yet.

Brittany was tempted to name her something ridiculous like Fluffums or Snuggly Bear—just to make him have to call her that—but she couldn't do that to any female even in the name of fun. Besides, the orange tabby with shimmering light green eyes, rescued from the local pound, was much too dignified for that.

Brittany had decided on Ariel.

Suspecting she was going to need her wine for what came next, Brittany took a fortifying sip before opening Brandon's box. Unlike when she'd gone through John's, it was strange to go through her brother's belongings. She barely knew him, whereas with John it hadn't felt that way.

It wasn't until she'd gotten to the bottom of the box that she saw the envelope addressed to her.

Tears filled her eyes even before she opened it. She curled up on the couch with her wine and Ariel in her lap and started to read.

By the time she finished, tears were streaming down her cheeks. She was so overwhelmed by what she read that she didn't even hear the door open.

"Jesus, Brit, what's wrong?"

Brittany looked up to see John standing there. Despite how happy she was to see him, she didn't move other than to hold the letter up to him. "Did you know about this?"

He'd obviously seen the opened boxes when he walked

in and realized what they were. He barely glanced at the letter before nodding.

Brittany's chest was so tight with emotion she could barely speak. "This is what you were talking about when you said I should have trusted him?"

John nodded again and sat down next to her. He was momentarily surprised when the kitten hopped on his leg before jumping off the couch, but he didn't stop to ask questions before taking Brittany into his arms.

Feeling those big, strong arms around her opened the floodgates. Her crying got harder—a lot harder—as she wept for her lost brother.

The brother she would never have the chance to apologize to.

The brother she hadn't really known.

The brother she should have trusted.

She had blamed Brandon for changing his story after their parents were killed, but he'd only done it to protect her. The Saudi diplomat had threatened to have her kidnapped and sold as some old man's sex slave. In the letter, Brandon apologized for what he'd done, saying that he'd only been eighteen. He'd been scared and hadn't known what to do.

But he'd never forgotten. After he'd become a SEAL he'd investigated and learned the whole story behind the cover-up and why the government had wanted to protect this guy so badly. The diplomat was a CIA asset, and they were using him for information about terrorists. He'd been of negligible use, stringing them along for years before they cut ties with him.

In the envelope, Brandon had given her all the information she needed, even suggesting that it would make a good story.

He'd just given her the starring centerpiece in the article she was writing on abuses of diplomatic immunity.

There was one more piece of information Brandon

had given her. The diplomat's son had been killed in a car accident a couple years ago, when his father was stationed in Pakistan.

When her tears had finally dried, she looked up at John. "Was Brandon ever deployed to Pakistan?"

John's expression went stony—maybe a little too stony. "I can't say."

She'd thought the secrecy thing would make her angry. After what they'd gone through, she was surprised that it didn't. She understood why he couldn't share things with her.

But she knew the answer anyway. There was something in his eyes. And maybe she knew her brother a little better now, too. Brandon had gotten his justice. It might not have been the way she would have done it, but she wouldn't pretend she was sorry.

God, how wrong she'd been. She would give anything to be able to go back and change things. "Why didn't he tell me?"

"I think at first he was ashamed."

"That's ridiculous!"

"He thought he should have protected you better."

"He was only eighteen."

John shrugged as if he understood Brandon's perspective. "After he found out the whole story about the cover-up behind your parents' death, he changed his mind. He wanted you to know the truth. But every time I asked him, he said he was waiting for the right opportunity." John looked at her. "He never stopped loving you, Brit. You were the most important person in the world to him."

Brittany felt her throat closing again. "Aren't you supposed to be making me feel better?"

He gave her that one-sided smile that she loved so much. "You will. But he wouldn't want you to feel guilty because of what you read in there."

No, she supposed not—especially because her brother had something to feel guilty for, too. So did John. "You lied to me."

John frowned. "How?"

She handed him the letter and pointed to the last section. "You told me Brandon didn't interfere five years ago. But he did. He told you to stay away from me."

John scanned the letter, obviously surprised by what he was reading. Brandon wrote that he was wrong to have interfered. At the time he hadn't known John as well, but there was no one he would have been happier to see her with. John finished and then shook his head. "Not exactly."

"What do you mean?"

"He didn't tell me to stay away from you. He gave me a choice."

Her eyes narrowed. "What kind of choice?"

"The 'state your intentions' or 'beat it' kind of choice."

Her eyes widened. "He told you to marry me?"

"Not in so many words, but that was the direction I needed to be heading."

Brittany made a "jeez" sound. "No wonder you went running for the Boobsie Twins."

He winced with a grimace—and not just at the bad joke. "Yeah, well, about that. That was kind of a lie, too."

Brittany was floored. "You didn't sleep with them?"

He shook his head.

"You're such an asshole!" She gave him a hard enough shove to make him grunt.

"Ow. What was that for? I thought you'd be happy. Would you rather I'd slept with them?"

"Of course not, but that was for letting me *think* you had. Couldn't you have just come to me like a grown-up and explained? Didn't you think I might understand? That I might not be any more eager to marry you than you were me?"

Something crossed his face that she didn't understand. He looked a little worried. "Yeah, it occurred to me. But I wanted something final."

"You wanted me to hate you?" He nodded. "Why?"

"Because I wasn't sure I'd be strong enough to stay away from you."

She eyed him, seeing that he was telling the truth. "You know, in a warped way that's kind of sweet."

He grinned, but then he looked at the clock and got the worried look on his face again. It was almost seven p.m.

"You expecting someone?"

"As a matter of fact, yes."

He looked a little green and appeared to be sweating a little.

What was wrong with him?

She was about to ask when she heard what sounded like a drum. No, not one drum—a lot of drums. Followed by a bunch of trumpets and flutes and the unmistakable tune of Fleetwood Mac's "Tusk."

Oh my God . . . he didn't?

She turned to gape at him, and he smiled sheepishly. *He did.*

"A marching band?" she said with utter disbelief.

He shrugged. "I still have some contacts with the USC band. I had your friend Mac call one of them."

The same USC band that had performed in "Tusk."

Brittany raced to the door to open it and felt the chills racing down her spine as she was blasted with the sounds of at least fifty members of one of the country's most famous college marching bands. Instead of Lindsey Buckingham on the vocals, one of the cheerleaders was singing.

Just say that you love me.
Just tell me that you'll marry me.

Brittany was too overcome to notice right away that they'd changed the lyrics of the last two lines of the chorus.

John stood to the side of the door, watching her reaction but careful not to let anyone outside see him.

She turned to him wordlessly, and he gave her a smile so sweet and uncertain that she thought her heart might burst through her chest.

He was worried that she would say no because of what she'd said a few minutes ago. But that was because she'd been twenty-two!

Instead of putting him out of his misery, however, she arched a brow and turned back to the band. Most of the block had come out to enjoy the unexpected entertainment, and they ended up playing a few more songs. She went out to thank them before finally returning to the house and to a clearly crawling-up-the-walls SEAL.

She barely had a chance to close the door before he blurted, "It doesn't have to be right away. I know it's only been a few weeks, but I just wanted you to know that I am serious about this. That marriage is where I want this to head."

"What about our jobs?"

He frowned again. "Mine is a little uncertain right now. Scott wants us to stay off the grid a little longer."

She understood. They still had a lot to figure out. "So is mine. What about after it's safe?"

"You don't want me to be a SEAL?" He looked devastated.

"I didn't say that. Do you want to be married to a reporter?"

"Not unless she's you." Seeing that wasn't going to be enough, he added, "I would never ask you to give up what you do. I'm sure there will be times when I don't like what you are writing, but I will never ask you to put aside your work for me again. I never should have done that. I hope you will forgive me."

She already had after the first fifty times he'd apologized at Kate's house while they were waiting for Colt.

"What if I decide to write an exposé on secret SEAL teams?"

He lost a little color in his face and swallowed as if he were eating a rotten egg. "As long as you weren't publishing anything you'd gotten from me, I would probably try to convince you not to, but if I couldn't, I would deal with it."

Good thing for him she never had any intention of writing an article like that. Not all conspiracies needed to be uncovered; some secrets kept him safe. He seemed to realize she was testing him and turned it back on her. "What about you? Are you going to be okay with me gone for months and not able to tell you anything about where I am or what I'm doing?"

It was her turn to swallow hard on something that wasn't very palatable. "Nothing? Not even a tiny hint?"

He crossed his arms in front of the spectacular chest she admired so much and shook his head. "Nada."

She made a face. "Then I guess I'll have to try to deal with it, too."

He grinned. "Does that mean . . . ?" He took her into his arms again. "Will you marry me?"

She smiled back at him and nodded, her eyes filling with tears of happiness. "But wait! Didn't you say something about naked and swinging a baton?"

"You didn't just make a dick joke in the middle of my proposal?"

She laughed. "I guess we'll have to leave that part out when we tell the kids."

"Kids? Don't you think I should get used to the cat first? What's its name?"

"Ariel."

It didn't take him long to figure out. *The Little Mermaid?*

She nodded. The statue they'd seen on their second sightseeing day in Copenhagen.

He bent down and covered her mouth with the sweetest, most tender kiss he'd ever given her.

A kiss that led to that naked-and-baton part of the proposal that she'd been looking forward to.

It was a long time later, when they were lying in bed, that Ariel came out of her hiding place. She'd apparently decided that John was all right because instead of seeking out Brittany, she snuggled next to him.

Traitor. Brittany knew she should have gotten a boy cat. "Maybe I should change her name to Brutus?"

He started laughing much harder than the joke warranted. His eyes were twinkling when he finally stopped.

"What?" she asked, leaning over to prop herself on his chest.

"Brutus is taken." She gave him a look that told him she had no clue what he was talking about. "I hope Ariel likes dogs, because I arranged to have the platoon dog sent here from Honolulu. Brand used to take care of him when we were at the base."

Brittany fell back on the pillow. Brutus. Oh jeez. So much for no personal life. She now had a kitten, a dog, a house, and a fiancé.

And she'd never been happier in her life.

Keep reading for a special preview
of the next book in the Lost Platoon series,

OUT OF TIME

Coming from Berkley Jove in fall 2018!

One

AUGUST 17

He'd been honey-trapped.

Scott sat at his recently acknowledged sister's dining room table, feeling as if he had the word "sucker" tattooed across his forehead. No one was saying it, but he knew that was what they were all thinking.

Kate, the aforementioned sister, was looking at him worriedly; her ex-husband and his ex-chief, Colt Wesson, wouldn't meet his eye (although Colt was probably grappling with his own demons right now); the recently arrived Senior Chief Dean Baylor was looking pissed off (which admittedly wasn't unusual); and the always-ready-with-a-wisecrack John Donovan had fallen into a rare contemplative silence. Brittany Blake, after being kidnapped and nearly killed, was resting in one of Kate's guest rooms, or she'd likely be thinking it as well.

How could they not? It was true. Scott had just had it confirmed from Natalie's compatriot's—or should he say *comrade's*—mouth right before he'd been killed. His girlfriend, Natalie Andersson, aka Natalya Petrova, had been a Russian spy who'd passed on the information that had gotten eight of Scott's men killed. For almost three months, he'd been mourning her and thinking of her as their savior, and she'd been the one responsible for their mission being compromised all along.

It didn't matter that she'd warned him and been killed. She'd been lying to him. Using him. *Fucking* him for information.

Shit, that hurt. Betrayal curdled in his gut like acid, eating away at him mercilessly.

He'd had no clue. She'd deceived him and betrayed him in the worst possible way, and he'd been ready to put a ring on her finger. A ring that would have taken him away from the Team that had been his life. If Scott had that damned ring with him right now, he'd throw it as far as he could into the Potomac, which ran outside Kate's swanky town house.

When he thought of how he'd held on to it like some sort of precious talisman, refusing to sell the Easter egg–sized diamond even when he desperately needed cash as he made his way out of Russia . . . it made him want to slam his fist through the table and turn the fine mahogany into kindling. Scott was an expert at controlling his emotions, but right now they'd been pulled too close to the surface and stretched taut to the snapping point. His pride hurt worse than the patched-up shoulder where he'd taken a bullet a few hours ago.

For the first time in his life, a woman had made a fool of him, and Scott didn't know how to handle it. It was a bitter pill for any guy to swallow. For a SEAL officer whose job it was to see things like this coming from a mile away, who was supposed to be smarter and savvier than everyone else, it was the worst kind of humiliation.

Kate had tried to warn him, but Scott hadn't wanted to

believe it. He'd defended Natalie, even when the coincidences piled up. Russian birth and adoption that she'd kept secret? So what? There were thousands of kids adopted from Russia—were all of them suddenly suspected spies? Phone contact with the same guy who'd targeted the reporter writing stories about the "Lost Platoon," and who also happened to be born in Russia and came to America via the same adoption agency as Natalie? Not enough. But when that same guy, Mikhail "Mick" Evans, kidnapped Brittany in an attempt to capture and kill John Donovan, all Scott's doubts had been put to rest. Brutally.

He could still hear the bastard's taunts as Scott tried to question him. "She played you like a fool. How long did it take for her to get in your bed? A few hours? And you never suspected a thing. Man, it was almost too easy."

Scott had wanted to kill him. But Donovan had done it for him after Scott had been shot and Mick had turned a gun on Kate.

For almost three months, while his men had been forced to scatter across the globe and go dark, Scott had been busting his ass, trying to figure out what had happened out there and how their mission had been compromised. He'd looked into everyone who could have known about the mission, followed leads that went nowhere, searching for motives or anything suspicious that could lead him to figuring out who was responsible for the deaths of eight of his men and the woman he'd loved.

But the person responsible for feeding the information to Russia about their mission had been right there in front of him the whole time. One of their own hadn't betrayed them; the leak had come from a Russian mole. His Natalie. No, *Natalya*—and definitely not his.

Maybe he should be relieved. He had an answer. The Russians were responsible. There wasn't anyone on the inside waiting to take them out. His men could come out of hiding.

But nothing could lessen the bitter sting of betrayal that filled him with anger and shame.

Sucker.

"If you won't go the hospital, at least let me call my doctor," Kate said. "I'm sure he will be discreet." She paused, staring at him in earnest. "You don't look good, Scott."

Not surprising since he felt like shit. But the pain from the gunshot was the least of it.

He and Kate had known they were brother and sister for almost three years, but it was still strange having someone worry about him. Scott had been alone for a long time. His parents had been killed in a boating accident when he was in his first year at the Naval Academy. Actually, his father had survived for a few days, which was how Scott had learned that he wasn't his biological father. He'd needed blood and their blood types had been incompatible.

Scott's seemingly idyllic family and happy childhood had been built on a bed of lies. The man whom Scott had loved and admired more than anyone in the world—who'd left Scott the family fortune—hadn't been his biological father. The discovery had devastated him. Scott had been angry at everyone—at everything—but especially at his recently deceased mother. How could she have betrayed his father, her husband like that?

He'd never given much thought to the man she'd cheated on his father with or the fact that Scott might have half siblings somewhere. He never would have known if Kate's ex-husband's jealousy hadn't led them to the truth.

"I'm fine," Scott assured her. "This isn't the first time Colt has had to patch me up."

But rather than reassure her, the mention of her ex-husband's doctoring made Kate look even more upset. But she didn't need to worry about Colt using his old corpsman's skills for bad. Whatever reason Colt might have had to want to kill Scott was gone. The only person

Colt looked like he wanted to kill right now was himself. Which was good. After what he'd done to Kate, the bastard deserved to suffer.

Colt had thought Scott and Kate's unusual closeness was because they were having an affair, and he'd only just learned that they were actually brother and sister. For years Colt had hated Scott—blaming him for the destruction of his marriage—but now Colt was facing the truth. There was only one man responsible for the mess Colt had made of their lives, and it wasn't Scott.

"What now?" Baylor looked at him, asking the question that was foremost in all of their minds.

The six survivors had been in hiding since their mission had gone bad, and Scott knew how anxious the guys were to get back to the land of the living and the frogman work that they all loved.

"Now that we know where the leak came from and who was behind it"—aka Russia and not someone inside—"we don't have to play dead. I will contact command and explain what happened. They can decide how they want to handle our sudden reappearance."

In an attempt to quiet the public interest roused by Brittany's "Lost Platoon" articles, equating the missing platoon of Navy SEALs with the famous Lost Legion of Rome, the navy had recently announced that a platoon of SEALs had been killed in a training exercise.

Baylor and Donovan looked relieved by Scott's decision. Colt not so much.

"You sure that's a good idea, Ace?" Colt asked with that lazy drawl that belied the savvy operator whose mind was always working every angle. Colt wasn't a part of their team anymore, but he still worked for the military in some kind of clandestine unit that Scott didn't know much about—didn't want to know much about, as he was sure it was of questionable legality.

It was the first time Colt had used Scott's call sign in

over three years, but if his former friend thought Scott was going to forgive and forget all that had passed between them, he was out of his mind.

Colt had been the senior enlisted man in Team Nine when Scott had joined as a young lieutenant. Colt had shown him the ropes and taught Scott everything he knew about being an operative. To most people their friendship didn't make any sense. Scott was by the book and believed in rules. Colt didn't. But somehow they'd gelled. Scott had looked up to him as an older brother, which made Colt's accusations and turning on him even more unforgivable. How could Colt think Scott would ever do that to a Teammate and a friend?

Scott and Kate hadn't betrayed Colt; Colt had betrayed them.

"We don't have a choice," Scott said. "Technically we've been AWOL since the explosion. Without a good reason not to come forward, we could have a hard time explaining ourselves."

Or defending themselves against a court-martial.

"I wouldn't be so ready to make a reappearance," Colt said. "Not until you learn the extent of the damage done by Mick and Natalie. We don't know what Mick was able to pass on to his superiors before he was killed. We also don't know the extent of their cell here in Washington. I suspect it was a small one since the guys Mick had with him when he took Brittany were more hired mafia thug than professional. But that isn't to say there isn't someone else out there. Who else knows there were survivors? Mick found out about Donovan but how about the rest of you? You guys are safer dead than alive."

"You think they might come after us again?" Donovan asked.

Colt shrugged. "I don't know. I just think it will be easier to find out why they went after you in the first place if you all stay dead."

"They went after him to shut him up," Baylor said. "The Russians don't want any survivors showing up to ruin their nice little story about what happened out there. Ivanov won't want to appear to be avoiding the war that he vowed to start if there were any more 'incursions.'"

But if that were true, coming out would be the safest thing for them.

Scott watched Colt's face. His expression didn't give anything away, but Scott could guess what he was thinking. "You think there's more to it?"

Colt met his gaze for the first time since learning that he was Kate's brother. "I think it's worth not jumping to any conclusions too quickly. Not until we know all the facts."

"Which could be easier to find out with help from the inside," Scott pointed out. He was close to his direct superior in the chain of command, the commander of SEAL Team Nine, Mark Ryan. Scott wasn't looking forward to explaining why they hadn't come to him right away.

Colt guessed the direction of his thoughts. He didn't have much regard for the brass in general. "Ryan might be your friend, but he's an officer first, and he'll do his duty even if he doesn't like it."

The same thing could be said about Scott. Once. But look at him now: scruffy, AWOL, and definitely not by the book, unless it was called "how to look like a lowlife." He didn't even recognize himself.

"What are you getting at Colt?" Kate asked.

"The government is going to be looking for someone to blame, and right now that's Taylor. They'll want to know exactly what and how much he told her."

Scott felt his spine go ramrod stiff and his shoulders turn just as rigid. Blood surged through his veins at a boil. "It sounds as if you are accusing me of something, Wesson." Colt didn't shy away from Scott's fury. Scott looked around the table at the other blank faces staring at him. "Is that what you all think?" He swore. "I didn't tell her a damned thing!"

The sound of his voice reverberated in the oval room, shaking the floor-to-ceiling windows, which were there to take advantage of the river view.

Suddenly, memories came back to him. Images. Snippets of conversation and clumsy questions when they were lying naked and twisted in sheets after she'd just brought him to his knees for the God-knew-how-manyith time.

When he was at his weakest.

I heard there is trouble brewing in Syria again. . . .

When all of his defenses had been shattered.

You'll tell me when you have to leave . . . and when you'll be back. . . .

When she'd fucked every ounce of sense from his head—both of them. The one he was supposed to think with, and the one that had been at her mercy from the first moment he'd seen her at that Capitol Hill bar.

Unlike most Teamguys, bars weren't stomping grounds for him. He didn't do drunken hookups or one-night stands.

But he'd made an exception that night. An accidental bump—at least he'd thought it was accidental—that led to a drink, a flirty conversation that had gotten closer and closer until somehow their lips were touching, and a scorching kiss that had lit his blood on fire. They'd barely made it out of the cab and into her apartment before her legs were wrapped around his waist, and he was sinking into her for the first time. The first of many times that night.

His face heated with some of that pounding blood. How could he have been so stupid? How could he not have seen it?

He'd been too damned bewitched by tilted green cat eyes, long, fluttery lashes, pouty red lips, high, sharp cheekbones, long, tousled blond hair, and a body that could have sold lingerie to a Mennonite.

But it hadn't just been her beauty that had attracted him. She was smart, and she knew it. She'd walked into the bar with the cool confidence of a woman who knew she could handle anyone in the room—man or woman. That had been freaking irresistible.

Which, of course, was the point. She'd been chosen to deceive and entrance. And like a damned glutton, he'd taken a dive right into the honey.

Over and over. He hadn't been able to get enough of her. He'd been utterly captivated, out of his mind with lust, and, for the first time in his life, head over heels in love.

As much as he hated to admit any of that, it was the damned truth, and he'd own it even if it made him the world's biggest sucker.

But he wasn't a complete fool. He'd never forgotten his job or what that meant. He hadn't told her a damned thing about what he did or where he went. He'd never told her anything that could be considered confidential or secret. His job was all he had left; he'd be damned if he let her take that from him, too.

Whatever information she'd passed on, it hadn't come from him, and he dared anyone at the table to suggest otherwise.

Colt didn't seem inclined to argue—a rarity for him. Instead he shrugged. "They won't believe you even if it is true, and you'll spend the next few weeks in some small room, trying to convince them otherwise."

Scott cursed; Colt was right. Scott would be the scapegoat, and proving that he hadn't told Natalie anything would take some time. Assuming he could persuade them, that is.

"Wesson is right," the senior chief agreed. "The way it looks now, they'll hang and tie you from the nearest rafter first and worry about right or wrong later."

"Maybe," Scott admitted. "But I'm not going to let

you and the rest of the team face AWOL or desertion charges just to save my own skin."

"I never try to second-guess better minds than mine," Donovan said sarcastically, referring to command. "But I'd wager charges against the rest of us will be the last thing on their minds. There's going to be all kinds of spin going on, but trying to punish us for not coming out right away, given everything that happened?" He shook his head. "No way."

"Dynomite is right," Baylor said. "They won't be looking at us when they have a nice fat target to aim at." Ak Scott. "We're safe. But if you want to avoid time in tha small room, you're better off getting your facts lined up first. Besides," the grim-faced Texan reminded him, "we're a team. We do this together, and you aren't going to be much help to us if you are locked up somewhere or spending all your time defending yourself."

"What difference is a few days going to make?" Col pointed out.

But Scott still wasn't convinced. They might be right but he had a duty as an officer not only to come forward but also to protect his men.

It was Kate who came up with the solution.

"How about a compromise?" she said. "My godfather is already involved. We could go to him and get his take. You'll have technically reported in to someone in the chain of command"—Kate's godfather, General Thomas Murray, was the Vice Chairman of the Joint Chiefs of Staff and one of the handful of people who'd been in the loop about their mission—"but we minimize who knows for a little longer."

It was a great suggestion. Two birds with one stone. Scott looked around the table, and the three men nodded their approval.

Kate made the call.

She returned a short time later. "He was shocked, bu

when I explained everything, he agreed with Colt," she said in a way that suggested that didn't happen often—if ever. "He thinks you should lie low a little longer. Your survival is miraculous but inconvenient, as it makes a delicate political situation with Russia even more precarious. The US is already on the brink of war, and if this comes out, it will only get worse. You aren't going to be popular with those in the administration who don't want war. Some in the White House will wish that you'd just stayed buried, and the secret of your mission along with you."

They all knew that, but somehow hearing it from someone in the general's position made it much more sobering.

"He offered to help in any way he can," Kate added apologetically, understanding the downer cast by her relayed message. "I told him I would keep him in the loop."

Scott nodded. He might take the general up on it. He was determined to do whatever he needed to do to clear his name. He might have fallen in love with the wrong woman, but he hadn't betrayed his country or his men.

He stood up.

"Where are you going?" Colt asked.

"To make some calls. I need to tell Spivak, Miggy, and Travis to hang tight."

But not for much longer. One way or another this was all going to end soon.

Scott had no intention of letting Natalie rest in peace. He could kill her for what she'd done. Too bad someone else had gotten to her first.

Ready to find
your next great read?

Let us help.

Visit prh.com/nextread